Nobody Said Amen

A NOVEL

by Tracy Sugarman

A MORRIS JESUP BOOK

PROSPECTA PRESS

A Morris Jesup Book of the Westport Library, Westport, Connecticut
Published by PROSPECTA PRESS
P. O. Box 3131
Westport, CT 06880
(203) 454-4454
www.prospectapress.com
www.westportlibrary.org

Cover art by Tracy Sugarman
Cover design by Miggs Burroughs
Book design by Barbara Aronica-Buck

Print edition ISBN: 978-1-935212-95-9
E-book ISBN: 978-1-935212-85-0

First edition November 2012

Printed in the United States of America

For Bette Keirn Lindsey,
Lake Lindsey, and
Charles McLaurin

Nobody Said Amen

Part One 1964

Chapter One

The cab left the bright neon of the highway from the airport and slowed sharply as it entered the darkened campus.

"You got a kid out here?"

The man in the back seat continued to peer into the darkness. "No," he said.

"Place's been deserted since graduation," said the driver. "Last fare I had out here was two weeks ago." He caught his eyes in the rearview mirror. "You sure of the address?"

Ted Mendelsohn checked Max's notes. "Yeah, I'm sure."

The car's motor echoed against the silent college buildings as the cab moved slowly ahead behind its probing finger of light. At the rise of a small hill, he tapped the driver's shoulder. "The hall should be right after the next turn. Let me off at the corner."

The driver shrugged. "If you say so."

As the car eased to a stop, two young black men with backpacks crossed from the darkness and trotted toward the single lighted building across the deserted green. The driver turned in his seat. "Not many people around. None of my business, but you sure you want to be out here?"

Mendelsohn watched the two slender figures as they loped into the bright entryway of the orientation building. "Yeah. I'm sure."

But from the minute he entered the orientation building, he wasn't so sure. He sensed he wasn't welcome. As his eyes adjusted to the bright light he saw he was adrift in a sea of khaki and denim, backpacks, knapsacks, and duffle bags, and realized that he was not only the oldest person in the room but the most over-dressed. He heard the hiss of "fuzz," then, "Watch it. FBI." What the hell was he thinking when he'd packed for the flight? Christ, he was dressed like he was catching the 8:12 to Grand Central for a meeting with Max at *Newsweek*. He knew the room was watching and judging. A guy twice their age in a suit and a tie with a Valpack? Going to Mississippi to register black voters? Pissed with himself, he worked his way through the press of bodies and found an uncluttered seat against the wall. He loosened his tie, shed his jacket and stretched his legs, still stiff from the flight. A hell of a way to start, Mendelsohn. He watched the students, and beneath the ripples of laughter and sudden shouts of recognition, he sensed a stifled tension in the room, and it had nothing to do with him. The volunteers looked tentative themselves, doing what he was doing, taking the measure of strangers who would soon be more than strangers.

He got up and crossed to the desk to sign in with the woman from the Council of Churches, remembering meeting her at the New York office. Holmgren? Holstone? "Holstein," she said with a grin. "Jean Holstein. Glad you could make it, Mr. Mendelsohn." She checked her pad. "Journalist. *Newsweek* magazine. Right?"

"Guilty as charged."

Her eyes drifted across the youthful faces in the chattering room. "Nice to have someone my age going with us, Mr. Mendelsohn."

He tried not to smile and held out his hand, "At our age, Jean, I think you can call me Ted."

A short, thin young Negro left a tight knot of blacks. He stood, seriously searching the throbbing hall before approaching the desk.

"Any word?"

Jean nodded. "A message for you, John. Mickey and Rita Schwerner just got in. They asked me to tell you to save them a beer."

The somber young man nodded, smiling for the first time. "Thanks, Jean. That's good news. We were hoping they'd make it out. They've been checking out the church fires, and they've had a rough time." He nodded briefly to Mendelsohn and trotted to the small black caucus. "Mickey and Rita are here." Each word seemed newly formed, perhaps a way to eliminate a stutter.

"Who are those kids, Jean?"

"SNCC kids, field workers from Mississippi. The Student Nonviolent Coordinating Committee. The young guy is John Lewis. He's in charge." And that was how the orientation week started for him in Oxford, Ohio, June 1964.

Later, a long week later, one of the SNCC kids, Dennis Flanagan, told him: "It was the seersucker suit you were wearing, man! Everybody saw you thought FBI," and grinned at the memory.

"No. It was the hat," insisted Bobby Willis. "Definitely the hat. Nobody but FBI guys have worn hats since Kennedy gave them up." So when Mendelsohn bought the table a round of beers they pounded the table, and when he announced his next trick, "the disappearance," they hooted and watched appreciatively as he stepped on his Panama straw hat and tossed it into the trash at the end of the bar. Bobby Willis said, "Nice, Pop."

On Saturday he called Max at his home in Yonkers. And Max sounded like Max. "Jesus, Teddy, why did you wait all this time to call me? You couldn't find a phone in Ohio?"

"I was adjusting, Max. Taking stock. Convincing the kids I'm not FBI."

Max laughed. "You? FBI? Over J. Edgar's dead body!" His voice dropped. "How's it going?"

"It's too soon to know. It's a deserted campus in the middle of Ohio farm country. You can smell the hay in the fields and see the stars at night. And you can watch the kids, almost five hundred of them this week, white kids mostly." He paused as a boisterous bunch of volunteers descended from the dining room. "I do. And they're from everywhere, Max."

"What about the reporters?"

"A few. AP. UPI. A stringer from the *Washington Post*. Not a story yet. Not going to be a problem."

"And Negroes?"

"Mostly field workers from Mississippi. The SNCC kids. They may be our story." A memory came unannounced. "You remember in '44 when our outfit arrived in Plymouth, England, after the bombing? You and I were on our first liberty and we ran into a group of RAF pilots? Well, these SNCC kids remind me of them."

Max said, "Talk to me."

"They're tough. They're cool. They're sinewy. They're knowing. And they're tired."

"I remember. And?"

"And they're glad these white kids have come to help. But they own the war they've been fighting. Like the RAF kids." He wanted to find the right words. "And it's not the white kids' war because they haven't been there. Can you remember that feeling in '44?"

"Yes."

"Then you remember. They loved each other. Not us. Same thing here. These white college kids are new troops, too shiny-new, maybe. But I can read the questions in the black kids' eyes."

"Like?"

"Like can these scrubbed kids make it through a summer in the Delta? Like can they really connect us to power in Washington? Can they find us bail money? Can we trust these strangers?"

Max cut in, irritated. "They don't trust the students? Why the fuck not? They've come to help. What's the problem?"

Ted hesitated. "It may not be a problem. The SNCC kids aren't hostile, they want to trust them. But for a lot of them hope has been something that melts in your black hand. It's going to take a lot of doing, in not much time. And it may be our story, Max." He looked at the phone that connected him with the commonplace world he'd lived in, a world that was somehow receding. "It doesn't feel like an Ohio campus, it feels like an arena in the middle of nowhere. It's a scary space filled with images painted by black field workers who've been shot at for trying to register blacks so they can vote in America. They're conjuring up a Mississippi the volunteers can't even imagine, that I can't imagine. The time's hanging suspended, five days, four days, three days, two till we head for Mississippi. Christ, it feels like our countdown on the ship before D-Day, Max. We both sweated our balls off. I'm twenty years older than these kids and I've seen a hell of a lot more than they have, but I find I'm just one more white guy staring at a Mississippi that the blacks insist that I see."

"You keep calling them kids," Max said. "They're not kids."

"They look like my son, Richard. And they look like my daughter, Laurie. They're kids to me."

"That's fine, Teddy'. Just don't write it that way. Keep some distance. You're working for *Newsweek*, not bucking for father of the year."

Ted hung up the phone slowly, lingering on the time he'd conjured up of him and Max together—'43? '44?—in England, and before that, at the midshipman school at Notre Dame. The sailor had told the new arrivals, "Follow me topside to the sixth deck," and Ted had hoisted his duffle bag and followed the other new midshipmen to their quarters.

At the end of the long corridor the sailor began to read the list of their new billets.

"McElroy, Frederick—billet 6A

McElwain, Jack—billet 6A

McKendrick, Alan—billet 6B

Mendelsohn, Theodore—billet 6B

Miller, Max—billet 6C

McCarthy. Brian—billet 6C."

Before opening his door Ted looked at the short, wiry midshipman-behind him in the hall. He looked like a young Jimmy Cagney. "Are you Alan McKendrick, my new bunkmate?"

"I'm Max Miller. And you're not Brian McCarthy, I'll bet."

"You're right." He held out his hand, laughing. "Ted Mendelsohn."

So Miller, a reporter-on-leave "for the duration" from *Newsweek*, and Mendelsohn, the school newspaper editor at Chapel Hill, nurtured a special friendship. In the four months at midshipman school, they discovered a mutual appreciation for good writing, Chicago stride piano, South Bend girls on Saturday leaves, Robert Benchley, and good jazz. On the long bus ride back to South Bend from Chicago, where they had heard the Benny Goodman band on a Saturday leave, Ted lamented, "It took a Jew to hire Lionel Hampton and Teddy Wilson for a big band. But Goodman will never get a booking in my hometown of Atlanta."

Max disagreed. "Nonsense. I'm Catholic, and I would have hired those guys. They're the best in the business."

"You're a mixed breed, Miller. Doesn't count. Only your old man was Jewish."

Max grimaced. "He was also a prick who ran out on my mother and me. That's why I got raised in the church." He tapped Ted's knee and looked quizzical. "Were you serious about Atlanta? Goodman's the hottest swing band in the country. They could play anywhere."

"Not with Teddy Wilson on piano and Lionel Hampton on vibes. There'd be a riot. If you were born and raised there, you'd know it. And it's not just Atlanta, Max. It's the South. My family's been there since Sherman burned the place. Believe me, I know." He'd felt edgy and sad. "Being in that audience today, blacks, whites, it didn't matter. We were just folks who wanted to hear great music."

"How did your people get to Atlanta? Why Atlanta?"

"My great grandfather, Elijah Mendelsohnn, was a farmer, piss-poor, in Austria. He had a cousin who'd immigrated to Georgia and opened a pawnshop in Atlanta during Reconstruction. The cousin made money pawning rifles from the Union soldiers who were going home, and he told Elijah to come. And he came, with Grandma Sarah and two Guernsey breeding stock. He dropped the second "n" in Mendelsohnn to be more like a Yankee, and bought a small piece of land outside Atlanta. He started a tiny dairy that grew into Eli Dairy, a name that fit better on a milk wagon than Elijah. So for a hundred years there's been an Eli Dairy." He looked at Max. "The family expects me to run it after the war."

"What are the odds of your doing it?"

Ted shook his head. "Same odds as you have for making Admiral."

When they received their commissions as ensigns, USNR, Mendelsohn and Miller were assigned to train naval amphibious crews for the coming invasion of Europe. In the long, anxious days and nights preparing for D-Day in the English Channel they shared a longing for sleep, a desire to get the damn war behind them, and unsettling fears about what was waiting for them in Fortress Europe.

On D-Day they hit the invasion beaches together but saw each other only one more time before Ted was assigned to the Normandy beachhead and Miller got orders to return to his ship and proceed to New York to prepare for the invasion of Japan. From that point on, the friendship was nurtured by V-mails and letters.

One letter from Max caught up with Ted when he returned to England after the beachhead had been secured.

Teddy,
If you get to London again, look up Alex Hanson, an old
buddy who's working for Yank Magazine. I'm seeing his sister,
Maggie, while my ship is in dry-dock at the Brooklyn Navy Yard.
Terrific girl, Maggie. You'd like her. You ever coming home? It'll
be lonesome in the Pacific without you, pal.
Max

After VJ-Day, Max was discharged and was eagerly embraced again by *Newsweek* magazine. When Ted's discharge papers came through, he found himself adrift in London, hungry to see beyond the beachheads and liberated ports of Fortress Europe that had been his truncated world since D-Day. He wanted to explore Rome, visit Vienna, cross the Alps, and, after the ennui of his goddam beachhead, enjoy Paree! And he wanted to write about this new world, not the one of marketing milk in Atlanta. When he met with Alex Hanson at *Yank* magazine, his stars started to come into alignment.

Yank was beginning its final months of publication, and was trying desperately to find the reporters needed to tell the liberation story. Hanson enthusiastically introduced him to the managing editor, and Mendelsohn was taken aboard. For six months he wrote a column for *Yank* that he called "Kilroy Was Here," vivid recollections from the sailors and soldiers who had liberated the beaches and braved the killing thickets and hedgerows of France. When Hanson sent the reportage to his new brother-in-law, Max, in New York, Ted received his first American assignment as a reporter.

Teddy,
When you're done with Fleet Street, Newsweek *can use you*
to tell our readers what our kids are leaving behind. Your word
pictures are as graphic as Bill Mauldin's drawings in Stars and
Stripes. *We'll pay you a hundred bucks a column, once a month.*
Tell us what you find in what's left of Hitler's Europe. Your press
card will be in the next mail.
Max

With the first paycheck from New York, Ted bought an English bike and began the personal exploration of Europe he had promised himself. Within 36 hours the tour was nearly aborted when he swerved into a canal trying to avoid a hurtling Red Ball truck convoy outside of Saint-Lô. He was scrambling out of the slimy water, hauling his wrecked bike, when the driver of the last truck in the 30-truck convoy saw him and wheeled the loaded truck off the rutted highway. The black GI leapt from the cab. "You okay?" He extended his hand and helped the bleeding and shaken Mendelsohn to his feet. "Good reflexes, man! I've seen worse slides into second base. You sure you're all right?"

Ted wiped the muck from his face and stared at the wrecked bicycle. "I made second safe, but my bike was out by a mile." With disgust he tossed the bike back down in the weeds and sank, exhausted, to the roadbed. "Thanks for the hand, Mac. You got a load to deliver. I don't want to keep you."

The driver squatted beside him, exploring the cut on Ted's forehead, trying to stop the bleeding with a handkerchief soaked from his canteen. "Doesn't seem deep. I don't think it's much to worry about. I got a truckload of medic supplies, but you're not going to need them." He sighted down the empty and silent highway, seeing only the clouds of dust from his convoy that still lingered like ghosts in the dusk. "Gotta catch up with the trucks in Chartres and then I got a detail to deliver to a place called Dachau. You know Dachau?"

"Dachau? Never heard of it. But if you're really going into Germany can I hitch a ride with you? I've been stuck in Normandy since D-Day and I'd like to see Hitler's playground and the Supermen. The Krauts have just been mostly the invisible bastards who've kept me from going back to Atlanta."

"Atlanta! You must be kidding. You're going back to see my mammy in old Dixie? You really from Atlanta? I can't believe that! I'm from the south side. Went to Carver High." He grinned. "Don't guess you went there, too. Wrong color, man. Name is Sam. Sam July."

Ted took his extended hand. "Ted Mendelsohn."

"Climb aboard. I can always use a back-up driver." July threw the truck in motion. "We ought not be out here alone. The krauts love to surprise us." He stared out the grimy windshield. "Watch the sky on your right." When the convoy came into view he lit a cigarette and passed Ted the deck. "What did you do in Atlanta?"

"I worked for Eli Dairy."

July slapped his hands against the wheel. "Best damn milk in all of Atlanta!" He turned and looked at Mendelsohn with a new interest. "Mendelsohn," he said, "Eli Dairy Mendelsohn?"

Ted tried to smile. "Eli Dairy Mendelsohn."

"My Grandpa Phineas on my mama's side had a route with Eli, horse-drawn," said July. "Horse's name was Moses." He laughed. "Used to let me feed Moses once in a while. He and Moses delivered for Eli for twenty-seven years." He smiled, watching Ted out of the corner of his eye. "Hey, now you can deliver for me!"

"I'm not as dependable as Moses," said Mendelsohn. "But I do land in the bulrushes."

They were laughing as they rolled into Chartres.

From Yank *magazine:*

KILROY WAS HERE

There is no way, no way I know, for an American born in the twentieth century to really understand what I am seeing. This is the concentration camp of Dachau, a German invention. It was erected as the very first camp for political prisoners by Adolph Hitler in 1933. Just beyond these bullet-riddled and now deserted guard towers is an unrecognizable nightmare world, created by the same nation that blessed us with Bach, with Beethoven, with Mozart. There is no way.

What I enter now is a killing ground, an extermination camp with a still-warm crematorium, rail tracks still shivering from the last transport of the men, women, and children who have been delivered here to be murdered. In front of me is a rotting pile of 2300 human corpses, and the riddled bodies of wild carrion dogs who had been feeding on the flesh, shot by outraged GI's when they broke into the camp, and the ashes of 400 innocents whose bodies were set on fire by the terrified Nazi guards as our troops stormed the gates. I wondered if some of them were Mendelsohns who never reached America. There is no way.

> *There was no way for General Eisenhower either. The unspeakable horror assaulted him when we liberated Dachau. In his fury he ordered our troops to go outside the camp and round up every German male in the village and march them slowly, one by one, through the entire slaughterhouse. The Nazi commandant was laid on the top of the rotting corpses, and the villagers were forced to spit upon him. Even for this five-star General, born in Abilene, Kansas, just before this century began, a man from a family rooted in Germany, there was no way. Dachau was such an obscenity that his very humanity felt assailed. No way to understand how his family's spiritual home could be so profoundly defiled.*
>
> *There was no way. There is no way.*
>
> *The guards who survived recalled that during the forced showers, when the tens of thousands of children, women, and men were suffocated by gas, the loudspeakers in the camp would play Bach. And Beethoven. When the next trains arrived, they would play Mozart.*

Mendelsohn was nearly overwhelmed by the human disaster he encountered everywhere, the cruel consequences of the Master Race mythology, the unspeakable barbarism it had unleashed. Dazed and shattered remnants of the Jews, Gypsies, and liberals who miraculously had escaped the fires of Dachau, Treblinka, Auschwitz, and Buchenwald filled every by-way and turgid refugee camp in the heart of Europe. It was a desolate and desperate journey into the dark heart of racism, and he wanted to capture that reality in his "Kilroy Was Here" columns that now had begun to appear in *Newsweek*. The heartbreaking powerlessness of the skeletal survivors seeded a fierce resolution. Mendelsohn knew he would resist the horror of racism whenever and wherever he found it.

On his last week on the continent, Max Miller had sent him a cable.

Teddy,
Soon as you can shake the clan after your visit home, there's
a chair for you at Newsweek. *Folks here are eager to meet Kilroy*
because your stuff has been so alive and on-target. We got a lot
to do, pal. Come.
Max

When he returned to Atlanta at the end of the year, Ted Mendelsohn was nearly a stranger to his family. Although they ravenously reclaimed him, he found the norms of Atlanta life stultifying and surprisingly difficult. He had changed, and Atlanta was changing. The city was racing into a buoyant postwar prosperity, reaching out to new suburbs and greenery. But beneath the euphoria, he could detect the old truisms of caste and race that he remembered from his childhood.

It was soon apparent that the subject of racism in any form was a source of irritation to his parents.

"Let the *schwartze* get the laundry, Teddy darling. You ought to rest."

He reacted abruptly and loudly, startling his mother. "Christ, Mom, stop that! Clementine is not a *schwartze*. She's an American who happens to be Negro!"

His mother's eyes widened; she was clearly wounded by the sharpness in his rebuke. "All right, darling. I understand. I won't use that word. I won't say *schwartze* again." She cocked her head, seeking to find the boy who had gone off to war, then smiled. "I should have my mouth washed out with soap."

Ted looked tenderly at his mother. "When is the last time you told me that, mom? Probably when I called Paddy McElroy a lousy harp when he called me a kike after Boy Scout camp!"

She kissed him then and walked briskly to the door. "Get washed up, Teddy. We're going to the club for dinner."

Relieved and grateful to have him home safe, she brought her young veteran into the social swim of the synagogue and the country club, eager to have him meet the young men and women who could relaunch him into the community. "He's very high-strung," she confided to her husband that night as they were retiring. "He's been through a lot." But fatigued by the daily struggle to keep Eli Dairy running through the long war when all the young men had been gone, his father was ailing now. Ted watched with distress as proud Irving Mendelsohn's strength seemed to be betraying him. "Help me, Teddy." The words were so needy that Ted became more and more involved with Eli Dairy. In his first letter to Max Miller after returning stateside, he wrote of his dilemma.

> *Max,*
> *The wandering Jew has returned to the family and to the South that still won't hire Teddy Wilson. I'm trying to pass the buck of Eli Dairy to a younger cousin who likes it here, but my old man is a hard case who believes in tradition, responsibility, loyalty, early bedtime, and the separation of the races. Not sharing much of that, I'm not getting much traction. As to the separation of the races, that's now a no-man's-land where conversation dies. So keep my seat warm, but I won't be able to use it until something changes.*
> *Teddy*

Irving Mendelsohn died late in December, and Max received another letter from Ted.

> *Max*
> *Life gets in the way of life. So much to tell you when we get together. Arriving with my sweetheart, Julia, and will call you from Grand Central. Dust off the chair.*
> *Ted*

In the Spring of 1951, Julia Berg and Ted Mendelsohn were married in the living room of Max and Maggie Miller. "Your wedding present is a year's subscription to *Newsweek*," toasted Max with great ceremony. "Oh, and something I almost forgot to mention. Kilroy here is getting the Washington beat, no shabby beginning." He grinned at the wide-eyed couple. "*Newsweek* thinks you and Washington will be a great fit, Teddy. We're planning on keeping you real busy. And that should keep

NOBODY SAID AMEN 15

your bridegroom close enough, Julia honey, so he can pick up the groceries on the way home!"

For four years the Mendelsohns reveled in the excitement and glamour of the postwar capitol, only retreating to the quieter Maryland suburbs to replant their burgeoning family in a greener soil. The Kilroy of *Yank* magazine became the now bylined Ted Mendelsohn of *Newsweek*, leading the frantic bifurcated life of the commuter. Dogged and determined to create the nest that Julia had dreamed of since leaving Atlanta, he seemed to be constantly racing home for picnics, birthday parties, parents' nights, and Little League games, all the demanding small-town happenings that seemed to overspill from the family calendar. Julia was radiant, intimately involved with the warp and woof of her kids' lives. But the world of the newsroom was beginning to tremble with a new urgency of a "cold war" abroad and a roiling civil liberties conflict where charges of "Communist sympathizers" were erupting from Senator Joe McCarthy and the House Un-American Activities Committee. When Ted found the names of friends and colleagues on "black lists" that made them unhireable, his eagerness to get actively back on the scene and in the field became ever more at odds with his insulated life in the suburbs.

Max was nervously alive to the tremors, goading his reporters to "dig harder, dig deeper, and dig faster. You're getting paid to keep us in front of the news, not sucking hind tit!" Max's demands became the frantic focus of Mendelsohn's life, and Mendelsohn's idyll on the outskirts of the world skidded to an end. As segregation was being challenged in the schools and in the public accommodations of the South, as pray-ins and sit-ins exploded, and as the right of blacks to vote in elections were being asserted and denied, Mendelsohn's bylines ricocheted from the Carolinas, Tennessee, Alabama, and Georgia, and back to Washington, where the Senate was still debating whether to pass anti-lynching legislation.

Briefly back at home, he found Laurie to be shy in his presence and Richard unfamiliarly cool. Julia tried to be welcoming, but her exasperation at the changes in the normal routines he had forced on their lives could not be hidden.

"What has happened to you, Ted? What is happening to us? You missed Richard's father-son banquet at the temple. Again. Last time it was sit-ins in Tennessee. This time it was Little Rock. Where the hell will you be when Laurie graduates? Damn it. It's not fair!" She sat, desolate, on the edge of the bed, next to his half-empty Valpack. "It's not what we planned, sweetheart."

He nodded. "I know that, Julia. I feel like I'm tied to a runaway train. I'm on the cusp of something that I feel I've got to cover, to understand. It's why I do what I do, darling. Why I'm not peddling milk. Why I'm a journalist. History is not waiting for me, and I find myself running like mad." His voice broke. "Looking like a stranger to my daughter and missing father-son suppers with my kid, whom I adore. Feeling guilty. And not knowing what to do about it."

Julia touched his hand. "I didn't marry Lowell Thomas. I married you. I love you, but I spend most of my time missing you." She rose and stopped at the door. "Your kids deserve more than that. Laurie does. Richard does. And so do I. Your job is becoming your wife, and the wife you married is becoming a goddam widow." As she left the room the phone rang in the hall.

Julia answered. "It's for you." Her voice was brittle. "It's your boss and good friend, Max." She handed him the phone, turned on her heel, and went swiftly down the stairs.

Max's voice was brisk. "The tickets for Oxford are at the airport, Teddy. Flight is at 7:40. Fly good and for Christ's sake keep me in the loop. Oh, and say hi to Julia for me. She was off the phone before I had a chance."

Everyone stood in the June sunshine in front of the Administration building, a puddle of humanity on the deserted Oxford, Ohio, campus. The talk was muted, people uneasy about what was about to take place. Kids smoked and shifted nervously, edging aside as Ted made his way over to Dale Billings, a young, black SNCC field worker who stood quiet and watchful on the edge of the lawn. "What are they going to do, Dale?"

Dale nodded toward a group of the staff who were carrying chairs from the dining hall into the center of the crowd. "They'll set up a make-believe lunch counter," Dale replied, squinting in the bright glare.

"Then they'll integrate it." He nudged Ted. "Like I was doing in Washington when we met. But this is about what happens when I do that in Mississippi." He nodded toward a stocky young black who stepped into the clearing. "That SNCC kid is Jimmy Mack. He lives in the town of Shiloh in the Delta."

Jimmy Mack held up his arms for silence, and Mendelsohn could hear the whir of the newsreel cameras that had arrived the day before. "This is the way you protect your body." His voice was flat. "The vital parts of your body are your head, your neck, and your groin. You can protect them best by curling up like a baby, your legs together, your knees pulled up to protect your gut and your privates, your hands and arms shielding your head and the back of your neck."

Mack bent forward, rolling into a fetal position, his arms lacing across his dark bent head and his hands cradling the back of his head and neck. The girl standing next to the reporter sucked in a deep breath. Mack rose from the lawn and led a volunteer from the crowd into the center. "Let me see you protect yourself." The student assumed the position, and the young black pulled back his sneakered foot, gently tapping the exposed areas of the supine volunteer. "Your legs, your thighs, your buttocks, your kidneys, your back can take a kick or a billy club. So can your arms and your hands. Your head can't. Your neck can't. Your groin can't. When your companion is being beaten or stomped while lying on the ground, you must protect him or her. You do it by shielding his head with your body. Your back can take it."

Ted became aware again of the whir of the newsreel cameras. Everything would be recorded for the great spectator public except the nausea and the outrage of having to learn the art of protecting yourself from a Mississippi lynch mob or from American police who were waiting to assault you. When he turned to Dale Billings he saw that the young man was standing, arms folded, watching him.

Ted's hand was shaking as he wrote in his notebook, seeking the words to convey to Max and *Newsweek* what he felt. When he looked across the tight circle of students there was not a sound. Their eyes stayed riveted on the tableau of a violence that until that moment had existed for them only in grade-B movies and tabloid spreads.

"It's a nightmare theater. The loveliness of this June afternoon won't be remembered by the students in the days and nights ahead in Mississippi. The sky is a delicate blue, and the sun-washed breeze is moving gently across the children who are play-acting on the green lawn. But it's a nightmare theater."

At the end of the week Ted called Max to let him know he was heading for Shiloh, Mississippi. "It's going to be a hell of a story," Max said. Then he added something very un-Max like. "Drive carefully Teddy. I've been to the Delta. You can bet your ass they know you're coming."

Chapter Two

A Trailways bus took them to Memphis, and when they got there Dale Billings, another SNCC field worker from Shiloh named Harold Parker, and Johnny Buckley, a red-headed volunteer from Seattle, joined Ted at the Hertz counter. The Hertz lady was blond and pretty. "Yes, we have a car for you. No, we don't have any with Mississippi plates."

Johnny Buckley leaned over Ted's shoulder and smiled at the woman. "You certain, pretty lady?"

Her eyes flicked from Buckley to the two Negroes waiting beside him. "I'm absolutely certain." Her voice had altered. "Why don't you try one of the other agencies? You planning a long trip?"

"Several weeks," Ted said. "Thank you. I'll check the other agencies."

She watched them move to the other rentals. "No, sir. No car with Mississippi plates." "No, sir. No car at all." The cool blonde stood, arms crossed, as Ted returned to the Hertz counter. "Ma'am, I'd like to rent a car with Tennessee plates." Deadpan, she reached for the form and filled it out. Without a word she pushed it toward him and held out a pen for him to sign with. As he thanked her, a small smile flitted across her face. "Y'all will find the car parked across the road in space 49." She paused just a moment, leaned back on the counter and crossed her arms again. "It's a yella Chevy. Bright yella, with Tennessee plates." With a dimpled smile, Buckley said, "Thank you, pretty lady." She looked at the engaging redhead and her eyes were clouded. "Y'can't fool 'em, y'know." When Buckley and Ted picked up the keys from the counter, Dale and Parker were already out the door.

The neat geometry of the Delta unfolded as they moved at 55 miles per hour into the heartland of Mississippi. Dwarfed cotton plants stretched in symmetric rows almost to the horizon, the dark soil between the rows cartwheeling like black spokes as the Chevy moved down Highway 49. Next to Ted, Dale Billings stretched his legs under the dashboard, looping his arm carelessly over the back of the seat. The attitude of repose was deceptive, for his eyes were quick and alert, scanning the road ahead and behind for any vehicles. "Take it easy," he cautioned. "The car traveling toward us could be the Highway Patrol who move up and down this route."

Ted's eyes moved once more to the mirror, once more to the road ahead and the approaching vehicle, and then to the shivering needle of the speedometer. *You can bet your ass they know you're coming.* For the first time he began to feel the tension in his neck. It was a Ford pickup truck. The two white men in farmers' straw hats studied their license as they sped past, one craning his neck to see who was inside the Chevy. As Ted read his mirror, the man next to the driver turned and watched them. Dale saw the Ford grow small in the distance. "They're gone, Ted. But watch your speed."

Watch his speed! Christ, he'd never monitored his speed so carefully in his up-till-now long life. He was getting a stiff neck watching his speed.

"Doesn't matter a hell of a lot whether you going fifty-five or sixty-five," said Parker from the back seat. "If the Mississippi Highway Patrol arrests you and says you were going eighty-five, you were going eighty-five."

"So why am I breaking my stiff neck going fifty-five, Dale?"

Dale Billings laughed. "Okay by me. Go eighty-five and we'll get there quicker."

"Maybe," said Buckley.

A Negro kid was sitting next to him, and he was driving down

Highway 49 in the Mississippi Delta. It was a new feeling, edgy, uncom-
fortable. Did Dale feel as exposed as he did? Safer if he sat in the back?
So approaching cars wouldn't notice? Ted was ashamed to think this
way. Christ, he couldn't take his eye off that damned rearview mirror!
He tapped Dale's knee and stepped on the gas. "Joe Louis said it, Dale.
You can run but you can't hide."

Dale laughed. "Look at that country out there, Ted. Good for running, terrible for hiding!" It was suddenly very clear. He couldn't work
down here this summer if he was going to be running scared. His story
was right here—young kids moving into "who knows what" to try to
register black Americans so they could vote. They were all silent now.
Just watching. And he had work to do. When they reached Clarksdale,
Dale made the decision for him.

"We're getting close to Klan country, Buckley. You get up here. I'll
hunker down in the back with Parker when we're approaching Shiloh
so it looks like it's just two white guys in the car. When you see the Kilbrew gas station on your right, Ted, take the next left and you'll pass
the Sojourner Chapel. Jimmy Mack said we'll meet there at seven tomorrow night." Dale's eyes swept the car. "Meanwhile, get to know the
families you'll be staying with."

Ted Mendelsohn breathed easy for the first time since he'd left
Memphis. He had brought the wheels they'd need. Now the baton had
been passed.

Chapter Three

On Sunday, right after service, Jimmy Mack had come up to Percy
and Rennie, bursting with the news. "They're arriving tomorrow, Mr.
Williams. Driving in from Memphis. Can you believe it, Sister Rennie?
And I'm hoping the journalist can stay with you. He's an older man than
the students, I don't think he'll be a bother. Has kids of his own up in
Washington, D.C. Got to know him a little at the orientation." Jimmy

had run out of breath then, looking expectantly at Mr. Williams. "Is it still okay with you?"

Rennie had looked at Percy, knowing he would do the Christian thing. And of course he had. As for her, if Jimmy Mack had asked her to do it, she would have anyhow. So on Monday Ted Mendelsohn had arrived with Jimmy Mack, and Percy had told him, "You are very welcome in this house." And Rennie had said, "You can share our granddaughter Sharon's room, Mr. Mendelsohn. She don't take much space."

"Mr. Mendelsohn is my father, Mrs. Williams. Please call me Ted." And it was done. "'Course Percy still calls him Mr. Mendelsohn and he calls Percy Mr. Williams," she told Jimmy later. But from the get-go, he was Ted to her and she was Rennie to him. She couldn't help laughing, watching Sharon. The way that baby was carrying on with that white man! Ted Mendelsohn never did seem strange to Sharon.

By Friday morning the rest of the summer volunteers for Shiloh were arriving, so Ted rose early, eager to move outside to get the feel of the neighbors about their coming. Rennie was outspoken and scornful of the two black teachers on the block. They had told her, "You shouldn't let that Communist stay at your house."

"I tol' them he's just a vetrin like my Percy. He's got kids. He ain't no Communist. He's a reporter." And when the electric company had come around and told her if she didn't get the Communist out of her house, they'd have to tote up her back bills and she wouldn't like that, Rennie told them to go read their Bible and study up on charity. "They all just scared folks, Ted, and they ought to be ashamed!"

Mendelsohn wondered how many others were like the teachers and the electric company. And how many Rennie Williamses there'd be to run interference for him. It was important to know because tonight was the first meeting at the Sojourner Chapel.

From behind her cracked glasses, Rennie Williams watched the tall reporter gathering his notebooks and camera, gulping the coffee she had warmed on the little stove. She smiled at the spectacle as he moved across their tiny living room, his head bent because the ceiling was very close.

"Hi, Sharon baby!" he called, and Rennie's little granddaughter came running, laughing, clasping his legs in her chubby arms. Rennie grinned, shaking her head. She'd never thought the ceiling was low before. But so much was new in her thinking since the white man had arrived. Mendelsohn squatted, taking Sharon's hand and then blowing on it to make her giggle. When he rose he paused at the screen door and called back to the kitchen. "I'll pick up the corn meal and hamburger meat, Rennie. I'm going cross-town near the grocery. See you later."

"Thank you, Ted." She watched him back the Chevy off the lawn and across the drainage ditch. Ted. The first white person who'd ever been in her house in 51 years. Ted. She couldn't help smiling, it was just too strange. Nice looking man, too. Dark, curly hair, but losing some. A little gray at the temples. She took the coffee cup and washed it under the one water faucet in the small kitchen. Better feed the family early tonight. Jimmy said the meeting would start at seven.

Right after supper Ted Mendelsohn headed for the Sojourner Chapel. Mr. Williams, Rennie, and Sharon would follow as soon as Sharon was fed and changed. Panting in the heavy damp of the late afternoon, he approached the chapel. It appeared nearly deserted. Only a gaggle of neighborhood kids playing on the baked clay out front, their shouts and cries mixing with the music of a single piano and the muffled sound of singing from inside. Mendelsohn paused, checking his notebook. Jimmy had said seven o'clock. Looking down the dirt road he saw several volunteers ambling toward the chapel, but hardly any blacks. Puzzled, he climbed the stairs and entered.

In the back of the room an elderly woman bent intently over an upright, out of tune, piano, playing and singing softly with two women companions, "Precious Lord, lead me on." Mendelsohn scanned the rows of empty benches that added to the melancholy of the unadorned chapel. The only color in the room was the faded lettering of a Sunday school poster and an American flag that hung limply in the oppressive heat on the wall behind the podium. He sat down on a bench near the entrance, listening to the thrum of the ancient piano and the gentle singing of the three old women. Outside the two windows behind the lectern, the brilliance of the afternoon glare dimmed, turning first to rose, then to lavender. Mendelsohn's eyes grew heavy. When the music stopped, he stirred and sat erect. The sky beyond the windows was turning to coal as the day expired. One of the women moved through the darkening room and switched on the naked bulbs in the ceiling.

Surprised to see Mendelsohn, she nodded and murmured, "Good evening, suh." She paused, then stepped closer. "Can ah help you?"

"No, thanks, I'm just waiting for the meeting to start. I was enjoying hearing you sing."

She glanced at the window and nodded. "The meeting should be starting soon. Trucks from the fields came back about a half hour ago."

When Mendelsohn stepped outside, Jimmy Mack was at the bottom of the steps, greeting the men and women of Shiloh who were filtering back from the fields or from the small houses down the dusky dirt roads. Jimmy had passed the word, summoning them to come to meet the volunteers who had just arrived, and they looked curiously at the group of northerners who waited just beyond the steps. Young! How young the volunteers looked! Some younger even than Jimmy.

"You know what you're doin', Mack?" a man asked, pausing at the door. "Look like some of 'em ain't even shaved yet."

Jimmy laughed. "They didn't come all the way to Shiloh to shave, Munroe. They're here to work."

"Well, I ain't seen this many whites this side of the highway since there was a raid on Huey Johnson's still back in '58. And these kids look like they not old enough to drink!"

Jimmy grinned. "Huey's still is long gone, Munroe. Naw, they're here to work, and we got a whole lot of work to do."

Mendelsohn lingered at the chapel door after Jimmy and the volunteers had moved inside and down the narrow aisle, standing tentatively on either side of the platform. He noted that the older women, chatty and smiling, most at home in the chapel, had moved confidently to the front benches, stirring the heavy air with their funeral parlor fans. Behind them were most of the young women and girls, many in bright summer cottons, giggling and whispering as they stole glances at the boys who lingered restlessly at the entrance, not yet deciding to settle in. When Mr. Williams led his family into Sojourner Chapel the elderly men at the rear obligingly made room for the deacon.

Like the rest of the old men, Percy craned his neck to see the volunteers. "They're Davids, come to slay Goliath," Rennie had said to Percy on their walk to the church, but Mr. Williams frowned when he looked at the young whites, noting that only Mack and Dale Billings were Negroes. He'd never before seen whites in Sojourner Chapel. When the door closed behind him, Mendelsohn estimated there were perhaps 150 souls in the uncomfortably warm room.

The wide-eyed volunteers stood awkwardly, scanning the faces of these strangers they realized they must get to know. But . . . all these women? All these kids? Jesus! What do they think we can do? Where are the men? There was a hush of expectancy as Jimmy stepped to the podium. With a loud slap of his hands he sang out in his husky voice: *"Go tell it on the mountain . . . "*

Startled, the crowd quickly responded: *"Over the hills and everywhere!"*

And now the clapping and singing soared as Jimmy brought the volunteers on to the platform with him, confidently exhorting the crowd: *"Go tell it on the mountain . . . "*

Mendelsohn's eyes misted, caught up with the wonder of this moment as every voice began to join in a sweet commonality not hinted at only minutes before. Here, in this wretchedly needy church, weary heads lifted and unbelieving eyes were shining. Filling the place with a joyous noise were the poorest of the poor and America's most favored children, smiling at each other and shouting out, *"To let my people go!"*

Mendelsohn watched Jimmy Mack, who seemed to throb with aspiration and optimism, believing in himself, but even more believing in all of them, making them braver.

"These folks on the platform with me," he cried out, "have left their own families to come to Shiloh because they think we are being cheated down here! They know, like you know, that we are being kept from registering to vote because Mr. Charley wants it that way!"

"Oh, yes!"

"And Mr. Charley's going to try to put us down whenever we stand up and say out loud, 'We want to have what other Americans have!'"

"That's right! Preach, son!"

"Well Mr. Charley's gonna have to stop all of these volunteers standing here when you go up the stairs at the courthouse to try to register because they're going to be right with you. And then the whole country will know about it!" He paused, searching the audience until he spotted Mendelsohn and waved him forward. Making his way up the aisle to the platform, Mendelsohn saw a look of pride in Rennie Williams as she held up Sharon to see.

Jimmy said, "This is Ted Mendelsohn, and you're gonna see a lot of him this summer. He's a reporter from Washington and he's here to tell the truth about Shiloh and the Delta, and what's happening to brave folks like you that want to change things!"

By meeting's end, each of the volunteers had been introduced to Shiloh, and the excited chatter of a new beginning seemed to follow them all as they began cascading out into the darkness.

The only light visible was across the highway at the Kilbrew gas station and Mendelsohn could see three men, silhouetted in the open door of the office, watching them exit Sojourner Chapel. Two cars idled at the entrance of the Kilbrew garage. Rennie Williams came down the chapel steps, carefully cradling Sharon, who was asleep in her arms. Mr. Williams followed behind. His head nodding, he stopped in front of Ted, meeting his eyes directly. "That was something I never saw before." His voice was gentle but firm. "I'm seventy-one, Mr. Mendelsohn."

The two idling cars suddenly raced their motors, wheeling to hurtle into the neighborhood. Screaming curses, the men in the cars hurled empty beer bottles at the lighted target of the open church door. Bottles crashed against the doorjamb, showering glass on the scattering crowd as Mr. Williams pushed Rennie and the baby to the safety of the darkened road. Ted saw them disappear behind a neighboring house. The summer volunteers froze at the door.

Jimmy yelled to Hollis Watkins, "Kill the lights!" Mendelsohn thought, *There's a smart kid, good reflexes he learned in Korea.* In the sudden darkness they watched the tail-lights of the two cars disappear down the rutted road. Johnny Buckley led a weeping child and her terrified mother across the shattered glass to the sheltering darkness beyond the road, then trotted back to the wide-eyed volunteers, who made a ring around Jimmy. "Who, Jimmy? Rednecks? Klan?" The questions hung in the dark.

"Rednecks? The Klan? Don't matter," Jimmy said sharply. "Get home and keep your lights off. Try and get some sleep. After canvassing during the day tomorrow, we'll meet at the chapel at eight, tomorrow night." With no further word, the students fled down the road but Mendelsohn could hear Dale Billings's voice, ripe with contempt, "Missafuckingsippi!"

From the shadow of the chapel, Jimmy Mack and Mendelsohn watched the two cars barrel back onto the highway, tires squealing as they swung into the gas station. Hooting and gesturing at the darkened chapel, the boisterous men disappeared into the office. A moment later the outside lights of the Kilbrew station were turned off. Only the pale light of the office window was visible.

Jimmy and Ted walked together, hugging the side of the road, half-waiting for another run by the cars from the Kilbrew station. When they reached the Williams house, Jimmy Mack touched Ted's arm in the dark. "They're coming back, but not tonight. Those bottles were just meant to let us know they're watching." He heard Mack's low chuckle. "Why don't you go meet the mayor tomorrow?" he suggested. "Let him know you're here, writing it all down. Let him know we're watching." His laugh was so surprisingly boyish, it startled Mendelsohn. It was easy to forget how young the always composed Jimmy Mack really was. "Time he welcomed you to Shiloh, Mississippi, Ted. Southern hospitality."

Chapter Four

When he left Mr. Williams's house it was barely nine o'clock in the morning, yet the yellow Chevy already felt like an oven. Little Sharon was pushing on the screen door, waving as though he was leaving her forever. Rolling down the dusty window, Ted waved back. "See you later, baby!"

Easing past the deserted Sojourner Chapel, he squinted through the shimmering heat at the Kilbrew station across the highway. Nothing seemed to move in the breathless air. The dusty town square was nearly deserted as he parked next to a lonely pay telephone outside the feed store, where he called the office of Mayor Burroughs. The secretary said that the mayor was not yet in, but she would take the information and make sure to tell him that Mr. Mendelsohn, a reporter from

Newsweek, wanted to meet him and would come to his office at 11:00.

The damp heat seemed to smother the town. When he got back in the overheated car, he eased out from the curb, and drove slowly around the square. Life in Shiloh appeared listless, its existence justified by the few stores and services it offered to the great plantations that stretched regally from horizon to horizon. Guarding one end of the square, the Tildon Bank threw its shadow, offering a brief blessing of shade to the black men who were now carrying bales from the Brion Brothers' feed store to waiting trucks, and to the few housewives making their way on the steamy sidewalk to the small Stop and Save grocery. Mendelsohn stared at the small, well-appointed bank building, the launch pad for the political behemoth of Senator Sterling Tildon. On the opposite end of Shiloh's melancholy downtown, a three-story tan building, the Shiloh Arms, stood rooted. Once the finest Delta hotel to be found by the drummers who came to do business with the great plantations, it was now shuttered, a plaintive echo of a more prosperous time in the '20s. On the parched town green, just beyond the gaunt, pigeon-stained statue of a Confederate soldier, the town constable coaxed a police dog from the police pickup truck, trying to exercise the reluctant animal in the sweltering air. East of the square were the comfortable, ample homes of the merchants and managers of Shiloh. With large, shaded porches nestling under great maples and elms, the neighborhoods were an oasis of cool green that ended abruptly at Highway 49.

On the other side of the highway was the Sanctified Quarter, home of the Negroes of Shiloh, where Percy and Rennie Williams lived. Ted had learned about the Sanctified Quarter before he ever came to the Delta. But now it was here before him, a visible history that was as exotic to him as it was tragic.

When the out-gunned and exhausted Confederate troops had been forced to flee south from the Delta, they left behind a smoldering land of burning buildings, thousands of abandoned fields with rotting cotton, and a hungry, bewildered, and rootless population of slaves. So when the pursuing Union troops swept through the cotton hamlet of Shiloh, they left behind a small garrison to secure the vital Delta crossroad and offer protection to the thousands who were newly free.

The Union encampment was on the Daniel Wilbur plantation,

adjacent to the one good wagon road that stretched north to Memphis and south nearly to the cotton ports on the Gulf of Mexico. Emboldened by the Yankee presence, Negroes from the Wilbur plantation took over the looted and abandoned granary and proudly christened it their Sanctified Church. It was the first black house of worship in the Delta that belonged to the parishioners. The small, unheated, and unlit building became, by its mere presence, the spiritual center for the throngs of ex-slaves who roamed the region as they foraged for food and shelter.

Three years after fleeing Shiloh, Daniel Wilbur, his wife, and his only son, George, returned from their long exile. To their despair, they found that their great plantation house had been gutted. From the remains of the veranda Wilbur could see, from horizon to horizon, the desolate ruin that had once been the family plantation. Thousands of his acres of cotton, the richest in the whole Delta, his daddy had said, bore only the rotted and desiccated remains of cotton plants that had died of suffocation by encroaching weeds, thirst, and disease. They too were the victims of the savage war. The powerless slaves, who had been forced for generations to keep the fields alive and productive, had abandoned the land they had nurtured and fled toward freedom. It was an irony that was lost on Daniel Wilbur. He knew only that he must rebuild the family legacy.

He surveyed the throngs of black men, knowing that without them the plantation could never be revived. And an agreement was reached that history would morally judge a hundred years later, an agreement forged only from a shared desperate need to survive. The ex-slaves became indentured servants to the old masters. For shelter and food they would once more drain the swamps and master the killing labor and suffocating heat of the cotton fields. For a pittance of a wage, they would once more become voiceless and powerless beasts of burden that could secure the legacy of the white aristocracy of the Delta. And when Daniel Wilbur commanded that they tear down their Sanctified Church and rebuild a greater granary, there were no black voices that said no. All that remained of the Sanctified Church, Dale Billings had told Mendelsohn, was the small overgrown burial plot that the Negroes had built in the lee of a stand of locust trees behind the church. Among the tangle of ivy and bayberry bushes one could still see a few remaining tiny rock headstones with some names still legible: Tobias, Daddy, Martha, January.

With fierce resolve, Wilbur had recreated the great plantation despite the turmoil of the Reconstruction years. He was demanding and autocratic with his family. His son, George, considered him an unloving man dedicated only to success, who had no empathy and was a stranger to compassion. Blacks who worked at the Wilbur place thought he was a hard taskmaster but a fair one. When Daniel Wilbur died in 1874, he left the thriving plantation of 3,000 acres to his son, a canny business-man who had managed the family fortunes during the hard years of re-building and was determined not to emulate his father. He decided early to enjoy his inherited wealth and travel abroad. So in the spring of 1875 he sold the plantation to an eager young Yankee banker who had come to settle his family in the Mississippi Delta. His name was Amos Tildon.

Mendelsohn eased across the highway, eager to see more of the Sanctified Quarter and to understand what it had become. Unadorned by street lights or paved roads, the black Quarter had sprouted like swamp weeds over the decades from depleted acres where cotton had once flourished. Few trees provided shade, and drainage ditches by the side of the dirt roads had to serve as sewers for the Quarter. On the metal roofs of the cobbled-together houses the Delta sun was blinding. As he had already learned at the Williams house, the stifling heat in the summer made the lives below almost unbearable. Yet in almost every sere front yard he noticed tin cans and discarded containers blossoming defiantly with petunias, nasturtiums, geraniums, and field daisies. And behind nearly every little house he could see a vegetable garden that might provide the tomatoes, okra, and beets that could be preserved for the cold months ahead.

Before six in the morning, Mendelsohn had heard the trucks from the plantations pick up the men, women, and children of the Quarter, carrying them miles out into the vast green sea of cotton where they would labor until dropped off back at the highway when the sun had gone. Mr. Williams, at 71, was still making that journey. "Work from cain't to cain't, Mr. Mendelsohn, suh," he had explained in his gentle voice.

"Cain't to cain't?" Mendelsohn asked.

The old man had smiled. "Work from cain't see in the morning cause it's too dark, to cain't see at night cause it's too dark."

Mendelsohn had nodded. "A long day. And how much do you make, Mr. Williams?"

"Mostly about six dollars a day. 'Course we got Mrs. Williams's garden out back, which carries us through most of the winter."

Mendelsohn recrossed the highway now, parked the Chevy in the shade of the bank, and stepped gratefully into the air-conditioned interior. It was very small, with only two tellers. Sterling Tildon's grandfather had opened this bank in the last years of Reconstruction, when times were cruel. Folks needed money, and land was cheap. With a little inheritance, Tildon had begun the acquisition of the land that now made up the largest plantation in the Delta. His father had expanded the bank in the 1930s and sent his son to Ole Miss, hoping he would choose a life in politics. And Sterling had not disappointed.

Mendelsohn moved across the marble floor to the building directory. Flanked by the Confederate Stars and Bars and Old Glory, it announced that Senator Sterling Tildon's office was on the second floor. On the third floor was the suite occupied by the White Citizens Council of Shiloh and the Shiloh Club. He slowly scanned the interior of the Tildon bank and then looked out to the sleepy, overheated square. So this modest fountainhead in this two-bit feudal town was the genesis of the extraordinary career of Senator Sterling Tildon. During all Mendelsohn's years covering Washington, this was the man he had watched with the most fascination as, step by step, he'd mastered the vast machinery of the United States Senate. When Mendelsohn approached the teller and inquired where he might find the mayor, the young woman pointed across the street.

"Our bank director, Mr. Roland Burroughs, serves as mayor, sir. Mornings he can be found at the City Hall yonder. Afternoons he is up on the second floor, next to the senator's Shiloh office."

Mendelsohn was panting when he reached the second floor of the small City Hall. Facing the landing, the glass door stenciled MAYOR stood ajar. As he loosened his tie and gulped for air, he watched the heavy, florid man in the office struggle to push up the large, shadeless window that framed the square. An ancient fan hung lifeless from the ceiling, and the morning sun flooded the room.

"Mayor Burroughs?"

The mayor turned, studying Ted over his glasses. "Yeah," he nodded. "I'm Burroughs."

"Can I help you with that window?"

"No. Takes knowing how. Damn window's older than I am." Mopping his brow, he moved from the window and made his way to the worn leather seat at his desk. "You must be the reporter." He slowly poured himself a glass of water from a desk thermos. "You want some of this?"

"No, thanks. Looks like you've been doing all the heavy lifting. I've just been moseying around, looking at Shiloh." Nothing stirred in the stifling office. "You mind if I take this off?" Mendelsohn shed his seersucker jacket and stood before the straight chair in front of the desk. "I just found out that you are also director of the Tildon bank, Mr. Mayor. Pretty large load to carry."

Burroughs arched his back, settling into the comfortable old leather, and smiled. "Been doing it for so long that it feels like ordinary. I sweat here in the morning and cool off at the bank in the afternoon. Well, take a seat. I'm always glad to have folks come and look over my little town. We're not big, but we're right in the heart of the Mississippi Delta. Richest soil in the world, richer than the Nile Valley. And if you can find it, the best moonshine that doesn't come from Kentucky. Hope you'll enjoy your stay. So what brings you to Shiloh?"

"Didn't know about the moonshine, Mr. Mayor. I guess what brought me here was Senator Tildon."

"Sterling! Well, I'll be darned. You know Sterling?"

"I know him like a reporter knows the heaviest hitter in the Senate. My beat's been in Washington for a long time, so I've interviewed your Senator Tildon on several occasions."

"So the Senator sent you here?"

"No. I'm covering the great debate going on about the Voting Rights bill that's tied up in the Senate."

"Oh, yeah, Sterling's been leading that fight. Looks like that commie bill will never get out of committee." He turned, squinting at the reporter. "Why you here and not in Washington?"

"Just the way a story unfolds, Mr. Mayor. You go where the story takes you. I left Washington to cover the meeting in Ohio where the civil rights workers from Mississippi came to orient the student volunteers who were coming down to work here. And when I met the group who were coming to Senator Tildon's home town, I decided to tag along."

Burroughs drained the glass of water and wiped his mouth with the back of his hand. His eyes remained still. "Just decided to tag along. Must be an interestin' job you got. Where you stayin'? Our little hotel across the square there hasn't been open for years. Don't get a whole lot of visitors down here. Not till this commie invasion this summer with those 'Freedom Riders.' You stayin' at the Motel 6 over in Cleveland?"

"No. I'm staying with Mr. Percy Williams over in the Sanctified Quarter."

The mayor's chair pushed back from the desk. "You're stayin' with Percy Williams?" His voice was incredulous. "With those commie kids, those Freedom Riders?"

"I don't think Mr. Williams could rightly be called a Freedom Rider, Mr. Mayor. He's deacon of his church, seventy-one years old, and never been out of Shiloh. Tells me he played with Senator Tildon when he was a boy, picking cotton at Tildon's place. His daddy did shares there."

"For a Yankee reporter, you seem to know a hell of a lot about this Delta Nigra."

Mendelsohn stood and carefully picked up his jacket. "You learn a lot when you visit someone's home town."

Burroughs wheeled in his chair, extricating a dusty ledger from the shelf. "You came by to sign the register?" He shoved the register brusquely across the desk. "Just sign your name and your company. *Newsweek* you said on the phone?"

The reporter signed the register, shoving it back to the mayor when he was done. "That's right. *Newsweek* magazine."

Burroughs squinted at the signature. "Mendelsohn. Not a name I ever saw before." He leaned back in his chair. "What kind of name is Mendelsohn?"

"Well, it's an all-right name. It was my father's name, Mr. Mayor."

"Not a name you see down here. Never saw it in Iwo Jima." He leaned forward, elbows on the desk. His face was flushed. "Never saw it at the VFW." His voice was hoarse. "Never saw it at the Legion Hall, Mendelsohn."

"Not a name that kind of slides off your tongue, Mr. Mayor? Well, maybe you need a title to remember it. I was Lieutenant Mendelsohn on D-Day at Utah Beach. And my cousin, Major Buddy Mendelsohn? He was killed with the 101st Airborne right behind my beach on D+ 2. Maybe that would have caught your attention way back before you didn't see any Mendelsohns on Iwo Jima. Or at the Shiloh VFW. Too bad there aren't any Mendelsohns down here in the Delta." He smiled. "Until now, of course."

"Until now, of course," said Burroughs.

Mendelsohn waited a beat and then sat back down on the chair. Very deliberately he took out his notebook and unscrewed his pen. "Enough about me, Mayor Burroughs. I'd rather talk about you. And about Shiloh. And about those three civil rights kids, Goodman, Schwerner, and Chaney who disappeared over in Neshoba two nights ago. They were heading to Shiloh."

Burroughs rose from his chair, walked to the window, and silently stared out. "I'll bet you would, Mendelsohn." When he turned back, his face was angry. "Three more victims of the Savage South for *Newsweek*, huh? You just lookin' for a story about trouble down here, aren't you? 'Spect this redneck mayor to help you? Well, Lieutenant, you came to the wrong place." He returned to his desk and sat down heavily in the chair. "Last time we had trouble down here was two years ago when some outside agitators, like those three you just mentioned, came into Shiloh and shot up some Nigra homes in order to get money and publicity up North." He snorted. "Worked, too. Gotta hand it to 'em. All the Yankee papers and networks were competin' to see who could vilify us the most. And your magazine did a photograph essay showin' those poor, mistreated darkies." He pulled out a stapled sheaf of papers from a desk drawer and dropped it in front of Mendelsohn. "You'll find it right on top. Just about broke your heart, Mendelsohn."

"So the disappearance of those three civil rights kids was just an accident, Mr. Mayor? I'm real interested in the answer because I was with those boys just before they arrived in Mississippi, and my magazine, the one you save so carefully, is not interested in bullshit."

"No. I don't think their disappearance is an accident. I'm like J.

Edgar Hoover who thinks they rushed off to Cuba so they can laugh at us. Mr. Hoover just bullshit too?"

"You shouldn't ask that of a Washington reporter. So your quote is that there is no trouble to report?"

"That's right. You can quote me. Mayor Roland Burroughs says there is no trouble in Shiloh, and we're not going to stand for any bein' brought here. Our Nigras are good people. We know them and they know us. There's nothin' these beatnik Freedom Riders can give them. They're happy folks, Mendelsohn. And they sure as hell don't want any trouble with the whites who they're going to have to get along with after the beatniks go home. What are they doing down here, anyway?"

"They're starting Freedom Schools to teach American history and black history and trying to register black voters."

"Freedom Schools? Why, hell, we're spendin' more money on the Nigra education in Magnolia County than in the white schools!"

Mendelsohn hiked back in his chair and looked at him. "You believe that, Mayor Burroughs?'

"Sure I believe it. Everybody down here knows that."

"Same folks who believe that Negroes are voting in Mississippi?"

"Damn straight! We've had Nigras voting in Shiloh for thirty-five years. Go ask your friend Senator Tildon. All his Nigras vote! Nigras who've voted all these years are fine folks. And we respect them. They know that these outside agitators are just stirring up trouble. Why, they're embarrassed that white girls are sleepin' over there in the Sanctified Quarter!" He rose abruptly and strode to the office door as the reporter gathered his notes and followed him. "There's never any trouble from the Nigras in Shiloh, Mendelsohn. Tell your Jew magazine that."

Mendelsohn met his eyes. "I'll do that. And I can quote you on that?"

"Yeah, Lieutenant. B.U.R.R.O.U.G.H.S"

Chapter Five

Jimmy Mack crossed the highway and followed a small tractor lane that led on to the Claybourne plantation, his mind filled with the images of last night at Sojourner Chapel, hearing still the crashing of glass, his thoughts racing to spread the word about the next meeting on Sunday. Urgent that the volunteers really get to know the community, and the folks get to know these white kids. Long as they're here, everybody in Sanctified Quarter is open to the kind of violence that happened at Sojourner.

The path dipped through a stand of pine into a hollow where a tractor had gotten mired in the brackish water of a swamp. As he moved to circle the tractor, a large white man crawled out of the brush carrying a heavy chain that he had attached to a tree. Startled, Jimmy stopped abruptly, recognized the man, and stepped forward.

"Mr. Claybourne!"

The tall, heavyset man dropped the heavy chain and turned to stare at the intruder. "Yeah. I'm Claybourne. But who are you? And what in hell are you doing out here on my spread?"

"I'm Jimmy Mack, Mr. Claybourne. Nephew to Justin and Lottie Mack? Your tenants? Don't suppose you'd remember me, but I used to pick here when I was still living in Shiloh."

Claybourne leaned back on the crippled tractor, wiping his greasy hands on a rag, studying the young black. "No. I don't remember you. Justin and Lottie are kin?"

"Yes, sir. Aunt and uncle. First time I met you was when you carried my aunt to the hospital over in Mound Bayou in '59. I think it probably saved her life. Her appendix had burst when she was hauling a full bag to the weighing machine. They said you picked her up in your arms and toted her to the car. They still talk about it. I met you when you came to the house to see how my aunt was makin' it."

Claybourne smiled for the first time. "You remember that? They're good folks, Lottie and Justin. Been working for the Claybourne place since I was a kid. You comin' to visit?"

"Hope to. Like to see them again and meet some of their friends out here on the place."

Claybourne's eyes were suddenly attentive. "Why'd you want to do that, boy?"

Jimmy cleared his throat. "We're havin' a meeting over in the Sanctified Quarter on Sunday afternoon, right after Vespers. I want to tell them about it, urge them to come."

Claybourne stood up, his hands on his hips. His voice was soft. "You a preacher, Jimmy?"

"No, sir. Hopin' to get to college soon. But, no, sir. Not a preacher."

"So it ain't a church meetin'." His voice rose and he stepped toward the young black. "Jesus, boy, are you one of those Freedom Riders? That kind of meetin'?"

Jimmy licked his lips, his mouth feeling suddenly dry. "It's just a meetin' to talk about voting, Mr. Claybourne."

"You mean a Communist meetin'?"

"No, sir." He stopped in mid-sentence as three black field workers came over the rise, halting in surprise.

Claybourne's voice rose. "You want my workers to go to a Communist meeting!"

"No, sir. Not a Communist meeting, Mr. Claybourne. Only about five percent of the Negroes here in the Delta have ever voted." His eyes moved to the three field workers. "Some of us think it's time they did."

Eyes averted, the men hurried past them now, nodding briefly to Claybourne.

"Some of you do, huh? Well, boy, you've got five minutes to get your black ass off my property. And those five minutes are a gift from Justin and Lottie. After five minutes I'm ringing up the Highway Patrol and reporting I've got an agitator here who's disturbin' my tenants. You don't want to be here when they arrive."

Jimmy Mack looked calmly at the furious man. "Do you figure that my leavin' is gonna keep these folks from voting, Mr. Claybourne? Things have been changin' since I got back from Korea. Lot of my buddies comin' back want a piece of the action. They think they paid some dues. This voting thing is happening all over the South, not just in Shiloh."

Claybourne thrust a thick finger against Jimmy's chest. "It ain't happening here, boy. Any of my Negroes go down to get registered will find their belongings out on the highway. Goes for Justin. Goes for Lottie. Goes for all of 'em. That's a promise you can repeat over at the Sanctified Quarter." He pulled a pocket watch from his jeans. "And you've got just three minutes left."

Ted was talking with Jimmy Mack on the porch of the Freedom House when the old roadster pulled into the yard. The Model A Ford was packed solid. Three young men from the front and two from the rumble seat exited the car and stood uneasily, surveying the old farmhouse. Jimmy stepped into the yard and approached the group.

"Hi," he said, "Can I help you?"

A lanky redhead moved forward. "This was the old Wheeler farm when I was growing up. Is this what's called the Shiloh Freedom House now?"

"Yeah," said Jimmy. "That's our outside name for it. Inside, it's still the old Wheeler farmhouse." He half-smiled, "but with books."

Ted joined Jimmy, squinting at the redhead. "Sorry, but don't I know you?"

The redhead grinned. "Yeah, Mr. Mendelsohn. I'm Timmy Kilbrew, Senator Tildon's summer intern last year. I met you twice when you came to interview the senator."

Mendelsohn laughed. "Of course! We even had lunch together once in the Senate dining room. If I remember right, your grandfather was visiting the senator and joined us."

"Grandfather Oscar was a fraternity brother of the senator at Ole Miss back in 1920. He's still with us. Pretty much retired but still active."

"In politics like the senator?"

"No. Just on the board of his church."

Mendelsohn said, "I'm glad to see you again, Kilbrew. Do you live in Shiloh?"

"Not according to my mother! I'm in my senior year at Millsaps College, and I don't get home much. In another week I'll be back in Washington working with the senator." His gaze moved to the blacks clustered over books in the yard, then back to the reporter. "I didn't know you ever left Washington, Mr. Mendelsohn. Are you on assignment?"

Ted said, "I'm covering the students who came down on the voting rights drive." He looked at the restless young men behind Kilbrew. "I guess you and your buddies are not part of the movement."

Kilbrew wrinkled his nose and stared at the farmhouse. "Certainly not." He nodded at the others. "We're all from Millsaps. We were just wondering who was living here and decided to drive over to see."

Jimmy said, "Why don't you get out of the sun and sit down on the porch?" His voice was careful. "We don't often have the chance to welcome white visitors. They're usually in a hurry to leave."

Timmy Kilbrew led the group to the shady porch. They stood, nervously scrutinizing the students in the yard and the piles of books on the porch, continuing their restless vigil even after Kilbrew settled on the top step. "We had questions and thought we'd come to the source for answers. Reading the papers about you doesn't help a lot. Are you really a Communist conspiracy like it says in the Clarion?"

Jimmy suppressed a smile. "Kind of a shabby place to have a Communist conspiracy. Not at what we're getting paid!" For the first time the young men laughed, and settled on the porch steps.

Kilbrew's eyes swept the gaggle of kids in the yard. "So, what are you hoping to do in Shiloh?"

"We spend most of our time talking with the families we're living with," said Jimmy, "trying to convince them that they have the right to vote down here. You have questions, Kilbrew? Ask away. We'll tell you what you want to know."

"Senator Tildon is leading the fight against the Voting Rights Bill and our group thinks that he's doing a hell of a job, protecting the states' rights to determine who should vote." Kilbrew gazed steadily at Jimmy. "It's fair to say we resent people who don't live here who come down and tell us how to live differently."

Jimmy said, "I'm sure that's true. Feelings run pretty deep, on both sides of the highway." He met Kilbrew's unblinking eyes. "About six hundred thousand Americans died arguing about that. But we didn't come all the way down here to fight the Civil War all over again."

Kilbrew pressed forward. "To a lot of the folks here, your coming down, acting high and mighty, feels a lot like an occupation we remember very vividly. It's humiliating. And we're not about to sit still for it."

Mendelsohn looked quizzically at Timmy Kilbrew. "Didn't think you were old enough to remember the occupation, Timmy. But that's your prerogative. That's what the courts are for. That's what the laws are for. That's the system we all established, and the Constitution we ratified. That's what brought me out of Washington."

"I'm old enough, Mendelsohn," Kilbrew said, his voice rising, "to recognize that you're down here covering only one side of the argument."

"That's not so," said Ted. "I'm a journalist. I get paid to do this. So I'm reporting about Negro Americans who are trying to achieve equality of the franchise, and honestly telling about the obstacles they have to overcome. The people have a right to know that."

"That's crap!" Kilbrew was clearly aggrieved. "Then the people ought to be told that white Mississippians are daily being portrayed as savages and brutes who hate black people because they object to race mixing. There's never a word about kindness and generosity by the white community."

Ted nodded. "That may be so, but the headlines are more likely to be about three nonviolent students who have disappeared and are probably dead. Or about the Sojourner Chapel which was attacked while I watched, by violent men hurling Coke bottles at the black parishioners."

Jimmy studied the faces of the Millsaps students, "Can you guys justify that violence?"

"Of course not!" snapped Timmy Kilbrew. "We believe in law and order, same as you. People who commit crimes should be held responsible. You may think of us as a lynch mob, but you're wrong. We just know from our history that the state is a better vehicle to provide law and order than a detached federal bureaucracy. We have our traditions and we respect them. We know our people and trust them to elect candidates who share those beliefs. Those are the people who vote in Mississippi."

"The people who vote in Mississippi," said Jimmy in a cool voice. "The people who have been allowed to vote in Mississippi."

Kilbrew turned to Ted. "Mr. Mendelsohn, you know that I work for a senator who has committed his whole public career to keeping the federal government off our backs. He believes that saving this state's integrity is a public trust."

Ted nodded. "That's Senator Tildon." He stood and walked with the students to their car. "So you believe that only white Americans should vote in our elections, Timmy?"

"No," said Kilbrew. "Just Americans who share our values." He climbed into the driver's seat and extended his hand to Mendelsohn. "I remember the old Wheeler farm very fondly," he said, starting up the Ford. "It was a friendly place. I'll tell Grandfather Oscar that I saw you at the Freedom House."

Chapter Six

The rooster outside Mendelsohn's window had startled him awake at sunrise, so Rennie's call from the bedroom door came as he was already dressing. "Somebody been messing with your car I think, Ted. I couldn't see, it was before sun up. When I went to the window, wasn't nobody there. But I heard somethin'."

Mendelsohn went outside and gingerly inspected the Chevy, flinching as he inched up the dusty hood and explored with his fingers under the dash. Rennie was watching from the window, so he waved reassuringly and then eased down, sliding under the car. Explosives? What the hell did he know about explosives? Nothing. And unless they were labeled EXPLOSIVES he'd probably not know them when he saw them. He crawled back into the driver's seat and stared at the ignition key, willing himself to turn on the motor. When he closed his eyes and turned the key, the Chevy purred to life. He was wringing wet and grinning with relief when he stepped from the car. Rennie and Sharon were smiling and waving from the house. And then he saw the slashed rear tire. With a sigh, the car tilted, the last air finally escaping. By the time he'd jacked up the car and removed the damaged wheel, he was greasy and dripping with sweat.

"No place to go except Kilbrew's," Rennie said. "Not that they'll be any help. Next place is seven miles away, up in Ruleville."

He left the Williams yard, pushing the damaged wheel before him. At the Sojourner Chapel he paused for breath and then headed across Highway 49 to the Kilbrew Gas and Auto Repair. "Anybody here? Hello!"

The door opened, and a demure young woman stood at the entrance. Carrying a small linen purse and dressed in a white cotton shift, she seemed foreign to the scene and appeared uncomfortable. She stared at him and then said softly, "Good morning."

"Good morning. Wasn't sure anybody was here. Somebody who can help me with this tire? I'm staying across the highway and when I came out this morning somebody had—" He stopped to look around the deserted station. "Well, this tube has got to be repaired and the tire replaced."

"My brother's gone on a service call, and I promised to keep an eye on things till he gets back. I don't work here. You can leave the tire if you want. Bobby Joe is pretty busy, so I can't rightly tell you if and when it'll get done." She paused, cocked her head and looked hard at Mendelsohn. When she spoke again, the timidity had gone from her voice. "I don't guess Bobby Joe is going to want to help you. You're one of those Freedom Riders over in the Sanctified Quarter, aren't you?"

Before he could answer, a pretty, blond, and pregnant woman emerged from the office and planted herself boldly in front of the office door. "We saw you when you first drove into the Quarter, didn't we, Em? You had another white boy next to you and two Nigras crouching down in the back seat." She chuckled. "Welcome to Shiloh. Population 3,107. The most vigilant town in Magnolia County!"

Mendelsohn had to laugh. "Thank you for the welcome." He dropped the tire, suddenly conscious in their presence of how he must look, and wiped his hands on his grimy jeans. "Well, I sure can't do much freedom riding with this damn tire, ladies. So I'm going to have to leave it. Maybe Bobby Joe will show a little Christian spirit. I'll appreciate it."

The pregnant woman smiled. "You don't look like the others."

"Beg your pardon?"

She flushed. "I said you don't look like the others."

He returned her smile. "I'm just like the others. I'm twenty years older than they are, but I'm just like them."

She laughed softly, turned briefly to her embarrassed companion, then pointed her finger at him. "Take off your sunglasses," she demanded. "I've got questions for you, and I want to see your eyes." Puzzled, but intrigued by the glint of brazen fun in her voice, Mendelsohn removed his sunglasses and stepped forward. "What would you like to ask me?"

Surprised by his willingness, she wetted her lips and pondered. "Well, Em and I were wondering . . . " She halted, then raised her chin, her green eyes flashing. "No, that's not fair. Not Em. Me. I was wondering what are you doing down here in Shiloh?" The woman's silent companion, lips parted and eyes wide, edged back to the entrance of the office.

"I'm spending the summer writing and taking photographs. I'm a journalist. And I'm covering the kids who came down here to work."

The blonde's eyes narrowed. "Who are you bein' a journalist for?"

"*Newsweek* magazine."

"*Newsweek* magazine! Up in New York City?" *Up in New York City* sounded as if she were speaking of the Land of Oz.

He tried not to smile. "Yeah. That's where the publisher is. He sends us working types out to see the country. That's how I got to Shiloh."

Excited now, she moved closer. A very feminine summer aroma of lavender and suntan lotion made his thoughts drift. Her face was very near. "Would you answer me honest?"

Her companion interrupted from the doorway, "Willy! What in the world?"

"It's all right, Em." She never took her eyes from his face. "Would you really talk with me?"

Mendelsohn stared. Where was this going? He hadn't been near a woman who smelled so good in—Christ! Six weeks? "Sure, Let's talk. What's bothering you?"

She pouted and frowned. "Well, we can't talk here!"

He gazed slowly around the empty station and asked innocently, "Why not?"

She exploded, "Because this is a gas station!" Taking a deep breath, she plunged ahead. "Would you come to my house?"

Em looked shocked but remained silent. Mendelsohn grinned and nodded. "Well, thank you. That's the first invitation I've had from the white community since I arrived in Magnolia County."

"Now don't start that!"

"Look, before I accept your kind invitation, you ought to know that if I come I'm liable to jeopardize your position in Shiloh. When I drive in or out of the Sanctified Quarter, people notice. You both noticed. And I'm often followed."

"Don't be silly. Everybody in Shiloh knows me. Just come." She pointed south. "You go down 49 past the high school. First road on the right. The Claybourne place. Anybody can show you."

"Thank you." He thought of what it would be like if Dale Billings met this woman, and could hardly suppress his smile. "Can I bring some of the kids I'm living with? You'd like them."

Her eyes widen in horror. "Heavens, no!"

He laughed at her vehemence. "They don't bite! When would you like me to come?"

Her eyes were bright with anticipation and she turned to Em. "Can Bobby Joe fix his tire by Wednesday? He'll need his car to get out to the plantation."

Looking very uncomfortable, Em stared at the blonde, then shrugged. "I'll talk to him."

The pregnant woman clapped delightedly. "Bobby Joe's never said no to Emily in his whole life. So why don't you come Wednesday afternoon, one-thirty. Em, you come, too." She extended her hand to him. When he took it, it felt smooth and surprisingly cool. She smiled. "My name is Wilson Claybourne. What's yours?"

Chapter Seven

Dale Billings was speaking to SNCC headquarters in Jackson when Mendelsohn dropped into the chair opposite. Billings was staring at the phone, seemingly unaware that Ted had even come in.

"J. Edgar Hoover said he's opening an office?" Billings's voice became strident. "Down in Neshoba? Be the first fucking office the FBI's got in Tildon's state if it's true! Keep me posted. It's lonely up here." He hung up and saw the reporter. His long slender fingers beat a tattoo on the old desk. "Nothing new on the boys." A sardonic smile creased his intent young face. "But the shit's hit the fan in all the big papers up north. Mickey Schwerner and Andy Goodman, two white guys, are missing. So Jackson says J. Edgar's gonna have to look interested. Word from Washington is he's going to open an office down here." His scornful voice filled the empty Freedom House. "After how many years? How many lynchings? How many burned down churches? How many black brothers gone missing or shot? Now two white civil rights workers, Mickey and Andy, go missing, and the FBI is going to open an office in Missafuckingsippi? I wish I could still laugh. It's fucking pathetic." He took a deep breath and pointed to the ham sandwich on the desk before him. "You want part of this? You been gone all morning, you must be hungry."

"Hell, no. Unlike some of my brothers, I do like ham. But that sandwich looks as tired as you." Even at the Ohio orientation Ted had thought Dale looked drawn, his eyes too large in his thin face. Railskinny, he thought. And the bottled intensity in the youngster seemed ready to spill now that he was back in the Delta. His fingers never seemed at rest, tapping a staccato accompaniment to his speech. The kid's been waiting for this summer, Ted reflected, feeling everything, and not taking care of himself.

He walked to the ancient ice box and took out a quart of milk and placed it next to Dale's sandwich. "Eat your lunch, Dale. You look like a poster child for the Salvation Army."

"Still being my Jewish mama, Ted?"

"Well, your kin are down in Tunica, so I'm the only man in Magnolia County that knows you don't know how to take care of yourself. So eat your pork and drink your milk."

Dale slapped the desk, his laughter cascading. "Mercy, mercy!"

"You've been on the pipe most of the night with Jackson? You've got to get some sleep. Things are just getting started down here now that the students have arrived. They'll need your help. Nobody knows Shiloh and Magnolia County like you do."

Billings raised his hands in mock surrender. "Breeding, Mendelsohn. How many people you know have cousins in Magnolia County, Missafuckingsippi? That's why I am so knowledgeable. Been a captive audience to my father's second wife whose family is still in Tunica, just down the road. I've been down here on school holidays since before Emmett Till was killed over in Money. That was a cautionary lesson for a nice northern Negro like myself. Lucky for me, I never learned to whistle. What I don't know, I can usually find out. Not talent, just breeding, Mendelsohn."

Dale Billings always broke him up. Ever since the magazine had sent Mendelsohn to cover the first demonstration when Howard students picketed the Woolworth's in Washington. Max had been prescient about its newsworthiness. Dale Billings had been the cheerleader, seemingly oblivious to the catcalls from a hostile crowd of whites that swiftly had gathered. His tough welterweight body was in constant motion, leading the students, *what do we want, when do we want it*, chanting, clapping, *freedom! freedom! now! now!* Celebrating the moment and making the others braver. Mendelsohn couldn't take his eyes off him. When the picket line passed his part of the crowd Ted had called out "Talk to me later, I'm with *Newsweek*." Billings was being hustled away by the police when Mendelsohn asked the cop, "What's he done?" The cop shouldered his way past him. "Butt out. What the hell is it to you? You with them?"

Mendelsohn had flashed his press card and the cop had grunted, "He's blocking traffic."

Dale had grinned at him. "*Newsweek*? Why'd I think you were with the *Amsterdam News* or *Ebony*?"

Since Mendelsohn was the only white reporter who showed up to cover the story, it started a long friendship with Dale Billings. When he'd run into him again at the Ohio orientation, the kid was hot to trot, couldn't wait to join the group going into Shiloh in Magnolia County. "Gonna be Communications Director, Ted!" And Ted had teased him. "Is the movement that hard up? Don't know if you can make the weight, Dale." And Dale had shot back "Pound for pound I'm the toughest kid on the block. But they made me Communications Director because I am so smart and communicate so well. But mostly," he laughed, "because I know where Magnolia County is in Missafuckingsippi!"

"What do you know about a family named Claybourne, Dale? It's a long story, but I've been invited to the Claybourne house. It's occurred to me that I may be getting set up."

"Invited to the Claybourne house? You kidding? Other than the Tildon place, Lucas Claybourne has the biggest plantation in Shiloh. Must have more than forty tenant families on the place. Lucas invited you?"

"Not Lucas. I met Wilson, Mrs. Lucas Claybourne, and she recognized a gentleman and invited me to visit her on this Wednesday afternoon. It's not talent, Dale. It's just breeding. What I want to know is, should I go?"

Billings cocked his head and his eyes grew serious. "Don't rightly know. Her husband gonna be there? If he is I don't know if you ought to go. If he ain't, I don't know if you ought to go. I'd watch my back, old timer. He ain't Klan, but he knows everybody who is. His wife, Willy? Been honey to all the Shiloh bees who wear pants and want to invite her into the hive for a little sportin'. But she's more fizz than sarsaparilla, and folks think Lucas keeps her on a pretty tight lead. But she's been news in Shiloh since she was Magnolia Cotton Queen in '56, first summer I came to the Delta. Beautiful chick, sexy. Got one kid, Alex, and has another on the way. What's she want with a wanderin' Jew like you?"

Mendelsohn laughed and started for the door. "Age adds a certain dimension of allure, son. I explained that I was twenty years older than you agitators and that might have done it. So in my estimation as an old and very experienced journalist, I think she wants to entertain me, not kill me. However, I could be wrong. And as Communications Director, I'd like you to make sure I'm right. So if I'm not back by four

o'clock, please come and get me. Or communicate with the new FBI office in Neshoba."

"And what will I tell *Newsweek* when they call askin' what happened
to old Mendelsohn?"

"Tell them I'm on the case and the check never arrived."

Chapter Eight

Bobby Joe Kilbrew nodded to Luther Lonergan. "That's him."

They watched from the gas station as Mendelsohn walked down
the dirt road and paused at the Sojourner Chapel. When he methodically kicked broken glass from the steps, the two men grinned. "It's too
bad we missed the fucker the other night, Luther!" Minutes later they
saw him start to cross Highway 49 then halt as four huge trucks carrying
newly sawed pines rumbled past. Bobby Joe squinted through the waves
of heat. "He looks younger than Em said." He picked up a tire iron,
swinging it like a pendulum into the hollow of his left hand, back and
forth, "Let me do the talkin'."

When the trucks passed, Mendelsohn trotted across the highway,
crossed the baking asphalt, and strode into the office. "Is one of you
Bobby Joe Kilbrew?"

"Yeah." The arc of the pendulum continued, ending each time with
a soft plop. "I'm BJ."

Mendelsohn grinned. "I'm the guy with the fucked-up tire. I think
your sister told you about it."

"Yeah, she did. Said this reporter from New York needed help."

"I sure do. Hard to do my job down here without wheels."

"Depends. What is your job down here?"

"Reporting. I write about what's happening so folks understand the
news." He smiled at the man at the desk. "So I need wheels to go talk
with people. If I wasn't staying so close, I would have had to use a car
to come talk to you."

"Luther and me've seen what New York reporters write about us rednecks." Kilbrew turned to Luther. "Ain't that so, Luther? Lot of us don't think those Jew reporters write very patriotic stuff." Kilbrew carefully laid the tire iron on the desk. His eyes met Mendelsohn's. "That what you do for work?"

"My boss sent me down to write about what's happening in the Delta now that the Negroes are starting to try to register to vote. He never said anything about rednecks, Mr. Kilbrew."

Kilbrew turned to Luther. "You hear that, old buddy? Reporter here says that niggers are tryin' to register to vote."

Luther grinned. "Naw. Sure haven't heard about no niggers here tryin' to vote, BJ. You sure you mean Shiloh?"

Mendelsohn turned to Kilbrew. "Were you able to patch the tube?"

"Yeah. Em said you was lookin' for a little Christian charity, so me and Luther here fixed the tube and replaced the tire. Hope your magazine's payin' for your little accident. Not really charity, but it was the Christian thing to do. Comes to fifty-six fifty. Cash. Tire's just inside the door of the garage. Luther'll show you where."

Mendelsohn took bills from his wallet and fished two quarters from his jeans. "I'm mighty grateful, Mr. Kilbrew." He placed the money on the desk. "About that accident to the tire." He looked at Luther and then at Kilbrew. "I've been driving for almost thirty years, and never saw a tire get into that condition. Either of you got any idea how that could happen?"

Kilbrew sat motionless, looking up at the reporter. "Yeah, I got a good idea." His tall, lanky body unfolded from his chair and he picked up the tire iron as he stood. "Luther tells me you're stayin' with Deacon Williams, over in the Quarter?" His large hand holding the iron pointed toward the highway. "Accidents happen all the time over there in nigger-town. It's a dangerous place for outsiders who don't know about how to avoid accidents, not bein' from nigger-town. Probably not too bright of Deacon Williams puttin' you up there, where these kind of accidents can happen. Some people 'round here, Luther for instance, and me, just don't understand why a good old Christian man who never had an accident before would do that for a Communist. Take that kind of chance. Got any idea how that could happen?"

Half-smiling, the reporter nodded. "Yeah, I got a good idea." He picked up an empty beer bottle that rested on the edge of Kilbrew's desk. Holding it by its neck, he patted his other hand. "Still had one bottle left, Mr. Kilbrew? If you got to ask the question how come Deacon Williams took me in, I guess you wouldn't understand the answer." His smile disappeared. "But you ought to understand this, Mr. Kilbrew. The FBI knows about my tire, and they know all about the attack on the So-journer Chapel because I told them. It's the kind of work a good re-porter does. And they know that my magazine is worried about the continued good health of Deacon Percy Williams who lives at number 17 on Mulberry Lane in Shiloh. I made sure they got it right." He re-peated the words slowly. "17 Mulberry Lane. Your Senator Tildon is eager to have our magazine's understanding, if not always its support, come election time. He sure wouldn't appreciate anything embarrassing happening in his hometown of Shiloh this summer. So let's hope that there won't be any more accidents." He stepped around Luther and tossed the bottle into the empty beer case near the door. It bounced but remained intact. "They don't break too easy, do they? I guess you really have to throw 'em hard. You don't have to come with me, Luther. I'm sure I can find the tire." He nodded to Kilbrew. "Remember to thank your sister for me."

Deeply troubled by the naked confrontation, Mendelsohn headed directly to the Freedom House, eager to share his concerns. Dale and Jimmy met him as he crossed the porch.

"What's happening, brother?" Dale asked. "You look unhappy."

"I just got my wheels back from Kilbrew and I think everybody in Sanctified Quarter ought to expect trouble. Those are mean bastards. The Coke bottles don't mean anything. They want us gone. Period."

Dale nodded. "Those guys play hardball. I'll pass the word through the Quarter and call down to headquarters at Jackson."

"I called the FBI and filled them in about the attack on Sojourner. I didn't get the impression that they were going to do anything but 'in-vestigate.'"

"We all could be long gone by the time Hoover's guys move on any of this," said Dale. "I think you should lay it all out for Dennis Haley, the sheriff, Jimmy. This is his turf. He ought to know that we expect violence when we have our organizing meeting. And Mendelsohn ought to go with you. The man from *Newsweek*." He grinned. "That's going to get the sheriff's attention."

Jimmy said, "Call him, Dale. Tell Haley that Mendelsohn and I want to see him and that it's urgent, even make it this afternoon. We can get some lunch at Billy's Chili before we go." He chuckled. "Wait till you meet Billy, Ted. He's tough, he's smart and he gives the Shiloh cops nothing but grief."

Mendelsohn settled into the uncomfortable booth at Billy's Chili with Dale and Jimmy. Billy, who had fought during the war in the battle for Anzio with a colored Sea Bee construction group, left two fingers of his left hand on Anzio beach. Now he pulled three beers from his ancient fridge and banged them on the table. "Law says I gotta serve these brothers," he said, "but don't say nothin 'bout I have to serve you. However, since you seem to be a kindly old white person who is a friend of these niggers, you may have a cold beer also. What you-all doin' this close to downtown?"

"They going to see the sheriff man, Dangerous Dennis Haley. All things to all people is Dennis," said Dale. "But you and I can just relax, Billy, and enjoy your Pilsner."

Billy brought a fourth bottle to the table, studying Jimmy with curiosity. "Why you do that, James? You lose a bet or somethin'?"

Jimmy laughed. "No, I don't owe the sheriff nothin', and he owes me, but he won't admit it. So I'm just taking our Wandering Jew reporter to make his presence known before the mass meeting. Figure it couldn't hurt."

"Power of the press, Billy," Ted said, and raised his glass. "To the press! Awesome in its potential but usually lousing up in performance. I invited myself to come."

Billy lazily surveyed the empty room then watched as a police car drove slowly by, paused, and eased back. When Billy jovially waved, the cruiser squealed its wheels and sped away. He chuckled. "Those meatheads been embarrassed by my cordiality since I got back from Italy in '45. Since I saw the real racial Supermen penned up like sick pigs on our beachhead, I was just never able to be a-feared of these local

Supermen. Gives 'em aches and pains every time I smile and wave. Here, piggy, piggy, piggy!"

Jimmy emptied his glass and untangled himself from the booth. "Time we go make nice to the sheriff, Ted."

Ted put some bills on the table. "Thanks, Billy. Any messages?"

Billy nodded. "Yeah, Tell him his Supermen got no manners. They never wave back."

Mrs. Skinner, the secretary, stood awkwardly in the entrance to the sheriff's office. "They're here, Sheriff Haley." She looked anxiously at her notes. "The New York reporter, Mendelsohn?" She frowned, checking her message. "And that Nigra organizer, Mack, Jimmy Mack."

"Well, send them in, Hilda." Haley smiled at her discomfort. "Not armed, are they?" When he noted her wide-eyed concern, he said. "Not to worry Hilda. Assassins don't make appointments first."

With affection, he watched her scuttle back to her office where Jimmy and Mendelsohn waited. He settled back in his chair at his desk. Hilda Skinner. She'd been with him at Shiloh High in '39 when he was coaching the football team and she was leader of the Pep Squad. And when he got back from the Pacific and got elected sheriff, she'd been the first one he hired. He chuckled, remembering how many years it took before she stopped calling him "coach."

Jimmy Mack in his dark glasses entered and Mendelsohn followed. "Come on in and sit down," said Haley. "Mrs. Skinner told me you had called and wanted to meet. Seemed like a good idea because Mack and I have seen each other about everywhere in Shiloh and we haven't spoken before." He turned to face the reporter. "You must be Mendelsohn, from New York. *Newsweek*? Why don't you tell me what you have in mind?"

"Not me," Ted said. "I think that you should be talking with Mr. Mack. He's the one with questions. I'm just a reporter."

Haley reddened, noting the rebuke, but nodded. "Mack?"

"I'm director of the Shiloh group that came here to help Negroes organize to get the vote, part of SNCC. I've come because I think the non-violent volunteers I brought here are going to be violently harassed at our first countywide organizing meeting. I'm hoping that you can help us avoid that."

"Have you been harassed down here, Mack? I'm very aware of what you've been doing, and I haven't observed any problems."

Mack took off his sunglasses and put his hands on the edge of the desk. "Yeah, Sheriff. I've observed problems." His voice was chill. "Last night our Sojourner Chapel was attacked by white men who threw Coca-Cola bottles that smashed the entrance of the church as Shiloh citizens were leaving a peaceful meeting. I watched the attackers' cars return to the Kilbrew station. When I confronted Kilbrew about the attack, he was threatening. We're about to have our first open-to-the-public organizing meeting, and we expect real trouble. Three of our SNCC workers have disappeared." He halted. "That's why we're here, asking for your help."

Haley remained silent, studying the two men before him. "It's right you came here. Violence in Magnolia County is not going to be tolerated, and this office is going to see that Magnolia remains peaceful. But I can't keep my eye on every redneck who is unhappy." He rose from his chair and went to a green file case in the corner, extracted several manila folders, and laid them on the desk. "These are letters sent to the mayor, by Shiloh citizens who are not violent. They're solid citizens, old families, complaining about your agitators invading their property and stirring up trouble with their Nigras. They want something done about it." He resumed his seat behind the desk. "The mayor was good enough to share them with his sheriff," he said, his voice chilly. "There's an election coming up this fall."

"Agitators?" Jimmy snapped, "My agitators are American citizens who have to go out on the plantations to explain to a lot of the sharecroppers that they have rights, guaranteed by the Constitution, to vote in American elections. The only way they can do that is to get out there, where the 'solid citizen' owners don't want them to be. I don't think agitator is the right word to use about that. But I can't promise that we won't keep on doing that until they get registered. Hell, once they're registered they can even vote for the mayor if they want to!"

Haley smiled for the first time. "I'll be sure and tell the mayor that next time he calls." The smile vanished. "Where and when is this public meeting you're worried about?"

"On Sunday next, seven o'clock, at the old Baptist schoolhouse."

"There will be no trouble. My officers will be there."

Mendelsohn stood up. "I'd suggest that they stay outside, Sheriff. I've covered meetings like this before. If the officers are inside, a lot of the Negroes won't speak up or take part in the meeting. The people who come there have a right to set the rules about who is allowed inside. It's private property, and the Baptists have offered it to the Summer Project."

Haley said dryly, "Thought you weren't going to be part of this conversation, Mendelsohn. Thought only Mack was going to speak."

Ted held the sheriff's eyes for a beat. "It's not my job, Sheriff. I'm just a reporter. I listen, take notes, and then tell the great American public what's really happening, and who's doing what to make it happen. What I feel I try very hard to keep to myself. That's what I get poorly paid to do."

"You like your work, Mendelsohn?"

"Yes, I do. Do you, Sheriff?"

"Sometimes," Haley said, standing up. The meeting was over.

Chapter Nine

On the way to the Claybourne plantation, Ted turned from the highway on to a straight patch of gravel that sliced through dizzying rows of young cotton plants. After a hundred yards he slowed the Chevy, caught up in the beauty of the green vista that seemed as vast as the sky that arched above, wondering what this must be like when the plants burst into cotton in the fall. In the distance, tiny figures moved between the rows, bobbing like dark corks as they edged forward, chopping out the weeds. In the overheated stillness he could hear the chunk, chunk, chunk of the hoes.

At an ancient weeping willow, the gravel road curved gently into the shade of a tall stand of old oaks surrounding a stately plantation house. It didn't look like Tara. Not a grand ante-bellum mansion that was built before Abraham Lincoln was practicing law. No, it was almost defiantly Victorian, a white soaring filigreed eminence that could be comfortably at home in Newport, Rhode Island, or on Beacon Hill in Boston. It spoke of old money, of an unquestioned sense of entitlement. Carpetbagger money? He'd have to ask. No great white columns like the ones David Selznick had arranged. Beautiful, expensive, comfortably inviting, but decidedly not Tara.

Ted had to smile, feeling relieved. On the broad, deeply shaded veranda embracing the house, he saw the woman from the gas station. Dressed in a pale green linen shift, she rose awkwardly from a porch swing and came forward to greet him. Not Scarlett, but a smiling Willy Claybourne.

"You found the Claybournes, and nobody chased you that I can see from here." Her eyes elaborately searched the empty driveway.

He grinned and nodded. "And none of the townsfolk have arrived yet to string me up."

"I heard you on the gravel. Come on in out of this heat. Welcome, Ted Mendelsohn!"

"Mendelsohn's too much to handle in this humidity. Brevity is all, my editor, Max, keeps telling me. Just Ted if it's all right with you, Mrs. Claybourne."

Her smile was impish. "What's good for the cat is good for the kitten. If you're Ted, then I'm Willy. Em's inside. Nobody's ever called her Emily. And I want you to meet my husband." She hesitated. "Lucas Claybourne. He's more traditional than I am. He'll likely call you Mr. Mendelsohn."

"And what do I call him?"

She slipped her hand under his arm and opened the door. "You could call him lord of the manor." She smiled wickedly. "But I wouldn't if I were you. I think Mr. Claybourne will do nicely for now."

Together, they moved down a cool, wide entry hall past four large, idealized oils of antebellum harbors in New England. Facing the entry to the living room a single portrait held a silent, self-important vigil. The man, painted in his elder years, was dressed in a great cloak and standing on the deck of a three-masted vessel under full sail. Ted stopped before the portrait, bursting with questions. "And who is this? He looks like Cotton Mather!"

"This gentleman is the very first Claybourne to reach the Delta," Willy explained. "Henry Percival Claybourne, great-great-grandfather to my husband, Lucas, on his father's side. Henry Percival was a very successful ship owner who made a fortune carrying supplies to the occupying Northern troops down here from his home port in Plymouth, Massachusetts." Noting the astonished look on Ted's face, she grinned. "One nation, indivisible, Ted! Everybody came from some place."

As they entered the living room, a large, heavyset man in his late twenties turned from his conversation with Emily. With his rumpled dark brown hair, soiled khakis, and muddy field boots, Lucas Claybourne looked like a slightly aging running guard from Ole Miss. He was deeply tanned from the Delta sun, a man who would be most at home outside, perhaps a little uncomfortable among the colorful chintz and floral draperies of Willy Claybourne's living room. He stood up, frowning, from a couch. A Bermuda fireplace held great pots of flowering fuchsia. Hands in his pockets, he quietly regarded Willy and the journalist.

"Luke, honey, come meet Mr. Mendelsohn."

Shake hands with the son of a bitch? Let Willy do it. His eyes remained still.

"Lucas!" Her voice was cutting.

Jesus, Willy! Just what the fuck is this Jew reporter doing in my house? What the hell do you want from me?

He remained stonily silent but finally he nodded. "Lucas Claybourne, Mr. Mendelsohn." He cleared his throat. "Wilson and Em were telling me about your meeting at Bobby Joe's station."

Ted smiled. "Well, if Miss Kilbrew here hadn't bailed me out with her brother, I think I'd still be there."

"Doesn't surprise me." His voice was deep and lazy. "Em's been almost family with us for a long time. Real close." The voice had a cool edge. "Anything her best friend Willy asks her to do, she usually obliges. Hard to turn down a friend. No matter what."

Mendelsohn nodded to Emily who stood stiffly by the fireplace. "When I went to pick up the wheel, Miss Kilbrew, I don't think your brother was very happy about the whole thing. So I'm really obliged to you."

She nodded briefly, her fingers picking lint from her skirt. "BJ's not my brother. He's a half brother. We're not a whole lot alike." Abruptly she sat back down on the couch.

"Mr. Mendelsohn needed someone to offer a little Christian charity, Luke, and that's what Em got BJ to do." Willy turned to Ted. "Em and I teach Sunday school together down at Shiloh Baptist, so I know about her good heart, Ted. But best I can remember about BJ from high school, nobody wrote 'good heart' in his yearbook!"

Irritated, Luke broke in. "Who the hell's business is it if BJ has a good heart? That what this journalist is tryin' to find out?" His eyes narrowed. "Willy and Em were tellin' me that's what you are. That so?"

Ted folded his arms. "I think of myself as a reporter, Mr. Claybourne. I think a journalist gets paid better."

"Why don't you all sit down," said Willy. "Mr. Mendelsohn works for *Newsweek*, Luke. They sent him down here for the whole summer. Whole summer sounds more like a journalist than a reporter to me!"

Luke Claybourne settled on the edge of the sofa, his eyes intent on the interloper. "A journalist?" He turned to regard Willy. "Never had a journalist in our home before. Em and I were just talking about that. My wife is full of surprises, isn't she, Em?" Emily reddened, but remained silent.

A young black maid entered the room, bearing a tray of glasses, a bucket of ice, and a pitcher of iced tea. Ted recognized her immediately: Eula, Jimmy Mack's girl. She had been with Jimmy the night they all had arrived in Shiloh. Her eyes flicked briefly to his and her head made an imperceptible negative nod. She paused behind the couch, waiting for Willy to notice her. "You can put it on the coffee table, Eula. Just leave the tray. I'll pour the iced tea. You could bring the cookies in." Eula nodded politely and silently left the room.

Ted watched Willy fill the glasses and settle on the floor, her back against the couch, and heard her mutter, "Lord have mercy," as she sought to get comfortable. "Two more months till the baby comes." Her eyes locked on his. Bright eyes, filled with curiosity, as if she were waiting for some yet unimagined curtain to go up. This was not a usual part of the afternoon entertainment, Ted thought. The lady seemed to have her own agenda, and he was the pigeon she had brought to the table.

And it was painfully clear that Luke Claybourne was not happy that Ted Mendelsohn was on the menu.

"You have a beautiful place Mr. Claybourne. I appreciate Mrs. Claybourne's invitation to come here."

"Thank you," Claybourne said curtly. "We like to think that we are hospitable to people that bear us no ill will. But we're not used to having journalists here. Are you planning on taking notes? Taking our pictures? Recording the exotic redneck flora and fauna of Magnolia County? Tell you the truth, Mendelsohn, I'm not sure how to talk in front of a—" He hesitated. "A journalist from New York."

Mendelsohn placed his glass carefully on the table. "I'm not sure you understand what I'm down here to do, Mr. Claybourne. I'm not an outrider for Martin Luther King or the NAACP or any of the other civil rights organizations. I'm down here to try to understand what's happening on the ground. And when I get a handle on what these student volunteers are feeling and doing, and what folks who live here are feeling and doing, then I'll write my story and send it to *Newsweek*. And if I still have questions, I'd like the chance to come back and talk to you."

"So you're just down here doin' a job, like Willy said?" Lucas eased back in the couch, his voice skeptical. "Willing to look on both sides of the highway?"

"That's true. But I don't want to misrepresent myself to any of you."

Willy frowned and exchanged glances with Emily. "Misrepresent? What you told Em and me wasn't so?"

"What I told you was so. But I didn't tell you enough. I'm not just a reporter who happened to get assigned to Mississippi."

Luke Claybourne hiked forward on the couch. His deep voice filled the space. "Didn't just happen to get assigned? That's what you're sayin'?" His voice rose. "Then what brought you here, Mendelsohn?"

"Me. I wanted to be here." The room was silent.

"What about *Newsweek*?" Claybourne's voice was a challenge. "That a little misrepresenting, too?"

"I've worked for *Newsweek* in Washington for a lot of years, Mr. Claybourne. When I told them I wanted to come here, they said go write your story. Take as much time as you need. I'm here as a reporter to cover what I think is going to be an important story. I thought you deserved to know that."

Luke Claybourne got up abruptly from the couch and walked the length of the room, pausing at the window. When he returned, his face was troubled. "I appreciate that, Mendelsohn, but you're not neutral. You're living in the Sanctified Quarter."

Eula returned from the kitchen. She moved quietly from person to person offering pastries, pausing at Emily's side as the usually reticent woman turned to confront Mendelsohn. "You're living with those niggers in the Quarter?" Em's thin voice was strident. "Sleeping with those niggers?" Her outrage echoed in the room. "And you came down here to do that?" Finally noticing the waiting maid with her tray, she motioned impatiently. "I don't want any!"

"Where better to try to understand what those students are learning and experiencing?" asked Mendelsohn. "So when Mrs. Claybourne told me that she had questions I might answer and invited me here, I was hoping to see from the inside part of the Delta I haven't seen."

Willy intervened. "I invited him, Luke, because there are a whole lot of questions I wanted to ask him, and he promised to answer them. That a good enough reason for askin' him here?"

Impassive, Eula remained standing. "Anything else, Miss Willy?"

"That'll be all," said Willy. Eula picked up the empty glasses, but paused at the kitchen door.

"Em's questions are fair, Ted," said Willy, "and we'd all like to get some answers."

Luke's powerful voice was vehement. "I don't know about the ladies, but I sure as hell want some answers, Mendelsohn." Elbows on his knees, he leaned forward, ready to charge. "Tell us how those beatnik freedom riders you're livin' with can presume to come into our state, not knowing squat about our people or our customs, and tell us how to live our lives."

The reporter shook his head in disagreement. "They think they're here to help Negroes in Mississippi change their lives, not yours." The two men seemed planted, facing each other across the coffee table. From the corner of his eye, Mendelsohn could see the solitary figure of Eula. "They think black Americans ought to know about their history, ought to know about their own heritage. And they sure as hell believe that they should have the right to vote."

"Who in hell asked them to come?" Luke looked at Eula by the kitchen door. "You ever ask them to come, Eula? Any of your kin over in Sanctified Quarter? No, indeed. I'll tell you who asked them to come. The Communists."

Em chimed in. "That's sure right. Bobby Joe showed me an article in the *Clarion* sayin' J. Edgar Hoover himself says these freedom riders are all Communist dupes. Saw it myself, Luke!"

Mendelsohn listened attentively before replying. "From what I've seen, I think Hoover's wrong. I'm getting to know these kids. I came with them. They're smart kids, and they're nobody's dupes. But some of them are more smart-ass than smart. One of the kids from Cornell, a pre-law student, was pulled over by the Highway Patrol when he was going 25 miles an hour down Highway 49 at midnight. He was so angry that he tried to lecture the patrolman about the patrolman's infringement of his constitutional rights. For his trouble, he was busted and sent to the work farm over in Sunflower. He's still there. I went to see him and he's a mess. A good kid who won't be smart-ass again while he's down here. But he's nobody's dupe. I'd bet my paycheck he's never met a Communist."

Willy shook her head. "It wasn't a work camp that made all those kids scruffy. I never saw white kids look like that. Where'd they find these characters, Ted?"

He shrugged. "Stanford, Harvard, Columbia, Howard. . . . Doesn't matter. They're middle-class kids who are stealing a summer to work down here. And they're not staying at the Jackson Sheraton."

"There's no excuse for being unclean. Soap doesn't cost much."

"No excuse? But there are reasons, Willy. Those kids are on the roads every day, knocking on doors, trying to register voters. Roads aren't paved in the Sanctified Quarter. The only showers they get are when it rains. Most of the kids do their laundry in kettles over the fire in the backyard."

Luke' s face was livid. "Not everybody in the Quarter does their laundry in kettles! A lot of them work for me. They live different from us. They are different from us." He paused, his eyes fixed on the reporter. "I know my people and they know me, and you don't know them and you don't know me. People down here know their place, Mendelsohn. We do. And the Nigras do. We've learned to get on to-gether over generations, and we don't need or want people ridin' in and tearin' up everything we've built."

"Amen!" Em's face was high in color. "Tell him about seeing the congressman's son, Willy."

Willy turned to Mendelsohn. "You act like you believe Mississippi is enemy territory, Ted. You don't really understand what we feel, or why we feel it. Early last week Luke and I were watching television and there was an interview with Robert Carter, the congressman's son. He had just arrived in Shiloh with your people. Looked like such a nice clean-cut kid. I said to Luke we ought to bring him out here, have him meet our son, Alex, get to know us down here."

Luke snorted in disgust, imitating Willy. "Let's bring him here! An-other great idea from the hostess of the Delta, Wilson Claybourne!"

Willy grew pink but plunged ahead. "Well, the very next day Em and I were drivin' through the Quarter on the way to pick up Eula, and we see Robert Carter, big as life, walkin' hand in hand with a nigger girl! I could have killed him!" She stopped, embarrassed by her out-burst. "Maybe not. But I wanted to!" Eula's attentive but serene expres-sion never altered. Silently, she pushed back on the swinging kitchen door and disappeared. No one but Mendelsohn seemed to notice.

"You just don't understand, Ted. I can see it in your face. But you weren't born and raised in a place that is mostly black. Every day, grow-ing up in Shiloh, I was surrounded by Nigras. Thousands of them. And I had to be special, feel special, or I would have drowned. I couldn't stand them shoving against me, touching me."

Em's voice rose in anger. "Willy's right! You don't understand. You judge. And magazines like yours crucify us. They read in your northern papers that we're all bigots down here. They lump us all together and never miss giving us a black eye."

"You're wrong," Ted said. "Mississippi gives Mississippi a black eye."

"That's what I mean!" Em interrupted, almost shouting. "'Cording to you, it's always us poor redneck fools who are wrong!"

When Mendelsohn broke the silence he sought to answer the

distraught Emily. "Let me ask you a question, Miss Kilbrew. What do you think my editor was going to do with the story I filed from Shiloh last week? I'd gone over to Greenville to check some court records and when I pulled out of the courthouse parking lot in the evening I was chased, ninety miles an hour, all the way back to the Sanctified Quarter. I had to outrun a souped-up pickup truck with two guys leaning out the windows with shotguns. Two shots I heard, but I wasn't counting, I was too busy watching my rear view mirror."

Em's brittle laugh hung in the room. "Down here that's what we call the good ol' boys just havin' sport."

Mendelsohn stared at Emily who busied herself with her glass of iced tea. "Sport?" His voice was acid. "When I made it back to the Quarter I hid my car behind the Chapel and spotted the truck that had chased me. It was parked at your brother's gas station. And when I reported what happened to the sheriff the next morning, he laughed. 'Somebody just havin' some good, clean fun.' I ought to lighten-up, he said."

Em lifted her chin. "See? Just like I said!"

Mendelsohn looked slowly at each of them. "That is the 'black eye' which will appear in next Tuesday's *Newsweek*. Three columns. And tell your brother, Miss Kilbrew, the story's going to run with my picture of the pickup truck parked in front of the Kilbrew gas station."

Fuming, Em stood and headed for the front door. "Thanks a hell of a lot for inviting me to your party, Willy." She nodded to Luke. "Great guest list, Lucas. Make sure Mr. Mendelsohn is invited to the country club." In a moment, the door slammed behind her.

Willy sat quietly, leaning back against the couch, her eyes still fixed on the front door. She appeared startled when Luke broke the silence. His voice was quiet and sober. The anger in the room seemed to have left with Emily.

"There are bad elements down here, Mendelsohn. And some of them are violent people. 'Spect you have a few yourself up in New York. But there are a lot of very frightened white folks down here, too." His eyes were questioning. "They watch these agitators coming in. They watch a whole stirring about voting and organizing and race-mixing. You don't have to be Klan to see all these things. Willy sees them. I see them. Not just Bobby Joe Kilbrew. None of us knows what's coming next. A lot of frightened people. As a reporter, you should know that. And they're not all black."

Eula opened the kitchen door and stood silent, waiting for Willy to notice. Willy turned and beckoned her. "Come in, Eula. I think we're done."

"Anything I can do before I leave, Miss Willy?"

"Just help me up from this floor. After seven months I feel like a lead balloon, about to burst." She laughed, "Can a lead balloon burst, Ted?"

Eula helped her to her feet and then turned to Luke. "Good night, Mister Luke." She turned and reentered the kitchen. They heard the back door close and Eula's steps fade gradually on the gravel outside.

Willy caught Luke's eye and gave a quick nod. The large man stood, and for the first time in the afternoon, a smile lightened his face. "Not sure this is the kind of southern hospitality you expected, Mr. Mendelsohn. But it's the kind you're going to find when Willy Claybourne is the hostess. Very little bullshit and a lot of uncomfortable questions, because my wife has a curiosity that doesn't stop. I've been trying to get used to it since I first dated her in high school. Usually I can ease the situation with some of my daddy's bourbon—which is exceptional." He grinned. "We've had the questions, but none of the easing. Willy and I would like to have you join us for a drink."

Surprised, Mendelsohn returned his smile. "Thank you. I'd be very pleased to do that." As Luke moved to a sideboard to pour the drinks, Ted turned to Willy. "Might I use your phone, Willy? A friend of mine expected to hear from me by four o'clock." He grinned as her eyes widened. "The kind of friend that worries a lot."

"One of those scruffy students who rarely showers?"

He laughed and picked up the phone. "How did you know?"

Dale's voice sounded tight and constricted on the phone, and Ted had to strain to hear. "Yes, I'm fine. Why do—? When? " Drinks in hand, Luke and Willy turned at the sudden urgency in Mendelsohn's voice. He began jotting notes. "Where? Of course. I'm on the way." When he hung up the receiver, he scanned the notes, and approached the Claybournes.

"Is there a problem?" asked Willy.

Mendelsohn handed her the notes. "They've found the station wagon that the three civil rights workers were driving." Her hand was shaking as she returned the paper.

Luke grinned. "Five will get you three that it was parked at the Havana airport. J. Edgar predicted it."

Mendelsohn tried to control his voice. "You'd lose. The wagon was hidden in the woods outside Meridian in Lauderdale County. It's been burned."

"Meridian? And what about the three outside agitators?" Luke's voice was aggrieved. "They leave a forwarding address?"

Mendelsohn stared at Luke. "Those three agitators are boys I was with up in Ohio at the orientation, Mr. Claybourne. James Chaney is a kid from Meridian. He's been working with Mickey Schwerner, a young man from New York who's been down here restoring black churches that have been torched. And Andy Goodman is a college kid from Westchester, New York, nineteen years old, who just arrived in Mississippi to try to register black voters."

Willy stepped in front of Luke. Her face was pale. "Where are the boys, Ted?"

"Nobody knows. They're simply gone, Willy."

"I think my bet is still a good one, Mendelsohn." Luke was replenishing his drink. "Can I pour you one?" Mendelsohn knew it was an afterthought meant to be gracious, but he recognized it as arrogance cloaked in good manners. He'd seen it before. Claybourne had the implacable confidence of a poker player who was so sure of the validity of his hole card that he didn't even have to show his hand before picking up the chips. Mendelsohn felt disoriented and sick at heart. James! Andy! Mickey! Just disposable chips? *Where are you guys?* His jaw was clenched. *Can I pour you one?* Go fuck yourself!

"No. I've got to get back. This is a very important story and my editor's going to be looking for me."

"Why important, Mendelsohn?' Luke's voice was unrelenting. "Three Commie kids playing hide and seek in the barbarous South? That's what you think is important enough to write about? You just lookin' for another black eye?"

"It's not a judgment call for me to make, Mr. Claybourne. I'm just a working stiff. If something has happened to those boys—" He hesitated. "Two of these boys are white. People up north will notice that. Some, unfortunately, are considered more equal than others up there. Just like down here. My editor taught me that." He turned to Willy. "Thank you for this afternoon, Willy. I hope Mr. Claybourne is right, that those three young men are hiding in Havana. It's a bet I'd like to lose."

Chapter Ten

Sunday already, and still no hint of rain.

Luke Claybourne sat down heavily on the top step of the porch. The sliver of shade from the roof cut the glare from the fields, but the sodden heat engulfed every corner of his Delta. He squinted at the shimmering silent fields and the implacable sky. It's never going to rain again. Not a damn cloud. Look at that sky. As unbroken blue as the plantation's green. Like Delta bookends this rotten summer. Rain! Please, Jesus, rain! Down by the roots it's caking and that cotton's getting browner by the minute. Should have listened to Roland Burroughs, that money-sucking bastard. *New sprinklers that can wet you down twelve, fifteen rows at a time, Lukie.* Lukie! Nobody'd called him Lukie since the old man passed.

"I've got almost forty families living off this place, and I can't take care of them and buy those goddam sprinklers, too!" His voice startled him. "Those contraptions give me the creeps just lookin' at 'em, like giant space grasshoppers, something from Buck Rogers." He looked at the crows, wheeling slowly in the heat. "Nothin's movin'. Nothin's growing. But it's something else. Shit, the weather hasn't changed in two months. It's not just the weather."

Irritable, he walked inside and poured a glass of iced tea from the sweaty pitcher. The bright cerulean of the unrelenting sky made him blink as it reflected off his glass. It's never going to rain again. He swallowed deep and sucked on an ice cube. It's not just the weather. It's Willy.

The thought surprised him, it was so ready. *Willy. I don't think it's the pregnancy.* She wants the baby, flounces all over town, telling everybody the McIntire-Claybourne union is declaring a dividend come September! She still makes me laugh. But something's changing. The way she listens when Dick Perkins carries on about ski resorts in Colorado or scuba diving in Mexico. Her eyes get big, like a kid. She looks like Willy McIntire again, my Cotton Queen. God, I want to touch her, squeeze her tight. And the way she looked at that reporter, a nosy Jew from New York who's slumming down here. But anything about New York is manna for old Willy. She hasn't been that interested in anything I've had to say in six months. Why be interested in the resident redneck? Six months and we've hardly touched each other, for Christ's sake. Who told you fucking would bother the baby, Willy? Doc Henderson never said that. Dick Perkins says she's restless, is all. Get her out a little more. Where? To Walgreens?

He emptied the glass and poured some bourbon from a flask onto the ice. Funny. Sundays always felt like Sundays. The whiskey was sweet in his mouth. Sweeter on Sundays? He smiled. Yes, Jesus! A door closed and he called, "Willy? You home already?"

"No, Mr. Luke, it's Eula." She paused at the door. His face brightened.

"Well, aren't you a sight for a Sabbath morning! All dressed up in your Sunday-go-to-meetin' clothes. What are you doin' here, Eula? You're never here on Sunday." He clinked the ice cubes and grinned. "It is Sunday, isn't it?"

She noted the flask and Luke's drowsy look. "For sure it's Sunday, Mr. Luke. Miss Willy asked me come and set up for the church ladies who are coming for luncheon. Be in your way if I start bringing in the dishes?"

He nodded. "Go ahead. You're not in my way." He heard the clatter of crockery being loaded on trays. The door swung open, and Eula stepped into the room. His eyes moved slowly over the beautiful dark woman as she walked gracefully across the floor. The harsh light from the window seemed to melt on the mahogany skin. His tongue hesitated as it moved across his lips. He groaned silently. Oh, to stroke that luminous skin, to touch it, to have his tongue glide slowly across those breasts that undulated under the pink blouse. Oh, Christ. Just once.

"Mr. Luke?" She turned from the table and stirred uncomfortably as his avid eyes met hers. "I best get started with the luncheon, Mr. Luke."

"You look so pretty in that pink blouse, Eula May. It's a great color for you. I never get to see you wearing anything but your uniform. I think we ought to dress you in pink."

She smiled, and suppressed a laugh. "I don't think Miss Willy would appreciate that, Mr. Luke, though she's the one that gave me her blouse for my twenty-first birthday." He was surprised by the sudden boldness of her gaze. "Way that you're looking, you probably recognize it!"

"Yeah, I do. But it looks a little different on you. There's more of you to fill it out. Twenty-one! God, you've become a beautiful woman while we weren't noticin', Eula! Seems like only last week you were still over in junior high school and you came here on Saturdays to help your mama, Josie. Twenty-one?"

"Miss Willy's going to be back in an hour, and I should get on with my work." She hesitated at the door to the kitchen.

Luke swung his legs to the floor and strode over to the table with his glass in hand. "Twenty-first birthday, and I didn't even know it! Calls for a celebration drink, Eula, honey. Some of my daddy's great moonshine." He held up the flask like a trophy. "Did Josie ever tell you about that still over in Tallahatchie? She and my daddy used to drive up in the hills in the old De Soto to get the 'shine. They'd come back real late, frisky and gigglin'."

He winked. "I caught 'em together one night and my old man pulled out his leather belt. Josie stood right over there, watchin'. He was just tappin' the leather into his hand. 'Lukie, boy, this is a little secret between you and me that your mama doesn't have to know about. What am I supposed to do with this belt now, son?'" Luke paused and looked mischievously at Eula. "And I said 'I'd put it back in your pants, pa.' He and Josie started giggling, and I lit out for my room upstairs." His laughter filled the room. "My daddy never did whip me, because he knew I could keep a secret." He lifted the flask. "Let me pour you a short one, girl."

"I don't drink, Mr. Luke. You know that."

"That's all right. Just sit with me a little. We never get a chance to talk. There's no big rush about doing the lunch." Damn, she looks good in that blouse! Hell, she's twenty-one, she's a nigger girl and knows the score, done it plenty times with that Jimmy Mack, I'll bet, long before this. She's Josie's daughter, for Christ's sake! Good. She's sitting down. Those eyes. Black as pitch. Never can rightly tell what she's thinking. He settled back as Eula perched tentatively at the end of the couch.

"Your kin and mine, Eula." His voice was intimate. "They've known each other well for a whole lot of years. Cared a whole lot for each other. Like I care for you. Now tell me, how is Josie? She was doing poorly a few months ago."

Eula smiled. "Thank you for askin'. She's feeling better. Doctor Henderson gave her somethin' for her arthritis that really seems to help. 'Course she's gettin' on, and nothing will really help very much."

Luke reached out, his hand carelessly resting on Eula's knee. "But you're not getting old, honey. Twenty-one! Prime of your life. Look at you. Like a ripe peach." His hand tightened on her knee and he edged closer. His voice was soft. "You been picked yet, Eula May?" His rough hand had moved to her thigh.

She looked at him with dark eyes as she deliberately removed his hand and rose from the couch. "I have work to do, Mr. Claybourne. It's late."

"Now wait a minute. You know there's nothin' better for a girl than to be picked by a man who cares about her. I care for you, Eula May. I do." As she stood up, he stretched out to restrain her and knocked over his glass of whisky.

Her face did not change expression as she went to the sideboard, returning with a dishtowel. She bent to mop up the spilled drink and Luke put his hand on her shoulder. His face was flushed. "Eula—Eula, honey . . . "

She straightened up and stared down at Claybourne, struggling to control the anger in her voice. "Mr. Luke, this did not happen. You're not your daddy. And I am definitely not my mama. House niggers are long gone. The moonshine may not remember that, but you do. We've known each other for too long a time for you not to know." She stepped back. "I've got to finish the luncheon and go on to church, Mr. Luke."

Furious and humiliated, Luke confronted her. "Why?" he taunted. "You got some sins to confess?"

"No, sir, Mr. Luke. And I don't plan to have any." She turned and moved swiftly toward the kitchen.

"Where the hell do you think you're going?" The fury in his voice made her turn. "You don't just walk out when I'm talking to you! Where are the manners your mama taught you, girl?"

"Mama taught me manners." Her voice was sharp. "But Mama came out of another time. You're right, Mama was very big on manners, Mr. Luke. Mustn't do anything that might make the Claybournes think we're not grateful. But Mama's manners aren't mine."

"Meaning what?"

"Meaning I'm all grown up now that I'm twenty-one. I make up my own mind about what is proper. I think it's good manners to respect the people that work for you. I think it's the proper thing to do. But then I guess I don't get frisky like mama did on your daddy's shine. Been too busy trying to get on to college."

"Don't you dare to preach to me, girl. Not in my house!"

"I don't mean to do that, Mr. Luke. You and Miss Willy have always made me feel welcome here. But a whole lot is changing right outside. I see it on the television set. I hear it over in the Sanctified Quarter. I read about it in the *Clarion*. And you don't seem to notice anything different."

"More preaching bullshit from the 'freedom fighter' you're banging in your room? Well, girl, listen hard. Miss Willy likes how things are here. Mr. Luke likes how things are here. And my niggers like how things are here. Any of 'em don't, the highway north is right at the end of the driveway."

"A whole lot of your Negroes are going over to Indianola and registering to vote, Mr. Luke. They're not heading north. And I'm not heading north."

"Goddammit! So it's true what I heard? You and Caleb Johnson and Rufus Marks went down to Indianola and registered to vote?"

"Yes, sir. We certainly did. On my day off last Thursday."

Luke pointed to the window. "If the three of you don't get your names off that list by tomorrow, girl, last Thursday will be your last day off at this plantation."

Unobserved, Willy had entered the room, halting at the door.

In disbelief, Eula stared at the enraged man. "You're firing Caleb and Rufus and me? For registering to vote?"

"You and Caleb and Rufus and any other ungrateful black on this plantation who's taking on airs and forgetting his place. We ought to help Eula get to college, Willy said. Another of her great ideas. College? You don't have any idea of what your place is, girl. I can just imagine what you'd be like after college! I said tomorrow, and I mean tomorrow."

Willy stepped between them. "You're doing what?"

Startled, Luke stared at her. "I've told Eula she gets her name off the voting rolls tomorrow or she's out of here for good."

"You're firing Eula?"

"Stay the hell out of this, Willy!"

"Oh, no, I won't. I don't tell you how to run the plantation. You do as you see fit. You always tell me it's your business. But this house is my business, and I will not have you firing Eula May. I need her and I want her here." She turned to face the black woman. "You promised me you would stay till the baby comes. I want you to keep your promise, Eula. I need you. You haven't finished with the lunch, and the ladies will be here in less than an hour."

"Yes, Miss Willy." Without a backward glance, she left the room.

Luke watched the kitchen door swing shut and wheeled on his wife. "Jesus Christ, woman. You really want to cut off my balls in front of that nigger?"

"That nigger? Eula? You're sending Josie's daughter away?" She stared, unbelieving, at Luke's flushed face. "Are you drunk, or have you gone crazy? Well, Lucas, she's not going. Do you understand? Eula's not going anywhere."

"Oh, yeah, I understand what you're saying. And you better understand what I'm saying, Willy McIntire. If you ever, ever, put me down in front of a nigger again, it will be your last day as Mrs. Lucas Claybourne."

Chapter Eleven

After the first week, Sheriff Dennis Haley had the police cruiser stop tailing the reporter. He knew the yellow Chevy was going to be following the volunteers as they ventured up into Drew, down into Indianola, over to Cleveland. When the volunteers from Shiloh gathered crowds with their freedom songs on the sidewalks in Drew, or in Sunflower or Ruleville, the Mack kid would work the crowd. When they'd stage a picket line in Cleveland at City Hall, Mack would be handing out the signs, showing them where to start, where to stop. If there was anybody to worry about, it was Jimmy Mack. And each time he saw Mack, he saw Mendelsohn, taking notes, taking pictures.

It became as predictable as the furious response of the local toughs. Each time, he'd call the local police chief, telling him to monitor the demonstration but not let it become a mob thing that could get real ugly. Too many Feds in the area who would notice. "We don't need the FBI on our backs," Sheriff Haley told them, "and you can stop your surveillance of the reporter. It's a waste of the taxpayers' money."

It was clear by now that the volunteers were nonviolent. But after every public meeting, anywhere in his county, he'd get the agonized calls from Mayor Burroughs. "What is your problem, Haley? Those Commies are organizing civil unrest right under your goddam nose, and you're not putting a stop to it? Magnolia County is going to be the laughingstock of the whole country!" Haley would hold the receiver at arm's length, staring at the circulating fan. "The White Citizens Council is meeting Thursday, talking about candidates for the fall elections. Your name is not real popular with the folks upstairs in my bank. Get your ass in gear, Haley. There are others in this community who seem to have more balls than the sheriff's office and will do something about the Reds if you don't." The sheriff would close his eyes and wait impatiently for the harangue to stop. "Thank you for the heads-up, Mr. Mayor."

The call from Dick Perkins made him smile. "You got a drink for the local carpetbagger, Dennis?" Ever since 1958, when Perkins arrived from Colorado to run the U.S. government's agricultural demonstration farm just south of Shiloh, Haley and Perkins had shared an affectionate but slightly jaundiced view of the reality of Delta life. As a result, they enjoyed each other's company. "I'm taking my latest foreign delegation to the bus terminal at five and I'm going to need some American talk and some Kentucky bourbon." After the latest tirade by the mayor, Haley could use a drink himself. And Perkins was good company.

"Come on over to the office," he said, "and if you don't have plans, come on home and have some ribs with Janey and me."

Mrs. Skinner, his secretary, had already left when Haley heard Perkins on the stairs. He turned his overhead fan to high, kicked off his shoes, and took out the Jack Daniels and a couple of glasses. His feet on the desk, he was lighting his after-work cigar when Perkins stuck his head around the door.

"This Mayor Burroughs' office?"

The sheriff grinned and motioned to the chair opposite. "No, he just left. He needed a high colonic for his rapid heartbeat caused by worry that the Bolsheviks are already here. You can have his seat. Matter of fact, I wish you'd have his seat."

Perkins poured himself a drink and settled down comfortably to enjoy it. "Thank you, sir. It's a just reward for doing the Lord's work one more day. I feel blessed. Two Brazilians, one Chileño, and two good neighbors from Ecuador are right this moment discussing how American know-how, as exemplified by the highly mechanized Perkins farm, can be replicated, turning South America into a fecund Eden. It is truly a wonderful thing that I am doing. And your invitation to visit Madame Jane and share your ribs makes this weary bachelor very happy."

Haley grinned. Perkins's arm's-length view of the life in Shiloh where he had chosen to settle was uncannily close to Haley's own, although he himself had been born and raised Delta. Being sheriff did that. Every time he got cynical, he found out it wasn't cynical enough. "Have you met the Ambassador from *Newsweek* yet?" he asked Perkins. "No? Well, his presence in our Shiloh is giving Mayor Burroughs all kinds of shit-fits. And Mayor Burroughs is giving this sheriff all kinds of shit-fits, threatening in his own way to let loose the savages to do the cleansing of the Bolsheviks. Did you know that *Newsweek* is a Bolshevik rag, Richard? No? Well, I think the next time I hear from the mayor I'll put you on the phone. It's past time to educate outlanders like you."

"Outlander? Sheriff, I am now in my seventh year as a plantation owner and taxpayer in Magnolia County, garden spot of America. And I don't take kindly to your characterization. In forty-three more years I will be considered one of your own. So watch your tongue. You got a little more ice? No, in answer to your question. In Colorado, *Newsweek* was not considered hazardous to your health. But we were an enlightened community at the university. We knew Reds when we saw them. Didn't even fire the ones Joe McCarthy said we should."

"What made you leave? Politics?"

"No. Helen's dying. After she was gone, the music went out and Colorado got a lot chillier. I decided to leave the ag school and make my fortune as a wily carpetbagger at the government's expense. I run their demonstration farm in Shiloh and then make a deal to lease the land from Washington with an option to buy. Smartest thing I ever did. So now, Dennis, I am doing well and doing good. For which I am truly grateful."

"Grateful, Richard, but not yet humble. You still have forty-three years to learn how. Maybe your friend Claybourne can help teach you."

"Luke?" Perkins laughed. "There are a lot of nice things about Luke Claybourne. He was very generous when I first came down. He and Willy made me feel at home. But humble? Not Luke. He got his road map on living from his daddy, and the old man never taught humble. When he died Luke had to take over and pretend he knew what he was doing. He became more like his old man than his old man was." Perkins added ice to his drink and settled back in his chair. "It wasn't easy for Willy, who's a lot more curious about the world out there."

Haley's eyes crinkled. "Ah, Willy. You never knew her family, the McIntires, Richard. They sharecropped at the old Sheridan place. They were gone by the time you got here. Poorest white folks I ever saw—four kids, a drunk for a father, and a mother who worked herself to death. After she died, the kids split, heading north. Only Willy stayed. The Kilbrews took her in and she and their daughter, Emily, started high school together. She and Em have been tight ever since."

"Luke said that Willy was the most beautiful girl he ever saw when she came to Shiloh High. Prom Queen. Cotton Queen." Dennis smiled.

"I remember her. Beautiful blonde. Wasn't a boy in Shiloh didn't have savage thoughts about Wilson McIntire. But Lucas Claybourne had the inside track. Growing up rich and a star linebacker at Shiloh High gave him a sense of entitlement that nobody could compete with. As for Willy McIntire, she loved Luke for all those reasons. But she was antsy. Gettin' used to Claybourne life was pretty daunting for a McIntire who never knew shit from Shinola. Luke's mama was old New Orleans money and Luke's daddy had a tight rein on his only son. Mama never did approve of Willy, and they didn't marry until she passed on."

"It's worked out," said Perkins. "You can get used to money. Besides, she really seems to love Luke. Got one kid, Alex, already and another in the oven to prove it. Willy's great. But she's going to be antsy all her life, I suspect. She's never really been out of the Delta except for her honeymoon with Luke in New Orleans. I keep trying to broaden their horizons a little, being kind of a genteel outside agitator. I've been trying to get them interested in some of the Delta blues I love. I'm going to take them to a juke joint outside of Clarksdale I heard of last week. A place called Fatback's Platter. Ever hear of it, Dennis?"

Haley looked up sharply. "Fatback's? Yeah. It's not a licensed joint because we're a dry state, so I pretend I don't know. Long as there's no trouble the Nigras can play their music and drink their 'shine. Besides, I got a small insurance policy, a man named Bronko, who makes sure that no trouble comes out of Fatback's."

"Bronko? What's a Bronko? Sounds like a Polish car."

Dennis laughed. "No. This Bronko is a half-Polish, half-Nigra off-duty policeman. He's a mean mother, but I'm never quite sure which half is turned on. He came to work for me about nine years ago when he got out of the slammer for beating up a Polack who happened to be his father."

"And that's your insurance policy at Fatback's?"

"Uh huh. He sure is. Nobody fucks with Bronko. He's a killer, Richard. But he owes me, so I keep him handy for emergencies. Hey, the mayor may be right. If the Bolshies act up, our little county will have Bronko to show them the light."

"And what does this mighty man do at Fatback's?"

"He runs the door and keeps away all evil so the sheriff can sleep well. Not many of your racial persuasion ever show up there. So if you're really going and you want to get in I'd suggest a fifty-dollar lubrication for the Bronko and a message from his friend the sheriff that it's okay."

He swiveled in his chair and looked hard at Perkins. "Luke really said he'd go?"

"I hunt quail with Luke, and he trusts me when I can get him to look up from his bountiful plantation for longer than the next weather report. It took a little persuading from me and a lot of persuading from Willy. But good 'shine will always be attractive for Luke, even if the 'jungle music'—Luke's description—isn't. But we're going Saturday night." He grinned. "If it's any good, Dennis, I'll take your Janey there some Saturday night. Being the sheriff, I don't think you'd be comfortable going."

"Bachelors like you, Perkins, give bachelorhood a bad name. No man's wife is really safe. It's okay for tonight, you can come home with me for dinner with Janey. I'll be right there. But when you go to Fatback's Platter, Janey's going to be busy at home with her sheriff."

Later, walking home from the Haleys, warmed by the hospitality and drowsy with the many drinks of the evening, Perkins remembered Dennis's sly voice: "Wasn't a boy in Shiloh didn't have savage thoughts about Willy McIntire." Perkins chuckled. Dennis Haley had nailed it. Savage thoughts. How could they not? That very first afternoon. . . . Jesus. Seven years ago, and he could paint a picture of it. It was his first visit to introduce himself to Roland Burroughs, the banker and mayor, a man he had to get to know. Burroughs was all hominy and honey, happy to meet the man who was going to run the experimental farm and introduce Magnolia County to the world's farmers.

After the meeting Burroughs had said, "I want to take you upstairs and show you the Shiloh Club. I want you to feel welcome here and meet the folks you'll want to know who use the Club." When they'd walked up the stairs he'd felt like he was back in Boulder, Colorado, at the Faculty Club. A busy comfortable bar, an inviting smorgasbord arranged before two large windows looking out across the town green, and the easy laughter and lilt of southern conversation, much of it from a table of women where the morning's shopping was piled on an extra chair. Nice. The kind of a room Helen would have liked.

As they'd approached the bar, Willy Claybourne had pivoted, carrying two Bloody Marys. She had nearly run into him and jockeyed quickly to save the drinks from capsizing. He'd had a quick vision of blond hair and wide green eyes.

"Oh, I am so sorry! Did I spill some on you?"

He had assured the lively and lovely lady that all was well and he didn't need repairs.

She'd grinned at him and said, "I was trying to help Sammy because the bar was so busy and so I—" She'd stopped, embarrassed. "I do go on. Forgive me. You probably want to get your own drink from Sammy. Hi, Mr. Mayor!"

Burroughs had laughed. "Hi, Willy. Before you mow any more men down, meet our new friend from Colorado. Richard Perkins. This is Shiloh's one and only Wilson Claybourne."

She'd cocked her head and smiled. "Hi. You are absolutely the only person I have ever met from Colorado. Did you ski to Shiloh?"

Before he could answer, Burroughs had said, "If those drinks aren't for us, then you'd better get on to your table!" Willy had paused and given them a brazen look, up and down.

"I would have taken you two for bourbon and soda. Or maybe just bourbon. No, these are for Miss Emily and me. Nice to meet you, Richard Perkins." He had watched her trim figure as she'd threaded her way to her table. And when the noon sun from the large windows caught the mop of blond curls, he—well, he could paint a picture. When he'd raised his bourbon to her across the crowded room, she had grinned and raised her glass in response.

Southern women. He never had figured them out. From the get-go, Willy was bewitching, knowing, teasing, feminine. What was it that made them different? Helen was a beautiful woman, sexy in her own way, but a little unattainable, not as aggressively female as a Willy Claybourne. More mysterious. But Willy gave him the impression she was attainable and reminded him that he was male every time he encountered her. From that first tangle with the Bloody Marys it was a given that they were going to know each other a lot better. The next weekend Luke Claybourne had invited him out to his plantation. He said his wife

had told him Richard Perkins was new in town and he wanted to make him welcome. And Perkins knew he wanted to go.

Chapter Twelve

NEFERTITI. The sign was tacked to the door, and caught their headlights when they came down the long winding road. Perkins pulled up alongside the line of dusty cars and trucks parked almost around the bungalow. He grinned at Luke and caught Willy's smiling eyes in the mirror. "This has got to be it. Welcome to Fatback's Platter, and songs by the Queen of the Nile, Nefertiti." When they opened the car door, the beat of the music from the cabin was shaking the place. A cluster of blacks crowded the entrance and Willy's hand tightened on Luke's arm.

"Richard, you really think we can take Willy in that joint?" Luke asked. "Last time I went to a juke joint like that I was drunk and had the whole football team with me. Got out by the skin of my teeth."

"Relax, Luke. I know a man who knows a man. Stay here with Willy till I call you." He strode across the yard and reached out to shake hands with the huge man at the door. Over the music Bronko's guttural voice was saying, "I told you niggers to stay back. You'll get in when I say you'll get in." He and Perkins put their heads together, and then Perkins waved Luke and Willy to join him.

"Comin' through," Bronko said, moving into the crush with Willy, Luke and Perkins in his wake. Startled at the sudden intrusion of whites at Fatback's, the crowd at the door grudgingly parted and the four stepped into the smoke and noise. As Bronko led them to a small table in the corner, dancers were leaving the crowded floor and a throaty singer's voice seemed to hush the place.

Nefertiti, the pretty, buxom, glistening woman at the mike, was singing, her eyes closed and her expressive hands making little circles to match the lyrics. Dressed in a scarlet gown that plunged tantalizingly over well rounded breasts, with a cascade of glass necklaces catching and reflecting the funky light of the room, she commanded the scene. With every tilt of her expressive head, the long dangling earrings trembled in the half-light. The alto sax groaned a rhythmic background, and a sinuous snare gave a shivering, suggestive accompaniment to the music.

> *Whoever said a good man is hard to find*
> *Positively absolutely sure was blind*
> *I've found the best man there ever was*
> *Here's just some of the things that my man does. . . .*

Laughter rolled like surf in the little room then subsided.

> *Why he shakes my ashes, greases my griddle,*
> *Chimes my butter and he strokes my fiddle,*
> *My man is such a handy man (oh, yes he is). . . .*

Willy tilted her head to catch the words through the noisy merriment in the room.

> *He threads my needle, creams my wheat*
> *Heats my heater and he chops my meat*
> *My man is such a handy man.*

Willy was laughing, her eyes bright, her hand tight on Luke's arm. She caught Perkins's broad smile as he ordered drinks for the table, and saw Luke frown, staring at the singer. "Oh, for God's sake, Luke," she protested. "Lighten up and have some fun."

Luke's eyes never left the woman at the mike. It really was her. How many years? Seventeen, maybe? He stirred uncomfortably in his chair. Long before I even met Willy . . . "Never-titty! Nefertiti! Jesus!" When he turned finally to Willy she was chuckling quietly as she followed the glistening singer. Verse after verse, the ribaldry built as Nefertiti grimaced and clucked, sharing the wicked fun of the words with every corner of Fatback's Platter.

Yeah you know my ice don't get a chance to melt away
Cause he sees that I get that fresh piece every day,
My man, my man is such a handy man . . .

Nefertiti's eyes grew large as she suddenly spotted Luke. Fanning herself with her large lavender scarf, she wrapped up her patter. Then she
pointed at Lucas, and the patrons howled. "I know that white man. And
I ain't kiddin'!" As the room roared its approval, Nefertiti blew kisses to
the crowd and moved with surprising nimbleness to Perkins's table, both
hands extended to Luke. "My, God, it really is you. White Lightning!"

Willy turned to Luke with a wide smile, her eyebrows arched. "Introduce us to your friend, darling." He was flushed with embarrassment
as he rose to greet the woman, but could not contain a pleased smile.

"A long time, Nefertiti. Hell, a very long time." As the voluptuous
woman enthusiastically embraced him, Willy exchanged astonished
glances with Perkins. "This is my wife, Willy, and my friend, Dick
Perkins." He clumsily extricated himself, but held the singer's hand.
"Willy, right after the war, Eula's mother had a gentleman friend—
Calvin—who used to come visit us at the plantation. He was a widower,
and loved Josie's company. He had a pretty, skinny little daughter he
brought with him—this lady. And every time he came, Nefertiti and I
were left to play together. I was about eight and you about six, Titi, first
time you came."

Nefertiti grinned and took Willy's hands in her own. "I knew your
man long before you did, Willy." Mischievously she rolled her eyes and
winked at Perkins. "We played a lot together!"

Reddening, Luke looked sideways at Willy, struggling to find a way
ahead in the conversation. "Last time I saw Titi," he mumbled, "I was
fifteen."

"A large fifteen, Willy! I mean a tall fifteen!" She shook with laughter and squeezed Luke's hand.

Shaking his head, Luke waved to the waiter. "We could use a drink
for the lady," he said, and everyone laughed.

"It took you a long time to get there, White Lightning. You used to
be a whole lot faster!" She smiled at his discomfiture and placed a wet
kiss on his cheek.

Perkins rose from the table, "C'mon, Willy, let's you and me let these folks reminisce. The music's too good to waste." He tugged her to the crowded dance floor. "Willy," he murmured. "Stop lookin' like that. You never played doctor when you were eight?"

She leaned back in his arms, and smiled at him. "How'd you know that, way out in Colorado?"

How clearly Luke remembered! The girl that had come with Calvin was fun! Right from the start, Nefertiti was pissy as hell, game for anything, a tomboy, and full of laughter. She looked more like a boy than a girl, he'd been glad to see. It was lonely during the summer, nobody much around, and he'd welcomed her company. His daddy was always way out in the fields, checking the pickers in the surplus GI jeep he'd bought when he returned from the war. There was nobody to hunt turtles with down in the hollow, nobody to fish for the catfish that were always there in the lower-40 pond, nobody for nothing. Damn near made him wish it was school time again. Then Nefertiti had showed up.

The first time he took her to the hollow for turtles, she tripped on a trailing vine from the willow and fell face down in the muddy water. When she rose, her face was so caked with mud that he burst out laughing. "You look like a nigger!"

"Well, what you think I is?" She'd scraped off the mud, then looked right at him. "I's a nigger." Then she'd made a comic face and giggled. "You fall in that nasty water and you looks like a nigger, too!"

"Didn't mean nothing by it," he said, feeling sort of bad. That afternoon they got three turtles while the Delta sun was baking the mud on their soaking clothes. "Gonna take off these nastys," she'd said and pulled off the T-shirt, shorts and underwear. At the little overflow stream from the pool she squatted in the water and washed the mud away. When she stretched out to dry in the sun, Luke pulled off his shorts and washed himself at the pool.

"Watch out for the biting flies," he said, lying down beside her. "They leave real big welts. Daddy says they can make you sick." He rolled on his side, his head only inches away from the girl. "Where'd you get a name like Nefertiti? Don't sound like a nigger name I ever heard of."

"Papa says mama named me. She thought I was beautiful like the

Queen of the Nile, papa said. That's who Nefertiti was. Don't much remember mama. She passed when I was three and a half. I remember her skin, real light. I loved it. Not dark like mine and papa's." She sat up, staring at Luke's body. "You got funny colors, light pink around your middle and dark brown on top. Sun doesn't make that much difference on me. I never saw a white boy's pecker before. Ain't very big." She rolled on to her back, her eyes closed against the sun.

Luke said angrily, "It's big enough. They get bigger when you're older." He grinned. "You ain't even got a small one. You look like a boy, no titties at all."

"You gets titties when you older, papa told me. I ain't no boy. I'm Nefertiti, Queen of the Nile!" Then she hooted with laughter. "And you ain't!"

"And you ain't Nefertiti, neither. Your name is Never-Titty!" The two of them started to laugh at his great joke when they heard the call from the house. "Nefertiti! Time to go home!"

Luke whispered, "Y'hear that? Never-Titty, time to go home!"

Giggling, she'd slapped him and pulled on her clothes. "Daddy never said that. You bad, Lucas."

Nefertiti lit a cigarette and settled back in her chair, appraising Luke. "You ever learn to use these, Lightnin'? Rememberin' your old man, I'd bet no."

"Daddy would have beat my bottom then. You remember him, huh?" She still looked so damn fine. Little Titi. . . . oh, man. "It was all so simple then."

Nefertiti nodded, a tear streaking her mascara. "And sweet, Lucas. So sweet." Her gaze moved to the dance floor. "And Willy McIntire turned out like that!"

Dressed in a soft green floral linen that billowed as she turned, revealing long, tan legs, Willy moved effortlessly in Perkins's arms. Her eyes were closed and her head was back, light catching her blonde hair. Nefertiti nodded and smiled. "Well, you always liked beautiful women. Girls, anyway. Leastwise till you went to Shiloh High and you lost my address."

"Don't shit a shitter, Titi. It was you that moved away to Biloxi with your father."

"Yeah. That's so. But the day you went off to high school I knew our playtime was over. And so did you."

He blew his nose hard in his handkerchief. "Must be all the smoke in the room," he muttered. It was sweet. He could see her still. It was never that simple sweet again. Damn smoke was getting in his eyes.

Richard Perkins and Willy had stepped back, watching the dancers grooving on a go-for-broke "Take the A Train." The unrestrained joy on the floor was infectious. "You game?" Richard shed his jacket, pulled down his tie, and held out his arms.

"No. But what the hell," Willy said.

Laughing, he swept her back out into the melee. She was still youthfully slender even in her pregnancy. Perkins brought her tight against him, then swung the surprised Willy out to the length of his arm as he found the beat and started to lindy.

Her lips parted and her eyes flashed as she discovered the passionate side of Dick Perkins. Lord! Oh, yes! Not like dancing before the long mirror when Luke was down in New Orleans, wishing . . . for what? She surrendered to the Ellington music, melding body to body. My God, I'd nearly forgotten. Wonderful! The crowded dance floor seemed to become a stage for the couple. The other dancers edged away and a rhythmic clapping started and didn't stop till "A Train" surrendered in a long wail by the sax. Still in his embrace, Willy took a deep breath, then slowly eased him away. "Well, Richard Perkins," she breathed. "You are full of surprises."

Nefertiti watched Luke as his eyes followed Willy and Perkins. When he turned back to her, she touched her glass to his. "You like that music, Lightnin'?"

"No. Jungle music, Titi. I'm too redneck for that stuff."

She smiled. "But not too redneck to teach this jungle bunny quite a few things my daddy never told me about."

He tilted his head, meeting her eyes. "The jungle bunny had quite a few things to teach me that I hoped my daddy was never going to know about." He laughed. "'Course our housekeeper, Josie, knew, ever since she found us in the tack room buck naked, and observed you admiring how much I had grown in those few years!"

She hooted. "Seein' was believin', but it don't mean a thing if it ain't got that swing, and we were both too scared to find out. Lordy, Lordy! That was when you were fourteen and I was twelve. I had to wait a whole year, Lucas, wonderin' and wonderin' how it would be."

"We couldn't wait that long, Titi. I was so hot for you that I borrowed my daddy's jeep and drove us out to that spot near the levee outside of Greenville. Even had moonlight on the river for that first time. You remember?"

"You're one crazy cracker, Lucas. You think a girl don't remember her first time?" She gazed at him tenderly. "Not that the first time was very successful, lover! You were so eager that you got there without me. That's the night I called you White Lightning! Christ, are you blushing? No need. We made up for that on more great times than I can remember." Her gaze drifted to the dancers on the floor. "Willy's one lucky lady, Luke."

When Perkins and Willy returned to the table, Titi rose and embraced Willy. "Last time my daddy brought me to Claybourne's, you came back with Lucas and I saw he'd found what he was waitin' for. Can we all have a nightcap when I'm done with the next set? Gotta go to work."

They started to applaud when she crossed to the mike and a loud voice called, "'I Would if I Could,' baby. Sing it!" Nefertiti grinned and held up her hand for silence.

"The old songs are the best songs, after all. Music, maestro." The snare started its roll and the bass took up the beat as the sax nestled close to the singer.

Now I would if I could but honey I can't no more,
Yes I would if I could but honey I can't no more,
I can't get no cooperation, the way I did before. . . .

"I like your friend, Luke," said Richard, grinning. "Now there are folks I know who would not believe what I have just seen with my own two eyes."

"The old songs are the best songs, after all?" Willy echoed, raising an eyebrow. "You think so, Luke?"

He didn't answer because Nefertiti's throaty voice cut through the smoky room. But his eyes met Willy's over the glass as he finished off the whisky.

Now you're gettin' slow and easy,
You're as patient as can be,
You don't ask for too much lovin'
And that's what's botherin' me.
Tell me, papa papa, just what are we waitin' for?
Yes, I would if I could, but I don't get a chance no more.

When the last car had pulled out of the parking lot, Bronko locked the door behind him and followed Nefertiti to the bar. "Pour us a sip, lover, while I tote up my riches," she said, methodically counting the bills and writing down the numbers like her daddy used to do. When she finished, she made a small separate stack and carefully slipped it into an envelope and handed it to Bronko. He grinned, enjoying the charade they played every Saturday night.

"And who gets the envelope, Titi?"

She closed the register, moved around the bar and sat next to him. She nuzzled against him, chuckling. "You get the envelope, lover."

He put his arm around her, and she lowered her head to rest on his shoulder. "And who keeps the envelope, Titi?"

She laughed like a tired child, pleased with their game. "Sheriff Dennis Haley keeps the envelope."

He raised her head and kissed her long and hard. "And what does Bronko get?"

She slid from the stool. "Bronko gets a sip, a taste, and a lot of lovin' from the Queen of the Nile."

He locked the bar and led her through the dark stand of trees to the little cottage that her daddy had built after the war. "And how come Bronko gets a sip, a taste, and a lot of lovin'?"

She led him to her bed. "Because Bronko is my handy man. Didn't you know?"

When he left, it was two in the morning and Nefertiti was deep asleep. Her gentle touch and tenderness was the only balm in the crabbed and lonely world of Stanley Bronko. She never wanted him there when she awoke, and he longed to stay. But he stole away from the room like a burglar. He hated that feeling.

Lucas Claybourne. White Lightnin'. Oh my God! Chilled, she had wakened at four, and slipped into her robe, staring into the darkness. After all these years, Lucas. She squeezed her eyes tight, conjuring that ghost from her fifteenth year. *Oh, Lightnin', don't go!*

Her eyes opened, searching the coal black room, but she saw only the pale gray square of the dawn window. Shivering, her body tingling and vividly awake, Nefertiti tapped out a cigarette and lit it. In the bureau mirror she saw its pulsing glow and crossed to light the candle beside the glass. Dear Jesus. Lightnin'. It was like a moan. You loved me. The tears came, glowing where they fell, staining the dark velvet skin. Her eyes, wide and frightened, stared back from the mirror.

Richard Perkins heard the hiss of the sprinklers as they moved down the rows, and without opening his eyes he knew that it was already fierce out in the fields. Six weeks since the last rain shower that moved up from the coast? His head was still full of images from the night. Nefertiti, so damned exciting, and good-hearted, fucked-up-priorities Luke. Wants to be his daddy, good white master to his tenants. He grinned, still fuzzy from the hooch at Fatback's. Poor Luke. He'd never seen a man turn that red. Luke and Nefertiti, the great white planter, redneck son of a bitch with his plantation playmate! He felt for old Lucas.

Perkins stretched, squeezing his eyes against the brilliant window. And Willy. Wasn't she something? Take the A-train. . . . His body stirred at the thought, and then he let the thought in and felt Willy, seven months pregnant, moving in synch, letting the music decide. For real? Or for now? Or was it just Willy? You are full of surprises, Richard Perkins. Christ, he hadn't let himself feel like that since Helen. His hand stretched out across the bed to nothing. An old habit. Dum de dum de dum. . . . How the hell did it go? Lonesome . . . .

Get the lonesome blues
Any time you're far from me,
Get the lonesome blues
Deeper than the deep blue sea. . . .

Blinking, he pulled up the blinds and looked outside. This sea was green, stretching endlessly under the glare. Only the sprinklers were moving, trembling across the hard-baked Delta earth.

The call from Richard Perkins came as Willy was finishing her coffee.

"Good morning, Willy. After such a big night I was afraid I might wake you calling so early."

"No chance of that, Dick. I've been up since seven. I had to make breakfast for Luke before he headed to the cotton broker in Jackson. Why did you call?"

"I wanted to make sure that the lindy and the A-Train had not derailed you last night. I felt a little responsible."

She smiled and sipped her coffee. "You were a little responsible. No. Not derailed, But maybe detoured. I haven't been on that kind of a trip in a very long time. It made me wonder where that train was headed."

There was a pause before Perkins answered. "Willy, I'd like to come over to talk. You mind?"

Willy put down her coffee. "You are full of surprises, Dick Perkins. Of course I don't mind."

Willy met him at the door with a grin and planted a kiss on his cheek. "My gentleman caller. Now how many women have gentleman callers before eleven in the morning! Do you want some coffee?"

"No, thanks. I'm not sure gentleman callers drink coffee. As a matter of fact, I'm not sure what gentleman callers do."

"They have assignations," Willy chuckled. "I read it somewhere and looked up the word. I don't think this is an assignation."

Perkins settled on the living room couch, watching Willy as she sat opposite him. "We've been friends for a very long time, Willy. I've come here a hundred times to see you and Luke. And this is the first time I've come to visit you alone. It's not the first time I've wanted to. It's the first time I've come."

She met his gaze. "I'm aware of that." Mischievously, she asked, "Do you think it was the A-Train that brought you?"

"No. I think it was because I've always felt something very important could happen between us, and until last night I didn't want to let that happen. This morning I knew that I want that to happen, Willy."

The merriment in her eyes faded. "Dick, we've been dearest friends. You've understood me better than anyone other than Luke. I love you like the dear friend you are and always have been." She smiled. "Maybe it was the bourbon and the Basie at Fatback's."

"Willy, it wasn't the bourbon and the Basie." He moved from the couch and crossed to her side. Gently, he raised her face and kissed her.

When Willy took his hands from her face and kissed them, her eyes were troubled. "Darling Dick. If wishes were horses . . . beggars would ride. And Willy Claybourne would still be Willy McIntire and Mr. Wonderful from Colorado would ride out of the west and take her out to the world, probably on a horse. You've told me so much about that world beyond the Delta. How I would love to see that world with you!" She sighed, and her eyes held his. "You know how to truly embrace it. But for now, I'm Willy McIntire Claybourne, wife of Lucas, who is struggling to hold on to a farm that's his life, mother of Alex and mother-in-waiting for a new Claybourne." She rose from the couch. "Dearest Dick, you brought me a beautiful gift of friendship when you came to Shiloh. I will always love you for it." She smiled wanly and held out her hand. "But wishes aren't horses."

Chapter Thirteen

Bronko let the water pound him, the throbbing shower bringing him back, but slowly. It had been a long night at Fatback's, near two when the sheriff's honky friends finally left. Mmm. Good lookin' broad.

That fast 50 from Haley's friend will help. Sheriff's been good to me. Hell, I been good to him, too. He smiled. Not as good as Titi! Mmm . . . . Jesus!

His eyes opened, the water cascading from his shaved head and his broad shoulders. Seeing the dark curve of his glistening stomach made him wince. He was putting on weight again.

He stepped from the shower, wrapped a towel around his shoulders, moved heavily to the sink and stared at the mirror. It always happened. He never knew how to stop it. His thick forefinger began to trace the curving, nearly white scar that started below his cheekbone and ended in the shadow of his ear. The buckle on Big Stanley's belt. Bronko spat into the sink in disgust and then lathered to shave. The soap made a clown's face of the heavy Negroid features and he searched the mirror. Two calculating blue eyes stared back at him. Fucking Polack eyes! Two Polack eyes and one Polack scar to carry for the rest of my fucking life. Should've killed that bastard when I found out he was the one who got her knocked up, but what does a kid know? Polack didn't know his whore was mulatto, light as the sheriff's wife. A great joke on everybody when I arrived. He spat in the sink, washed away the lather, and buried his face in the towel. How many times did he use the belt and the buckle on both of us? Throwed the old lady out, and me with her. She grabbed the next bus for N'Orleans and left me with the Sisters and I didn't catch up with Big Stanley till I was eighteen at the work farm and he was a guard. He smiled at his image. Introduced myself by poling him with my rock hammer, woulda killed him then but they jumped me. He gone now, don' matter leastwise where. I'd still be servin' time weren't for Haley.

Haley summoned Bronko that afternoon. "My friend Dick Perkins tells me you took good care of them at Fatback's. You did good, Stanley. Any trouble out there?"

Bronko shook his head. "Not likely." He placed the envelope on the corner of the desk and watched the sheriff slide it into his jacket pocket. "People don't mess with me, Sheriff. And I don't mess with them lest I got to."

Haley settled back in his chair, studying the huge man. "Sit down,

Stanley. I had a visit yesterday from the reporter who's in town. You know who I mean. Tall guy named Mendelsohn?"

Bronko nodded. "Shit, he been everywhere those agitators been. No missin' him. Yeah I seen him."

"He came to see me with Jimmy Mack. You know Mack?"

"I know who he is. Hell, at this point everybody know who he is. Seems like as many people know him as know me, and I been takin' care of business round here for a long time. He's a tough little bugger. But this ain't his turf. Maybe I gotta remind him of that."

"That could be a real problem, Stanley. And I don't want any problem I don't need to have with the mayor on my back. It's why I called you in."

Bronko frowned, stirring uncomfortably in his seat. "So what you want from me?"

The sheriff rose from his chair and went to the large town map hanging on the wall. "You know that Baptist school used to be over on Summit?"

"Yeah. It's been empty for three, maybe four years."

"Well, Mack's made a deal with the Elders to use the school as an organizing center, and they're going to have a big public meeting next Sunday night to open the place. Folks going to be coming in from a whole lot of places."

"Organizing the niggers for what? To tear up the place?"

"Organizing the farm workers in a union, Stanley. The mayor's all upset about it, but there's nothing legal we can do about stopping it. And there are a lot of Klan who are gonna be all upset about it, and there's nothing legal they can do to stop it either. But that doesn't mean they're not going to try. So we got to know what the hell we're doing every minute of that meeting. I want you and all my deputies at that Baptist school Sunday."

"I wouldn't miss it. I want to know what niggers are goin' to show up for that agitator. So what did Mack and the reporter want from you?"

"They wanted me to promise that the police will stay outside because it's a legal meeting on private property. And if it is, the reporter said we got no right to be inside unless we're invited in. They think the police will be intimidating to a lot of the people who are coming."

"Well, who gives a shit what they think? They're agitators!"

"I do." His voice was metallic. "I said that no police are going to come in unless there is trouble. And I meant nobody, Stanley. What happens at that meeting is going to be reported every damn place, and we are not going to fuck it up. You are not going to fuck it up, Bronko."

"You want me to play nice with these Communists?" His voice was incredulous.

"I want you to protect my ass, Bronko. That's what you are paid to do."

Chapter Fourteen

Summer had moved across the Delta. The dwarf cotton plants had stretched in vain, seeking the rain that never came. Dirt had caked in the fields but it was hidden by the myriad of leaves that now touched row on row. Mendelsohn drove slowly through the Sanctified Quarter and out to the highway heading north to the Claybourne plantation, passing Martha Honey, Jim Dann, and a clutch of volunteers from the Freedom School, still walking the dusty roads, fanning out, one more time, to talk freedom with the blacks. They walked slowly now, finally in rhythm with the ebb and flow of breath here in the Mississippi Delta. The kids had ceased to be remarkable to white Shiloh. And Andy and Mickey and James? Almost too painful to think of. Where were they? At every dark crossroad, at every strange car that wheeled into the Quarter, at every dusk when the Angelus chimed, at every passing over-heated day, at every finish of an exhausting week, the nagging, terrifying question that mirrored that whole summer: Where were they? When the town constable passed with the police dog pacing in the truck bed now, it occasioned hardly a glance from the blacks or the white students. Now FBI agents moved in their black cars through the languorous heat. And the TV networks had crews on the ready, their antenna trucks in shady places where they could find the students and the blacks. Ted

Mendelsohn heard a lot of whispering that the FBI might have found some talkers out in the country who maybe remembered certain things, and he was trying to check it out. Andy, Mickey, James . . . Where are you, guys?

Even the caravans of committed blacks going down to the County Courthouse had become routine. But now July was melting into August and the tempo of activity at the Freedom House was freshening. Jimmy Mack had decided the nagging uncertainty was stifling the mission they had come for. It was time to challenge the very heartland of the Delta. Mack organized a Freedom Meeting for his dusty troop in the abandoned Baptist school. "It's not a mile from the White Citizens' Council headquarters, Ted! Freedom Train's a-rollin', and it leaves on Sunday. Everybody invited to come!"

Ted watched the black youngster, so vulnerable, daring a future he couldn't imagine, striding forward without a map or a back-up. "Jimmy, how about my coming with you and we go visit the sheriff before the meeting?"

Jimmy grinned and nodded. "Don't know that I need someone to ride shotgun in planning for a nonviolent meeting, but it couldn't hurt."

Apprehensive, Ted had called Max. "There's never been such a meeting in Indianola. These kids are putting themselves on the line, half a mile from the White Citizens Council headquarters. I don't know."

Max interrupted with exasperation, "They're not kids! They're organizers, for Christ's sake! They're not your kids." He hesitated. "Just write your story. And be careful, Teddy."

Ted had replied, "Stay tuned. And have some bail money ready." Now he eased past the courthouse, studying the faces of the townspeople. The facade of the white community was as monolithic in August as it had been in June. If there were strains of passion or conscience within the structure, they sure as hell remained fraternal secrets. They all shared the handshake. Only this morning he had wired *Newsweek*:

> *The overt hostility of violence has been replaced by the quiet intransigence of the sheriff and the police. The white face the students have learned to know so well remains unmoved and*

unchanged. It's as full of loathing and hate as on the day they arrived.

And yet there were the Claybournes. And what of them? He wheeled onto the gravel driveway of their home and parked in the shade of the great willow, wanting to walk a ways. From day one, Lucas and Wilson Claybourne had posed more questions for him than they had answered.

Eula sauntered out on the veranda, seeking in vain any errant breeze. Mendelsohn spotted her and waved from the walk. Jimmy's girl, still here, in the belly of the beast? Smart as hell, and looks so fine. "How's it going, Eula? You're still here?"

She came to meet him. "Things are going well, Ted. I've moved in here because I promised the Claybournes I'd help them till the baby gets here. Another month, I suspect." She grinned. "That's my excuse. What's yours?"

"Being a conscientious member of the press. I trust your bosses to level with me and tell me what they think. Not many white folks I've met are like that. I'm trying to wrap up the story about Goodman, Schwerner, and Chaney, Eula. Those kids are still missing."

"That's just so awful. I have cousins down in Meridian, friends of the Chaney family. I met James in the spring." Her eyes clouded. "He was so excited about the northern students coming down here."

Ted nodded. "But people forget so quick. The only reason my boss is hanging on to the story is because two of those kids are white and from the North. But news is news only because it's happening today. And they've been gone now since June."

They walked together and paused at the step to the veranda. Eula touched his arm and raised her troubled face. Her voice had softened. "Do you think James and the others are dead?"

"We may never know. It's the kind of a story that's not new in your Mississippi. You remember Emmett Till? Just fifteen years old?" He wanted to reassure the girl but couldn't find the words to do it. His gut was roiling at the obscenity of the crime, but when he spoke it was with the dispassionate advice of a journalist. "Maybe this will be different. More people are paying attention this time. We can only hope."

Eula's silence made him turn. When she looked up, her eyes were damp. Ted knew she was not thinking about Emmett Till.

He squeezed her hand. "Jimmy is going to be fine, Eula. People are watching now." He glanced at the house. "Are the Claybournes home?"

"Miss Willy is. Let me tell her you're here. She'll be glad to see you."

Mendelsohn chuckled. "But not Mr. Luke, huh?"

She smiled. "Mr. Luke refers to you as the 'Hebrew gentleman caller' or the 'red journalist,' depending on what you wrote that week. But he's not home. He's out in the fields, worried sick about the drought. Swears he'll never even make a crop this year less it rains. Over breakfast this morning he asked me, 'What in the world will all our families at Claybournes' do if we can't make a crop?' And I sure didn't have an answer for the poor man. His friend Dick Perkins is inside, waiting for him to come back. Come on in."

He followed her down the long cool hall, hearing the hoarse rasp of Louie Armstrong coming from the living room.

Moonlight shining on the fields below
Banjos humming so soft and low

A lean man with salt-and-pepper hair was bent over the phonograph, holding a small pile of records. He straightened, smiling, and moderated the sound as Ted and Eula entered the room. Eula said, "Mr. Perkins, this is Mr. Mendelsohn, the writer from *Newsweek*? Let me go get Miss Willy."

Perkins set the records on the table and walked over to greet him. "It's nice to meet you, Mr. Mendelsohn. Friend Claybourne has told me about you, and so has Willy. From New York, right? I'm surprised we haven't met before this." His smile was knowing. "You must be the outside agitator that Lucas described."

"I think Mr. Claybourne refers to me as the Hebrew outside agitator, Mr. Perkins. But I am unmistakably he." He settled in an easy chair. "I'm just a working stiff, hardly a card-carrying agitator. But the Claybournes have been very hospitable. Are you the Perkins from the Perkins plantation?"

Perkins sat down in a facing chair, holding up a hand in protest.

"Well, I prefer to be known as the Perkins from the Perkins farm. I never could get comfortable with the word plantation, Mr. Mendelsohn."

"Not a son of the gallant South? Maybe you're the outside agitator!"

"I'm afraid I'm a son of the gallant West. I arrived here seven years ago from Colorado and bought my farm. One of the last carpetbaggers."

Mendelsohn glanced at the phonograph. "I never thought I'd hear Satchmo in this living room, Mr. Perkins. Lucas Claybourne would call that jungle music."

Perkins smiled. "Nobody's beyond redemption, Mr. Mendelsohn. I'm determined to broaden Luke's horizons. Willy has a lot more daring."

The reporter nodded. "Yes, she has. She picked me up at a gas station and invited me home. That doesn't happen a lot in New York, and I've found that it doesn't happen down here with an outsider at all."

Perkins threw back his head and laughed. "No. I think maybe it's never happened before! She's a woman with great curiosity and no sense of fear. I took the Claybournes to a juke joint in Clarksdale to hear some Delta blues, something I like a lot. And Willy loved it! She even got me out on the floor with her. I don't think Luke quite appreciated it, but he's a harder case. It's why I brought some Leadbelly, Armstrong, and B.B. King for my friend to listen to—if he'll listen." He measured the reporter. "With a name like Mendelsohn, you must like music. Do you like the music from the Delta?"

"I like all kinds of good music. I haven't really heard authentic blues since I came down to the Delta. I've been running practically on empty down here, chasing this story about the boys' disappearance."

Perkins frowned and leaned forward. "We don't usually get a lot of northern journalists down here. Of course we don't usually have the kind of story you've been covering, either. A sad business."

"A sad business? You think it's a sad business?" Angry and impatient, Mendelsohn got up and turned to face him. "Do you know that's the first time anyone white in Magnolia County has said that? Three innocent kids, grabbed and probably lynched, and nobody this side of highway 49 seems to think that's a sad business. Don't you find that astonishing?"

Perkins remained silent, watching Ted struggle to rein in his anger.

"I've been down here long enough to not be astonished, Mr. Mendelsohn," he said quietly.

"A sad business, but nothing to be astonished by? You don't find that troubling?"

Perkins frowned. "You're putting words in my mouth. I didn't say it wasn't troubling. I'm an agricultural expert, not a clergyman. I worry about improving the soil and making the harvest more bountiful. I leave the perfectibility of the human condition to those who are better qualified."

Mendelsohn took his seat again, but perched at its edge. "Point taken. But after living in this garrison society on the other side of the highway, I begin to wonder how come most of the wisdom I find down here is among the least educated and least favored. And smart white people like Lucas Claybourne don't seem to know the score. Being a carpetbagger, Mr. Perkins, maybe you have a perspective I can't seem to manage."

"Carpetbaggers are just businessmen who know a good thing when they see it, Mr. Mendelsohn. They don't come to change the situation, they come to exploit the situation. I'm just one of those businessmen, not a seer. I try in my own way to do no harm, like a doctor. I do know this much. If you think Lucas Claybourne doesn't know the score, you're sadly mistaken. In some ways, he's one of the most savvy political people I've ever met. But he comes out of a different history and a different values system. No, the Lucas Claybournes clinging to this Delta know the score. They just don't like the score."

From the hallway they heard Willy's cheerful exclamation: "Satchmo!" The two men rose, watching with amusement as she came into the room. Dressed in a long bathrobe, a towel wrapped around her hair, she entered in a rush, pausing only to call to Richard, "You brought us Louis!" Half closing her eyes she lifted her arms to an imaginary partner and danced across the room, stopping to plant an affectionate kiss on the smiling Perkins. She turned to greet Mendelsohn. "Sorry I took so long, Ted. I was in the shower when Eula told me you were downstairs. I see you've met our friend Richard." Taking Perkins's arm, she said very formally, "Richard is our compadre, Mr. Mendelsohn." She grinned and looked for assurance from Perkins. "Compadre, right?"

Perkins nodded. "Compadre. You now own two Spanish words, Willy."

She laughed as she noticed the quizzical look on Mendelsohn's face. "The other one is 'si.' And that one Richard has forbidden me to use when we get to Mexico and meet those hot-looking Spanish types. He's very protective, Ted. He's the only man in the world who has been able to persuade Lucas to leave Shiloh and fly off on a vacation in Acapulco once the baby has arrived. And we're going!" She paused. "Forgive me, Ted. I haven't even offered you a cup of coffee. Eula! We're all dying for some coffee. What brings you here so early in the morning?"

"I wanted to say thanks to you and Mr. Claybourne before I go back to New York. My boss wants me at the office, and who knows when I'll get back to Mississippi. You made me welcome, and I appreciate it."

"It was our pleasure, Ted. Sit a minute and you'll be able to see Luke." She smiled and winked at Richard. "Those two seemed to have a lot to talk about!"

The front door swung open and Luke rumbled into the room. "Eula, get me a cup of coffee!" He stopped and surveyed the three sitting around the coffee table. "Looks like you're waiting for a fourth for bridge." As he settled heavily into a chair, Eula brought a large carafe of coffee.

"Hot off the fire, Mr. Luke," she said. "And the cream is fresh from the barn."

Luke lifted his cup. "Dick, you and I gotta talk. You been out in those fields? More like bakelite than soil. It's gonna kill us if we don't get rain," he growled, "and soon." He turned and faced Mendelsohn, his face impassive. "Haven't seen you in weeks. Thought you would have left since they never did find those missing kids." For the first time he ventured a brief, satisfied smile. "I haven't won my bet yet, but my hole card still looks good. You gonna hang around to write about the labor organizing these pinkos are starting that's gonna break our balls?"

Mendelsohn put down his coffee. "Not my beat, Mr. Claybourne. I'm heading back to New York this weekend and just stopped to say goodbye to you and Mrs. Claybourne."

"You could write a story about this goddam heat. I don't think it's been this hot for this long since your Hebrews built those pyramids."

He slumped dejectedly back in his chair. "Nothin's growin' out there, Dick. If we make a crop it'll be a large miracle. And now my Nigras are talkin' union! Union! And we haven't had a rain longer than a piss in three months."

"You're hurting worse than you had to, Luke," Perkins said. "You should have invested in those automated sprinklers when I told you to. No way of surviving this kind of drought without automation. You'd have to hire on twenty times the hands you have now to keep those plants healthy."

Luke exploded from his chair. "And what about the forty families I got to feed now, for Christ's sakes?"

Willy rose and came over to refill Luke's coffee. "Darling, don't get so upset."

"I'm not upset. I'm worried is all." The querulousness had retreated from his voice. Looking deeply troubled, he returned to his seat. "I owe it to them, Richard. They've been with our family from the get-go. Nothin' to do with union. Everything to do with responsibility. My daddy taught me about what they owe me and what I owe them. It's sad, but the money's not there for them and the machines. End of story." He turned to the reporter. "What do you know about this union thing?"

Mendelsohn raised his hands. "Never heard about it till last week when I was down in Jackson at the FBI office. All I heard was rumors that a union might grow out of the Freedom Democratic Party that's been organizing around the state. The talk in Jackson was that it might start up here in the Delta. The whole history of organizing sharecroppers in Mississippi never got off the ground in the '30s when the AFL tried. The guess in Jackson is that, if it happens, the SNCC kid Jimmy Mack, who's leading the voting drive, might get involved. When I asked him if it was true—" He fumbled for his notebook. "Mack said, 'When we get the vote we'll elect people who will bring justice to the Delta. My job is to make that happen.'"

"Son of a bitch! I knew there was gonna be trouble the minute I saw Mack coming on to my place. Said he was going to see Lottie and Justin and meet some of their friends, Willy. 'Just a little organizing meeting,' he said. Yeah. A little meeting to castrate us. What are they lookin' for, Mendelsohn?"

"In Jackson they're saying a dollar fifteen an hour. That's the minimum wage. Is that a lot?" The question was asked innocently.

"Is that a lot?" His jaw tight, Claybourne glared at him. "Do you have any idea what folks get down here for workin' in the fields?" In exasperation he turned to Perkins. "Can you believe it, Dick? A dollar fifteen! That's going to hurt the Nigras. Hurt them bad. In the end they'll be the ones to suffer. Help me explain it to this journalist from New York so he understands."

Perkins nodded. "Luke's got forty tenant families, Mendelsohn. Except for the littlest kids, all of them go to the fields. Each one's got to get paid. Only Senator Tilden's got more tenant families than Luke."

Willy intervened softly. "Luke's worried we'll have to let a lot of them go if the farm hands organize, Ted. A dollar fifteen an hour is a whole lot more than seven dollars a day. And we have long days down here in the Delta."

Perkins added, "That's an arithmetic that looks staggering to folks here in Shiloh, Mr. Mendelsohn. And if you're not mechanized, you depend on those huge numbers of stoop labor."

Luke shook his head in annoyance. "They're not stoop labor. They're people, families. And I'd have to run twenty of them off my place." He looked at Willy. "And Jimmy Mack's family among them. I'd hate like hell to do it, too. What's going to happen to those families? Just forget them? Christ. I've known most of those folks all my life."

Perkins's voice was sympathetic. "It's not personal, Luke." He turned to Mendelsohn. "The old plantation system created a monster of cheap, unskilled labor. Without it, those fields out there would still be swamp and scrub, and the country would be importing cotton from all over the world instead of exporting it. Luke's daddy got rich on it. And some of us have done very well enjoying the fruits of all that labor. It was a system that worked then. But it's got to change now or it'll strangle the South."

Luke snorted, "Well, thank you, Dr. Perkins, for that enlightening sociological analysis. How come none of us rednecks who've been living with this exploitive system all our lives seem to have your remarkable insights? After all, you must know something we don't since you came from the great cotton state of Colorado!"

"Stop that, Lucas." Willy's voice was like a slap. "Richard was simply commenting on what he's seen. You make it sound like he's attacking you."

Claybourne's angry silence seemed to fill the room. Mendelsohn stood up and extended his hand to Luke. "I've got to get back to New York, where there are no cotton fields. I'll tell them what I've learned, Mr. Claybourne." He shook hands with Willy. "Thanks for the coffee and the good conversation, Willy."

As Perkins rose to say goodbye, the front door slammed and a shrill woman's voice called out, "Willy? Luke? Are you here?" They could hear footsteps in the hallway and a distraught Emily burst into the room.

Frightened, Willy exclaimed, "Em! What in the world . . . ?"

Shaken and pale, Emily stopped at the door, struggling to speak. "It's Bobby Joe." The words were like a cry.

Luke strode over and brought her to the couch. "It's all right, Em. Take a deep breath. Now, what about Bobby Joe?"

She licked her lips and cleared her throat, her frightened eyes on Luke's concerned face. "Mama says he's been arrested." Her eyes darted to Mendelsohn and then to Willy. "Willy, mama said it was the FBI that came and took him away. 'For questioning,' she said."

Willy was silent, but Luke spoke sharply. "About what, for Christ's sake? Questioning about what, Em?"

She began to weep. "Something about those three civil rights workers."

"Can I use your phone, Willy?" Mendelsohn crossed to the telephone table. "I'll call an agent I know down at the FBI in Jackson and check it out."

Everyone strained to hear as they watched him scribble notes, speaking at length on the phone. When he hung up, he looked at the distraught Emily. "I'm sorry, Miss Kilbrew. Your brother was picked up as a material witness to murder. He's being held in Jackson at a federal facility."

"Murder? Bobby Joe? That's ridiculous!" Luke's voice was hard. "What are you talking about, Mendelsohn?"

"It's not me, Mr. Claybourne." He held up his notes. "It's Mr. Hoover's FBI. They say that someone in the Klan finally talked. And this morning they found the three kids."

Willy's eyes widened. She put a comforting arm around Emily who was sobbing now. When she spoke her voice was thin and quiet. "Where, Ted?"

"Buried in an earthen dam in Neshoba County. They'd been executed, Mr. Claybourne." He turned and left the room, nearly colliding with a startled Eula. In another moment he was running on the gravel to his car.

The call from Max was waiting when he got back to his room. "Tell me everything, Teddy. Hoover's office is trumpeting about how FBI vigilance broke this case. That sure as hell will have to be proved, but meanwhile we've got the inside track on what it all means to the blacks, the whites, and the whole country. It's your narrative, baby, and I want you to wrap it the way you see it, hear it, touch it. James Chaney's funeral is early next week in Meridian, and I want you there. This story has legs and it's going to go on for a long time. But I want the heart of this story. And I've got my best guy to tell it."

Chapter Fifteen

Jimmy lay still, his eyes tracing the pale yellow under the edge of the shade as it started to brighten. Almost real dawn. His hand moved gently along the soft curve of Eula's back, and he felt her stir.

"Jimmy," she murmured and rolled over to face him. Her hand found his face and pulled it to her. "Jimmy." Her breath was sweet. Inches apart, they lingered, searching each other's faces, pleased with what they saw. Without a word she moved into his arms. Jimmy, Jimmy. The dream had scared her, and she was not going to share it. He kissed her. A long kiss and the tip of her tongue aroused him. His hand moved to her breast and he looked at her. She was smiling, and he answered her smile with a shake of his head. "Oh, baby, I want to. I always want to with you. But I can't. I've got to get out of here. It's almost seven." She took his hand from her breast and kissed it. "There's more where that came from," she whispered. She sat up and reached for her robe.

"You best get out of here before the rooster wakes the Claybournes," she said. She watched him climb into his jeans and pull the T-shirt over his shoulders. What good shoulders. She grinned and pointed to the door. "Time for my rooster to get out of the hen house."

He leaned back against the door. She could see his troubled face in the light that began to flood the room. "We didn't finish what we talked about last night, baby. I want you to be at the organizing meeting at the school on Sunday. It's really important to me that you come."

Eula crossed from the bed and stood before him. "You know I can't, Jimmy. If it wasn't for Mrs. Claybourne, I would have been thrown off the plantation already, just for registering to vote. If Luke Claybourne found out I was at a union-organizing meeting, I would be out of this job. And Willy Claybourne would back him up."

"But I need you. I need your support, " His voice was insistent. "Everybody in the Sanctified Quarter knows we're a couple. How will it look if my girl doesn't show up at the most important meeting of the summer?"

"I can't help it, darling. I need this job. And I'm hoping the Claybournes will help me out with my college expenses if I get into Delta State."

He put his hands on her arms, his head touching hers. His voice was a supplication. "But can't you see, baby, that this organizing thing is bigger than that? This is the whole future of the Delta. Maybe even Mississippi. Maybe even the whole South. We have to show solidarity or this won't work. It's risky for everybody. But sometimes we have to take risks to make any gains." When she remained silent, he found himself angrier than he ever thought he could be with this precious woman. "Christ, you knew James Chaney. You knew he was out there somewhere, taking risks. He's dead, Eula!"

She flinched, and tears filled her eyes. "I pray for James. And I so believe in what you are all trying to do." Her eyes were beseeching him. "I love you, Jimmy. But I just can't do it with you."

Unbidden, the hateful words spilled out from him. "Do you want to be somebody's house nigger for the rest of your life?"

She closed her eyes as if he had slapped her. "No, of course not.

That's why I want to go to college so that what happened to my mama won't happen to me."

"But you going to college just helps one person, honey. You. Organizing is going to help all of us."

Eula wiped away the tears with an impatient hand. "No. You're wrong. My going to college is so I can help our people, all of us, which is what I plan to do."

Jimmy gently wiped away a final tear. How much he loved this woman, and what kind of craziness were they living in? He blinked hard so as not to weep himself. "And what about us? You and me?"

Her voice trembled. "We'll just have to see."

He opened the door to leave and then stopped. "You know I love you, Eula May. I have right from the beginning. And one day I want us to be married. I want you to be the mother of my children."

Through new tears, she struggled to answer. "I love you, too, Jimmy. And I'm very proud of what you're doing. But I'm not ready."

"When will you be, Eula?"

Her voice was small and forlorn. "I don't know. All I know is not now."

Chapter Sixteen

The days leading to the mass meeting were melting away, and Jimmy was in a dizzying rush to put everything in place; calls to the preachers, meetings with the nervous volunteers, strategy sessions with SNCC headquarters, establishing a minimal security for the Baptist school. And then this stupid arrest, which could shatter everything!

Jimmy was furious with himself. He should have known better. Hell, he did know better, and he wasn't thinking. Trying to build support for the upcoming strike with blacks on the senator's plantation, for Christ's sake. Of course the police would be watching. Jimmy glanced at Dale Billings and muttered, "Sorry, brother." They stood rigid, blinking in the light of the police car as the two officers stepped from the car and approached them, hands on their holsters. The taller one said, "Put your fucking hands on the hood and keep them there. Now!" They leaned over the hood as he patted them down. "They're clean," he said.

The shorter policeman pulled out his notebook. In a soft voice he said, "All right, boys, give me your names."

"Dale Billings."

"Mack. James Mack."

The taller one grinned. "Jimmy Mack! No shit!" He pulled Mack by the shirt and hustled him roughly into the back seat of the cruiser. Very deliberately, the other officer finished his writing, then turned to Dale,

"Get in the back seat. You're both under arrest for trespassing."

The tall cop watched them in his rear view mirror. "You niggers so dumb you go agitating on the Tildon plantation?" Jimmy groaned and closed his eyes and Dale stared straight ahead. "Luther," the tall one said. "This is the Jimmy Mack that's the organizer. The organizer!" He hooted. "Just another dumb fucking nigger."

At police headquarters the two were booked by a sleepy sergeant and led up steep iron stairs to an open cell at the top. With a lopsided smile Dale said, "Bet you didn't know you were just another dumb, fucking nigger, brother." He aimed a playful punch at Jimmy who shook his head desolately.

"I was so busy thinking about the mass meeting I wasn't paying enough attention. Man, I'm real sorry I brought you with me."

Dale grinned. "Missifuckingsippi, Jimmy bro. They been grabbing everybody. Nothing personal. Just hope the senator's folks we met are gonna come to the meeting." He nodded to the open cell door. "They don't seem very worried that we're going to escape."

There were voices down below and the slamming of doors. "Dale Billings!" It was the tall policeman at the bottom of the stairs. "Get down here." When Dale stepped from the cell and looked below, only the two policemen were visible. Jimmy could hear Dale's feet on the iron steps and then only the murmur of voices. There was a sudden shouted gasp of pain, a groan, and the sound of someone falling.

"Hey, Bronko, get this nigger out of here! And bring the mop." Now it was the softer voice of the policeman called Luther. "Jimmy Mack!" Jimmy stepped from the cell and looked below. A huge black policeman was half lifting, half dragging, a dazed Dale out the door. "Come on down, Jimmy," said Deputy Luther Lonergan.

Jimmy stared. The two policemen looked ridiculously tiny, their white faces turned up to his cell. "Don't let me piss myself," he prayed. Unbidden, he watched his feet move down the iron stairs, and suddenly he was standing between the two policemen. The two white faces filled the room. "Where is Dale Billings?" he asked, looking at the tall one. The large face never changed expression.

"Getting some help from another nigger. Now I get to ask the questions." He cocked his head. "Are you a Negro or a nigger, Mack?" His eyes widened, waiting the answer. Jimmy met his eyes. "A Negro." The unexpected blow from Lonergan exploded against his jaw, sending him sprawling on the cement floor. The tall cop swung back his boot and kicked him in the ribs. With a gasp, Jimmy retched, spitting blood on the floor. His teeth felt loose. You bastard! Lonergan reached down, grabbed his collar and hauled him to his feet. Very quietly he said. "My turn to ask a question, Jimmy. Are you a Negro or a nigger?" Jimmy's left eye was closing and a roaring was deafening in his ear. I am gonna be sick. His right eye finally focused on the policeman's face. The words choked in Jimmy's throat and he spat out more blood. "A Negro." The tall policeman swung his billy club, striking Mack's arm with such force that he toppled to the cement, and a scream erupted from his throat. Gasping for breath and clutching his damaged arm, he tried to rise but failed. From where he lay he looked up the iron stairs, trying to stop the whirling room so he would not be sick. As the room steadied, he saw the huge black policeman standing, arms folded, and expressionless. "Are you a Negro or a nigger, Jimmy Mack?" One of the cops . . . which one . . . doesn't matter . . . they're going to beat me till they kill me . . . they got to hear me say nigger. The second kick in the ribs robbed him of all decisions. Panting, desperate for breath, Mack groaned, "Nigger."

Through the rosy mist of his bleeding eye he saw the black policeman impassively observing. Lonergan chuckled, stepping back from the prostrate Mack. "We're done." With contempt, he beckoned to the waiting Bronko. "Get this nigger out of here." The two officers left the room and Bronko came slowly down the stairs.

"A Negro or a nigger." Bronko spat the words. Like my old man . . . nigger, nigger, nigger . . . never got tired of makin' me say it. Beat the shit out of me for not being a white Polack like him. He never knew the whore was half black herself. Surprise, surprise! He couldn't believe it when I decked him with the hammer. Surprise, surprise! Shoulda finished the son of a bitch. That blue eyed bastard gone now, left while I was doin' time. Knew I'd kill him when I got out.

He paused when he reached the prostrate Jimmy Mack. "Some niggers don't never learn. Say what you gotta say and do what you gotta do later." He dragged the wounded man to the door and shoved him into the night. Bronko's thick finger slowly traced the white scar on his cheek as he watched Jimmy stagger to the highway. He took a lot of licks 'fore he said nigger. That black motherfucker is a tough bugger. If they don't kill him first, he gonna give me a lot of trouble.

Chapter Seventeen

Eula didn't hear the tapping till she turned off the water at the kitchen sink and reached for a towel for the pile of dishes. She frowned, brushed the damp hair from her eyes and looked at the wall clock. Ten-thirty. Who in the world at this hour of night? The tapping was louder and more urgent. She dried her hands on her apron and cautiously approached the back door.

"Jesus, baby, open the damn door. It's me."

"Jimmy!" She swung open the door and leaned back against the wall as Jimmy staggered into the kitchen. "My God, what—?"

He swayed, blinking in the sudden light, clutching his arm. "Help me to the chair, baby."

She hurried to his side and helped him reach the kitchen chair. "You're bleeding! Your eye! What—?"

"Later, baby." His voice was strained. "Don't be frightened. Get some ice. The bleeding will stop in a minute." Exhausted, he tilted his head back and closed his eyes. A hacking cough rumbled from his chest and his damaged arm dropped to his side. "They kicked me in the ribs." A groan escaped through his clenched lips. "It hurts so much to breathe, baby. And I can't use my right arm. I think something's busted."

"Who? Never mind who. We've got to get you to a hospital. You could have a punctured lung!" Eula emptied ice onto a dishtowel and hurried to his side. "Don't talk. Stay quiet, Jimmy." She put the compress on his closed eye and across the discolored cheek and nose. "Hold this with your left hand, darling. I'll be right back." Beneath the pounding pain, he heard her voice calling upstairs. "Miss Willy!" Her voice sounded tiny and at a great distance. "Miss Willy!" As he started to cough again, the kitchen ceiling light seemed to dip and swing, so he closed his eyes tight. With the darkness, the pain shooting through his arm was magically turned off as he fainted.

They found him on the floor by the chair. Eula knelt beside him, cradling his head. "Under the sink, Miss Willy. The ammonia bottle. It will help." Willy handed her the bottle, staring at the unconscious boy on the floor. When Eula placed the ammonia under Jimmy's nose, he began to cough, and his good eye flew open. "Stop!" The command was hoarse. "I'm all right, baby. Help me to sit up."

Eula helped him to sit erect. "He's hurting bad, Miss Willy. He can't use his arm, and he's having trouble breathing."

Jimmy blinked. "Sorry to mess up your kitchen, Mrs. Claybourne." He was interrupted by a rough cough. "I don't like to mess up Eula's good work." Unexpectedly, tears ran down his battered cheek. "You really don't need this beat-up nigger in your kitchen."

"I don't know what's happened to you, Jimmy. Eula can tell me later. But we've got to get you to the Shiloh Medical Center, and right now. Your cough sounds terrible."

"No." His voice was unexpectedly loud. "No."

Impatiently, Willy said, "Just give me your hand, Jimmy. Eula, get your arm under his and we'll get him to my car."

With a groan, he finally was able to stand. "Give me a minute," he pleaded. The two women stopped. "We're not going to the Shiloh Medical Center." Jimmy's voice was firm.

"Of course we are." said Willy. "You need help and that's why we're going."

"They won't let me in the door. Talk to her, Eula."

Eula nodded. "Not even the Emergency entrance." Her voice was tinged with anger. "There is no colored entrance at the Shiloh Medical Center, Miss Willy."

"But he's hurt. Hurt bad! Don't be silly, Eula. If Luke were here he'd damn well get him in the hospital. I'll take him."

"Don't matter, Miss Willy. Jimmy's black, and he won't get in. Waste of time. Only place he can go is over to the colored clinic in Mound Bayou, about forty minutes away. I know a doctor we can wake when we get there."

"No time to argue," snapped Willy. "Let me tell my sister to keep an eye on Alex till I get back." She moved swiftly out of the kitchen, returning with her car keys "You know the way, Eula? Sit next to me and we'll let Jimmy stretch out in the back seat." When they made it out to the car, Jimmy hobbled into the back seat. As the two women got in the front, Willy said, "Who did this to you, Jimmy? It's barbaric! I'm going to call the police soon as I'm back."

"You don't have to call them, Mrs. Claybourne." His voice was muffled. "They already know about this nigger."

"Don't talk like that, Jimmy, "she said sharply. "How do they know that?"

"Because they were the ones that beat me." In the dim light, Eula saw that he was crying.

"Dear Jesus." Willy's eyes glistened as she met Jimmy's in the rear view mirror. "I'm so sorry, Jimmy," she said, and started the engine.

When Willy returned, Lucas met her at the door. "Christ! Do you know it's almost three o'clock in the morning? I didn't know if you were dead or alive. Been out of my mind worrying. All your sister knew was you'd rushed out and would be back later. I called everybody. Went to ask Eula and she was gone. Are you all right?"

She slumped wearily into a chair and closed her eyes. "'I'm sorry,

Luke. Wasn't time to leave you a note. And there wasn't a phone in Mound Bayou I could get to."

"Mound Bayou? What in the world were you doing in Mound Bayou? Are you crazy? There's not a white soul in that whole town!"

"I didn't go to find that out, Luke." She raised her eyes. "I went with our Eula to find a doctor who'd treat a black man who'd been severely beaten."

"A black man who'd been severely beaten. And you took him to Mound Bayou." Incredulous, he simply stared at his wife.

She nodded. "It was Jimmy Mack, and he'd been terribly beaten. We didn't know how bad. He was having an awful time breathing."

"So Eula's Freedom Fighter got beat up by some nigger and Eula got Miss Fixit to go running? You put poultices on the poor man?"

She raised her head and met his gaze. "No, Lucas. He was arrested by two policeman of the Shiloh police force as he came off the property of Senator Tildon. And when they got him to police headquarters, they beat him."

"He was trespassing on Tildon's property? Stealing? Selling dope?"

"No. He was trying to organize Tildon's workers to vote." She shook her head. "That was what he was doing there. He and that boy, Dale Billings. Trying to get people to vote."

"Should have been arrested, Willy. That's private property. I would have had him arrested myself if he was caught on Claybourne's."

"He was beaten, Luke. Cut in the face, beat on his body, kicked in the ribs. That the price for trying to organize in Shiloh?"

"There must be more to the story, Willy. This isn't Russia. Police don't beat people for trespassin' in Magnolia County."

She began to weep, her shoulders shaking as she buried her face in her hands. Alarmed, Luke knelt next to her, putting his arms around her. "Willy, it's all right. Whatever you been through, it's over. Come on to bed. We'll talk about it tomorrow."

She raised her head, trying to see Luke through the tears. "There is more to the story. I heard Jimmy tell it to Eula. They beat him, Luke, and they kicked him, one after the other, until he'd say 'I'm a nigger.'" The tears began again. "Are you a Negro or a nigger?" Stricken, she stared at her husband. "And then when they were through, they threw him out of headquarters. How he got back to our place, Lord knows. I don't think he remembers himself."

Luke frowned. "Where is he now?"

"We left him with old Mrs. Thompson over in the Quarter. She was a nurse in the war down in Gulfport with the colored troops. Said she'll see he gets some rest. She has some morphine if the pain gets too bad."

"And Eula heard that whole beating story from Jimmy Mack?"

Willy massaged the back of her neck, trying to compose herself. "We both did, Luke. I'm a witness. She's a witness. You can talk to her in the morning. She's back in her room, worried sick if Jimmy will be all right." Her voice rose in anger. "And I want you to call the sheriff. Dennis Haley's got to know what his police did in his headquarters last night!"

"Willy," he protested. "It's almost four o'clock! I'll call him later in the morning and tell him we want to see him." He helped her to her feet. "Enough damage done for one night."

"Come in Willy, Lucas." Dennis Haley held open the door and motioned to the seats beside his desk. "Sit down, folks. Tell me what's troubling you. You sounded really upset, Luke."

"I'm more than upset, Dennis. My wife was told that two of your officers, Shiloh policemen, severely beat and kicked two of your prisoners last night. You know anything about two Nigras being busted last night for trespassin' on Senator Tildon's property?'

"Yes. I got the report from the sergeant on duty last night. It was on my desk this morning when I came in. Sergeant Meyers booked James Mack and Dale Billings before he went home. The charge was trespassing. No mention of anyone being beaten. They were supposed to be kept overnight as a warning against any further trespassing. You know, Lucas, there's been a lot of incursions onto the plantations by these Freedom Summer kids. But the two policeman who arrested them kicked them out early this morning."

"Is that the usual practice, Dennis? Two Shiloh police arrest the men, then dismiss the charge and release the prisoners in the middle of the night?"

"No. I'd say not. But Butler and Lonergan have been with the force a long time. When I questioned them, they said Shiloh taxpayers shouldn't have to pay to house and feed two nigger agitators. Since trespassing was the only charge and the sergeant had left, they used their discretion. Not usual, Luke, but it doesn't seem like a reason to make a fuss about it. What's the problem? Them two boys your niggers?"

Willy answered. "No. They don't work at Claybournes. But your policemen are not telling you what happened last night!"

The sheriff looked at Luke and then at Willy. "You saw what happened last night, Willy? You saw those two boys?"

"No," she said impatiently. "I only heard what happened last night. And it was only from Jimmy Mack. Dale Billings had disappeared by the time Mack was beaten and released. And Mack said it was your policemen who beat him, Sheriff. I was carryin' him to Mound Bayou clinic for medical assistance when he told my maid, Eula, and me the story."

"You believe that story, Lucas?" Haley rose and went to the door. "Butler! Lonergan! Get in here!" A moment later the two policemen entered the room, removing their hats. Butler nodded to Lucas. "Mr. Claybourne." Lonergan remained silent.

Haley closed the door and resumed his seat behind the desk. "According to the sheet, you both were involved with the arrest of James Mack and Dale Billings last night for trespassing at the Tildon plantation. That right?"

"Yes, sir," said Butler. "Caught the niggers about eight o'clock comin' out to the road. Lonergan and me had staked out the place, hearing that agitators were likely gonna be there." He grinned at the sheriff. "Was easy as shootin' fish in a barrel."

"There's a story going 'round that you beat those two prisoners at this headquarters." Haley eased back in his chair. "You got any light to shed on that, Butler?"

"No, sir. I sure don't."

"You, Lonergan?"

"That's bullshit, Sheriff. 'Scuse me, Mrs. Claybourne. Don't know where a story like that would come from. Course, there's a whole lot of riff-raff in Shiloh this summer. Cain't know what they'd say or do to make us Christians look bad. Those two niggers sayin' now they was beat up by me and Butler? They run a little and fell down a little when we busted them." Smiling, he turned to look at his partner. "You beat up those nigger agitators, Butler, when I wasn't lookin'? Shame on you if you did."

Haley spoke sharply. "That's enough smart-talk. You deny beating Mack and Billings?"

"Course I do, Sheriff. Like I said, it's bullshit."

The sheriff turned to Willy. "Mrs. Claybourne, you've heard these two police officers deny the charges. Seems like it's James Mack's word and story against theirs. You know of any witness that saw this alleged beating happen?"

Willy looked at Luke. "There is one, Dennis," he said. "A colored officer named Bronko. Stanley Bronko."

The sheriff frowned and nodded toward the door. "You men are dismissed. Send Bronko in."

Butler and Lonergan went in to the Day Room where Bronko was watching the television. "Turn off that goddam television and get your black ass in to the sheriff's office," said Butler. "Haley's orders."

Bronko turned his great head and looked at the two policemen. Slowly, he stood and faced them. "My friend, Sheriff Haley, wants to see me? Why he want that? You two honky mother-fuckers trying to mess with me in Haley's headquarters? You can kiss my Polack ass."

"I don't gotta answer your dumb nigger questions, Bronko. Sheriff said to send you in. But before you go in, you ought to know that me and Lonergan just explained to the sheriff that nothing happened here last night worth rememberin' about those two prisoners we brought in."

Lonergan planted himself in front of Bronko. "You pretty tight with Sheriff Haley, ain't you, boy? Well your friend could be in a peck of trouble if anything happened in his shit hole of a headquarters to any of the prisoners brought in. So Butler and me reassured him that we didn't see nothing. You want to go on bein' Haley's pet coon dog and go on bein' scratched, then you didn't see nothin, neither."

"Don't mess with me, Lonergan." Bronko's voice was low and guttural. "Don't need you tellin' me what the fuck I gonna do. I broke honkies like you in half when they messed with me. Don't believe me? Ask the sheriff." He picked up his cap, pushed Lonergan aside, and left the office.

When Bronko entered Haley's office, Luke whispered to Willy, "Isn't that the guy who ran the door at Fatback's?" Willy nodded, watching the large man come to attention in front of Haley's desk. "At ease, Deputy Bronko. This is Mr. and Mrs. Claybourne. Came in this morning because they heard a story that Jimmy Mack and Dale Billings, who were picked up for trespassing, were beaten in this headquarters last night. Mr. Claybourne seems to think you might be a witness to that." Haley paused and looked steadily at Bronko. "That's a very serious crime. It would certainly be a terrible discredit to this office, particularly since this office is the first to hire a colored officer in the whole Delta. Did you see Mack and Billings last night?"

Bronko nodded. "Yes, sir."

"Did you see Deputy Butler or Deputy Lonergan strike either of those prisoners?"

His eyes locked on Haley's. "No, sir. Who say that they did, Sheriff?"

"James Mack told Mrs. Claybourne that."

Bronko's eyes moved lazily to Willy. "Why you believe Jimmy Mack, Miz Claybourne? He just a full-of-himself nigger, trying to get some size here this summer by agitatin' good colored folks who're just tryin' to get along. You an' Mr. Claybourne know wasn't no trouble here 'fore those troublemakers come here. Jimmy Mack is just trouble."

Haley nodded. "Thank you, Deputy Bronko. You're dismissed."

When Bronko left the room the sheriff escorted the Claybournes to their car. "Sorry about all this, Willy. I'm not saying you didn't hear what you say you heard. But according to my officers, any bruises Mack and Billings got were from running and falling. And the only other officer that was present says nothing happened here at the station. My hands are pretty much tied."

Lucas met Haley's gaze. "Willy doesn't make up alibis for agitators, Dennis. She knows what she saw. She knows what she heard. And she told the truth. Willy doesn't know how to lie."

Willy paused before entering the car. "You've got three police officers working for you that are lying to you, Dennis. Guess you'll have to figure out why."

Chapter Eighteen

When Willy Claybourne walked into the kitchen, she sifted through the fragrant pile of laundry that was stacked on the kitchen counter. Head down, Eula was concentrating on the ironing, the dark hand skillfully moving the iron across the damp laundry.

"Eula, honey, did you see my white blouse with the scalloped ruffle around the neck?"

The iron kept moving, edging carefully around the last of the dinner napkins. In the silence, Eula's eyes remained locked on her work.

"I asked you a question." Willy's voice was annoyed. "Did you see my white blouse? The one Luke says makes me look like a schoolgirl?"

"No, ma'am." The iron kept moving. It was so quiet they could hear the slight hiss as the heated iron moved across the moist fabric.

"What's this no ma'am and not looking at me when I'm talking to you?"

Eula very deliberately set the iron on its stand and raised angry eyes to Willy's.

"What is all this, Eula? Are you all right?"

"No, ma'am."

"You're not? What's the matter with you?"

"It's not me. It's Jimmy."

"Oh, sweet Jesus. Jimmy!" Willy sounded relieved but clearly embarrassed. "Forgive me. Is Jimmy okay? He's been all right since he was treated at Mound Bayou, isn't he?"

"His body is healing." There was a huskiness in her voice. "But his heart and mind are something else." Tears glistened in Eula's eyes. "And so are mine."

"You?"

"Yes, me. I'm aching for him. Jimmy's always been such a proud man." Her voice was almost a whisper. "You ever seen your man humiliated?"

"My Luke? Humiliated? You must be kidding. You know him better than that."

"Yes, I do. But you and Mr. Luke don't know my man. And that's probably why you don't understand."

"Understand what?" Her voice had risen. "I did everything I could. I got him to the hospital in Mound Bayou that night. What else could I have done?"

"You did." Eula nodded and unplugged the iron. "And we're both grateful for that. He was hurt so bad, and he needed help so bad. But it doesn't end there."

"End? What in hell is that supposed to mean?"

"Not one thing done about it. Not one word! Not one reprimand! Not one arrest! I think that you and Mr. Claybourne ought to speak out, force the sheriff to arrest the cops who beat Jimmy up! Claybournes own the second biggest plantation in all of Magnolia County, know all the most important people in Shiloh! You play bridge with the sheriff's wife! Can't you get some justice for my man who was beaten almost to death?"

"Well there must have been—"

Furious, Eula interrupted. "Must have been what? A reason? There's no reason, Miss Willy. The only reason is that Jimmy's skin is black."

Willy protested. "He must have done something to make them."

Eula stared at the woman. "Yes, something." The words were angry. "Something real criminal, like trying to register people to vote."

Willy's face was pale as she struggled to reach the distraught woman. "Eula May, I've never seen you like this before. Yes, that was a terrible thing that happened to Jimmy. And Luke and I both feel awful about it. You know we went to see the sheriff the very next day. But we don't go around telling the sheriff what to do. He's got a town to control and there's a lot of stuff going on right now, with these organizing meetings that Jimmy seems to be setting up to talk about strikes. Why, that could ruin everything for everybody. Even for you."

"What does that mean?"

"You know exactly what I mean. You're planning to go to college in February, and you know I'm planning to ask Luke to help you with expenses. I know you want that."

Eula untied her apron, slowly folded the ironing board and then turned to face Willy. "There's wants and wants, Mrs. Claybourne. And what I want most is to be proud of who I am and what I stand for. And right now, where I stand is not in this kitchen." She moved past Willy and opened the door to the yard.

Willy's eyes widened. "If you walk out, Eula . . . "

"I just did." The door slammed behind her.

Chapter Nineteen

By Thursday his eye was beginning to open sufficiently to focus. Jimmy paced restlessly in the dusty upstairs section of the Freedom House. Three more days till the mass meeting. The arm still throbbed but he was able to catch and squeeze the softball that Dale lobbed to him from his mattress on the floor. "Catch, brother! Much better." With a series of grunts Dale rose from the floor. "Gonna put the tin cup and the pencils away till we really need 'em."

Though Jimmy's face was still swollen, he cracked a broken smile and tossed the ball back. "Nobody'd buy them anyhow, looking like we do." He went to the window and tugged it up. The sounds of kids laughing and the softer calls of the Freedom School teachers meeting below in the yard washed into the stifling room. "Did you notice that the girls kept the kids away when we limped in, Dale? We're role models, man. Not supposed to look like D-Day survivors! Linda said go on upstairs and clean up so you don't scare the hell out of the class. 'What class?' I asked. 'How nonviolence can win,' she said with a straight face. Broke me up, man, and I tried not to laugh because of the cracked ribs."

Dale limped to the window. Grinning, he turned to see Jimmy's worried face. "Did Linda explain to you how that's supposed to happen?"

Jimmy groaned and resumed his restless tour of the attic. "Gotta be accomplished without me coughing or laughing because if I do either you're going to have to run the mass meeting. Doc Dorsey at Mound Bayou said there's nothing really to do about busted ribs but outlast 'em." He stopped and turned to Dale. "No bullshit. You really think anyone's gonna dare to come when they hear about us?"

Dale raised his hands helplessly. "Brother, we'll get a better idea at our meeting tonight when we hear from the plantations." He watched Jimmy closely, concerned about the deep worry that was etched on the young face. "Flake out, Jimmy. Been a tough week, and gonna be a long night tonight."

It was Eula who came by that afternoon to tell Percy and Rennie Williams about the beatings. "It was awful, Sister Rennie. Dale and Jimmy, beaten, kicked." Her voice broke. "Humiliated." Tears shone in her eyes. "My Jimmy. Beaten till he said, 'I'm a nigger.'"

Rennie's glasses caught the light, shielding the fierceness of her eyes as she gently led Eula to a chair. "Sit a minute, honey. You look wore out." She turned to Percy. "Made him say nigger, Percy. Sound familiar?"

Mr. Williams ran a glass of water at the tap and brought it to the shaken woman. In his soft, old man's voice he said, "Who, Eula? Them Kilbrews?"

She shook her head. "Not the Kilbrews, Brother Percy. The Shiloh police. They cracked Jimmy's ribs, and he hurts just moving. His mouth is a mess, he says. But thank heaven he and Dale are alive. They're both resting at the Freedom House, keeping out of sight till the mass meeting on Sunday. They both want to be there, and I'm worried sick about what's going to happen to them. They're meeting with folks tonight from the plantations, making plans for the walkout. Ted Mendelsohn thinks that the Klan's likely to attack the Freedom House, wanting to show that they're still in business in Magnolia County." Eula met Percy's steady gaze. "How can nonviolent civil rights workers protect themselves?" When the old man remained still, she rose to leave, her young face desolate. "Troubling times, Brother Percy. Thank you both for listening."

After supper that night Percy said he was going out. "I want to talk with my old friend Thomas, who I ain't seen in too long."

Rennie paused and gave him a long, searching look as she was putting Sharon to bed. "Sister Livia say Thomas just had his seventieth, thank the Lord. Thomas is getting along, Percy, and so are you. Best you remember you ain't boys no more. You both are the only two colored vetrins in Magnolia County still around from the Great War." She finished laying the child on her bed and turned a questioning face to her husband. "Ain't time for you two to go out hunting for possum yet. What you want with Tom McCormack?"

Percy said. "Don't need possum to talk to Thomas. Want to talk with him about the Lord's work. Used to talk about things like that when we were sloppin' mules in the cavalry for General Pershing in 1917."

"You were younger then, Percy, case you forgot."

"Well, the Lord ain't done with me yet, Sister Rennie. And Tom never been to church since the first day of his life. So it's always interestin' talking with Doubtin' Thomas about the Lord."

When he got outside Percy moved swiftly to the wired chicken pen in the rear. He moved the rooster aside with an impatient foot and reached into the ancient army footlocker where he kept the chicken feed. His hand felt the oilskin package and hauled it into the darkness of the yard. When he glanced at the bedroom window he could see Rennie bending over his sleepy granddaughter. Knowing he was alone, he unwrapped the well-oiled shotgun.

Thomas lived a quarter of a mile down the dirt road that curled past the Freedom House. Like Percy, Thomas and his wife Livia still went to the fields when the arthritis let them. Rennie didn't go now that their daughter, Beccah, had left Sharon with them. Percy's job as deacon of his church meant Saturday Vespers and Sunday services and a little Sabbath time with Rennie and Sharon. He owed them that. Thomas never came to church so Percy rarely had a chance for the long talks they had relished when they were young, single, and in the same colored unit in the cavalry. Only when work in the fields was over after the frost came would the two of them go into the hills south of Shiloh, looking for possum, squirrels, and, if they were lucky, maybe a bear to stretch the sparse harvest of the little gardens that Rennie and Livia cultivated. They enjoyed hunting, and they made each other laugh. Even more, they loved arguing.

When Percy rapped on the door, Livia greeted him with a broad smile and a hug to her very ample bosom. "Percy! How you doin? Thomas!" Her shout echoed in the still night. "Look who come callin'!" With a sudden look of alarm, she stepped back. "Sister Rennie okay?"

"She's fine, Livia. Havin' a time with Beccah's Sharon!"

Thomas came to the door and the two men walked out into the moonlit yard, settling on a low wall made from the stones that had been removed years ago when Livia planted her garden. "Ain't like you, Deacon, to come this late." Thomas glanced at the moon. "Gotta be almost ten o'clock. You ain't goin' out tomorrow on the truck?"

"Maybe. Maybe not." Percy shot a quick glance at his friend. "Got a lick of work to do tonight and it's getting to be a little late. You might want to give me a hand, Thomas, even though it is work that the Almighty might think is okay. That something that's against your irreligion?"

Thomas threw back his head and laughed. "What the hell you talking about, Deacon? You going through changes like Livia did? Just because I don't join your quivering congregation don't mean I'm irreligious. I just have a deep distrust of signing up for anything, 'specially since you and I got rolled by the United States Army, who kept us shoveling mule shit longer than any Christian or Hebrew or Muslim ought to shovel. Just what kind of work you got in mind?

"You don't go to my church, Doubtin' Thomas, but I've seen you at some of the meetings at Sojourner when Mrs. Hamer was preachin' voters' rights. You seemed more than interested, and singing, arm in arm with Jimmy Mack and those volunteers, 'Ain't gonna let nobody turn me 'round.' Was you, wasn't it?"

Thomas looked at his friend. "It was, Deacon. Something I never thought I'd see in Shiloh." His eyes shone. "Young folks, black and white, made no difference, sayin', 'Stand up! We'll stand with you!' I like that Jimmy Mack. He walks and talks the same way in the Sanctified Quarter as he do in the middle of town. I like those kids who come down here, scared shitless and doin' what they ought to be doin' anyhow. If churches were like Sojourner Chapel and preachers were like Fannie Lou Hamer, I'd be leadin' the choir, singing 'We Shall Overcome.' But most of those preachers aren't like that, Deacon. They're not like you."

"Those kids are doin' the Lord's work, Thomas," Percy said softly.

"And Jimmy Mack and Dale Billings were beaten half to death by our Shiloh police earlier this week."

"Goddam!" Tom McCormack stood up, the moonlight catching the ruff of white hair fringing his dark brown scalp. "Is Jimmy hurt bad?"

"He's got some broken ribs and some loose teeth, Thomas. And Dale was banged up real good too. But they're at the Freedom House tonight, workin' out plans for the mass meeting Sunday and the walkout next week." Percy stood up and joined McCormack as he paced the yard. "Our police and our Shiloh Klan really believe they got a license to 'liminate people who are peacefully trying to change Senator Tildon's Magnolia County. They beat Fannie Lou Hamer in the jail over at Winona. Made two Negro trustees do the beatin'. Broke Mrs. Hamer's heart, but never stopped her from keepin' on. Now they beat Mack and Billings in our jail. And tonight, if Mr. Mendelsohn is right, Kilbrew's people might be going to burn the Freedom House."

Thomas halted abruptly. "Do Mack and Billings know the Kilbrew people are coming, Deacon?"

"Mr. Mendelsohn told 'em what he'd heard down at the FBI in Jackson."

"Those boys ain't Gandhi. And the Delta Klan ain't the British. Nonviolence ain't gonna stop those crackers. These kids got no guns to protect themselves!"

"Well, Thomas, they got mine. And I thought if it wasn't against your irreligion, they might have yours."

Chapter Twenty

For the two months before Jimmy Mack headed for the orientation meeting in Oxford, Ohio, he had been deeply troubled. His conversations with Bob Moses had persuaded him that he could handle the coming Freedom Summer project in Shiloh. "You know every back alley and tractor path in Magnolia County," Moses said. "Just find yourself a place for your Freedom House." He had observed the young Mack from the first day he had come to Greenwood, impressed from the beginning with his quiet confidence and alertness. "You're going to be a sergeant with green troops, so you need a place you all can care about. And a lot of those students have never been south of Atlantic City." In his characteristically soft voice, he had added, "You're going to have a busy summer, Mack. Keep us in touch. We've all got to make it to September." But finding a place for a Freedom House in the fishbowl of Shiloh had worn him to a frazzle. The shambles of the farmhouse he discovered a half mile from Sojourner Chapel had come like a miracle. He had walked past the doddering building a hundred times, never seeing it for what it could be, only as the sad memory of a long-ago home. But as the trip to Ohio came closer, Jimmy's vision sharpened as the possibilities for a Freedom House kept diminishing.

In the Sanctified Quarter only Sojourner Chapel had seemed large enough for any kind of meeting, but it could not work as an anchor for the every day, every night work of Freedom Summer. They'd need some rooms for classes, even a modest library since the Shiloh library was off limits to blacks. On a Sunday morning late in May, with Shiloh still asleep, he paused and examined the ancient building, then approached the drooping porch. He broke open the nailed front door and moved through the moldering rooms that had once housed two tenant families. Room by wretched room he tested the floors and struggled to open windows that had not been open since the Depression, when the last family had fled north.

When he explored the attic he found that the stifling rooms were dry, testament that the roof had remained intact over the decades. Filthy but relieved, Jimmy emerged knowing the decrepit place could be made to work. This could be the Freedom School! When he saw Bob Moses at Oxford, he was exuberant. "We got the place, Bob. Now all we got to do is teach the kids about America."

When the Freedom School teachers arrived from Oxford, they had attacked the place with the enthusiasm of kids on a holiday. With soap, suds, mops, and brooms they'd transformed the wreck into a livable approximation of a headquarters. With saws, hammers, and lumber from the remains of an abandoned outhouse they built shelves for the mound of books they had brought from Ohio. Jimmy and Dale had watched the place emerge, thrilled that kids and the elderly were coming to meet the young invaders, discover the books, and join the classes. Black history and American history were becoming friends to these Delta residents who had known only the cramped and distorted versions in their old and obsolete school books.

All summer, from dawn to dusk, the Shiloh Freedom House was a noisy, exciting, and buoyant terminus for the volunteers who worked as teachers and those who moved daily out on the dusty roads seeking to enroll black voters. Dale's desk inside the front screen door was the place where contact was vigilantly maintained with Freedom Summer headquarters in Jackson and bail sources in the North. But at night the Freedom House was usually deserted, a lonely farmhouse once again. Jimmy fretted because he knew that the building was too close to the highway. The only security they had to protect themselves from vandals was their own vigilance. There was no one to call if an attack were to come. Not the police. Not the Highway Patrol. Not the clergy. Not the press. Not the congressman. Not Senator Tildon. They knew they were alone.

On Wednesday evening, Ted Mendelsohn had been the first to arrive for the meeting with the blacks from the plantations. As he approached the Freedom House he could hear Dale Billings's voice inside speaking on the phone to Jackson. "Two white cops. Harold Butler and Luther Lonergan. L.O.N.E.R.G.A.N. Yeah. Works on his days off at the Kilbrew station."

Jimmy had stood waiting on the step for Ted, eager to explain the night of the beatings to him. "I know you heard from Dale. He's been passing the word. But don't write a word yet, Ted. Please. Don't make the sheriff antsy with a news story. Nobody's got to know that doesn't know already. I've been working toward Sunday's mass meeting all summer. People are already scared. Wait till Sunday's meeting is over."

Mendelsohn blanched at Mack's swollen face, and was shocked by the pleading in the youngster's voice. He so easily became his son, Richard, more vulnerable than he would ever admit. He studied Jimmy's face in the dusk. "They did a job on you, didn't they?" He swallowed hard. "If you don't tell Max, my boss, I won't. Not yet, I'm a reporter,

Jimmy. But not yet." Mack said nothing but turned and led the way into the house.

By nine o'clock the plantation people were all there. Hollis from the Wilson place in Inverness; George Purdy from the Milton spread in Indianola; Billy Jamieson from the Shott plantation in Drew; Marcia Hudson from the Stevens plantation in Ruleville; the Gator twins from the Gordon spread in Cleveland; Sharia Thompson, very uncomfortable in her pregnancy, from the Claybourne plantation; and Tucker Livingstone from the Tilton plantation. Dale Billings watched attentively from his small table, and Jimmy stood, his back to the door. Mendelsohn sat on the steps leading up to the attic, his notebook on his knee.

Jimmy said, "Before we start, you all heard about Mendelsohn by now. He's been our lifeline up north, gettin' our story out all summer. Said he wants to talk to you all."

Mendelsohn scanned the group, struck once more by how young these serious faces were. "I'm not the only one in Magnolia County that's been keeping track of you all summer," he said. "It's not a secret that you all have been working to get out the vote on your places. The Klan knows it. White Shiloh knows it. And everybody is betting on whether you walk off the plantations to protest the apartheid or don't. I've been taking the temperature of the town as the pressure's been building toward your walkout, so I wasn't really surprised when those two cops grabbed Jimmy and Dale. They want to make folks' minds up for them if they've been thinking of coming to your Sunday meeting. And tonight, on the way here, it looked at the Kilbrew station that something was coming down, probably soon." Mendelsohn's voice was staccato in the silent room. "Pickup trucks with shotguns flitting in and out like flies on sugar. Now that the FBI found Mickey and James and Andy, those rednecks are worried. I think it's a sure bet they know you might be meeting here tonight. But I wouldn't advertise it with your lights on. I left my car behind the Chapel and came here through the backyards. I don't think anyone saw me, Jimmy. But I can't be sure." He paused, aware that his role as a reporter, not a participant, was now on a fragile line. Frowning, he settled back on the stair, his eyes riveted on his notebook.

Jimmy spoke sharply. "Kill all the lights except the one on Dale's table and stay away from the windows. Give me your numbers of folks that will be coming on Sunday. Make it quick and Dale'll get them down. Hollis?"

"Seventeen families, Jimmy."

"George?"

"Eleven from Milton."

"Billy?"

"Shott's twenty-two coming to dance, Jim!" The roll call stopped as Jimmy held up his hand for silence. Dale snapped off the light. In the sudden silence they could hear the racing of a motor as a truck wheeled from the highway, turned into the connecting dirt road in front of the Freedom House and skidded to a halt 20 feet from the porch. Out of sight at the edge of the window, Jimmy watched as two men left the truck and slowly circled the house.

"Dark as a Scotchman's pocket," one of the men was saying. "Not a single pussy in sight." They remounted the pickup and cut across the yard to the road. In another moment the men and women in the Freedom House watched the tail light of the truck swerve back on to Highway 49, heading north. Jimmy gave a long relieved whistle, then resumed the roll call.

"Marcia? How many are coming?"

"Ten for sure. Two maybes."

"Twins?"

"Fifteen if they really come. Some folks heard about you and Dale."

"Sharia?"

"Lucas Claybourne gonna shit when we come, Jimmy. Twenty-eight!"

"Tucker?"

"We're all coming Sunday. And it's gonna make people drop their drawers in Washington when Massa Tildon's darkies go public and demand the vote!"

They filed quickly out of the house and melted into the darkness of the Sanctified Quarter. Mendelsohn was the last one. "You need anything, Jimmy?" He stopped short, laughing at the absurdity of his words. "Like give you a blood transfusion?"

Jimmy simply grinned and grimaced. "I look that bad, huh?"

Ted waited at the door and watched Jimmy limp to the stairs. His words sounded choked and shaky. "Be careful, kid. See you tomorrow."

Dale and Jimmy climbed the stairs to their mats in the attic. "I'll take the first watch," said Dale. From their window they saw the reporter slip out the door and move swiftly across the moonlit yard.

Chapter Twenty-One

Across the dirt road and parallel to it, the cotton on the Peterson spread ran from the west a quarter mile beyond the Freedom House all the way east until it touched Highway 49. From where Jimmy could see out his attic window, the endless rows of cotton resembled a vast dark sea, and the tiny twinkling lights of the plantation house far beyond looked like the lights of a passing ship, seemingly at the very horizon. In the moonlight the walls of cotton plants looked black, with only a pale luster where errant clusters of cotton caught the moon.

Behind the first row of plants, Percy Williams lay stretched flat on the ground. In his line of vision he had a direct shot at the edge of the porch. He had watched intently as the organizers left the meeting. "You see that, Thomas? No Jimmy and no Dale. They still inside. You comfortable, Thomas? Could be a considerable wait, even if Mendelsohn was right and they comin' at all."

Thirty feet down the row Thomas grunted. "Comfortable ain't the word, Deacon. Didn't say nothin' about comfortable when you mentioned this hunting trip. Least when we went after possum we took some decent corn to make things prettier." He chuckled. "When's the last time you and I pulled picket duty? Outside of El Paso, wasn't it? August 1917. Our reward for losing track of those sixteen stupid mules you thought we'd tethered that we didn't!"

Straight across the road was the edge of the Freedom House. Anything approaching could be caught by either of them. Percy shifted his weight from his elbow, resting his shotgun on the hard baked earth. He smiled in the dark, his eyes moving along the road—waiting for what?

Percy said, "Wasn't '17, Thomas. Was '18. After we got back from France. It was the same summer I met Rennie."

"But it was the deacon that fouled up, right?"

"I wasn't no deacon then. Just a lonely nigger who was thinkin' about Rennie rather than tethering those damn mules. For a drinking man, you got a long memory, Doubtin'."

It was nearly two o'clock when the headlights swept across their attic window as two pickup trucks pulled off the highway and turned into the dirt road. Dale watched them pass and in a moment he saw them edge onto the lawn. When their lights were turned off, they became silhouettes against the muted landscape of the endless cotton fields beyond. He heard the slam of the truck doors. As he strained to see, he was suddenly aware of the trilling throb of the cicadas. And then he saw the six figures move from the darkness. "Jimmy. Jimmy!" He nudged Mack with his boot. "Wake up. We got visitors."

Percy's gun tracked the two pickup trucks as they crept by their hedge of cotton plants. "Three men in each cab, Thomas," he hissed. He'd seen the drivers carefully surveying the darkened house. A hundred yards past, they had curled off the road, backed up, and pulled onto the edge of the Freedom House lot. The trucks seemed poised for a run toward the highway. When the headlights went black, he edged forward, gently easing the plants aside with the barrel of his shotgun. He watched as three shadows descended from the cab of the truck and joined the other shadows from the second pickup. The moon had waned, but the starlight laid a pale patina of blue on the yard. The air had chilled, and Percy shivered slightly. When he peered over his shoulder, he saw that Thomas's shotgun was aimed at the truck to his right. Beneath the drum of the cicadas, he heard Thomas's soft whisper. "Locked and loaded, Deacon?"

Percy nodded in the dark. "Locked and loaded."

The six men huddled at the rear of the truck. Suddenly, a reedy, rasping voice tore the silence. "Fore you touch the Cross, bow your unworthy heads!" In the half-light they could see a stooped old man with long white hair sweep off his wide-brimmed hat and lift his sunken face to the heavens. His voice rose in supplication. "Lord, make us your servants. Let us be your scourge and your sword. Give us the strength of soul to burn away this abomination. Help us, Jesus, to cleanse this race-mixing hell with your pure fire so that every Christian will know Thy will be done. We thank you, Jesus, and together we say Amen."

Percy and Thomas could clearly hear the low murmur of "Amen." Two men nearest the tailgate climbed into the bed of the truck and hauled off the greasy tarpaulin that had hidden a six-foot wooden cross.

A man's voice grunted, "Goddammit, Harold, pick up your end! It's a heavy son of a—"

"There will be no blasphemy!" The old man's voice was full of rage. "This is the Cross He died on! Have you no Christian respect? Hand down the shovels and the pick. Fast! Gonna start gettin' light soon." The old man laid the pick on his bony shoulders and started across the yard. "Tierney, Holcomb, Gordon, bring the shovels." The curt words were commands. Thomas could see the two figures in the truck bed as they struggled to unload the heavy cross.

"Goddam Preacher! Christ's disciples and God's messenger going to carry shovels and a pick, and you and me left to carry all the heavy shit! Least they coulda done was carry some of the gasoline." When the two men got the cross to the ground, they leaned it against the truck. One of them handed a bottle from the truck bed to his panting companion. "Have a taste, Luther. Preacher gonna be digging for a while."

Luther Lonergan took a long, thirsty swallow and handed back the bottle reluctantly, wiping his mouth with the back of his hand. He stared across at the Freedom House. "Jesus Christ, Harold, what a fire that old farmhouse gonna make! Any jigaboos left inside gonna be toast!"

Harold guffawed. "Burnt toast!"

"Preacher would say 'Burnt offerings!'" Luther Lonergan picked up his end of the cross and chuckled. "That's what that Christer would say. 'Burnt offerings!'"

From the attic window, Dale and Jimmy watched them plant the cross fifty feet from the porch. Two of the men returned to the trucks, carrying the bags containing the gasoline that they placed around the whole perimeter of the farmhouse. The third carefully delivered a dripping pail of gasoline to the site.

The preacher's voice rasped its instructions; "Soak the beautiful Cross well. I want its light to touch the heavens. And when the defilers and fornicators come to this cesspool in the morning light, they're going to see that Jesus never sleeps and never wearies. Pray with me. Dear Jesus, accept the work of these poor sinners and bless us." He stepped back and nodded to the man with the pail. With a great heave the gasoline was poured across the lumber. "First His Cross," said the preacher. "Then the pestilential sty." He dropped a flaming package of matches at the foot of the cross. With the rush of flame, Dale and Jimmy could see every vivid detail of the six men as they stared, transfixed, at the spectacle.

Jimmy and Dale saw the first flashes in the dark field beyond the road. Then suddenly the startling explosions of firing. Pow! Pow! Pow! Yells now, and the shattering of glass. Christ, the trucks! The windshields. Shit! The hornet sound of bullets striking metal . . . From where? Goddammit! From the house? No—no, somewhere else!

The men were running across the yard, trying to reach their guns, ducking as the explosions continued. No one paused to hear the screamed entreaties of the preacher who ran after them. "Torch the house! It's Satan's work! Torch the house!" By the time they reached the smoking trucks and scrambled aboard, the firing—from where?—had ceased. Weeping, the preacher was hauled into the bed of the second truck. Its windshield shattered and a rear tire deflated, it limped toward the dirt road.

When the two trucks had reached the highway and were heading north, Dale and Jimmy came out to the smoking yard. They stared across at the cotton fields, but there was no movement. Grinning and shaking their heads, they put out the flames on the cross with the soaked remnants of a farmhouse rug. "Let's pick up those bags of gasoline," Dale said. "But leave the cross. Something for the kids to see."

"Yeah," Jimmy agreed. "The cross got burned but the Freedom House is open for business! When they ask us what happened here, what the hell do we tell the kids about nonviolence?"

Dale laughed. "Just say the Lord works in mysterious ways."

Chapter Twenty-Two

Rennie was pouring coffee for Percy and herself when Mendelsohn joined them. "You stay overnight in Jackson, Ted?"

"No. Got back late yesterday and stopped over to see Jimmy at the Freedom House. He's going to be okay. When I came back here the house was dark, so I tried to be quiet. Didn't want to wake Sharon. Where is my roommate, Rennie?"

"Playing with the Allen child next door. Everybody here was sleepin' late so Sharon and me ate without you-all. Let me get you some coffee. Mrs. Allen says she thought she heard shots middle of the night. Told her I didn't. Either of you hear anything?"

"Shots?" Mendelsohn looked at Percy. "No. Not me. You, Mr. Williams?"

Percy shrugged. "Mrs. Allen ain't always a dependable listener, Rennie. Wouldn't give it too much worry what she said."

Mendelsohn finished his coffee. "And what are you doing home on a Monday, Mr. Williams? Thought you'd be out on the truck this morning. Not the Sabbath yet."

"I had some unfinished business to take care of last night, Mr. Mendelsohn. Took longer than I figured. Was kind of wore out s'morning and decided not to go to the fields."

Rennie wiped her hands on her apron and cocked her head. "Funny kind of business, Percy, that kept you and Thomas out till four in the morning. You think my man been cattin' around, Ted?"

Percy chuckled. "Well, it's a kind thought, Rennie, that you thought I might and that I could."

"Never said nothing about might or could. But I got long memories about you and Thomas McCormack. Was a time, Ted, that for sure the deacon and Thomas coulda and probably did!"

"Blessings on both of you," Mendelsohn laughed and moved to the door. "I'm going over to the Freedom House. Doing a story on the school. Anybody want a ride over?"

"No thanks, Mr. Mendelsohn," said the deacon. "I'm a little old to go to the Freedom School. But tell Jimmy hello for me."

Mendelsohn skidded to a stop in the yard and walked slowly toward the black skeleton of the cross. Jimmy watched him take out his notebook and the Leica, shooting it from every angle. Jimmy leaned against the door jamb as the Freedom School teachers begin to arrive, startled and aghast at the charred wreck of the burned cross in the yard. But by the time they drifted to the sagging porch, they were competing with gallows humor.

"You starting a new church, Jimmy Mack?"

"No, man."

"It's the Shiloh Church of the Parboiled Cross. Right, Mack?"

"No, man."

"It's sculpture, stupid. What the hell's the matter with you? This is a statement! Correct?"

"No, man."

"An attitude!"

"No, man."

"A profound commentary on Freedom Summer by one of the great artistes, James Mack, well known primitive."

"You got it."

Mendelsohn laughed, scribbling in his book. Smart-ass kids!

Once they were all on the porch Jimmy turned to the reporter. "You were right on the money, Ted. We had visitors last night." He scanned the attentive but impassive faces. He'd watched them like a shepherd, every step of the way from Ohio.

When he and Ted followed the volunteers into the Freedom House, Jimmy murmured, "They always surprise me. The Delta makes you a veteran real quick." He shook his head and grinned. "Come on in and let's get started. You want to use the phone to report our invasion, go ahead. Nobody but the Klan and us know anything about it."

Max wouldn't get off the phone when Ted called. "How do you know it was Klan? And what do the cops think? And 'persons unknown' shot up the trucks at the scene? Maybe you could get a few answers, for Crissakes? And is the mass meeting going to take place Sunday? And are the blacks walking . . . ?" It went on and on. "And are you okay, Teddy?" It was only the last question that he knew the answer to. Maybe.

Chapter Twenty-Three

For weeks, they'd been walking the dusty roads. Shiloh, Ruleville, Shaw, Drew, selling hope to folks who never had reason before to buy it. Dodging the highway patrols, the Klan, the sheriff, scratching every day to build support for the voter registration drive and to make the strike a reality. It had been tedious and dangerous work, and the unwarranted arrests of ten of them in Drew had tested their morale. They had been penned in a tiny old cement jail, just off Highway 49. The barred windows were easy targets for any firebomb coming from the highway, so there was a long, miserable night of waiting till dawn when they were transported to the odious work farm in Sunflower. After a week of cold grits and bed lice in the greasy mattresses, they limped back to the Freedom House and returned to work.

"They were one pitiful-looking group," Ted told Max. "Filthy and lice-bitten. But these scrubbed kids I worried about back at Oxford are tough. Not a guy or a girl split and went home, and they had every reason to if they chose. Like Mack says, they surprise you."

Watching the animated children at the Freedom School, Jimmy knew that the example of the optimistic volunteers was opening hearts and minds to possibilities that stretched way beyond their world of cotton fields. More and more local black high school students were joining the forays into hostile or indifferent neighborhoods. Buoyant now, Jimmy led them, knowing that no burning cross could rival this new, consuming fire that had been ignited.

For him, the ultimate prize had always been to carry this activity into the heart of Indianola, the very birthplace of the hated White Citizens Council. Through the sweltering summer, he tried to find any safe building that could accommodate both a Freedom School and a Community Center where political organizing could be held. The day he found the empty Negro Baptist School only one mile from the courthouse, he was like a kid at Christmas opening his first present.

"Man, I've been walking past this wreck without really seeing it. It's great, Dale!" He gazed at the prize with a smile and opened his arms wide. "It's not only great, brother Dale, they can't burn it down. It's brick!" The church Elders had been reluctant but were finally persuaded by the enthusiasm and boldness of Billings and Mack.

"Gonna change Indianola, Jimmy?"

Mack shrugged and grinned. "Maybe. Least it's gonna shake it up!"

When Jimmy's leaflets announcing MASS MEETING AT THE BAPTIST SCHOOL SUNDAY NIGHT hit the streets, every black and every white in Indianola had gotten the word.

On Sunday afternoon Jimmy joined Mendelsohn at Rennie Williams's house for the ride down to Indianola. She had hurried from church after Vespers, rushing up the rutted road yards ahead of Mr. Williams, who was walking with Sharon. Perspiration stained her church dress and she mopped her shining face as she entered the room. Finding the two of them, she broke into a wide grin. "Praise Jesus! You all are still here." Looking suddenly alarmed, she asked, "Meetin's still on, ain't it, James?"

Jimmy nodded. "Seven o'clock at the old Negro Baptist School in Indianola, Miz Williams. Don't rightly know who's going to dare to show up, though. There's never been a mass freedom meeting in Indianola. Folks gonna be there, Ted?" His eyes were masked by the dark glasses. "I've never felt less sure about anything."

Mendelsohn held open the door as Mr. Williams and Sharon arrived, and he swept the squealing girl into his arms. "What does the Good Book say about ye of little faith, Rennie?" he asked. "Tell James that the Lord will provide for his children. Even in the shadow of the White Citizens Council!"

"From your lips to Jesus's ear, Ted." She rescued Sharon from his arms. "The Williamses are all coming for sure. And the Lord will have to provide the others. Still room in your car?"

"It's reserved seating, Rennie," said Mendelsohn. "I'm leaving in thirty minutes. Stop worrying, Jimmy. You're our leader. I told Max on the phone, 'Mack is gonna make some history tonight.'"

Jimmy grinned. "And history's written by the winners, right?"

"You're damn right. And by *Newsweek*!"

Johnny Buckley and Harold Parker were still arranging the benches in the hall when the first kids begin to drift into the yard from the surrounding neighborhoods. By six-thirty, groups of teenagers were crossing the yard from the street, their voices animated and their heads bobbing. By seven o'clock, the old church school was packed with an exuberant crowd of hundreds of blacks. The walls were lined with people who couldn't find seats. The elderly sat scattered through the crowd, their eyes bright with excitement and wonder. A large group of the middle-aged husbands and wives, some with tiny children in their arms, chatted quietly, waiting for the meeting to begin.

"First time this summer we got folks at a mass meeting in the Delta who are not too old and not too young, but right in the middle," said Harold Parker. "How come they show up in this White Citizens Council town and don't show up in Shiloh?"

Johnny Buckley leaned against the wall at the front of the room, surveying the buoyant crowd. "We'll have to ask Jimmy when he gets here. Maybe it's because Indianola's bigger. Folks aren't as exposed here as in Shiloh."

Dale Billings grinned. "It feels like Indianola has spent the whole summer hearing about the circus, and the circus has finally arrived. Jimmy's on the way from Shiloh, probably driving like mad." He looked at the hundreds of blacks in the room, and when he spotted Eula he waved her to his side. "Did Jimmy know you were coming?"

She smiled. "No. I figured he had enough on his plate without worryin' about his lady. It'll be a surprise."

Dale shook his head and laughed. "I hope I can see his face when he walks in!"

The sheriff parked near the entrance to the long, overgrown driveway of the church school and settled back, watching the Negroes gathering for their meeting. Some of the elderly touched their caps, murmuring "Evenin', Sheriff," as they eased by, but most strode past with no acknowledgement of his presence. Dennis Haley wasn't the worst son of a bitch they'd suffered through, but he was nobody they could count on when nobody else was watching. Haley was old news, but they knew him.

"Puttin' on a little weight, ain't he?"

"Honky gettin' fat on the drippins from Fatback's Platter, and the sisters' joint out at the junction, and Just a Lick over in Bell Hollow."

"No strain, no pain, long as he got that Polack nigger to do the heavy liftin'. And a lot more if you wanna know."

"Shit, ain't that Bronko on the porch?"

Two cruisers eased past, guarding the perimeter of the churchyard. Butler and Lonergan got out of their car and leaned on its hood, smoking and joking. Tim Forrest and Tommy Thompson sauntered from their cruiser and moved with the crowd toward the porch.

The sheriff had told Bronko to park out back and to stand by in case there was trouble. "You're not the most popular officer I own in this part of Indianola. Make yourself scarce," he'd said. But there Bronko was, bigger than Christmas, letting everybody know he was there. Dennis Haley cursed, "Goddammit, there go Lonergan and Butler. . . . and here comes trouble."

Bronko pushed his way through the clutch of bodies on the porch and positioned himself at the top of the step as though he wanted Mack to know that he'd have to mess with him if he made any waves. His eyes were roaming the crowd when Lonergan and Butler approached. They were watching him, grinning, heads nodding. They stopped, an island of blue, at the bottom of the steps.

"Thought you was supposed to be in the back of the bus and out of sight, nigger. You didn't hear the sheriff?" Lonergan smirked, turning to view the people crowding behind. "Maybe this darkie is just coming to join his brothers at the picnic, Butler."

"It could be. Maybe he is the boy who shot up your truck Wednesday night, Luther. You a good shot with a shotgun, Bronko?"

"Blackbirds of a feather, Butler. Could sure be old Bronko pullin' picket duty out at the Commie House. Where were you Wednesday night, coon dog?"

"Fucking your mother, you redneck prick. Get off my back and let these people by."

The high Delta sky was lavender with dusk when Jimmy led his group across the porch and made his way slowly through the noisy congregation at the door. He stopped abruptly and broke into an exultant "yes!" as Eula stepped out of the crowd and took his hand. Wordlessly, he embraced her and led her to a seat beside the platform. His dark glasses swept the crowd. He was shaking his head as he and Mendelsohn made their way around the packed benches to stand next to Buckley against the wall. "You see what I see, Johnny? In Indianola?"

Dale Billings had watched him enter and with a wide grin led the crowd into song: *Black and white together . . .*

They responded with a rush of sound, and the exultant voices lifted in unison: *We shall not be moved!*

Jimmy stowed his sunglasses in the pocket of his jeans. His eyes were wet and shining. As the song filled the hall, his voice sounded harsh and shaken in Mendelsohn's ear. "Man! This is Indianola!" His voice broke, "I thought there'd be ten people here. Look at them! In Indianola!" For Jimmy Mack this was the most incredible moment since he had entered the Movement. Five times he had been jailed in this town, beaten like a dog, powerless to change it. Here, now, was the reality of every fantasy he had dreamed during those lonely, frightened nights in the Delta. His tough, compact body moved with the powerful urgency of the words.

Just like a tree that's planted by the waters,
We shall not be moved!

Dale Billings let the song subside. He sensed that the familiar music had eased the strangeness that always accompanied a first meeting. His boyish face nodded approval to the eager crowd. "I'm going to introduce you to one of the persons who has been leading the freedom fight here in Mississippi for—" He stopped abruptly. An angry murmur had started near the door. Dale resumed, his voice uncertain. "Well," he said "We've got an unwanted guest in here."

People rose from their seats, and benches scraped shrilly on the wooden floor as the crowd strained to see. A woman's hoarse whisper skittered along the row: "It's Bronko!" An alarmed cry sounded and was repeated around the hall: "Bronko!"

Dale moved swiftly along the wall toward the huge black policeman who had shouldered his way into the center of the room. Rennie Williams touched the arm of the woman who had first spread the word.

Her frightened eyes swung toward the hulk of the man, and she pulled Sharon closer.

"Who is Bronko?"

The woman's chin rose and her eyes were angry. "He's a stone killer. Killed two brothers down in Yancy a year ago and Harley Hines over in Wells last April."

With his heavy, dull face and enormous hands, Bronko stood like an animal at bay. His jaw was lowered and he stared furiously at Dale Billings, who blocked his path. The noise was shrill in the hall, and Dale's voice was drowned in the surging sound. Jimmy reached his side as he was repeating slowly what he had already said. As if to a slow child, he patiently explained that police were not needed or wanted. "Don't you understand? The sheriff promised us that the police would stay outside."

The deputy seemed not to comprehend, and the great hulk stood transfixed. Jimmy's voice rasped through the excited babble. "This is church property. You have no right to be here."

Bronko's pale blue eyes shifted from Dale to Jimmy Mack, and they narrowed in recognition. His thick neck strained at the blue collar, and one heavy hand moved slowly to rest on his holster. His face was shining from the steamy heat of the room as he studied the two young blacks. Silence had suddenly surrounded the three men. Bronko's voice could be heard clearly. "I know you. You the two niggers I saw at the station house when you was arrested." He wheeled and shouted to the room, "These two agitators are bringin' you trouble! They godless men who using our colored folk to bring Communism here. You all know me. I been seein' to your safety for a lotta years. Now you best leave right now 'fore someone gets messed up 'count of them. You don't have to stay and listen to 'em. I'm stayin' right here to make sure they don't preach rebellion." The crowd responded by stomping and chanting, "Go!" Bronko's eyes widened as the crescendo of noise broke about him.

Jimmy pointed to the door, his vibrant voice scissoring through the din: "You got to go!" He turned and pushed his way through the agitated crowd to the front of the heaving room. The nervous tumult ceased as he raised his hand for attention, his whole attitude taut and controlled. Ignoring the deputy, he addressed the back seats and benches of the room. "Before we start here, I'd like for you to know that this is church property. We've got an agreement with the sheriff that says we don't have to put up with any policeman inside. Now it's up to you whether you want him here or not."

Feet scraped on the floor as everyone stood, and a wave of noise roared through the room: "Go! Go! Go!!" The children had frightened half-smiles on their faces, but they screamed the word louder. "Go!" It seemed that every throat in the crowd was unleashing its accompaniment to the barrage of sound that assaulted the policeman. Ted Mendelsohn watched the fury on the faces of the old men and women. My God, they were yelling "Go!" to a Mississippi policeman! They cut the air with the word they had never said aloud: "Go! Go! Go!"

Fascinated and frightened, Ted saw Jimmy turn his back as the deputy's fingers tightened on his holster. As Jimmy made his way clear of the milling people, Bronko followed in his wake like an armored ship. Now he stood, hand on his holster, just below the podium. The light spilled across his enraged face and touched the white helmets of the Indianola police as they clustered beyond the step in the dark. The metallic chatter of the police car radios sounded lifeless and lonely in the long, hushed room.

Jimmy's young face was alight with excitement. He seemed to dismiss the presence of Bronko, speaking instead to the assembled crowd in a voice that was almost conversational. "I'm not unmindful tonight that many of you are here against the will of your folk. Kids are here against the will of their parents. Women are here against the will of their husbands. And many men are here against the will of their wives. And I understand why they were all against your comin'—because black people have been killed in Mississippi for saying they want to vote! Black people have been killed in Mississippi for comin' to a Freedom Meeting!"

There was an angry murmur throughout the hall and a voice called "Yes!" and another, "Preach, son!"

"But I know something's happening, something's changing. For better than two years we've been trying to get a meeting in this town so you could say out loud, in public, what you been sayin' over the years as you crouched by your beds, prayin'. Say out loud that you are tired of

being pushed in corners. Tired of the way you are living. Tired of havin'
Mr. Charlie tell you when to move, how to move, and where to go! But
now something's changing. You're not askin' Mr. Charlie when and
where and how. You're here tonight attending a Freedom Meeting! In
Indianola!"

His eyes locked on Bronko's and there was a timbre to the voice as
it rang out. "To me that's a great thing! A great thing!" His eyes were
shining with his pride in the people. He gestured toward the huge policeman before him, his voice ripe with scorn, and he hurled his words
at the glowering man. "I'm not unmindful of the fact that right here in
your city we have a sheriff's deputy who should be pickin' cotton!"

There was a gasp of disbelief and every eye was on the silent tableau
of the two poised men. Mendelsohn eased out the door and raced, panting, to the sheriff's car. He pointed to the silent hall. "Somebody's going
to get killed if you don't stop it!"

Dennis Haley stared at him and then scrambled from the cruiser. As
Mendelsohn fought to catch his breath, he heard Haley shouting, "Lonergan! Get your men in there and bring that stupid bastard out of there!"

Inside, time seemed frozen. Bronko's great head turned and he
licked at his heavy, lower lip. He stared at Mack. "I could kill you!" he
growled. His voice became a bellow. "This is an unlawful assembly. You
are all witness to this Communist mockin' the police! Y'all leave now
or you gonna be arrested!"

But the hush in the stifling room was torn only by Jimmy's mocking
voice. "Not unmindful," he cried, "that right here in your city you have
a sheriff's deputy who is not qualified to be a sheriff's deputy!"

Preach, Jimmy! Tell it! The room roared with laughter and passion:
Go! Go! Go!

Now Jimmy's voice fell, inviting the confidence of the rapt crowd.
They strained forward to hear. "You know," he said almost casually.
"Once when I was arrested up in Leflore County, a white official told
me, 'If a white policeman shoots a Negro, you have a racial crisis. But
if a Negro policeman shoots a Negro, you don't have a racial crisis.'" He
stopped. For a long moment there was complete silence in the room.
Then Jimmy's throaty voice spat out the words: "And that's why they
hired Bronko!"

A single breath seemed to suck through the audience, and then was expelled with a sigh. *"Yes! Oh, yes!"*

No one in the hall even noticed that the policemen had arrived, pausing at the door and unsheathing their guns. A roar seemed to fill the space, a wild mixture of relief, laughter, scorn, and admiration. Tears stood in the eyes of the oldsters, unbelieving half-smiles on their lined faces. They watched this boy, this David, come to battle. And they cried.

When the room quieted again, Jimmy shifted his tack. "For years I've known that we aren't the type of people who are scared. Our ancestors killed lions! They ate the meat of animals that would tear men apart! We're the same people that fought on foreign soil in two wars and in Korea. We're not afraid! We weren't afraid to go over there and shoot people who never did the things to us that these white people in Mississippi have." He was motionless, searching the wide-eyed faces of the youngsters who bunched along the walls. "Then why don't we shoot the white folk here?" The voice stopped again, and he took a half step closer to the teenagers. He spoke softly to them, and they nodded gently. "Because in this movement we don't hate. We love. Because even in Mississippi we're Americans. Born here. Raised here. In this movement we are going to win by being nonviolent. Because the soil out there is enriched with the tears, the blood, the bones, and the sweat of our ancestors. We own this country much as anybody else. America is sacred to us. America is a land that we want to live in."

His voice was vibrant with hope and full of wonder. He leaned toward the children and his young voice was joyous. "What's happening today is real. Not something you're reading about. It's happening *right here*! You are doing things that people before you would not have dreamed of doing. You are *here*! You won't say, 'I heard about it.' Or 'Somebody told me.' You'll say: I was right there! I saw it! My feet were in that place when history was made!"

The room erupted, shouts of *"Yes!"* ricocheting off the old walls until Jimmy raised his hands for silence. "Tomorrow," he said, "our feet are heading for freedom! Tomorrow our feet are walking off massa's land and they're not walkin' back until we get the vote and justice comes to those fields. Bible says a man is worthy of his hire. We been worthy for three hundred years, and we are tired of waiting." His aching arm came slowly up from his side, and he pointed at the threatening figure of Bronko. "And no paid killer, black or white, is gonna turn us around!"

Bronko stood transfixed. His eyes were frightened now as the lurching, shouting crowd surged from the rear toward the podium. Mendelsohn could only stare. As if in a nightmare, the room quieted, and all he could do was watch helplessly as Stanley Bronko's hand closed on his heavy service revolver and yanked it from its holster. With two shaking hands he lifted it and aimed at the man who was debasing him. "I'm going to kill you, you mother—"

"Drop your gun, Bronko!" As the startled deputy wheeled to see, the explosion of Lonergan's .45 crashed through the room. Bronko's surprised eyes stared at his erupting chest and the gun fell from his lifeless hands. Without a sound from his open mouth, he tumbled headlong into the aisle.

Chapter Twenty-Four

Mendelsohn checked his watch. It was nearly one o'clock in the morning when Sheriff Haley concluded his questioning. "Don't leave town, Mack. You too, Lonergan. There'll be an autopsy hearing, and the FBI says they want to have a sit-down with you both." Jimmy sat facing his desk, almost too exhausted to raise his head. Lonergan, still flushed with the electricity of the shooting, stared straight ahead, his eyes holding on the sheriff's angry face.

"Come on, Jimmy. It's time to go home." Mendelsohn offered him a hand and helped him to his feet. All Mack's vitality seemed depleted. The sheriff shook his head in disgust. "Get him out of here. He's brought nothing but trouble since he arrived. Now I'm going to have to deal with the whole goddam U.S. government and one more story about the violence-prone Mississippi policemen in your Commie magazine."

"There weren't supposed to be any policemen in the hall far as I can remember. Is that how you remember it, too, Sheriff Haley?"

Mendelsohn paused at the door. "It doesn't matter. I'll tell the FBI all about it. They said they would wait for us outside to make sure Jimmy got home okay." He turned and looked at Lonergan. "You can't be sure there'll always be a vigilant policeman like Officer Lonergan to cover his back."

Nefertiti buried her head, pulling the pillow tight against her ears. But the ring, ring, ring went on like a hammer hitting an anvil. Ring, ring, ring. She shuddered and then surrendered, snaking her arm to the trembling phone.

"It's Dennis." She rubbed sleep from her eyes and squinted to read the clock by the bed. Dennis? She growled into the receiver. "Do you know it's four o'clock? In the morning?"

"Course I know. Wasn't important I wouldn't be calling. You awake, Titi?"

"Awake? Yeah, Dennis. I had to wake up to answer the phone. What's the problem? You didn't get my package? I told Bronko—"

"Don't know what you're talking about. No package I know about. No. This is about Bronko."

"Why are you telling me? He works for you." She frowned. "Bronko in trouble?" There was silence.

"Bronko's dead." She sat bolt upright, staring at the clock face in the darkness. This time yesterday he was leaving her bed. "Bronko is dead?"

The sheriff's voice was chilly. "Yes. And we have to talk. I'll be there in an hour. Make some coffee."

Ted Mendelsohn got up early that Monday. The clamor and reverberation of the organizing meeting and its riotous ending had robbed him of any hope for rest. The image of Bronko's hand pulling out his gun had kept appearing as he stared into the dark, longing for sleep. His skin felt chilled in the damp dawn and he pulled on an old sweatshirt. A somber Rennie was in the kitchen, pouring water into the ancient percolator. She put it on the stove and sat down heavily in the single kitchen chair. The old woman looked at Mendelsohn over her cracked glasses.

"You ever see anything like that?" Her voice was sorrowful and quiet. "All my years ain't never seed a man shot dead right in front of me. Tore up. Like a big rag doll. Layin' dead not six feet from my Sharon." Tears clouded her glasses and she took them off, drying her eyes with a stove towel. "What that child gonna remember, Ted? And Jimmy Mack could just as easy been layin' dead, too." Her chin lifted and an uninvited smile suddenly brightened her damp eyes. "But you ever hear speechifying like that? Lordy! 'You were there! No one ever have to tell you. You were there!' That boy possessed, Ted! You saw it. I saw it. And Godamighty, Eula saw it. Man she loves most in the world 'bout to die. And he almos' got taken away by that Bronko. Passes understanding." She got heavily to her feet. "You want some coffee?"

"No coffee for me. I have to meet Jimmy at the Freedom House before the walkout starts." Mendelsohn took the trembling woman into his arms. "Sometimes man proposes and God disposes, Rennie. We both saw man's best and worst last night. And sometimes it does pass understanding." He released her and she patted his chest in embarrassment. Mendelsohn paused at the door. "I don't imagine Sharon's going to remember much about last night, Rennie. It happened so fast."

She nodded. "Hope that's so. You tell James he did good last night."

At the Freedom House, he read the *Clarion*: NEGRO LABOR ORGANIZER SAVED BY HEROIC ACTION OF LOCAL WHITE SHERIFF'S DEPUTY. Wordlessly, Mendelsohn held it up to Jimmy, his stomach growling, and picked up the telephone to call New York. "How the hell do I explain all this to Max?"

Jimmy said, "Before you call in your story, you ought to know a few things. That 'local white hero' who shot Bronko was one of the two who beat Dale and me at the station house. He's the guy who ordered Bronko to throw us out of there when they were done."

"Why are you telling me this?"

"Because Bronko was the only witness to the beatings, and Lonergan knew it. And those two hated each other's guts. I saw it that night after the beatings. My guess is he was probably worried that this nigger cop would use it against him given the opportunity."

Mendelsohn remained silent, holding the receiver. Jimmy finished his coffee. "Now the opportunity is gone. The black rogue cop is dead, and Law-and-Order Lonergan is alive and very well." He cocked his head and regarded the reporter. "Probably in for a promotion. You find that interesting?"

"Yes. But Bronko was this close to killing you. And Lonergan saved your life, Jimmy."

Jimmy stood up and stretched. "And two nights ago that pecker-head would have burned me alive if he had the chance."

"What are you talking about?"

"Dale and I watched the whole Klan cross burning from the attic. The guy who brought the gasoline to burn down the Freedom House was Officer Lonergan. If somebody hadn't shot up Lonergan's truck, Dale and I would have been lost in the ashes."

Mendelsohn stared at Mack. "And you call that interesting?"

"Yeah. What's even more interesting is that, if Lonergan finds out there were two witnesses who saw him light the fire, he's going to come looking for them." The astonishment on Mendelsohn's face made Jimmy grin. "You ever heard of the Mississippi whoo-who bird, Ted? Interesting bird. He flies in ever diminishing circles till he disappears up his own asshole."

Mendelsohn had held the receiver in his hand for a long while, and now he carefully placed it back on the hook. A question surfaced that he had hardly acknowledged. "You don't seem particularly happy that Bronko was killed."

Jimmy frowned. "I'm not. He was just a colored man doing a shitty job to get along. A man like me has a certain sympathy for that. If you're black and born in Mississippi, you know that man. He's you. Back then. Now. Maybe tomorrow. You don't get happy when he's shot dead like a dog." A wry grin started on his serious young face. "Besides, we only had one black cop in the whole Delta. Some black folks took a lot of pride in that, though they were embarrassed when he killed blacks for the Man. And now we're back to square one. There's no black cop in this Delta. Just white cops, like Lonergan, who can kill blacks for the Man."

"And you think he will?"

"I think he will try."

Chapter Twenty-Five

Lonergan closed the cruiser door and turned to Butler. He slapped his partner's thigh and chortled. "I wasn't out of bed yet when the phone rang." He grinned. "It was Roland Burroughs himself! Your mayor!"

Butler turned off the ignition. "You're shittin' me?"

"No. Wanted me to know that my resolute action at the Communist meeting was exactly what this police force has been needing. Best public relations thing that's happened to Shiloh in forty years. Wants me come to the White Citizens Council meeting Thursday night. His guest. Thinks the gentlemen at the Shiloh Club would enjoy meeting a Shiloh policeman who's not afraid to do what's got to be done." He threw back his head and laughed. "Finally gonna let one of the Klan meet the country club boys!"

Butler grinned. "Leave your white sheet at home, buddy. He knows you got it. His guest! Those white glove types don't invite us lower-order grunts for drinks 'less there's a reason. What's the reason?

"If it ain't admiration, maybe it's politics, partner. Be nice to me. I could be your next boss!"

"Dropping that Bronko bastard sure turned you on, pal. They gonna make you Pope?"

"You can kiss my ring, Butler."

"And you can kiss my ass, Lonergan. When's your truck gonna be fixed up? I don't plan on being your chauffeur."

Lonergan stretched luxuriously and lit a Camel from the crumpled pack in his breast pocket. "Preacher called, said he checked the trucks at Kilbrew's and they'll be ready tomorrow morning. The holy man is still pissed off that we didn't take down that Communist whorehouse. Wants to know who shot out our tires for the Devil. I told him that it was probably Bronko. He said it was too many shots for one sniper. That was the preacher's specialty in the Bulge in '45. At least two guns, he said."

"So what does the old bastard want us to do?"

"Burn out the Freedom House and all those Satan vipers, he said.

Burn 'em out or they're gonna kill us. Find 'em." He stared at Butler as he blew out a long stream of cigarette smoke. "The preacher's a mean prick. We don't want to be on his shit list, partner."

"And?"

"And maybe we should find who ruined his party."

The sun was just starting to touch the tops of the trees behind the deserted Fatback's Platter when Dennis Haley parked in the clearing behind Nefertiti's cottage. He scanned the yard and noted it was safely out of sight from the highway. He paused, listening to the cooing of a mourning dove back in the woods, then walked to the door and turned the knob. Hearing the rush of the shower, he grinned and stepped inside. He folded his long frame into the one easy chair and turned it to face the bathroom door. He was lighting a cigar when Nefertiti, with only a towel wrapped around her hair, stopped abruptly at the bathroom door.

Looking past the flame of his match, Haley lazily let his eyes move across the shining and sumptuous burnt sienna landscape of the woman.

She answered his stare without blinking, standing motionless. "You almost done, Dennis?" Her voice was flat. "Learned a long time ago that a boy with a hard-on can't be kept waitin' too long. Looks like you been waitin' too long."

"You can tell from over there?" He put his cigar on the edge of the table and opened his arms wide. "I think you ought to be a lot closer 'fore you rush to judgment." His smile was fixed, but his voice was commanding. "I mean now, Nefertiti."

She remained standing, but began to dry her hair with the towel, then slowly moved the towel, caressing the drops of water from her breasts, her stomach, her thighs. When she was done she moved past him and stretched out on the bed, her eyes locked on his. "You just walk in the door? That's it?"

"That's it, Nefertiti. I just walk in the door. And you welcome me. Simple."

"Funny," she said. "I took you for the sheriff, not my handy man." Her mocking voice crooned:

"Why, he shakes my ashes, greases my griddle,
chimes my butter and he strokes my fiddle,
my man is such a handy man. . . ."

His voice was angry now. "I think you should remember that. The sheriff. The honky who lets you operate on this lily pad, case you forgot. Your handy man is now very dead, Nefertiti. Too dumb to live. No hard-on at all. So you may just have to settle for a fine white stallion who appreciates what you've got, you black bitch."

"Someone like the sheriff."

"Spitting image." Without another word he unfastened his holster, placed it next to the cigar on the table, and began to undress.

"You gonna tell me what happened to Stanley?" The gaze from the bed was steady.

"Lesson for you, Nefertiti. He didn't have the sense to do what I told him. And it got him killed." He dropped his clothes on the floor and poured two glasses of whisky as he watched her in the mirror. "Your handy man thought he was a black Polack Wyatt Earp, riding into town and confronting the bad guys, all against my orders. Pulled his gun on Jimmy Mack, who was making a speech at the mass meeting."

Her eyes were wide. "Bronko was going to shoot him?"

"The *Newsweek* reporter thought so and came running to have me stop it. I sent my best cop, Lonergan, inside to get the dumb bastard out, and the next thing I knew Bronko was dead and the FBI was all over my back. You know what I'm going to have to deal with now? Christ!" He approached the bed carrying the drinks. "Your handy man was hired to cover my ass, Nefertiti, not to lay my woman. And now I've got to find a new messenger who won't mess with what's mine."

She emptied her glass. "Like me."

He raised his glass in an elaborate toast. "Like my sepia Queen of the Nile." She was silent as he sat heavily on the edge of the bed. His deep voice throbbed in the stuffy room. "So this is how the drill is going to go from now on. I'm gonna have Harold Butler start handling the door here at Fatback's and then bringing me the rent."

"You're crazy. Everybody knows he's Klan, Dennis. You think he's not going to have trouble at our door?"

"Butler can take care of himself." He knelt on the bed, staring down at her as he opened his arms wide. "And he'll take care of me, too. Unlike your handy man, he won't even try to get in this bed, Nefertiti. Unlike your sheriff, he can't stand niggers."

Chapter Twenty-Six

Billy's broom was sweeping the dregs of the night before across the curb when the cruiser pulled up and stopped. Billy leaned comfortably on the handle and benevolently waved the two officers toward the open door of Billy's Chili. "My goodness, two of Mississippi's finest, coming for breakfast at my modest establishment. How in the world can I show my appreciation, gentlemen?"

"You learn to talk like that when you were in Italy, boy?" Butler asked. "Don't sound like wop talk. Sound like wop talk to you, Lonergan?"

Lonergan grinned. "Sounds more like uppity-nigger talk, Butler. Course we never been in Italy, fighting to get laid with white Eyetalian women, like Billy here. So could be. Is it true her old man shot off your fingers on the way out the door, Billy?"

Billy laughed and held open the door. "Certainly good to see you relaxed and happy, officers." Smiling, he led them to a booth facing the grill. "I understand you had a heroic confrontation last night. Saved Deputy Bronko from being killed by an unarmed black man named Jimmy Mack by killing Bronko yourself." The two police sat down in silence. "Must have taken some moxie to do that. You fellas call that a 'fire fight'? When we weren't laying white Eyetalian women at Anzio, we used to call those uncomfortable shoot-outs 'fire fights.'"

He moved behind the stove, flipping hotcakes and turning sausages in the pan. "At any rate, Billy's Chili is happy to offer a free breakfast to the brave man who gunned down Deputy Bronko, a colored man who was not a patron of these premises. My clientele just didn't like having the place get a bad reputation by letting in just anybody. You might say we discriminated against that black officer. Hope that wasn't breaking any law. Could that be why you're here this morning?"

Butler said, "Deputy Lonergan, here, is the hero, boy. He gets the free breakfast. And I get the free breakfast because I'm hungry. That sound like a good plan?"

Billy laughed. "Certainly does. Put up your feet and stay a while. I got these hotcakes and pork sausage on the grill." He paused. "No offense, you gentlemen enjoy pig sausages? Not everybody likes pigs."

Butler turned to Lonergan. "You take offense, Lonergan?"

Lonergan's smile faded. "We'll have the sausages, Billy."

Billy and the two settled in the small booth toward the rear. Butler poured coffee into the saucer, waiting for it to cool as Lonergan's eyes settled on the gun, hanging in plain sight, over the hood of the stove. He pushed his hot cakes away and walked over to examine the weapon.

"A carbine! Damn, that's a fine little gun. Don't see many carbines down here." He returned to the table. "Know you gotta have a license for that carbine, Billy."

"Yes sir, Deputy Lonergan. Certainly do. Got it in '46 when I returned to Indianola after my extreme exertions caused by layin' white Eyetalian women on the Anzio beachhead. On certain other occasions I used that little carbine in the hills behind the beachhead and got attached to it. I have the license with my discharge papers in the back room. You like to see it?"

"I certainly would. Right now."

Billy turned in his seat and called to the closed door. "Z, baby, would you bring in my gun license please? We have a guest here who's eager to see it." A slender, blue-eyed, olive skinned woman with luxuriant black hair framing her oval face brought the small certificate to the table and paused behind Billy's chair. When she smiled, she revealed small, bright teeth behind her full, pink lips. Billy hid a smile behind his coffee cup as he watched the two police stare at his wife. He'd seen this reaction before. "Z, say hello to Deputy Lonergan and Deputy Butler. I don't think they've met you yet."

"*Buon giorno*, Signori," Z smiled. "I mean good morning, gentleman." She turned to Billy. "Gentleman?"

Billy chuckled. "Gentlemen." He pushed back his chair and put his arms around Z. "My Italian wife is just getting comfortable with English. But she's learning faster than I learned Italian at Anzio."

Butler was the first to speak. His voice was shrill. "This white woman with the nigger hair is your wife?"

Billy regarded him with a humorous detachment. "According to Chaplain Amos Grenville, Commander, U.S. Navy, who married us at the Anzio City Hall on August 22, 1944, this white woman with the nigger hair is my legal and beloved wife. Would you care to see the papers?"

Butler scraped back his chair and headed for the door. "Screw you both! I've seen enough filth for one morning." The door slammed behind him.

Lonergan remained seated, his eyes fixed on Billy's wife. "You called her Z, Billy. What does Z stand for?"

"It was her name in the Partisan group we worked with behind the beachhead. I'd heard about this sharpshooter in the hills that was picking off Germans, only name I heard was Z. Didn't find out it was a woman for ten days. Didn't find out it was a beautiful woman named Natalia till I met her when we secured the beach. Got married a week before our outfit shipped out for Normandy. It's taken a long time to get her here." He squeezed her shoulder. "But she's a keeper."

Lonergan said "A sharpshooter. You like the carbine, Z?"

She smiled. "Yes. A nice light gun. But I like a longer rifle for the sharpshooting. Yes?"

Lonergan said sharply "Tell me where you were last Wednesday night, Z."

Her eyes wide, she turned to Billy. "Where?"

Billy smiled. "Wednesday night Z worked with me till we closed up about two. We must have had thirty, thirty-five people here saw us working. Why do you ask?"

Lonergan gathered his hat and stood to go. "There's been some sharpshooting out near the Communist house, Billy. Shot the shit out of my truck. You hear anything about that?"

"No, Deputy Lonergan. All I heard about was poor Bronko. A lot of action for Indianola. Natives must have been restless."

"And you'd let me know if you hear anything? "

"What a question. I'm sure you know the answer. Say goodbye to Deputy Lonergan, Z."

With her arm entwined in Billy's, she followed the officer to the door. "*Arrividerci, signor.* Goodbye."

Chapter Twenty-Seven

Lonergan pulled in opposite the Freedom House, and parked across from where his truck had stood on the night of the firing. "We were right there, Butler. Preacher's truck was right behind us." They stepped onto the baking road, shading their eyes from the noon sun. The lawn of the Freedom House was dotted with groups of black kids with their teachers. On the porch they could see the journalist, Mendelsohn, talking intently with Jimmy Mack. When Mack spotted their cruiser, he and Mendelsohn disappeared inside. Lonergan walked slowly around the cruiser.

"All the shots hit my truck on this side, away from the Commie house. None came from over there."

Butler grunted as his eyes swept from the school to the road to the cotton fields. "So they came from the cotton. All we got to do is look through this haystack for a goddam needle with a name on it."

"Or names. Preacher's sure there was more than one." Impatiently, Lonergan pushed the nearest cotton plants aside and began to search between the rows. "You move east a hundred yards. I'll move west. 'Less the shooters were marksmen, they must have been in the first few rows."

"You think they left us a note? Shit, man, it's a hundred degrees out here." He stopped short, bending down to pick up an empty five-shot stripper clip. "Well, lookee here. A souvenir, Lonergan!" He walked toward the deputy and stooped again. "And some 30-06 shell casings! You ever see this kind of stripper clip?"

Lonergan squinted and then nodded. "It looks like the stripper clip from an old Enfield rifle. My grandpa brought one of those back with him in '18. Now who the hell still has an Enfield? Most of them got replaced by Springfields during the first war. Grampa said they were glad to unload the old Enfields, so he brought his home for hunting." He continued his search and finally found more empty casings at a spot opposite the near end of the house. "Damn if the preacher wasn't right. Two shooters, and they had us in a barrel."

Sweating and hot, they returned to the cruiser. Lonergan cranked down the windows and headed for the station. He grinned. "The mayor's gonna be really pleased about this."

Frowning, Butler lit a cigarette. "Another merit badge for Mr. Wonderful. You know, Lonergan, the guy who found the clip and then found the casings was your partner. You might tell the mayor."

"What do you take me for, partner? Course I'll tell him. We talk a lot, me and the mayor." He grinned at Butler's sour face. "One thing I don't get, though. Those shooters had us in their sights, close range. They shot out the tires, the windshields." He turned to look at Butler. "How come they didn't take us out?"

Butler watched the cotton rows cart-wheeling by. "Don't know, but they'll be damned sorry they didn't."

Old Oscar Kilbrew was dozing in his hammock when the cruiser pulled up at the curb. Lonergan led the way to the broad veranda, and when he spotted the old man he tapped gently at the screen door. "Mr. Kilbrew, sir, could we have a minute of your time?"

Kilbrew blinked and then raised his head, struggling to sit erect on the sagging hammock. "That you, Deputy Lonergan? Come on up. Who's that behind you?"

"Deputy Butler, sir."

"Always glad to see Shiloh's finest. Can I get you gentlemen a cold drink?"

Lonergan looked at Butler then said, "No, sir. We're only stayin' a few minutes. We're investigating a shooting incident that took place out at that Communist school the other night. Thought maybe you could help us."

Butler said, "I remembered you were one of the old veterans of

World War I still alive in Shiloh, you and Senator Tildon. But that don't help us much. We're tryin' to figure out who else came back to this town from the war who might have brought back an old Enfield rifle with him. You any idea, Kilbrew?"

"It's Mister Kilbrew, Deputy. Why d'you want to know that?" The reedy voice was coldly sarcastic. "How you so sure that two old veterans still alive in Shiloh didn't do the shootin'? Think we're too old to do that? You think Senator Tildon and I couldn't have shot up the Communist school if we wanted to?"

Butler flushed, his eyes darting to his clearly embarrassed partner. "Like we said, just doin' an investigation."

Lonergan stepped forward. "I'm sure the deputy didn't mean no disrespect, Mr. Kilbrew."

The old man turned to face Lonergan. "Nobody seems to know their place anymore, Officer Lonergan. I know you've got a job to do. How can I help you?"

"Down at the end of the Green there's a stone marker to 'Our Heroes from the Great War.' Your name is on it. Senator Tildon's name is on it. Col. Jeffrey Tollin is on it, and I know he died in 1938 when his place burned. But there are two other names at the bottom of the marker: Thomas McCormack and Percy Williams. You knew these men?"

Kilbrew smiled. "Course I knew them. We were demobilized at the same time. We were all in the cavalry. Used to march with those boys every Armistice Day. What do you want to know about those two old colored gentlemen?"

Butler burst out. "Niggers? Them two, McCormack and Williams, are niggers?"

The old man turned to Lonergan. "Tell your partner that Tom McCormack was wounded rescuing our horses when we were in the Argonne, and was decorated for it. He was made corporal and his buddy, Percy Williams, made staff sergeant in the colored platoon attached to our battalion." He turned to the flustered Butler. "They are not niggers. They are veterans, colored veterans."

Lonergan suppressed a thin smile. "Whatever you say, sir. Butler and I are just tryin' to find who might have shot up the trucks at the school the other night. You think those two have old Enfields?"

"Probably. Most of us dragged 'em home when we were demobbed. Think I still have my gun out in the shed somewhere. Just can't imagine either of those two old timers shootin' up anything bigger than a possum!

Mc Cormack and Williams hardly even go out to chop anymore." He paused. "Why in the world would they go out to shoot up trucks? Only thing I've heard about Deacon Williams is that he's keepin' that *Newsweek* reporter. Heard it from my boy over at the gas station."

Lonergan said, "It's time for us to go, Butler. We'll go talk to them, Mr. Kilbrew. Thank you for your help."

Ted was talking with Percy Williams in the tiny living room when he saw the cruiser pull up on the road. He watched Officer Butler step warily from the car, eyeing the sanitation ditch he had to step across in order to approach the Williams front door. Wrinkling his nose at the odor from the open sewer, Butler stepped carefully across the ditch and walked past the tin cans full of plants that brightened the nearly grassless yard. When the impatient knocking started, Ted said, "You've got company, Mr. Williams," and stepped back as the deacon opened the door.

"You sure took your time." Butler shoved past Percy, halting as he saw Mendelsohn, pivoting back to the old man. "You Williams? Percy Williams?"

"Yes, sir." His voice was gentle. "I am Percy Williams."

"Get in the car, grandpa. Takin' you to the station." When Williams didn't move, Butler said. "You hard of hearin', nigger? I said get in the car. Now."

Mendelsohn stepped closer. "Why are you taking Mr. Williams to the station, officer?"

Butler said "I don't have to tell you why." Looking around the barely furnished room, he said, "You're the Jew reporter staying in this house? Jesus Christ!"

Ted said, "Mr. Williams, unless you are put under arrest, you don't have to go with this man. You have a warrant for Mr. Williams?"

Butler hesitated and saw Lonergan approaching the house.

Hurriedly, he blurted, "He's not under arrest. We just want him to come to the sheriff's office to answer some questions."

Mendelsohn asked "Are you willing to go with this officer to the sheriff, Mr. Williams?"

Mr. Williams looked at him. "I don't want no trouble, Mr. Mendelsohn. I'll go with the officer."

When Lonergan pounded on the door, Butler swung it open, his hand clutching Williams's arm. "Got the suspect right here, Lonergan."

Mendelsohn stepped forward with his note pad. "What is your partner's name, Deputy Lonergan? He never mentioned it."

Lonergan gave Butler a withering look. "Butler. And you must be Mendelsohn from the magazine." He noted the pad and said, "We're just taking Williams in for some questions. He'll be back soon."

When Lonergan opened the rear door of the cruiser, Percy's eyes widened. "What you doin' here, Thomas?"

Tom McCormack said, "Just goin' with you to talk with the sheriff." As Lonergan closed the door, Mendelsohn came to the side of the car and nodded to the two men in the back seat. Butler gunned the motor and curled out onto the dirt road. Mendelsohn checked his watch and made a note on his pad.

Lonergan eased the cruiser off the highway at the edge of the cotton field. The Freedom House seemed deserted, and the burnt skeleton of the cross stood alone in the yard. He watched the two men in the back seat, who sat motionless, quietly meeting his gaze in the rear view mirror. "Thought maybe we'd have a little talk before we get to the sheriff," he said, turning off the ignition.

Butler hiked himself around so he could face them. "This place look familiar?"

"Yes, sir," said Percy. "That's the Freedom House over yonder. Took my Sharon there for finger-painting two Saturdays ago."

Butler growled, "You playin' with me, boy? Finger-paintin'? Don't mess with me, nigger. You own an Enfield rifle?"

"Yes, sir. Had it since '18."

Butler grinned at Lonergan. "Now we're getting' somewhere. You ever bring your Enfield out here when Sharon was doin' her finger-paintin'?"

"No, sir. Never did that."

Tom Mc Cormack spoke up, "Percy and I both have Enfields. Earned 'em, too. That the question you wanted to ask us? No big secret. Used to march with them on Armistice Day." His voice was challenging. "Against the law now for coloreds to own Enfields?"

Lonergan intervened. "No. But it's against the law for niggers to shoot up two trucks with Enfield rifles. So the real question is did you niggers shoot up the two trucks with Enfield rifles?"

McCormack said, "We want to talk with the sheriff about that." Percy looked at Doubtin' Thomas who simply patted his knee.

Butler exploded. "You want to talk with the sheriff? Some reason you can't talk with Lonergan and me? You shoot up those trucks, nigger?"

McCormack said, "We might know a lot about who did the shooting, and the sheriff would probably like to know that."

Lonergan's eyes narrowed. "And you think you could maybe not take the rap for the shooting by talking to him?"

Thomas said, "Depends I guess on the value of what we might give the sheriff."

Butler said, "Lonergan, don't bargain with these bastards! You want to know what they know? Let me take 'em out in the cotton for ten minutes and you'll find out. They got nothing to give Haley."

Percy Williams suppressed a smile as he realized where Doubtin' Thomas was going. "Well, Officer Butler, we could help the sheriff find who the Klan are that burned that cross over yonder."

Thomas said, "Bet we could do that, Percy. I sure don't want to go to jail myself. You agree with that?"

"Yes. Rennie and Sharon would have a hard time doin' without me. So maybe we got to talk with Sheriff Haley, Thomas."

Lonergan said, "You think you know who burned that cross?" His words lingered in the cruiser as Thomas calmly looked from Lonergan to Butler.

"Do you think Percy and I know that, Officer Lonergan? Because if we knew that, might be hell to pay for the people who burned the cross." It was silent in the cruiser. The afternoon was fading and the first lights far across the field were coming on in the shotgun houses of the tenants.

In a gentle voice, Percy suggested "What with those three students lynched, seems there's a lot of pressure on the sheriff and the mayor with the FBI all over Shiloh. Don't you think so, Officer Lonergan?"

Lonergan looked at Butler's enraged face then shook his head. "Yeah. I do. And I think it would be hell for those people."

"'Less that information got lost along the way." McCormack's voice was steady. "Old colored gentlemen tend to forget a lot of things. Course a lot of things worth forgetting."

Butler was furious. "You gonna let these niggers . . . ?"

Lonergan finished the sentence. "Go home."

Chapter Twenty-Eight

Mayor Roland Burroughs's morning had been a disaster. First Aggie calling from Tildon's office in Washington. Was it true? A killing of a black cop? And then the FBI thundering up the stairs like a posse. You dumb hick bastards don't know how to protect your own cops? And the Jew reporter, asking questions. He should have known shit would happen on Dennis Haley's watch. Indecisive bastard! Burroughs's jacket was drenched and he felt the sun beating hard on the back of his skull as he hurried from the City Hall to the blessed coolness of the bank. Christ! Would it ever rain? He squeezed his eyes tight, visualizing the rows upon rows upon rows . . . the miles of steaming earth and blackened roots . . . his beautiful verdant Delta a-simmer with heat . . . cracking, splintering, dying of thirst. . . .

And when he pulled open the door to his office, there, slumped in his desk chair, was the massive presence of a glowering Luke Claybourne. At the opening of the door, Luke raised his chin and muttered "Hi, Roland."

Panting, Burroughs pulled off his sweat-stained jacket and hung it on the clothes rack, half out of breath from his exertions. "Luke Claybourne." The words sounded like a dirge in his ears. Jesus! Not today!

"You don't look a hell of a lot like a banker. Get out of my chair and let an aging banker-mayor do his work. Planters and other misfits sit over on this side." He frowned, searching his desk calendar. "Did we have a date?"

Claybourne moved ponderously around the desk. "No. I've needed to see you for three days and you've been harder to find than a rainstorm."

"I've got a town to run, Luke. You so into that Wild Turkey you don't remember that? I'm not allowed to forget it for one damn moment."

Claybourne was clearly irritated. "You been talkin' to Willy? No, I'm not into the Wild Turkey. Only drinkin' time I have is when she's doin' her Jesus thing on Sundays."

Burroughs pulled down his tie, settled back in the worn leather, poured two glasses of water from the carafe, and slid one over to Luke. "You don't have to wait till Sunday for this." For the first time, he smiled. "I saw your little lady on the square two days ago. She doesn't look like the mother of two kids, Luke! Still looks to me like the Cotton Queen of Magnolia County!"

Luke grunted. "Part of my job description is to keep her lookin' like that. And she takes to it like a hen to corn. You can check it out at Neiman Marcus." Abruptly, he rose from his chair and walked to the tall window facing the square, studying the sky. "Not a goddam cloud." When he returned, he placed his elbows on the desk and stared at Burroughs. "Roland, I got to talk to you about our 4,000 acres. Something you know something about."

Burroughs laced his fingers and studied the desolate man before him. "Yeah. I know a good deal about Claybourne's. Known about it since your daddy and I returned from the Pacific in—'46? Yeah, Spring of '46. Your grandpa met us at the gate." He chuckled. "What kept you so long, Lucas? Killin' Japs in Tarawa shouldn't take that long!"

"Roland, I got no time for reminiscin'. The plantation's in trouble. Big trouble. You gotta help me."

Burroughs rose and went to close the office door, pausing to observe Luke carefully. Luke returned his searching gaze.

"No, I'm sober, Roland. I haven't had a real drink since the drought started. Me and my niggers been too busy tryin' to save my crop. And the truth is . . . " — he spat the words out — ". . . we ain't gonna make a crop." His eyes were stricken. "My soil's as hard as a coon's head, and what cotton we got is as brown as his ass."

Burroughs' mouth tightened. "I'm right sorry to hear that, Luke. Right sorry."

"Sorry doesn't help! Two years of drought? Sorry doesn't start to spell it. I need a loan, Roland. Two fucking years! I'm tapped out, and I can't afford to lose my field hands."

Burroughs remained silent. When he spoke his voice was grave. "A whole passel of places in the Delta are finding it tough, Luke. We're carrying more paper on more plantations than any time in our history, and we've been at it since 1878. Between the drought and the Nigras talking union and continuing to leave the Delta, there's a lot of hurt out there. You're not alone."

Luke was on his feet now, his face livid. "You mean misery loves company? Well, I don't. I got almost forty tenant families counting on me to keep Claybourne's open. Other people have to figure out their own way to do that."

Burroughs angrily met his gaze. "Some of the them have, Lucas. Some of them read the signs and got out, taking a bundle of government money with them. Your friend Dick Perkins was first in line. Told me yesterday he's selling his acreage to HUD and now the Feds are bringin' in affordable housing across the highway where it used to be cotton."

"Folks like Dick Perkins didn't grow up here, Roland. Never felt the obligations that go with having a plantation. Cotton was just a business opportunity." His eyes were furious. "That wasn't my daddy and that's not me! Leave folks high and dry who have worked your land for decades? Generations? How do Christian folk do that?"

Burroughs rose and faced him across the desk. His voice was quiet. "They do it by being smart, Luke. The Delta's changed, is changing, gonna go on changing. And the only ones who are gonna survive are the ones who recognize what's happening. They're the ones who invested in irrigation systems so they could survive the drought. How many years have I been telling you to mechanize, Luke? Every time, you told me, 'Get off my back. I'm running Claybourne's like my daddy did.

And I'm gonna take care of my niggers like my daddy did.' Well, I can't bail you out this time. This well has run dry."

Luke stood, "Can't bail me out, or won't bail me out?"

"Can't and won't, Luke. Bank can't hang on to the past and expect to survive."

"You selfish son of a bitch!"

Burroughs' face was suffused with sadness. "I loved your father. But God helps those who help themselves, Lucas. Banks, too. I'm right sorry, son." He walked slowly to the door and held it open. "Send my best to your little lady."

Luke let the door slam behind him. He leaned against the wall, fighting to restrain the hot, angry tears that were threatening to humiliate him. He walked swiftly through the bright cool of the busy bank lobby, nodding automatically to neighbors, eager to leave the place. *You bastard! I loved your father!* The words repeated and repeated, a sarcastic dirge. I *loved your father.* His mouth felt sour, and he paused to wipe the sweat from his face. A husky black man crossed from the Green and approached the bank. He stopped short on the sidewalk, recognizing the planter. Carefully, he stepped aside.

"Mr. Claybourne."

Lucas blinked and gruffly stuffed his damp handkerchief into his pants pocket as he stopped in front of Jimmy Mack. "Well, look what the good Lord has brought me. Jimmy the Organizer. The man who's pulling the plug and helping us sink. Just who I wanted to see after visiting my friendly banker." His voice was bitter. "How lucky can one man be in a single morning?"

Startled by the man's fury, Jimmy remained silent but Lucas was not yet drained. His eyes raked Mack's go-to-meeting clothes and settled on the impassive black face. "Why y'all dressed up? Goin' to a funeral?"

"Not mine." Jimmy started to pass but Lucas raised a hand to restrain him.

Do not touch me, Claybourne." His voice was firm. "Do not."

Lucas dropped his hand. "Just wanted a chance to talk with Justin's nephew, Jimmy Mack."

"The last time we talked I think we were on a more informal level, Claybourne. Then you just called me 'boy.'"

Lucas reddened. "Did, huh? And you called me 'Mister Claybourne,' if I remember correctly. You were a little more polite beginning of the summer. But your memory is better than mine."

Jimmy folded his arms. "I'm cursed with a good memory, Claybourne. I can remember almost exactly our last conversation. *Boy, you're not here to see your colored gal, you've got three minutes to get your black ass off my property.*"

Lucas rubbed his chin, his eyes watchful. "Said that, did I? Well, I thought our little Eula could have done a lot better than a rag-tag civil rights agitator. But no harm done. You left."

"Yes I did. And your little Eula stopped being your little Eula and left, too. Beats all, doesn't it, Claybourne? Just another house nigger bein' pushy, I guess."

Luke's eyes kindled. "A house nigger? A live-in whore? You sayin—" He broke off and moved toward Mack. "Eula May was never a house nigger. She was our housekeeper. That was my house and Willy's house. And you got a hell of a nerve suggesting that!"

"And you never . . . " Jimmy halted, picking his words carefully. "Ain't a colored man I know in the Delta who doesn't have nightmares about his woman who worked for old massa in the big house. Even if we pass a civil rights bill, it won't make those nightmares go away."

"There are a whole lot of nightmares, Mack. And they come in all colors." He looked over his shoulder at the bank. "Old massa's got a few himself." Calm now, he turned to leave. "What business you got with Burroughs?" He smiled for the first time. "You organizing his help?"

"Not any of your damn business, but I'll tell you anyhow. Mr. Burroughs wants to talk with me about the new housing Washington's planning for the Delta. Seems to think I might have some connections that could help."

Luke stared. "Connections."

"It should be good for the economy, Burroughs says. More of a future than chopping cotton or organizing workers. You agree?"

But Claybourne was walking rapidly away.

Only when he was about to leave the highway to drive his truck up the long drive to the house did Luke Claybourne become startlingly awake. Christ! He stared at the driveway, blinked and shook his head as if to clear away the jungle of sorrowful underbrush that had been his companion on the long ride home from the bank. Instead of turning, he gunned the Chevy down the steaming macadam, swinging right on the caked dirt work road that snaked across the plantation. As he eased the truck between the endless rows of wilt and mildew, the unendurable frustration filled the cab like the moist heat from the fields. With a groan, he leaned his throbbing head back on the flaking leather and killed the engine. Send my best. . . . How did it go? *Send my best to the little lady.*

The summer afternoon silence suspended over Claybourne's plantation was as warmly familiar as the comforting curve of Willy Claybourne's back, the little lady's back. When the angelus carillon from St. James's Church in town broke the silence, it startled a flock of blackbirds that rose helter-skelter from the field, then wheeled and disappeared. He reached for the doorless glove compartment and pulled out the dregs of a half pint of Jack Daniels. *Here's to you, Daddy's best friend, you bastard.* When he had drained the Daniels, he stepped from the sweltering cab, stared up at the unforgiving sun, and hurled the bottle into the parched ranks of brittle, suffocating cotton. And then he knew where he was going and why he was going, and he began walking up the hard dirt road.

The cottonwood tree reached above the fields like a sentinel. It must have died before he was a kid, but it had been a pole star for Luke from his earliest rememberings. From there, he could always find his way home, however vast the seas of green had appeared to the little boy. At a curve in the road, the land dipped suddenly, descending into a brackish wetland where scrub trees and wild roses, poison oak and dark green ivy tangled around the pale ocher cottonwood. Imperious, the tree lifted long black fingers to the sun and ghostly white fingers to the Delta moon. And just beyond was the bright blue circle of the catfish pond.

In the odorous mud he found the large flat rocks. He knew he'd find them. They had always been there, and only Daddy and he knew which was which.

"The one with the fossil on the dark side of the slate is yours," Daddy had said. "It was yours when you were here two million years ago and this was the bottom of the ocean."

"And I was a fish?"

"No. You were a little crustacean. Here's your picture." And Daddy had taken his finger and followed the tiny ridges of the little fossil on the rock. And when he had laughed Luke knew he was just teasing, and that was okay.

"There ain't no ocean here, Daddy."

"No more," he had said. "It all dried up."

"And how do you know which rock is yours, Daddy?"

"It's the one that's bigger than yours."

"But I have the fossil."

And daddy had smiled and nodded. "And you have the fossil."

And every time they came to the cottonwood to go catfishing, they'd find the large rocks and sit on them. Lots and lots of times.

He climbed up the bank. Old smells from the tangle of raspberry bushes made him pause, breathing deep, smiling as he remembered the raspberry taste of Never Titty. His eyes moved across the matted weeds, just the same as when the bank was Never Titty's Court. He laid his hat on the damp ground and stretched out on his back, his drowsy eyes searching the black stain of the dead cottonwood as it scraped the sky. *I'm guarding the castle from my watchtower, Titty. Protectin' the Queen.* And, bold as brass, she'd piped: *Your queen is as beautiful as Nefertiti, Queen of the Nile.* And then she had run to the pond and splashed down, squealing, on the shiny mud. In his ear he heard his daddy like it was yesterday. *You be nice to that little nigger pixie, Lukie. She trusts you.*

He closed his eyes and was surprised to find they were wet. He beat the earth softly at his side. *You bastard, Burroughs. I love this place. I love all of it.*

Chapter Twenty-Nine

At two in the afternoon, Fatback's Platter was as forlorn as the tuxedo in the window of Sol's thrift store near the Trailways station. Even the crystal ball that would send shards of color drifting across the dancers once darkness reclaimed the room was a silent, cool, gray presence. Nefertiti surveyed the empty dance floor and the deserted tables with their ungainly chairs piled on them. It was her favorite hour. Luxuriously, she unwrapped the Havana cigar from its silver sheath and bent to the match, drawing in the rich taste. Her drowsy eyes moved across the tableau, visualizing the scene tonight when the place would throb and the calls would cut through the music: "Sing it, Titi! Yes! Yes! You go, girl!" Slowly, she exhaled, sending a mist of blue into the edge of sun at the end of the bar. How she loved this room. Everything was perfect. No. She squeezed tight her eyes, seeing again the holster and the heavy hands. Not everything. Sheriff Dennis Haley would never let it be perfect. Ever.

When she heard Z's car crunch to a stop, she shook herself and moved down the bar to the bottle of Chianti Classico which she had brought from Jackson as a special gift for Z. She poured two glasses of the ruby wine and held them aloft as Z entered through the sudden blazing light of the front door and paused, letting her eyes adjust to the shadowed stillness of the bar. When she saw Nefertiti she grinned broadly. "Ciao, Titi!" and crossed swiftly to embrace her. She took the two glasses and retreated to a corner table. Nefertiti smiled, savoring this familiar ceremony with this exotic creature Billy had brought to Fatback's when she arrived from Italy. All her life, Nefertiti had been a man's woman. No woman had been allowed that close in her 30 years. But the past months had disclosed that there was a strong presence inside this olive-skinned Italian, a woman like herself who had traveled a long distance to find out who she was. Nefertiti brought the bottle and settled happily in the facing chair. She lifted her glass. "*Mia amica d'Italia!*" Z laughed, and their glasses touched. "My American friend!"

Nefertiti bent to relight her cigar, noting an unfamiliar tremble as she dropped a match and struck another.

"And how goes your world, Sister Titi? *Bene?*"

Titi's eyes lifted briefly and held on her friend. Then she resolutely shook out the match. "You don't miss much, do you? Bene? Not so bene, Z."

Z's voice was gentle. "I heard about Bronko. I'm so sorry, Titi. He was important to you?"

"He was. We never talked much. Talk wasn't what he did. He was so damaged, so damn confused. Maybe more like me than I admitted. Important? Hell, I don't know. We were comfortable together. He was there for me. But I never let him stay till morning." Frowning, she glanced at the front door. "And now he never will."

"You will miss him, I think. Who will handle your door? He was a very strong man."

"My silent partner will tell me who. And I will pretend it's okay. It's the way it is."

Z's hand covered Titi's. "Women here are like women back home. Not quite separate. Not quite equal. So we have to make our own rules sometimes. *Lentamente.*"

"*Lentamente?*"

"Slowly." She smiled. "The men find out later. Maybe also your silent partner?"

Titi's laugh was brittle. "My silent partner doesn't learn and doesn't forget. What he remembers all the time is what he owns."

Z refilled their glasses. Her eyes seemed to be viewing another landscape. "I knew such a man. He was rich and very powerful. And he owned land in Umbria that was larger than any plantation in the Delta. His family had owned it since the fifteenth century, a present from the pope. Three hundred years before your Revolutionary War, Titi! In Italia we had serfs centuries before there were any slaves in America." Her lips curled. "People have owned people for a long time."

"How did you know such a man?"

"His name was Sforzi. Count Ricardo Sforzi. My father had been on the Italian Olympic team in 1932 and won a gold in rifle shooting.

It was a great Italian victory. The count was on the Olympic Committee and when the games were concluded he hired my father to be his game-keeper. It was an incredible opportunity. So my mother, my father, and I moved into a house on Sforzi's land, and we became part of what the count owned. The war had started in 1939, but it never seemed to touch us in any way, perhaps because the count seemed to be a friend of many in Mussolini's fascist party. My childhood was spent with my father, hunting and shooting in the mountains, and I was well taught. My mother became part of the household staff. We paid for nothing. I was schooled there. The count was very attentive, and seemed to take a special interest in me. And when I turned sixteen, my father was told by the count that now I was to move into his quarters. He had waited long enough."

Titi's eyes filled. "And your daddy could do nothing. You were to be a house nigger."

Z drained her glass. "My father said my daughter will move into your quarters when her tutor leaves on Friday afternoon. And on Thursday night he led me through the mountains to a group of partisans who were fighting the Fascisti. He gave me a rifle and his blessings, and he went back to confront the count on Friday. My mother was put off the land and my father was arrested. He died in prison two weeks before the liberation. My mother lives with relatives near the Anzio beaches where I fought with the Partisans and met Billy."

"And you came to Mississippi to be free? That may be a first." Titi's smile was ironic and sympathetic. "You are like your father. You ought to get a gold for that!"

Chapter Thirty

Sampson Sparrow, looking fashionable in his red vest and black bow tie, continued wiping off the Shiloh Club bar when he saw them enter, his eyes quickly measuring the room. Most of the White Citizens

Council regulars were already huddling at the end of the bar or seated at the tiny tables, chatting and laughing. One scanned the *Clarion* that was lying on the bar, then held the newspaper story aloft and called over to another, "Where would they have taken that Nigra cop if he wasn't dead, Mike?"

The man hooted. "Not in our backyard! Directors at the hospital would've all had coronaries. Maybe they would have left him with the NAACP over in Cleveland. They're always looking for new members."

As laughter rocked the room, he read aloud from the *Clarion* story: "'Without a moment's hesitation, Deputy Sheriff Luther Lonergan faced down the rampaging, rogue Negro as he wheeled to fire his weapon. The white deputy's aim was true, and the life of James Mack, the Negro labor organizer, was spared.' Who the hell hired this crazy Nigra and gave him a .45? You any idea, Gene?"

The mayor's Town Counsel held up his hands. "Not my table. A question we might ask Sheriff Haley if he gets here. All I know is he'll be buried in the Nigra boneyard over in the Sanctified Quarter."

Sparrow, the elderly Negro bartender, watched as they passed the *Clarion* story from hand to hand. That poor blue-eyed nigger, he thought. Nobody gave a damn when he was breathing and nobody gives a damn now that he ain't. A mean mother, all in all. But they sure as hell used him. The old man grunted and shook his head in disgust. Who gave him the .45? Amazing how these men only knew what they wanted to know.

When Deputy Lonergan and Mayor Burroughs entered from the staircase there was a moment of surprised silence and then a ripple of applause. With a broad grin, Burroughs led his guest to the bar. "Two of the real stuff, Sammy. One for the mayor and one for the hero."

Sammy nodded. "Yessir, your honor." He swiftly poured two tumblers of bourbon. Burroughs said, "Sammy, this is Deputy Sheriff Luther Lonergan."

The bartender slid the drinks forward, his eyes on the flushed face of Lonergan. "Yessir. I recognized him from the *Clarion* picture. He's the hero who saved the Negro labor organizer and shot the Negro deputy sheriff." His voice was so cool and flat that the mayor frowned and Lonergan's eyes widened.

"Sammy your name, boy? " The deputy's voice was very quiet. "I like to remember names, boy."

"The name is Sparrow, Deputy Lonergan. Sampson Sparrow. And I'm old enough to be your father, sir." Without another word he turned and moved down the bar.

The policeman turned to Burroughs, his face livid. "Did you hear that old nigger?"

The mayor shrugged and smiled. "Don't let Sammy rile you, Luther. He's been pouring drinks for the Shiloh Club since Senator Tildon's daddy was still running the bank downstairs. Not worth getting upset about."

Moments later, when Sheriff Haley came in the door, the mayor tapped on his glass and addressed the noisy room. "Gentlemen, I'm glad that our sheriff has joined us because I want to propose a toast to a man who has made us all proud. Our police force and the town are going to benefit from his dedication. I give you Deputy Sheriff Luther Lonergan!"

The glasses were raised. "Lonergan!"

The mayor raised his hand and in the silence he led Lonergan to a nearby table. "Resolution is everything." He turned to the sheriff. "Don't you agree, Haley? Your Deputy Lonergan is the personification of resolution." He paused and then grinned. "Hell, you can't be irresolute if you're going to ride a Bronko!"

As appreciative laughter broke around him, Sheriff Dennis Haley looked over at the beaming Lonergan. He leaned back on the bar and said, "Sammy, get me a scotch. I didn't know we were going to be celebrating such a special occasion." When the mayor put his arm around Lonergan's shoulder, Haley called to the watchful Sparrow, "Make it a double." Sparrow served the drink and crossed his arms, his eyes bright.

Haley raised his glass, nodded to the mayor, and gazed at Lonergan. "Here's to Deputy Lonergan. A good deputy, willing to learn. I got great hopes for him, Mr. Mayor. He's a great shot, for openers."

Burroughs cupped his chin in his hand and stood beside Lonergan as Haley's voice sliced through the room. "I didn't know one of my boys was the personification of resolution, of course, but then the boss is always the last one to find out." The room grew very quiet. "Thank you for pointing that out, Mr. Mayor."

"Now I don't think that tone is helpful, Sheriff." Jamie Steinkraus rose from his seat opposite the bar. "I know Senator Tildon takes a lot of pride in the reputation of his town and this county in keeping its composure under all the stress of this Commie provocation. Seems to me, by being resolute, Deputy Lonergan removed a dangerous rogue officer and was a model of courage under pressure. The mayor was just expressing our gratitude. No reason for sarcasm, Dennis."

Mayor Burroughs interrupted. "I don't think the sheriff was being sarcastic, Jamie. We're all under a lot of stress, with the press on our backs and radicals invading our property. I'm sure the sheriff's doing the best he knows how. I don't want to be a Monday morning quarterback, but maybe the best judgment wasn't used when that Nigra thug, Bronko, was hired."

Lonergan suppressed a smile as Haley reddened. Burroughs shrugged. "Must have had a good reason, Sheriff Haley. I'm sure the folks here would like to hear it."

Haley drained his glass. "Law and order. The reason I hired Bronko was to maintain law and order, Mr. Mayor. Lot of folks are out there these days questioning the laws we've maintained here in the Delta for a hundred years. Not all that easy with the Feds looking under our beds spite of all the good work Jamie's Senator Tildon is doing in Washington. And that gets us to the order part." He paused, letting his eyes travel the room. "I get paid by you to see that order is maintained and that the thousands of our dark brothers who we want in our fields are not in our streets. Or in our beds. I found a black man who owed me and seemed to understand that. In the last five years, four black agitators were eliminated by Deputy Bronko. I don't remember anybody here calling the office and saying your black deputy shouldn't have done that, Sheriff. With all due respect, if my white deputies had done that, there would have been blood in Shiloh. I don't think our good senator would have liked that story, Jamie, with an election coming up. The dirty laundry was handled, gentlemen. I didn't expect thanks. It's what I get paid for. But I don't appreciate being made the goat now or at any time. You want a new sheriff? There's another election coming up. That's for your

White Citizens Council to decide." He turned his back and placed his empty glass on the bar. "Goodnight, Sammy." The old man nodded politely.

"Goodnight, Sheriff Haley." His eyes stayed on Haley as he walked out of the silent room.

The sheriff summoned Deputy Harold Butler to his office late the next afternoon. "Close the door. Got some private business to discuss. Take a seat." Butler nodded and settled warily in the chair opposite Haley's desk. "It's after hours, Harold. Thought you and I should get to know each other a little better." When the sheriff took out a bottle from his desk and offered him a drink, Butler's eyes widened and a relieved smile creased his face.

"Thanks. 'Preciate it, Sheriff. Been a long, tough day. Lot of shit hitting the fan after the shooting at the Commie meeting."

Haley nodded. "Not the best thing that could of happened when the FBI are all over the Delta looking for those agitators. Now the Feds, the reporters, and everybody wanting their name in the paper are kicking up sand. Your buddy Lonergan seems to be riding it full tilt."

Butler answered slowly. "Well, Sheriff, I work with Lonergan. Wouldn't describe him as a buddy, exactly."

Haley's eyes were unblinking. "What'd you think of the shooting, Harold? You were right there. Think it was a just shot?"

Butler emptied his drink and looked boldly at the sheriff. "I think Lonergan was trigger-happy, Sheriff. Wanted to blow the nigger away and make his mark. End of story."

Haley chuckled. "Not necessarily the end. Mayor Burroughs seems pretty fond of your partner. No telling what'll come of it. Lonergan seems to be feeling no pain." He leaned forward and refilled Butler's glass. "I guess you could call killing Bronko a career move."

Butler studied his drink. "You don't mind my askin', why you sharing this with me, Sheriff? Lonergan don't mean nothing to me. I'm just the guy who didn't shoot Bronko, and got no career move." He looked up, suppressing a smile. "You have something in mind?"

Haley grinned. "Nothing subtle about you, Butler. You call it like you see it. I like that."

Butler crossed his legs and leaned back in his chair. His tone was confiding. "People who know me always say that, Sheriff."

Haley nodded. "Doesn't surprise me, now that I'm getting to know you, Harold." He leaned forward, resting his elbows on the edge of the desk. "Matter of fact, I know quite a lot about you."

Butler watched in silence as the sheriff finished his drink and then walked around to the front of his desk to stand over him. "I know about you and the Klan preacher. I know about you and the Kilbrews. Even know that it wasn't your Klan unit that took out those three Commies, Goodman, Schwerner, and Chaney. Being a sheriff in the Mississippi Delta means you know a hell of a lot about a hell of a lot." He slowly returned to his seat. "And I know about the statutory rape of that fourteen-year-old in 1957 when you got busted from the Marines in Manila." He sat down heavily and refilled the glasses. "A man makes mistakes, Harold. I think we all pay our own dues and I'm not passing judgment. Nothing I'll ever mention again. Just want you to know that the people I choose to work for me are looked over and looked after."

Frowning, Butler licked his lips and cleared his throat. "Like Bronko?"

"Like Bronko. He was rotting in Parchman Prison before I cut him loose. Then he did what he was supposed to do for the sheriff, and he was taken care of. That Polack nigger was more important to me than you were or Lonergan was. Now my handyman has been blown away by our resolute Lonergan." He pounded the desk in irritation. "And, goddam, everything has got to be sorted out all over again!"

Watchful, Butler locked his hands behind his head and eased back in his chair. "And you want me to be your new nigger?"

Haley's eyes were hard. "Only if I say so. Then you say, yessir. And when I say jump, your answer is, how high, boss?"

Butler's anger rose and his voice was tight. "Yessir." He wiped his mouth with a stained handkerchief while watching the sheriff. "We're talking day job or after-hours job?"

"We're talking about you being there for me when I'm not there. We're talking about you being my pickup man, my enforcer, the man who has my back. Anybody who has to know, gets to know that the sheriff's man is Harold Butler. You're not going to win any popularity contests. You're just going to get rich."

"And how do I not get dead like Bronko, instead of rich like you say?"

Haley smiled thinly. "You don't let killers like Luther Lonergan get too close."

It was dusk when Nefertiti walked Z to her car. As Z started the engine, a battered Chevy careened off the highway and skidded to a stop. Harold Butler studied the two women through his dusty windshield and then got out of his car. He stared in distaste at Fatback's Platter, then, turning his back on Z, he said to Nefertiti, "Sheriff says you and I got to talk. Inside." He turned on his heel and walked into the bar.

Z frowned. "I know that man, Titi. No black shirt, but a Facisto." She looked sympathetically at her friend. "You going to be all right?"

Nefertiti nodded. "I think my silent partner has sent me a special delivery." She patted Z's arm and smiled. "Been handling that kind of redneck since I was wearing bloomers, Z. Not to worry. We'll talk later."

Butler was behind the bar, pouring himself a whisky, when she came into the shady room. "No," she said. "That's not the way it's going to be." Her words echoed in the empty room. She walked swiftly to the bar, picked up the bottle and returned it to the shelf.

Incredulous, he stared at her. "What the hell are you doing, nigger?"

She picked up the phone at the end of the bar. "Get me Sheriff Haley." Her eyes never left Butler. "Sheriff, there's a honky son of a bitch that has just walked into my establishment, drunk my whisky, and called me nigger. That's right, Sheriff." She paused. "Butler? Your name Butler, boy? Sheriff Haley wants to talk with you."

Butler hesitated, then took the extended phone from Nefertiti's hand. "Yessir. Yessir." His face was scarlet when he hung up. "Sheriff wants me to find out what you want me to do." He swallowed hard. "Then he wants you to call him."

"I'll call him when I'm ready. It's good we understand each other, Butler. Save a lot of problems for you, for me, and for the man we both work for. But when you're at Fatback's, you're working for me. You call me ma'am. You pay for drinks. You're not a customer. You run my door and keep it clear and see there are no problems for the sheriff. And after work you get paid by me and deliver a personal envelope to Sheriff Haley. And leave. Any questions?"

Butler shook his head, his eyes locked on Nefertiti.

"Fatback's opens at seven. You be here on time and the sheriff will be happy, something we both want." She left him and began to set up the tables. It was starting to get dark.

Chapter Thirty-One

Luke had watched, not daring to believe, as a sooty indigo rim of clouds began to finger the blindingly blue sky. As he squinted in the noon glare, he avidly tracked the ascending veil of gray, and his face cracked into a broad smile when he heard the far, far murmur of thunder that seemed to moan and then hurtle into a booming explosion over the endless rows of parched cotton. The dusty, weary plants bent before the foreign wind that suddenly raked their leaves. A blinding rip of lightning plummeted toward the distant field, and a crashing clap of thunder rattled the tin siding on the weighing machine. The racing storm clouds pell-melled across the sky, drowning the sun and sending gusts of water to pound against the side of the barn. His head back and his mouth open to the blessed water, Luke tore off his drenched shirt and jeans and raced out into the fields, his boots sloshing in the racing currents of water gathering between the rows.

"Willy! Willy! Come out! Come out!"

The lightning that suddenly painted the shadowed laundry where Willy Claybourne was folding the linens startled her. When the clap of thunder seemed to explode just outside, she heard Luke's yell and raced from the cellar to the porch. Breathless, she stepped out into the driving rain and saw Luke dancing, naked as a child, in a puddle. When he spotted her, he screamed, "Come on in!" His laughter was almost lost in the wind. "The water's fine!"

Giddy, she abandoned her sodden clothes on the step and went running to embrace him, her eyes bright in the light of the flashing lightning. "Lucas! Lucas!" And they tumbled, hilarious with the wonder of it all, to lie panting on the mud, their eyes turned to the cascading heaven.

"Thank you, Jesus!" Willy shouted.

After midnight, she heard the rush of wind fitfully subside and the pelting rain become a steady murmur on the roof. She rolled on to her side and looked at Luke. He slept like a boy, defenseless and nearly smiling. He could sleep through a tornado, she thought, and her gaze moved to the blind, inky window. There is weather, she thought, even in a marriage. Not just because he's a farmer. She rolled on her back, knowing that sleep would not return. Because he's his mother Lillian's boy. Because he's his daddy's son. Because he's laced to this land. Because he married Willy McIntire. And it's never been just fair weather for us. Never was for me. Maybe never will be for Luke. But, glory be, it's raining!

When Mendelsohn drove to the Freedom House it was pouring like he hadn't seen in the Delta, and it matched how he was feeling. The burned cross had tilted like a drunk in the wet clay and the place looked deserted and sad. Dale Billings met him on the porch and told him Jimmy was on the way. He heated up some cold coffee and they watched it rain.

Billings was beginning to look at the road ahead, feeling excited but sad. "I'm going back to Washington and law school. But I'm feeling guilty as hell about leaving."

Mendelsohn nodded. "You're not alone. I never felt so bad about wrapping a story and moving on." Jimmy Mack arrived, slogging through the mud, arm in arm with Eula, soaked to the skin and laughing. It was Eula who broke the news.

"We're getting married! Mr. Williams is going to do the honors at the church on Sunday after Rennie finishes her teaching at the Sunday School." She grinned, "Dale, you're going to be the best man."

Mendelsohn took Eula in his arms and kissed her. It was a nice finish for his story. Or was it a finish? What the hell was it about this forsaken part of the world that grabbed hold so hard and bothered his sleep? He shook his head to clear it and said, "It calls for a celebration! And Max Miller is taking us all to lunch."

They drove through the wet to Billy's Chili. Z embraced Eula and then Jimmy when she heard the news. "Billy, we're invited to the wedding! We'll close up after Saturday night. How wonderful!"

"We'll bring the cake," Billy said. "Tell your boss, Max, he's ordering the booze." He looked out at the drenched and deserted street, pulled down the shade, and locked the door to close the place. "What do you like to eat?"

When they finished the ribs, the greens, and the sweet potato pie, Z brought in the Chianti and the toasts were made. Dale Billings raised his glass.

"To Eula, who must be the bravest or dumbest woman in the world. And to Jimmy, who's about to find out!"

Z said, "To Eula and James: *Buona fortuna* and a *buono viaggio* for many many happy years! Ciao!"

Mendelsohn clinked his glass with theirs. "This is the unlikeliest courtship I've ever witnessed, and I intend to come back and report on the sequel. On behalf of brother Max and your humble servant, we wish you everything good."

Jimmy took off his dark glasses and kissed his fiancée, a very public act for a very private person. Then he stood up.

"To Eula," he said, "who's going to Delta State in the fall and will make us proud, and who's willing to let me tag along! I'm a lucky guy."

It was Eula who had the last word. "To my Jimmy. To our Jimmy. We love you."

Chapter Thirty-Two

By Saturday, the rains had passed, and the whole Delta seemed to breathe deep, watching the steam drifting from the fields. By Sunday, there was no trace in the parched earth that the rains had ever come. Luke haltingly walked the rows with Justin Mack, stooping often to reset the more fragile plants that had been ripped out by the torrents of the past week. Head bowed, Luke continued his desperate vigil, row after parched row, as Willy waited on the step of the porch. She watched as Luke finally left the field with Justin. Together, they stared across the land until the old man turned away, lightly touched Luke's shoulder, and shuffled toward home. As the light began to fade, Luke made his way to Willy on the porch. He never uttered a sound or raised his head when he settled heavily beside her. It was dark when she gently took his hand and led him into the house. There would be no crop this season.

The wedding celebration for Jimmy and Eula went on through the sun-embroidered afternoon. Rennie Williams and the ladies outdid themselves, for the last time, with platters of chicken, fried catfish, okra, all the fixings, and gallons of iced tea. For the summer volunteers, it was like the Last Supper, something to be savored and remembered. The tenderness and love being expressed was so naked and unashamed that Mendelsohn wondered if he, the Shiloh families, and the volunteers would ever know its like again. Mixed with the laughter were lingering looks and embarrassed embraces of affection, saddened partings with dear friends they had never known when the summer was borning in Oxford. Their backpacks piled high, the volunteers waited for the Trailways bus that would lead them home to the rest of their lives.

Sharon clung to Mendelsohn's legs, trying to keep him from leaving with the students. "Now, you stop that, honey," said Rennie, blinking rapidly behind the cracked lenses of her glasses. "Ted's going away for a while, but he'll be coming back. Ain't that so, Ted?"

Mendelsohn nodded, curling the child to his chest. "I'm not leaving yet, baby. And when I do, I'll be coming back," He watched the kids he had lived with, survived with, for three months on the black side of Highway 49, and tried to remember what they had been like back in Oxford. Who could have known? And who could have known that there were black Shiloh families like Rennie and Percy Williams who would dare so much to shelter and care for them? They had been strangers to his whole American existence, but would now be a treasured part of who he was. It was only after the bus had inched out into the highway that the wedding party reluctantly began to drift away.

The police cruiser was idling at the curb outside the churchyard. Leaning against the hood, Lonergan and Butler watched the crowd of townsfolk disperse, and remained silent until Jimmy, Eula, and Mendelsohn approached. Lonergan flipped his cigarette away and stepped in front of them.

"Mayor Burroughs sends his congratulations, Mack. Hopes you'll have a happy life together. He told me you're going to be working with the Washington people that are coming soon. Said you shouldn't hesitate to call on him if there's anything he can do to help."

Eula's hand tightened on Jimmy's arm and her eyes widened, but she said nothing. Jimmy nodded. "Yeah. Well, tell Mayor Burroughs thanks, and I'll be in touch . . ." His eyes flicked from Lonergan to Deputy Butler and held for a beat. "If this Negro needs him."

When the police car pulled away from the curb, Jimmy grinned. "Just gave myself a wedding present, Mendelsohn."

Ted grinned. "I'm sure you'll enjoy it. Something to remember."

Eula watched the police cruiser move down the highway. Her voice was pensive. "Something for Lonergan and Butler to remember, too."

Jimmy turned to Mendelsohn. "I have to meet the HUD people in Jackson tomorrow. You want to ride down with me? I want to pick your brain. You're my man in Washington, Ted. You know these kind of guys."

Ted cocked his head and smiled. "You've got nothing to be nervous about. This is your turf, kid. You've earned it. You know more about this corner of the world than they do. But I can't, Jimmy. Max is waiting on my wrap of Cheney's funeral in Meridian before sending me to interview Mandela in Cape Town." He shook his head, his eyes desolate. "All of this, this whole toxic, incredible summer, all—" His voice broke.

"It's just another story to Max. And when I get to see Mandela and write about the horrific apartheid in South Africa, all of it will be just another story for Max." He shook his head, angry and frustrated. "And it's not Max I'm frightened of. It's me. I feel like the world is skidding past me, and all I can do is take notes"

"Don't be so hard on yourself. You've been a lifeline for us, and a megaphone. We can't do that ourselves."

Ted blinked hard and searched Jimmy's face. "I've gotten a hell of a lot more than I gave. I've gotten to know you, and Eula, and the Claybournes, and Rennie Williams, all the people I've come to know and care for in this American wilderness. Victims, heroes, and too many of them damaged or dead like Mickey and Andy and James." He shrugged and cleared his throat. "But it's just another story for Max, soon to be yesterday's newspaper."

Chapter Thirty-Three

Reverend Gladsome Neeley had seen Willy Claybourne at the Johnny Reb Day parade when he'd finished his invocation on the town green. It was the only such parade in the Delta, so folks showed up from all the cotton towns halfway to Jackson. She was there with her boys, Alex and Benny; the reverend had christened them both. Willy's blond hair was tucked beneath a lavender sun hat that softly shadowed her face. No way to miss Wilson Claybourne. She moved with the quiet assurance of a beautiful woman who had always been beautiful. Gladsome and Willy had been friends since she had moved in with the Kilbrew family and started at Shiloh High. His mother had encouraged their friendship. "That child has seen more grief than a good Christian should ever know about, Glad. Be a good friend." And his father had welcomed her into the Bible studies class at the church, knowing full well the girl had never been in a church before.

For the shy Gladsome, Willy had been his first real crush. When she found Luke Claybourne, it had been a terrible disappointment for him. Being 18, Gladsome bemoaned his luck and went off to the University of Virginia and then Yale Divinity School. The friendship with Willy had revived when he was summoned by his father to take over as his assistant pastor. One of his first duties upon succeeding his father at the pulpit was to marry Lucas and Willy Claybourne. Luke went to church only for weddings, christenings, and funerals, and never did understand Willy's Sunday ritual of attendance. But for Willy, who longed for the ordinariness of a childhood that had been denied her, Sunday church filled some of that emptiness.

When the plantation had been lost, Luke seemed to be nearly drowning in frustration and guilt. Willy's need for something or someone to sustain her led her to seek Gladsome's counsel.

"I've never felt so helpless, Glad. I watch Luke leave for Parchman Penitentiary in the morning, and I think: I made him do that. And I weep once Alex goes off to school."

"There will be better days, Willy. You and Luke are going to make it. You are there for each other."

Her response was sodden. "I've never felt so alone."

"Willy, you never were raised in the church, never known Jesus as part of your life. Church has been something social for you, like the Shiloh Club, like the PTA, just a place to be part of the community. Now you've been stripped of so much that was material. And you feel naked, but you're not, Willy. Starting from now, you have a friend in Jesus. Every day."

"How do I find Him, Glad?"

He had taken her hand and knelt. She blinked away the tears and knelt beside him. "Pray with me, Willy."

When the student volunteers of Freedom Summer had arrived in Shiloh in June of 1964, Oscar Kilbrew was alarmed. He urged Rev. Neeley to convene an urgent meeting with the church Elders. Gladsome, noting the agitation in his caller, had readily consented, but asked his wife, Martha, to take notes and listen. He sensed it would not be an easy meeting. It was to take place at the elderly Kilbrew's home.

Oscar, who had been a parishioner when Gladsome's father was still the minister, nodded curtly to Gladsome and Martha as they entered his living room. "Good Evening, Martha, Gladsome. Since we've all known each other for a long time, I think it's good if we have a frank exchange of views about this worrisome invasion of our town."

Gladsome nodded. "I certainly agree, Oscar. It is worrisome."

Kilbrew said, "If it's worrisome, then everyone in town has got to do his part to deal with it. Do you agree?"

The minister sensed a tightening of tone in Kilbrew's voice, and a nervous shifting among the five Elders. "Of course. The whole country is watching Magnolia County this summer, and Shiloh in particular. How we stand the spotlight will be a measure of our character."

Kilbrew frowned. "Frankly, Gladsome, I think our problem may not be character as much as patriotism, fealty to our country and to our Mississippi."

Neeley's eyes widened. "What in the world are you suggesting, Mr. Kilbrew? That your minister is not patriotic?" His voice was so strident that Martha looked up hurriedly from her note taking. She could see the throbbing vein in her husband's neck and the unusual flush on his face. His voice dropped. "I am certain you are not implying that. What is it you wish to discuss with me and the Elders?"

Kilbrew said, levelly, "I am questioning your judgment, not your patriotism, Reverend Neeley. I leave it to others to judge what is patriotic in these terrible times. My son, who runs the garage, has told me that a colored who works for him, and lives in the Sanctified Quarter, reports that a radical minister who is counseling these local Communists is planning to come to services on Sunday. At their meeting, the minister told the group that he had known you at the Divinity School at Yale and was certain that there would be no problem attending our Sunday services. He showed the group a picture of a rally at Yale celebrating the Brown v. Board of Education decision in 1955. You were on the podium."

The room became still. Pale, Martha halted her writing and stared at her husband. Kilbrew's voice broke the silence. "That was you?"

"It was, Mr. Kilbrew. The whole Divinity School felt it was an advance for our country toward solving racial segregation. I do believe that. It's the law of the land, sir."

"You believe that racial segregation should be abolished?"

Gladsome met his furious gaze. "I believe that every society must work to make the world that Jesus offered us. None of us are perfect. But it's part of our task as Christians to help bring that world. I do not apologize for being on that podium."

Kilbrew was on his feet now and the other Elders rose behind him. "Those radicals are not coming to our church. Not this Sunday. Not any Sunday. The minute they sit in our church, your contract will be nullified. You understand that?"

Gladsome stood and faced them. "This church is not your church, Oscar. And it is not my church. This is the Lord's church, and as long as I am minister of His church it will be a welcome place for anyone coming to pray here." He beckoned to the shaken Martha and when she joined him, he nodded to the Elders. "Good evening, gentlemen. I think we are done here."

On Sunday, as Gladsome stood at the top of the steps welcoming his parishioners, he saw a knot of people cross the highway and start up the walk approaching the church. A white man in a suit, wearing a clerical collar, led four young black men and women and two white student volunteers to the base of the steps. The man waved and called, "It's Bill Farley, Reverend Neeley! I haven't seen you since New Haven. You have a pretty town, but it's a whole lot warmer here than in Connecticut. If you don't mind our perspiration, my friends and I have come to pray with you."

Gladsome saw the parishioners stiffen by the door, their eyes wide. When Farley's group started up the steps, he heard a murmur at the door as Oscar Kilbrew and the five Elders stepped out of the church and made a phalanx of bodies before the entrance. Taking a deep breath, Gladsome started down the steps and shook hands with the other minister. "Welcome, Reverend Farley. We're about to start."

Oscar Kilbrew held up his hand. "Stay right there. The clerical collar doesn't fool anybody. We know who you are and what you are. And you are not welcome here."

Gladsome said, "Mr. Kilbrew, these people have come to pray in the Lord's house. This church has never—"

Kilbrew interrupted. "I'm not talking to you, Reverend Neeley. I'm talking to these Communists who are here to embarrass and destroy us. This man Farley is living with Nigras in the Quarter and sleeping with Nigras in the Quarter, and he can go pray with Nigras in the Quarter."

Farley held up his hands in peace and turned to the young people behind him. "We'll have our service at the Sojourner Chapel." He looked up at the Elders. "You are very welcome to come," he said, then retreated down the steps.

Gladsome watched in silence, then looked at the Elders. "I have never before felt ashamed of Shiloh until this Sabbath. You have made me ashamed. I will take the advice you gave my Christian brothers, Mr. Kilbrew. I will go with them to the Sojourner Chapel, and I will pray for you."

Across the highway, a television crew from NBC filmed Gladsome Neeley as he caught up with Farley and the volunteers as they re-crossed the highway.

When the story broke, YALE MINISTER DENIED ACCESS TO MISSISSIPPI CHURCH, it raced across America, one more piece of evidence that segregation was not going to go away quietly in the South. The NBC story was seen as an urgent call for solidarity among the beleaguered whites like Oscar Kilbrew and the Elders. Fearsome change was at their very gates, promoted by radicals from the North, and circulated by a corrupt press that was determined to destroy their vision of what constituted a good society. A call went out from the Elders for a new minister. In the local paper Oscar Kilbrew, chairman of the Board of Elders, announced that the replacement for Rev. Gladsome Neeley would arrive before the end of the summer.

The firing of Gladsome Neeley was the line in the sand for the white community. Black riots in the northern cities were evidence enough to white Shiloh that segregation was not only justified, but had to be staunchly defended. The calls for "segregation ever, integration never" were soon back in the Mississippi press. Luke, sensing a growing restiveness in his black prisoners, confronted Willy.

"Your Jesus thing is your Jesus thing, Willy. But it's not just your Jesus thing. Your friend, Neeley, is kicking the hornet's nest and getting every black in the Delta riled up, every black in Parchman riled up. That's playing with fire, Willy, and it's goddam dangerous. The sooner that rabble rouser, Neely, leaves Shiloh the better. Your 'born again' meetings with this pinko are over."

Willy felt abandoned, knowing that her long friendship with Gladsome Neely could not continue. Her note to Gladsome said only, "Thank you, dear friend. Pray for me." Not even Em could know her sense of loss. She was left now with only her Jesus. For Gladsome, Willy's turning away was a wound that never really would heal.

When word reached the Sanctified Quarter that there was unusual activity around the Kilbrew gas station, Neely was visited by Rennie Williams. On that very night, Gladsome Neeley packed Martha and his kids into the old Oldsmobile and headed north on Highway 49 for Memphis.

Chapter Thirty-Four

It was dusk when Jimmy returned from Jackson. Eager to share his news with Eula who would be waiting at the Freedom House, he left from the Trailways station and cut across the highway near Sojourner Chapel. A familiar figure came from behind the building, tonelessly singing. Jimmy stared at the man through the early darkness.

When you wake up in the morning and your prick doth stand
From the pressure of your bladder on the prostate gland . . .

"Ted?" Jimmy's shocked voice echoed in the churchyard, but the song continued.

If you can't find a woman, find a clean old man,
And you'll revel in the joys of copulation!

Mendelsohn belched and laughed, "At your service. C'est moi, Ted the scrivener." He wagged his finger, "Whoever you are. In the dark they are all the same." The lurching figure had stopped, staring through the darkness. "Why, it's Jimmy! Have I got a drink for you!" He extended a nearly empty bottle of bourbon. "For you, brother."

"You okay, Ted? Jesus, you look like hell."

"Sure you won't join me? Misery loves company, and I'm sad and I'm miserable." Mendelsohn put an unsteady hand on Jimmy's shoulder. "And I'm going to leave this wilderness, Jimmy. On the next bus or sooner."

Jimmy took Ted's damp hand and led him to the steps of the church. "Sit down. Now hand me the bottle."

Jimmy took a large swig of the bourbon. "You want this back? It's almost a dead soldier."

Ted's voice had become melancholy. "No. Had enough. Had enough booze. Had enough Missifuckingsippi. Wanna go Manhattan. Point me toward the bus station."

"Later. Where you been?"

"Yeah, that's the question, Jimbo. Where I been?" He put his head in his hands. "New York called this morning. Max said after the Chaney kid's funeral to come home. He had sent me photos from the FBI of the three kids when they excavated them from the mud the Klan buried them in." He took the bottle from Jimmy and emptied it. "You don't want to see them, Jimmy." He rose from the steps, his hands thrust deep in his pockets. The slur had gone from his speech. "So at ten this morning I'm in Meridian. Ten in Meridian. . . . They ought to put that on my tombstone. In that crummy little overheated church, I saw where I've been, the whole long, hot summer. Watching Chaney's mother. That woman refused to weep, Jimmy! She was that furious, watching his kid brother agonize and cry like I never heard a kid cry. The boy looked like my Richard at that age. Hearing Hollis or Stokely or who the hell else shout out, 'I'm sick of burying my friends! I'm never going to another funeral! They want to kill us all.' And I watched me taking out a notebook. Goddammit, I did. I took out a notebook. Dear diary, dear editor: What I did on my summer vacation." He spat on the ground. "I wanted to take out a machine gun, Jimmy, and just blow the hell out of all the racist bastards I've had to write about all summer. When they started to sing 'We Shall Overcome,' I bolted out of there, blind, and was hit with a Coke bottle! The redneck was leaning against his truck, grinning. 'You got black pussy in there, nigger lover?' I beat the son of a bitch to the ground, Jimmy. I was not non-violent. I was not a spectator. And I kept on beating him till the sheriff pulled me away and stuck me in the back of his car. 'I thought you were a reporter. You gone crazy? Let's get you the hell out of here. Where you think you are? Manhattan? That guy was a Kilbrew. They'll kill you.' He had his deputy drive my car to the Sanctified Quarter. Said 'have a nice day.'"

"And you're really leaving, Ted? Who's gonna tell our story?"

"You are." He sat down hard on the step. "Everybody in America discovered Mississippi this summer. It's a lot more important that you stay, that you keep making the story. They got plans for me in New York, then Cape Town. So, yeah, I'm out of here, Jimmy. A lot of unfinished business, kid." He stood and put his arms around Jimmy. "We'll keep in touch. I'll be watching."

> *Sept. 30, 1964*
> *Cape Town, South Africa*
> *Hey, Jimmy,*
> *For two days I've been in the belly of the beast here and Robben Island makes Parchman Prison look like heaven. Only revisiting Mandela justifies being exposed to these bigoted bastards. It sickens me to realize that this hell will be Mandela's home for the rest of his life. But he remains full of plans, strategies and hopes for the future! What the hell is it in the human spirit that is so unquenchable?*
> *Ted*

> *Oct. 15, 1964*
> *Shiloh, Mississippi*
> *Ted,*
> *Just got back from the Democratic convention in Atlantic City. Feeling so lousy about what I saw that it's a bad time to be checking me out on unquenchable human spirit, man. It was our*

moment, and the whole world was watching my folks standing up and listening to our Fannie Lou Hamer crying, "Is this America? We are tired of being tired. We want our freedom and we want it now!" Proud? You bet your ass we were proud! And we were screwed by Rev. King and Humphrey and organized labor. LBJ told Humphrey, you want to be vice president? Send these trouble-makers back to Mississippi. And all our old friends asked us to take two damn seats at the convention, and Fannie Lou said, We don't want two seats. We are all tired. And we went home. End of story. Like I said, it's bad timing.
Jimmy

Oct. 22, 1964
Washington, D.C.
Jimmy:
Your letter reached me this morning. Bad news travels slow, and that's rotten news. I thought that the only lousy stuff in Atlantic City was the saltwater toffee, but journalists are the last to know about most everything. I do know that it's not the end of the story. There's no end if you decide there's no end. Mandela taught me that. All he wanted was inclusion for the Africans in their own government. But when he was betrayed they locked him away for life on Robben Island. From his cell he said America needs to know how we're struggling. I told him there were people like Jimmy Mack who already knew that and are fighting for their freedom. He made a fist. "Tell Mack that he's not alone." I'm on the way to New York to cover the elections. Keep the faith.
Ted

Chapter Thirty-Five

After the swelter of Robben Island, Mendelsohn was shivering even in the crush of the crowd at the Inaugural. He put up his collar against the wind that howled up Pennsylvania Avenue. He was always getting back when it was too hot or too frigid in this town. But today, he wanted to be here, in Washington, to see that Texas roughneck take over. Where was he going to take us? Son of a bitch has a vision. It always surprised him that he was that perceptive, almost religious, about education. Never know what is real or just manipulation. He reached the curb and was hailing a cab when a loud voice said, "No taxis for wandering Jews." When he turned he was embraced by an ebullient Jimmy Mack.

"Ted! What the hell are you doing here? When did you get back?"

Mendelsohn stepped back, grinning, alight with the serendipity. "It's been too long between drinks, Mack! And I've missed you. Follow me." The bartender welcomed Ted and looked curiously at his companion.

"Rudy, meet Jimmy Mack. A great friend from Mississippi. A real person, not another reporter." Rudy shook hands and waved them to a booth. "Usual for me," Ted said.

"Whatever he's having is fine. Make it two," said Jimmy.

Ted settled back on the bench, his eyes intent. "Don't even know where to start. How's Eula?"

"Doing great. She is in top management at Parchman. Really loving penology, and they're happy to have her."

"And you? You here for the Inauguration?"

"For that cracker? After he screwed us at Atlantic City? Not likely. I'm here on business." He reached in his jacket, extracted a card and slid it across the table.

J. MACK CONSTRUCTION CO
James Mack, President,
Shiloh, Mississippi

Ted stared at his friend, an unbelieving smile on his face. Speechless, he simply raised his hands.

Jimmy laughed. "You don't recognize an entrepreneur when you see one, honky?" He retrieved his card and replaced it in his wallet. "Your government money in action, Ted. I'm now building houses for HUD in Magnolia County. And our headquarters is a quarter-mile from Sojourner Chapel." He raised his glass. "We drink to Dale Billings, the happy man whose industry as a Washington lobbyist from Missifuckingsippi got us to Senator Bobby Kennedy, and thus into the generous heart of HUD."

Ted smiled and held his drink aloft. "To Dale! I guess he graduated law school at Howard like he said he would."

"He did," nodded Jimmy, "three tough years of hitting the books. And after graduation he accompanied the new senator from New York to show him what he didn't know about Missifuckingsippi. It was stunning. That trip changed Bobby's life, and mine."

"And Mack Construction got born, with Kennedy as midwife?"

Jimmy grinned. "It's how come, for the first time in our long relationship, I can pick up the check! Thank you, Dale."

Chapter Thirty-Six

Jimmy watched Joe McDonald's old truck make its way through the pools of water that collected along the edge of Highway 49 and groan to a stop. From the bed of the truck, he saw Spencer Thompson help his wife, Silvie, and three children on to the roadway, hauling their family possessions in sacks through the puddles, hunching their shoulders against the frigid rain. Thompson raised his arm in thanks, and the truck moved slowly down the highway. The Thompsons moved into the drenched field and in a minute were lost to sight as they plodded on the path through the cotton that led to home.

Mack was drenched to the skin by the time he reached the

Williams's house. Rennie, clucking her concern, hustled him to the
stove where every burner was alight, struggling against the raw December damp. Percy took the thin blanket from his bed and carefully
arranged it around Jimmy's trembling shoulders.

"It don't help to get sick, James."

Rennie poured a hot cup of coffee . "Drink this hot as you can.
Percy's right. It don't help to get sick."

Jimmy pulled the blanket tight around him and looked at his elderly
friends. "What did I do wrong?" His voice was desolate. "Wasn't supposed to end this way."

"Didn't do nothing wrong," said Rennie.

Jimmy drank the coffee and handed the cup back to the old woman.
"Sister Rennie, I just watched Spencer Thompson and his family get off
in the slop and go home to the Armstrong place. That's the seventy-sec-
ond family to come back to Shiloh after the walkout. Seventy-two, just
here in Shiloh! By Christmas the whole thousand we got to leave the
Delta will be back. Brother Percy, what did I do wrong?"

Percy pulled a kitchen chair close to the stove and folded his hands
in his lap. "You didn't do nothing wrong, James. You're a young man,
and you can't do the remembering I can." His eyes focused somewhere
beyond the tiny kitchen. "Remembering covers a lot of years of wrong,
James, and you didn't do nothing to add to it."

Rennie sat on the stool by the door, her eyes glued to her husband.

Percy said, "My first recalling's of a mission room, Baptist probably,
just south of Greenwood. I remember lots of children around, and hungry, being hungry a lot. And my name was Seven Williams." He grimaced. "Didn't have another name but Seven till I was tall enough to
go to the fields on the Douglas place."

Rennie wiped her glasses and chuckled. "And I remember when the
man at the weighing machine said 'You ain't even seven years yet. How
come you got Seven for a name, boy?' And you said, 'They told me at
the mission house I was number seven child of Zeke Williams.' And the
weighing man said, 'You look more like a Percy than a Seven,' and he
wrote it down." She laughed. "Percy Williams! Who knew that name
was gonna be mine one day!"

Percy didn't join the laughter. "Wrong! Pitiful and wrong! Never

knew my mother or my father? Never had a Christian name but Seven?"
His voice was sharp and he looked at Jimmy. "Seven? That's the kind of
wrong goes way, way back, James."

Rennie's voice was soft. "Never meant to say otherwise, Percy." She
drew her stool closer. "Deacon and I shared a lot of trouble, Jimmy. We
grew up together on the Douglas place. We saw a lynching before we
was teens, right on the Douglas spread, Horton Tyler, and that poor boy
was there for days before they cut him down." She blew her nose and
cleared her throat. "There was a whole lot of wrong, Jimmy. Between
Percy and me, we had maybe three years of schooling, and that was
when there was no work for us to do in the fields."

"We were cheap picking machines, not worth teaching." Percy's
gentle voice was cutting. "And that's how Mr. Charlie wants it. He ain't
going to have us organize to change things. He's got the politics in his
pocket, and he's got us in December, cold and hungry. It ain't your fault,
James. You made us all believe that we could change it, something we
never believed before. And that's not wrong. But till the politics change,
walking out don't matter."

Part Two 1968

Chapter Thirty-Seven

Luke was sure that '68 was going to be as dismal as the year it was burying, as damp as the chill that seemed to settle in his shoulders and soul. The damn clock had moved his world into an endgame he couldn't win. Every day of the past three months had showed him that. The torrential rain had drowned any hope he had for reviving the plantation. He stared at the darkening window, seeing only the endless highway he had been running up and down: the dripping motel signs, the canal-like roads, the near-empty hardware stores, the pathetic bars, and the closed faces. Tomorrow was the bank's deadline, and his hands were still empty. It was time to tell Willy. . . . Way past time. He heard Willy's 'Sleep tight, darlin's!' as she tucked the boys into bed, and then footsteps as she moved to the stairs. Luke settled back in his armchair, his drink forgotten on the coffee table, and watched her descend. For the thousandth time, he marveled at those wonderful legs. Christ, it was like the first time he saw them at the cheerleading rehearsal at Shiloh High.

She saw him and smiled. "Why're you sitting in the dark, darlin'? I've got something to show you. Turn on the lamp. We've heard from Dick Perkins. Wonderful news!"

Blinking in the sudden light, he took the letter from Willy's hand.

Dec. 20, 1967
Gulfport, Mississippi
Dear Willy and Luke,
Merry Christmas! Hope this finds you and the boys well and that the rains have finally ceased. The Lord could provide an ark for Noah but not an ark for the Claybournes? No justice, and no rest for the wicked, Luke. Let's hope for kinder weather in 1968, good friends.
Saying goodbye to you both was one of the hardest things I've ever had to do. I've spent more than a decade of my life in the Delta, and the gift of your friendship helped make the transition from my life in Boulder so much happier. I did not expect to find

*that kind of intimate friendship again. I will always be grateful
to you both. But I've become convinced that I have to move on
with my life. The chapter of the Colorado carpetbagger is really
finished, and the demonstration farm had ceased to be the challenge it once was. As I think you know, I felt I was treading water,
and the world was moving out of reach. That's why I headed to
the coast, looking for something I could care deeply about again.
I think I've found it. Time will tell.*

*Spending my first holiday season here on the casino Gulf
Coast is a culture shock. A green Christmas here means your
number's been coming up and you're doubling down on your bet!
Not as homey as Shiloh or as snowy as Colorado, but fascinating
all the same. The old farm already seems a lifetime ago.*

*I've bought an interest in the Silver Spoon Casino here in
Gulfport and am planning on running a real Delta Blues room
for the players, not immodestly to be called "Richard's Rook." I'm
planning on coming up after New Year's, eager to see you both
and to renew acquaintance with your old friend, Nefertiti, Lucas.
I have some plans that could include her if she's free. The Rook
will be a few steps more elegant than Fatback's Platter, and if the
blues are half as good as what we heard at Fatback's, it will be a
joy to run. Might even get you back on the dance floor, Willy.
We've kept our fans waiting too long!*

*I'm working through the arcane politics necessary down here,
trying to get a casino license in Mississippi. It's a civics lesson I
never learned in Colorado. (Never was taught the going price for
a Mississippi congressman!) But there always seems to be a way
for a born carpetbagger like me to find a place by the fire if the
locals like what you've got in your carpetbag. So look for me in
January and we'll make plans to get you both to Gulfport as special guests of Richard's Rook.*

*Happy holidays to all Claybournes, and warm wishes for a
peaceful Christmas and a green New Year from your old neigh-
bor.*

Dick

When Luke raised his face from the letter it was flushed. He dropped the letter on the table and stared at his wife. "That's wonderful news."

Willy tilted her head, her brows furrowed. "Of course it is. Dick's getting launched, it sounds like an exciting opportunity, and he wants us to come down to see it. Yes. I think that's wonderful news. And I don't understand why you don't think so."

He refilled his glass. "It's been so long since I met good news, baby, I don't think I'd recognize it." His voice sounded bitter and hollow in the room. "Sit down and have a drink yourself. You may need it. We can drink a toast to our good friend on his wonderful news."

When she settled down next to him on the couch, he filled a second glass with the bourbon. When she spoke, her voice was tight. "What is going on? You're scaring me, darlin'."

"Remember that loan I asked the bank for, for the next planting season, just so we could pull ourselves out of the hole this rotten weather has put us in?"

"Course I remember. You were going to see Roland Burroughs."

"It's about Burroughs." He handed her the drink. "The son of a bitch turned me down."

"Roland turned you down?"

"Oh, yes. In a heartbeat. Lectured me like I was a snot-nosed kid, not knowing how to manage. Told me I should've invested in mechanizing Claybourne's stead of taking care of my niggers!"

"But it was his advice that made us buy the last five hundred acres! At our dinner table he said we were going to feed and clothe the world and get rich doing it. Right at our table he said that."

"Well, now he's pleading poverty. Can't and won't bail us out."

"What does that mean? We need the loan till this weather breaks and we can get back to normal."

"Normal." Luke's voice was desolate. He rose and walked across the room, leaning back on the bar. As his eyes found hers, she was startled to see how troubled they were. With difficulty, he cleared his throat. "There is no normal, Wil. I'm a cotton farmer. There's being lucky and being unlucky. It was the drought for two years, and the floods last year and now. I can blame my luck, but it doesn't help." He met her eyes. "Wil, there's not going to be a loan. And there's not going to be a crop."

"But there must be others—"

"I asked every planter I know from here almost to Memphis before I went to Burroughs. Didn't want to give him the satisfaction of turning me down. But everyone's in the same boat, and the boats are all sinking. Foreclosure is threatening at least a third of them, and we're part of that third."

"Foreclosure? Losing your daddy's place? My, God, Luke, what are we going to do?"

"I'm going to have to get a job."

"A job?" Willy paled and her voice trembled. She frowned as the words seemed to catch in her throat. "What kind of a job? All you know how to do is run a plantation."

"I don't know what else to do." Luke's words hung in the stale air of the late afternoon as he settled beside her on the couch. Willy's arm tightened on his heavy shoulders. "For the first time in my life, Wil, I don't know what to do." His eyes searched hers, seeking an answer. "Ever since my meeting with Burroughs, I've been scouring the Delta, looking for something, anything. And all I've found is a lot of snickering. Claybournes been riding pretty high in the saddle for a hundred years, and some folks have a nose for blood."

"Oh, you don't deserve that."

"It's not a matter of deserving. It's a matter of what I got to offer, and I don't have much. The places that are hiring are looking for kids with college degrees who'll work cheap. You remember, Wil, I was too smart to go to college, couldn't wait to take over Claybourne's."

Tonelessly, she echoed, "Kids," and stared, as if seeing him for the first time. "Our kids! My God, Alex is almost ready for college and Benny will be one day soon. What will we—?" She stopped as Luke took her in his arms.

"It'll be all right, Willy. I heard that they're hirin' at Parchman, and I think I might be qualified."

"Parchman Penitentiary? Doing what?"

"They're hirin' guards." He felt her become rigid, and her voice became shrill.

"A guard? Luke, you can't. . . . The abuse you'd take, the danger! Guards have gotten killed over there." Abruptly, she pushed him away. "You can't do that!"

"Now listen. I gotta take whatever I can get, and that's what I think I can get. Besides, it's safer now. They used to use prisoners they could trust to help guard, and that always caused trouble. It's why they're looking for guards."

Willy was crying now, and her look was self-accusing. "If it wasn't for me you would have gone to Ole Miss like your daddy wanted! A guard at Parchman Penitentiary. Dear Jesus!" Impatiently she brushed away the tears. "How do you know you can even get that?"

"I don't. But I'm going in the morning for an interview, and everybody in Magnolia County knows who the Claybournes are. They know I can handle a gun and handle men, too." He wiped away a lingering tear on her cheek and raised her chin. "Besides, I always knew you had an eye for a man in uniform!"

She moved into his arms. "Oh, darling, I am so sorry. I am so terribly sorry."

Chapter Thirty-Eight

When Jimmy heard the key in the lock he glanced at his watch and put down his newspaper. Bearing groceries, Eula burst into the room, then plumped them on the table and crossed to kiss her husband. "A long day," she groaned. "Too long. And then I remembered we didn't have the makin's for supper. We have some cold beer on ice, which would be helpful." She dropped on to the deep sofa and smiled for the first time. "Go make your woman happy."

Jimmy crossed to the fridge and brought two frosty bottles, settling next to Eula. "You're late, baby. I was beginning to get worried. Glad you're home. I don't cotton your hanging around Parchman a minute longer than you have to."

"I know that. I'm sorry, darlin', I just couldn't get away a minute sooner. It's been a real crazy day."

He glanced at his wife. "Crazy how?" He grinned. "Somebody tryin' to bust out of Parchman? That's not new."

"Nope." She returned his smile. "Somebody tryin' to bust in! An old friend of yours from the bad old days."

"Say what? Who?"

She shifted so she could face him "Lucas Claybourne. I kid you not. Luke! He wants the guard job and I think I'm going to hire him."

He stared, speechless. After finding his voice he exploded, "You are what? You're going to hire that racist bastard? As what? Executioner?"

She burst out laughing. "Jimmy! Times change. This is not Shiloh in '64. There's a whole lot of history with me and the Claybournes." She rose and walked toward the kitchen, picking up the groceries as she went. "We can talk about it at dinner, or it'll be midnight by the time we eat. Executioner!" Her chuckle lingered in the room as he followed her, leaning against the door frame.

"Don't humor me. I'd rather talk about Mr. Charlie and your long history with the Claybourne family." His sarcasm made her turn.

"Jimmy! What in the world—?"

"You floor me, Eula! How can you even consider hiring a man who treated you like a house nigger?"

"Stop that!" Her eyes were bright with anger, and her smile had gone. "That's not fair." Her words were level. "It wasn't like that. I'm a woman that a lot of men tried to take advantage of. I know how to handle a Luke Claybourne. When I had to, I damn well did!"

"Come on, baby. He never tried to get you in bed with some help on the college tuition?" The words were biting, "How close did Mr. Charlie get? I've often—"

Eula raised her hand and closed her eyes tight. "Jimmy, stop right now."

But Luke's words cascaded, unable to cease: "Wondered what would have happened if Miss Willy hadn't come home."

"What do you mean, what would have happened? How dare you?"

He stepped closer, his eyes fastened on hers. "How dare I? Listen, Eula, lots of women—"

Furious, she slapped his face, and then stepped back, appalled. But the words poured out. "Damn you! After all our years together, you're still wondering?" Jimmy could only stare at his enraged wife. "I'm not lots of women. And if you don't know that by now, you never will."

"You think that's an easy question for a man to have to ask his wife? For me to ask you? It's heart-breaking." He shook his head, trying to shake a scene he had never anticipated. "Too damn many scars . . . too many nightmares." His voice was desolate. He began to leave the room, then turned to face her. "Baby, I never should have asked. I'm sorry." He opened his arms and tried to embrace her. "I love you, and I trust you beyond anything."

Eula angrily pushed him away. "No, you shouldn't have. You sure as hell should apologize."

"I do. From the bottom of my heart, I do."

She leaned back, her elbows resting on the stove. "It's time you get over it, lover." Her voice was steady. "If you don't know me better than that, maybe it's time to rethink the whole thing."

Shocked, Jimmy stared at her. "Don't ever say that, baby."

"Scars and nightmares," her voice faltered, "on both sides of the bed, Jimmy." She held out her hand.

Chapter Thirty-Nine

Luke took out his wedding suit and brushed the lint from the dark lapels. He was married 13 years ago. Jesus, 14! Didn't have to worry how I looked, they were all gaga lookin' at Willy. His calloused hand ran over the fabric, making him smile. Willy looked good enough to eat that Sunday. Couldn't keep my hands off her. Gladsome gave me a look and whispered, "Not yet, Lucas. I haven't finished the ceremony yet!"

Luke chuckled and struggled into the trousers and then the jacket. A little tight around the shoulders, but not too bad. He walked to the mirror. He'd gotten thicker, but that was okay for 33. He showed his teeth to his image, then frowned and turned away. It's too good a suit to wear to Parchman but it's what I got. "Still looks fine," Willy said at the church for Benny's christening, Alex's christening too. It doesn't say a hell of a lot about our social life, Willy girl.

Already sweating, he kissed Willy goodbye and very slowly drove the 13 miles to Parchman. The fields still haven't come back, he noted, and the rains keep coming. Gladsome Neely's God sure hasn't paid me any mind. Two years of drought and then two more years of flooding rain? Fucking biblical.

Not my goddam problem anymore.

The parking lot was still baked tar. He edged the jeep next to the main building. His mouth felt dry, and he hoped there was some water inside. You've got to talk, Lucas. And you've got to talk good. He pulled open the heavy door and took a very deep breath of hot, stale air. Be there for me, Daddy.

The long hall was deserted, his steps echoing ahead and behind, confirming his sense of isolation. His black Sunday suit felt as funereal as it had when he wrestled to button the white shirt with his calloused fingers.

He paused at the barred window overlooking a barren and deserted prison yard, seeking some solace from the sterility of the endless corridors. Beyond the wall with the guard standing sentinel, he could see the beginning of the prison farm, still a pale green carpet. In the glass's reflection, he nervously adjusted his sodden tie and wiped away the sweat that was soiling his collar. A door at the end of the hall swung open, and a uniformed guard stepped out and lifted his chin.

"Claybourne?" The sound reverberated. "You Claybourne?"

Luke nodded. "Yeah, I'm Claybourne."

The guard squinted, watching closely as Luke approached. "I know you? You look familiar. You related to the folks at the Claybourne place over in Shiloh? My brother used to truck some of their cotton down to Gulfport, and I'd ride with him sometimes."

Luke returned his gaze levelly. "Nope. Must be another Claybourne."

The guard shrugged. "Must be, you say so. But I seen you someplace." He stepped back, holding the door. "Sergeant will see you now."

Luke entered the office and hesitated. A woman with her back to the door was concluding a conversation on the telephone. "My appointment just walked in. See you at seven." Eula turned in her chair and stopped abruptly, her eyes narrowing. "Well. Mr. Claybourne."

Relieved and surprised, Luke laughed aloud. "Eula! Eula May! Hot damn. If that ain't something! So this is what happened to our Eula. We heard you went on to Delta State after you left the plantation. But then we lost track of you."

"The governor picked me out of the graduating class. Needed a smart black woman from the Delta." Her voice was cool. "Please sit down, Lucas."

Luke grinned appreciatively. "Couldn't have picked better, Eula honey. You ought to see the boys now." He fumbled at his wallet, extracted a picture of Willy and their sons, and handed it to Eula. "Alex is almost as tall as Willy."

Eula smiled and silently returned the photo. Luke cocked his head and smiled at her. "You're sure still lookin' fine. It's good to see you, Eula."

"It's good to see you, Lucas. And how is Miss Willy?"

"Willy? Well, you know Willy, she's fine. Keeps on keepin' on."

Eula leaned back in her chair, examining Luke's application. "When they sent along your request for a job interview, I thought there must be some mistake." Frowning, she placed it back on the desk and looked frankly at Luke. "I thought maybe it was a Claybourne I never met. But it really was you."

"Yeah," Luke cleared his throat. He felt parched and irritable, eager now to get the interview over. "Well, I don't want to keep you, Eula. It's great seeing you again. Wait till I tell Willy!" He forced a smile. "She missed you, girl, since the day you left us. Now I'm supposed to talk business with the sergeant. Is he in?"

"Lucas, I am the sergeant. Sergeant Eula May Baker. I still use my maiden name. You didn't know?"

"You're sergeant—Hey, this some kind of joke, Eula?"

"Not a joke, Lucas, though I thought it might be when I saw the job application from an L. Claybourne. And if it wasn't a joke, I wasn't sure we should be having this meeting. And right now, I'm less sure than before."

Unblinking, Luke returned her gaze. "Why not?"

"Because the man I hire is going to be working for me. And if it's a white man I hire, he's going to be surrounded by black men who will hate his guts because he's a white man, and he's holding the key. And he is going to have to take orders from a black woman." She eased back in her chair and regarded him calmly. Her voice was dry. "If memory serves, Mr. Claybourne, I find it hard to believe that you can do that, take orders from a black woman who will be your Supervisor. And I'm not at all sure I want you working for me."

Luke stiffened. "Well, that sure as hell makes two of us." His voice was cutting. "You? My boss? Jesus, wouldn't my daddy howl at that! How many years were the Bakers workin' for Claybournes? More than either one of us wants to remember."

"I'm not interested in remembering," she said dismissively, and stood up behind her desk. "So you want to cancel this meeting? That's okay with me. I need a new guard, but I don't need to import a headache from the bad old days."

Glowering, he looked up. The insulting nerve! This hectoring black woman was Eula? "Would I like to cancel this meeting? You're goddam right I would. But the truth is, if I had the balls my daddy had, I'd have been out of here by now. I can just hear him, Your colored maid gonna be your boss, son? Jesus!"

"Why are you here?" Each word was like a pebble striking the wall. "You didn't come all this way just to be insulting. What is the reason?"

He sat motionless, his eyes pinched closed. Then the words spilled out, surprising him. "Because I'm losing the plantation. Because I've got a wife and two kids to feed. Because I'm a planter with no place to plant, and no hirable talents that I know of. Because I need a job." He stood up and his voice filled the space between them. "Because I need this job, Eula. I need it."

"Simple as that, huh?"

"Not simple." His voice faltered. "Just as plain as I can say it. I hate havin' to ask for the job. I hate havin' to ask you for the job. But it's the truth, Eula May."

"I believe you, Lucas. You never lied in all the years I knew you. You took advantage. You sure as hell took advantage. But you never lied." She sat back down, her elbows on the desk. "So let me be just as straight with you. If you come to work here at Parchman, I'm Sergeant Baker, only Sergeant Baker. And I will be your supervisor. And you will be Officer Claybourne, only Officer Claybourne. Eula May was left in Shiloh when I moved on."

"For God's sakes, Eula . . . "

"And Mr. Luke and Miss Willy are names I remember with a lot of fondness. But I left them in Shiloh, too. You'd be well advised to leave that baggage before you seriously think about working here. Parchman Prison is a serious place, but a very long way from the Claybourne place. Parchman and Mississippi have both moved on."

He remained seated, staring at the woman across the desk, shaking his head in disbelief. Silently, he rose and moved to the office door. He reached for the knob, hesitated, and then dropped his hand to his side, his head bowed in resignation. Humiliated, he remained motionless.

"I need a strong man to work with the violent men I have to be responsible for." Her voice was quiet. "And I need an honest man who can recognize dishonesty when he sees it. These men will dissemble any chance they get in order to get an advantage. And any advantage can lead to violence. And I won't tolerate that." Her eyes met his when he slowly turned to face her. Her voice was unsparing. "And when an inmate calls the white ex-plantation owner guard a mother-fucking honky son of a bitch, I've got to know that that guard is a grown-up who knows himself well enough not to strike back. I've got to know that with absolute confidence. His job, and more important, my job, depend on that."

"And you think I can take that?"

She studied his face and nodded. "I think you can. Prove me right. If you work as hard at that as you did at keeping your tenants from starving, yes. I think you can."

Embarrassed at finding his eyes misting, he wiped his perspiring face. "Can I sit down for a minute?"

"Of course. Let me have the guard get you some water."

"Thank you."

He paused. Only the noise of the mower moving across the sere lawns outside filled the room. Luke's eyes met hers. "Thank you, Sergeant."

Chapter Forty

The call had shaken Emily Kilbrew. In her dreams, Willy's life as Wilson Claybourne was the one she desperately wanted for herself. Claybourne plantation was what the good life was, what it looked like, what it felt like. Willy McIntire's life had been magical since she came to Shiloh, and the plantation was a wondrous place where gentility and generosity had a permanent home. And now Claybourne's was to disappear? In all the years, she had never heard Willy so distraught.

When Emily pulled up to the entrance of the house, Willy was sitting on the steps, looking for all the world like a motherless child. When Em got out of the car and settled beside her, Willy dropped her head, her shoulders shaking. When the storm subsided, she impatiently wiped tears away and embraced Emily. "I'm glad to see you. I needed to see someone from my real life." She shook her head in disbelief. "I don't know, Em. Every single thing I thought was so seems to have pulled loose. I've never felt so lost."

Emily's arm tightened around Willy's shoulders. "Parchman? You said Luke is looking for a job at Parchman?" Her voice was incredulous. "My God, what next? My poor brother is sitting in a federal prison waiting for trial, and Lucas Claybourne is going to Parchman Prison, lookin' for a job? It's madness, Wil!"

"Been madness for a long time." Willy's vacant eyes searched the withered expanse of the cotton fields beyond the drive. "You remember when they blew up the black Sunday school and killed those four little girls? We were teaching at church school, and we said it must have been done by somebody crazy?" Her troubled eyes sought Emily's. "Then it turned out that it was the Klan. Be honest, Em. Was either of us really surprised?"

Emily took her hand from Willy's shoulder and stood up. "Bobby Joe swore to me that it wasn't the Klan." Her voice was brittle. "You can't believe everything you hear, Wil. Just because they say it's the Klan doesn't mean it's so." Her eyes were pleading. "It's been them against us for so long, it's hard to know what's real—hard to know who they are."

Her voice broke. "To know who we are. I hate it, Wil! I love what we have. I love that we are special, that we have a tradition, that we aren't mongrel and common. And I hate their arrogance, their superiority. And I'm sickened by their mingling! Don't they have any racial pride?"

Willy frowned and her words were level. "When those three civil rights workers disappeared, you and I and Luke and all our friends agreed that they didn't get murdered, they just ran off to Cuba. And then the FBI paid off Bobby Joe's friend, and we find out it was the Klan that murdered those kids." She stood and faced Emily. "Madness, Em? It's not madness, it's murder. Thou shalt not kill!" Emily's eyes widened, but she remained silent. Willy's voice rose." Children being butchered in a Sunday school for what? Those three civil rights kids going to investigate why someone burned down a poor black church, a Christian church, and they get lynched? For what?" She reached out and brought Emily to her. Her sorrowful voice was like a child's. "Are we crazy, Em?"

"Maybe. You turn on the TV, you look at the national magazines, and you feel like you're in a zoo and the whole country's laughing at you. And their heroes are nigger preachers grabbing the spotlight and scruffy beatniks walking on our town green, just asking for it, making us do things we never wanted to do."

Willy stared at her friend. "Things we never wanted to do? You believe that? You knew, and I knew, and everyone I knew believed that the Klan would take care of it, purge the devils, scare off the Communists. Protect 'our southern way of life.' We just agreed to not look." They sat in silence, feeling words had disarmed them.

When Emily finally rose to leave, she said, "Mama's been beside herself ever since they took Bobby Joe away. Four years ago, and to her it seems like yesterday. So I took her to hear the tent evangelist over in Shaw, a wonderful preacher, Wil. He's going to be there for ten days. And he made us feel so much better. He told Mama, 'Christ lets you in whenever you want to come in, You can start over,' he said. 'You can get born again." She knelt beside Willy. "Maybe Jesus does have an answer."

Willy took her hand. "Remember the passage from Mark we were teaching the kids at the church school? 'Suffer the little children to come unto me, for of such is the kingdom of God.' You think God knows about Mississippi? If He does, maybe that 's why everything is coming apart. Maybe this is our punishment, Em, for being deaf and being blind." Her voice was resigned. "There are none so blind as those that will not see."

Emily shrugged. "Sounds like an Old Testament God, Willy dear. All about punishment and eye for an eye. You and I were teaching about the love of Jesus. You and Luke never harmed a soul. I'm sure Jesus loves you."

"Heaven's not a free lunch. If Luke gets a job at Parchman, he'll be paying plenty. But what about Willy McIntire Claybourne? How does she find a way to pay back?"

Emily said, "I don't know. Maybe you'll come with Mama and me to Shaw next Friday and meet the preacher. He did say Jesus is the Light and the Way."

Chapter Forty-One

From her desk, Eula watched the unexpected shower that was darkening the scattering of dry brown leaves along the prison road. Frowning, she turned to the report that lay next to her phone. Damn it. What a rotten present this was.

When the call came from the infirmary, her voice was sharp and impatient. "And prisoner Marlow? Good. Keep me advised after you conclude the procedure. Yes. Immediately. Thank you, doctor. Have Officer Claybourne report to me when you're done." The rain was spattering the windows, driven by a rising wind, and she worried about the drive home later. But first was this near-disaster in the mess hall.

When Lucas knocked, she told him brusquely to come in, and eased back in her chair. He paused, then stepped briskly to her desk, removed his hat, and stood at attention. Eula stared at the bandage on his cheek in silence.

"Officer Claybourne, do you know why you are here?"

"Yes, ma'am."

"Yes, Sergeant." Her voice was metallic.

Lucas flushed. "Yes, Sergeant."

"And how long have you been a corrections guard at Parchman, Claybourne?"

"Five months, three weeks, Sergeant."

"After five months no guard of mine should have the problem that you have right this minute. The problem that I have right this minute." She held up the report. "What happened in the mess hall today will not happen again, Officer Claybourne. Not ever on my watch." She returned the report to the desk. "Not ever while you are in my charge. Do you understand?"

"Yes, Sergeant."

"Good. At ease, Claybourne. Sit down." Eula pulled a yellow pad from her desk, unscrewed a fountain pen, and shoved them both across the desk to Luke. "I want a complete statement from you on everything that happened this noon in the mess hall. Everything that was said. Everything that was done. And it's important that it be exactly right because there were witnesses." She leaned forward, her face inches from Claybourne. "If Marlow loses his eye, and the doctor says he may, this could be very serious for you and for me." She sat back in her chair and studied his face. "The doctor said you needed ten stitches and were very lucky. How did it start?"

He perched on the edge of his seat and met her angry eyes. "The prisoners at the table said it started when Big Al Marlow accused Sammy Bones of stealing his barbecue. There was a lot of hollering and I ran over from my end of the hall to see what was going down. It was just before the end of my shift and I didn't want any trouble. When I reached the table, Marlow had Bones in a chokehold and was pulling a shiv out of his sock. 'I'm gonna carve your lyin' face like a slab of barbecue.' I pounded on the table with my billy club and told him to let Bones go and give up the shiv. 'I'm giving the orders,' I said. 'Let him go!'"

"And what happened?"

"He shoved Bones away and tried to grab my billy. He laughed at me and waved the shiv, showing off for the men at the table. 'Come and get it, you—'" Lucas paused, his eyes searching Eula's.

"All of it." Her words were staccato. "I want to hear all of it."

Lucas swallowed and moistened his lips. "He said, 'Come and get it, you honky motherfucker. Your wife good pussy for the niggers that worked on your farm? Come on, honky! Come on!'"

"And what did you do? Exactly, Claybourne. What did you do?"

"I said, 'No son of a bitch has ever called me a honky motherfucker before, and you're the last one that ever will.' And that's when he tried to cut me. I ducked, he caught the side of my cheek, and I nailed the bastard twice with my club. He started bleeding and he dropped on the table. That's when the other officers came running up."

"And that's all?"

Claybourne nodded. "They took me and Marlow to the Infirmary."

"Are you all right?"

"Yeah, it looks worse than it feels. I'm sure I'll be fine." Luke stared out the window, seeing something beyond the icy rain. "Marlow is bad news, Sergeant."

"I know. Remember I warned you about prisoners like Marlow." Eula's voice had softened. "Five months ago."

Luke nodded. "I remember, and I've been keepin' an eye on Marlow, but he didn't cause me any trouble until today."

"But today you didn't follow the book, Claybourne. The minute you spotted trouble, you should have been blowing your whistle for backup. Parchman backup. You allowed it to become a one-on-one situation that could have ended in a riot. We can't have one-on-one in Parchman. We sure as hell can't have black and white in Parchman. We can only have the Parchman way, and you're being paid to do it the Parchman way. And you can't allow it to become personal, to lose it when a prisoner calls you a honky motherfucker. He's probably been called nigger his whole sorry life. Personal won't cut it here."

The room had darkened. Eula rose and walked to the door and closed it. She turned to face Lucas, "This conversation is off the record, Lucas. It never took place." She returned to her desk. "I care about you and Willy and that's why I want to ask you, are you sure you want to do this? This is not like giving orders and running the plantation."

Luke remained silent, looking at his hands. "No, Sergeant. I'm not at all sure I want to do this." He raised his eyes to face her. "But it's what

I can do. I don't have many choices. I've got Willy and the kids. And when I looked around, this was all there was."

"It can't have been easy to come here and find I was to be your boss."

"It wasn't. At first it wasn't." He smiled. "But you know what Willy said when I told her? She said, 'It's only right. That's the way it should be.'" He chuckled. "That's the way 'born-agains' think, I guess. Maybe I agree with her."

Eula was startled. "Born-again? Willy Claybourne is a born-again Christian?"

"It happened after we lost the place. When the bottom dropped out, we were so damn lost. Tell you the truth, when she said she found Jesus it was like a door opened for her. I didn't have a clue what she was finding, still don't. But she changed. Says she wants to pay back. It eats at her." His eyes searched Eula's. "Why does she think she owes?"

Eula smiled. "Willy Claybourne." Her eyes drifted to the window. "I miss her. She has a lot of talent, and she'll find a way. But what about you, Lucas? You might think about moving on. Delta State has wonderful new courses in aquaculture, and you're a smart man. You could probably ace those courses."

"Smart? Yeah, I was too smart to go to Ole Miss when I could have." His jaw tightened. "I inherited a plantation and didn't need to know anything other than how to make a cotton crop. Lotta good that does me now."

Eula moved to the door. "Think about Delta, Luke. It might be just the ticket."

Luke joined her. "Thank you, Sergeant. Christ knows I could use a ticket." He laughed. "Christ knows—Jesus, I sound just like Willy!"

Chapter Forty-Two

The news of Robert Kennedy's assassination came as Ted Mendelsohn and Julia were at the dining table, lingering over coffee. The television was murmuring in the corner. Ted frowned. "What did he say?" Julia hurried to turn up the volume. "Death came as Senator Kennedy was leaving a campaign stop here in California putting an end to . . . " Ted stared at the screen, struggling to process the incredible. Bobby dead? No! And, of course, yes. Sickening, bloody, heart-stoppingly, yes. Those monsters, those stupid, vile monsters, had torn that sweet man apart. Oh, my God.

He choked on the bile he tasted, not even hearing the raucous ringing of the telephone. Julia answered, "Yes, Max. We did. Can you believe—?" She paused, sitting down hard next to the table. "Of course, He's right here." Wordlessly, she held out the receiver.

"Teddy?" Max's voice was husky, almost unrecognizable. "Meet me at the office at eight tomorrow. We have to talk."

The night was dismal. Bobby gone? Bobby gone. The saddest word in the English language, gone. Malcolm gone, King gone. Now Bobby? Guns. In the hands of monsters. Gone. When Ted said goodbye to Julia at dawn, he felt he had not closed his eyes since supper.

The door to Max's office was open, and the news desk just beyond had a hushed urgency, voices muted even as the machines were spilling out the details of the latest American tragedy. Yes, in the kitchen . . . yes . . . can you believe? . . . yes . . . oh, my God, and yes, the widow is on the way . . . yes, yes. . . .

Max stood, staring out the window, looking across the Hudson toward Newark, then north toward Harlem, expecting—what? He turned when he heard the door close behind Mendelsohn.

"You look like an unmade bed," he growled.

"I am an unmade bed. Unslept in."

Max moved to his desk and poured two cups of coffee, sliding the sugar to Ted's side.

"How did Julia and the kids take the news?"

"Julia seemed stunned. 'You knew him,' she kept saying, 'and you knew John. You knew both of them. And you knew Goodman and Schwerner and Chaney,' and then she started to cry. 'You have two kids, and this is your world? This is our world?' And the kids were frightened. Richard's home from college and was remembering he was in social studies class when the teacher told them the President had been shot in Dallas, and Laurie asked me if she should still put up the Martin Luther King poster I had brought her from Washington? She is scared."

"And I'm scared, too," said Max. "First they nailed up the one Jesus we've got in this country who was marching with the garbage workers. Now they got Bobby, who might have stopped this idiot war. Where do we go from here, Teddy?"

Ted shook his head, studying his old friend. "If I had a clue I'd tell you. This is our country, Max? With maniacs who kill people like John and Bobby and Martin?" He moved ponderously to the door. "And you want me in Chicago to interview the Black Panthers?" He turned to Max. "Is this the best job you've got for an old friend?"

"It's a living," Max said. "It's what we do."

Chapter Forty-Three

The call from Dale Billings had been uncharacteristically abrupt. Eula frowned, "It's for you, baby. It's Dale." She handed the receiver to Jimmy, pausing at the kitchen door.

Jimmy nodded. "Of course. We'll see you when you get here." Eula watched Jimmy slowly hang up.

"He sounded terrible, Jimmy. Is he okay?"

"He's grieving, Eula, disoriented and grieving. He wants to come here next Saturday. I told him to come. He'll be here by suppertime. Is that a problem?"

"Dale? Of course not. Ever since Bobby was killed I've been wondering how he was, where he was. The call came from Hyannis, Jim."

"He went back to stay with Bobby's kids after California. Now he wants to see us."

Dale Billings had changed. Jimmy knew his old friend, and he struggled to identify the difference he saw. The tailoring was a whole lot better. Gone were the jeans, the denim shirt, and the tentative beard. The unruly hair was barbered now, making him look a little taller, and he had added some pounds. The restless Dale ebullience that had once brought heat and laughter into the room were gone. Now there was a tentative quality that Jimmy had never before spied beneath the loud, often profane bravado. His friend looked sad.

"Welcome home to Missifuckingsippi, pal. Long time no see!"

Dale walked straight to Eula and took her in his arms. He held her for a long beat and turned to Jimmy. "Not sure it's home. But it's so good to see both of you."

"Let me get some cold stuff," said Eula. "You look like you could use it, Dale."

When she left the room, Jimmy pulled up a chair opposite Dale. "I'm so sorry about Bobby. I know how tight you were with him, ever since you showed him the Delta. The country's going to miss him."

Dale remained silent, studying his hands. "This country doesn't deserve him. This country devours its young." He looked at Jimmy and smiled for the first time. "That's a quote from Ted Mendelsohn, the old man of the mountain who knows things."

Jimmy chuckled. "Ted would be pleased to know you're quoting him. Do you think he's right about the country?"

"It's hard to know. But we're stuck in the Big Muddy, kids keep getting killed in a war we shouldn't be in. Martin said that, and the country killed him. Bobby tried to say that and the country killed him." His eyes glistened. "Stokely said it and went off to Guinea and changed his name to Kwami Ture. He just left Missifuckingsippi and Alabama and the Black Panthers and Miss Liberty and split." He grew silent again as he watched Eula bring in the beer.

Jimmy lifted a bottle and said, "To better times," and Eula said, "To you, buddy. We're glad you're back."

Dale said softly, "Bobby was so good with his kids."

Later in the evening, after supper, he began to wander the room, seeking to frame the questions he had been asking himself, repeatedly, since the night in the kitchen in Los Angeles when Bobby was killed. Could we have known? Should I have been closer after the speech? Why did the Arab kill the one guy in America who had learned not to hate? And much later, What the hell do I do now? There were options, and for days they had intruded on every quiet moment. Leave? Go to Africa and fight for a pan-African future? Write a book about fighting Third World wars? Go to Oregon, where there were communes, with good people he knew? Run for mayor here in Shiloh? Hang up his shingle and practice law in Washington as a civil rights advocate? Get involved with the new Kennedy School of Government burgeoning in Boston?

Jimmy and Eula listened as he spoke, exploring avenues he might take, or not. "I was working for a man who had it all. The wit, the heart, the intellect, the family background, the money to make it all happen. And it all turned to shit!" And the final question, only half articulated in a faltering voice, "What qualifies me to even play in that league?"

"Everything," said Eula. "You've been paying your dues for ten long years, Dale. Everything."

Jimmy nodded concurrence. "You've seen so much up front, in the action, close to the center of gravity in this damn country. You know the stakes, you know the players. You even know when the deck has been fixed. And you're in the position to pass that knowledge along, shape it, change it maybe. You loved Bobby for a reason. That didn't get buried with him. I think you know the answer, Dale. You're a born teacher. If they'll take you, the new Kennedy School sounds like the place. You'd be working with the best and brightest young people in the country, most of whom don't know what lynching, beating, harassing, surviving, organizing is all about. Teach them by telling your story. It's an American story they should understand."

"And celebrate," Eula said softly. "They need to know."

Chapter Forty-Four

It was dark when Luke left Parchman, and the road was slick, something daunting to drivers in the Delta . He strained to see the treacherous road, swerving to avoid the oncoming careening autos. By the time he pulled into his driveway his eyes were burning with fatigue. When he stepped into the house, Willy rose to meet him. "You look beat. Are you all right?"

"Yeah. Just another terrible day at Parchman. The roads are glass and the drivers out there are lunatics. I'm just bushed."

She led him to the couch. "Come put your feet up. Got something amazing to tell you."

"Amazing? What could be amazing?"

Her eyes shone with excitement as she curled up beside him. "A half hour ago I got a call from Eula May Baker! My God, I haven't talked to that woman in years!" She hesitated and then plunged ahead. "After she walked out I swore I'd never speak to her again. And that's what's so amazing. In five minutes we were talking like we used to at the plantation."

He watched his wife quizzically. He hadn't seen Willy this animated since they'd sold the house. "She said Jimmy's doing well with the Mack Construction Company. Did you know that?"

"Not really." His voice was flat, but she seemed not to notice.

"It was just so great hearing Eula's voice!"

"Yeah? I hear her voice every day, and I don't always welcome hearing it."

"Oh, come on. You told me she's been fine since you started working at Parchman."

He nodded. "Sergeant's been more than fair. It's the work I hate. Wearing this monkey suit. Dealing with those creeps every day. But what did she want with you?"

"It's the most exciting thing, darlin'. Eula wants me to start working with the women at the prison!"

"At Parchman?"

"Yes. To start a women's group where they can talk about whatever is bothering them. Kind of like a ministry where I could help them deal with their problems."

"You . . . at Parchman?" His voice was incredulous. "Is Eula crazy?"

"We were very close once, Luke. She knows I'd be good at it." Her eyes kindled. "And I know it, too."

Luke said, "You're as crazy as Eula. Dammit, Willy, get it through your head. I don't want my wife working in Parchman Prison. That place is a landmine just waiting to explode. Don't you understand that?"

"I understand that. What you don't understand is that I really want to help these women." She walked away from the couch, then turned to face him. "Who do you think Christ was talking about when he said 'the least of these'? They've been short-changed all their lives, and being in prison is just one more dehumanizing act."

"'Dehumanizing?' His enraged voice was a shout. "Why do you suppose 'the least of these' are in there? Because their mamas weren't nice to them? Because they swiped some beef jerky from the Seven-Eleven? They're in Parchman because they killed a guy with a kitchen knife, because they robbed a gas station with a shotgun, because they were dealing dope outside the high school, because one of them drowned her baby to stop her crying. These are violent people, Willy, and I won't have you exposed to that."

"I'm not stupid. I know these are desperate women. They've led desperate lives. I can help them, Luke. I know I can."

"Listen, Lady Bountiful, whether you think you can help them or not, I'm your husband, and I don't want you there. I won't have it."

"It's not your choice. You're doing something with your life. I need to do something with mine, something I can feel proud of. Working with the women at Parchman is what I want to do."

"They're whores, Willy! Murderers! Eula Baker must be out of her mind." His face was flushed. "What qualifies you to even get in the cell with them?"

Willy touched his arm and her voice was quiet. "Because I understand where I come from. Much as you would like to think so, I wasn't always the Magnolia Queen. Long as I can remember, my McIntire family was as dirt poor as some of theirs. You don't know what hopeless is.

And if you hadn't come along and rescued me in high school, Lord knows what I might have become."

"Like what?"

"Like Sadie Perkins who runs the whorehouse over on Newcomb. Her family did shares on the same plantation we worked. Or like some of those ladies you find so fascinating down in Jackson. Neither of us are pure as the driven snow, honey. Sadie Perkins's way would have looked like an easy path out of where I was."

He glared at his wife. "I doubt you would have made a good whore. You haven't got the talent for it."

She was angry now. "Obviously, you know more about whoring than I do." She began to move past him to the door and he seized her arm.

"I'm not going to argue about this," he said. "I don't want you working at Parchman. Period. End of discussion."

Willy calmly confronted him. "No. You don't understand. Willy McIntire Claybourne is gonna do what she needs to do." When he raised his hand to strike her, she seized it and slowly pushed it down. "Don't you dare, Lucas. Don't you ever goddam dare."

Chapter Forty-Five

The guard left Willy at the door of the women's section on that first day at Parchman. "They're all yours, Mrs. Claybourne. Watch your back." She stepped inside, and he lingered for a moment, holding the door open behind her. Five black women lounged around a table with soft drink bottles and coffee cups. Their conversation was muted, focused on two of the women who were angrily arguing.

"You doing same inside as you did outside, stealing anything not nailed down. Like you stole my Henry!"

The woman opposite shrugged and laughed, turning to the others. "You hear this bitch? Says her toilet paper is same as Henry!" When the guard closed the door, the banter stopped and the women swiveled to face her.

"Good morning," Willy said. "I'm Wilson."

There was silence until one woman said, "Sergeant Baker said your name was Willy. She wrong?"

Willy smiled. "My growin' up name was Wilson. To my friends, I've always been Willy. We're not friends yet, but I'd like you to call me Willy."

"Your name ain't Willy. It's Wilson Claybourne. Recognized you minute you came in. Yeah, the Claybourne plantation. My Aunt Livia used to work there till she got fired. What you doin' here? This ain't the country club." No one laughed.

Willy said, "I didn't want to go to the country club. I wanted to come here." Her eyes met theirs as she scanned the table. "This shit hole *is* Parchman Prison, isn't it?" For a beat there was silence and then laughter erupted.

"Oh, yeah," said one. "This shit hole is Parchman Prison!"

A large, very dark woman with a scar from her eyebrow to her lip poured a cup of coffee and handed it to Willy. "What do Willy Claybourne know 'bout shit holes?"

Willy nodded thanks and took the cup. "Long 'fore I was Willy Claybourne I was Willy McIntire. And we had a shit hole for a toilet when my family worked shares at the old Stennis place. And if any of you remember Stennis, you know he never offered anyone choppin' cotton a cup of coffee. Even cheated on the weigh-out scale."

The dark woman nodded. "Coffee? You lucky you got water! He was a mean son of a bitch." She tilted her head and examined Willy. "I remember there was a cracker family named McIntire used to pick, must have been you. Only family that wasn't colored in this part of Magnolia that worked those fields. We worked Stennis summer of '41. Never figured out which was worse, old man Stennis or the cotton-mouths in his back forty!"

Willy grinned. "First snake I ever killed was with a hoe at the Stennis place. Was just before my first period. I thought for a long time it was the snake made it happen!"

The scarred corner of the woman's mouth lifted and she chuckled.

"Wasn't no snake, girl! I'm Lena. Why don't you pull up a chair? You can meet all these losers. Just don't believe anything they say."

Willy laughed. "I don't see losers. Just some women stuck in this Parchman shit hole."

After the first three sessions, Eula concluded that Willy's ministry was working. A house mother sometimes, she could also cuss them out like a top sergeant. Willy was giving her people a taste of outside, an ear that listened and an eye that recognized some of the past that had distorted their lives. The first time Eula heard them singing, "Jesus loves me, this I know," she knew Willy was reaching them.

"Yeah, Jesus loves you," Willy said, "but you got to love yourself. Why would your old man want you back? What boss would hire you? You got to be ready to leave here one day."

Slowly the volatile temperature of discord was lowered, and the violence in the Women's Section declined. Sergeant Eula Baker's new ministry program with Willy Claybourne was the gossip of Parchman. Lucas watched his maddening "born-again" wife from a distance with a mixture of jealousy and pride.

And then there was the visit from the governor. Eula had told Willy he was coming, his first visit to Parchman since his inauguration.

"He's heard good things from Dora Walters, his Prisons Department Director, about our program. The governor wants to check me out and meet you." She had grinned. "Walters said the governor remembers you as Magnolia Queen when he was a student at Ole Miss." Willy had been embarrassed, but Eula had kept on. "You don't have to wear your ball gown or your crown, Willy!"

Willy had recovered quickly. "It will be nice meeting a man who wants to talk to me. Luke seems to have forgotten how."

The governor, tall and rather courtly, had stood up when Willy arrived at Eula's office. "You've had a remarkable six months, Mrs. Claybourne. Mrs. Walters has kept me in touch with Parchman developments and Sgt. Baker has been describing the changes you've brought to her Woman's Program. It is impressive." He smiled, "I never thought the Magnolia Queen had to be anything but beautiful."

Willy grinned. "Thank you, sir. There was nothing in the job description that called for anything more, Governor."

He had invited her to sit and talk and was remarkably candid. "When you attain the prize of the governorship of Mississippi, you also inherit the fact of Parchman Prison." He had smiled wryly. "And that's not a gift. As you know, Parchman has had an ugly history. Hearing good news from this facility is a rarity, Mrs. Claybourne, so I took this opportunity to meet you." He stood up and extended his hand. "I wish you continued success with your ministry."

Driving home that night, she recalled the governor's compliment. "You've had a remarkable six months." Exhilarated and exhausted, she shook her head and thought, "You don't know the half of it, Governor."

The last six months had damn near cost her her marriage and her sanity, trying to build trust with discards who had never been trusted, let alone finding a new neighborhood for one son who missed his friends and another who was mad at her that he was going to be in a strange school. Remarkable? You could say that. She peered into the gloom as she slowed the Chevy and turned into the gravel driveway, eager to get home. It had been the most remarkable six months of her life.

A month after the governor's visit, Eula summoned Willy to her office. A slender, light-skinned black woman prisoner stood defiantly before her desk. What distinguished her was the intensity of the appraisal in her dark eyes. Willy had the feeling that both she and Eula were being imprinted and catalogued behind the intent young face.

Eula said, "This is prisoner Minny Lou Thompkins. She'll be housed in your unit." She sat back down behind her desk and her eyes locked on the seething young woman. "Prisoner Thompkins, you can make your time here as difficult as you wish. Or you can use it to your profit. That's up to you. I will take your request for a headscarf and pass it to my superiors for their decision. Making demands and shouting, as you did upon arrival, will not hasten their decisions or mine. You've been convicted of a very serious crime, and you will have to pay for that here in Parchman. You will be treated like every other prisoner." The Sergeant handed the woman's file to Willy and glanced at the wall clock. "Your meeting starts in fifteen minutes, Mrs. Claybourne. Take the prisoner with you and introduce her to the women in your group." Willy was struck by the concerned gravity in Eula's eyes. Prisoner Thompkins had clearly made her presence known.

Willy held the door to the meeting room open and the prisoner stepped in, stopping to stare at the women at the table. "I want you to welcome Minnie Lou Thompkins. She's new to Parchman," Willy said, and turned to face the prisoner. "I'm Wilson and I'm here to lead this group. In this room we're free to say whatever we want, Minnie Lou, and what's said in this place stays here. We don't discuss it outside." She motioned to a seat but Thompkins remained rooted, standing alone, her arms tightly folded against her chest. Willy moved past her and took her seat at the table as the women held hands. "We start our meetings this way, Minnie Lou." Willy tilted back her head and began to sing, "Jesus loves me . . . "

One by one the voices of the women rose to join her
Jesus loves me,
This I know,
For the Bible tells me so.
Little ones to Him belong.
They are weak but He is strong . . .

Now the voices rang out in unison, filling the room:

Yes, Jesus loves me!
Yes, Jesus loves me!
Yes, Jesus loves me!
The Bible tells me so.

The song wavered to an end, and the women stared at the still silent woman. Willy said gently, "Minnie Lou, I'm sure you must know this hymn. Why don't you sing with us?"

"I don't sing about Jesus." The words were dropped like stones.

Cleo hooted, "Who the hell this bitch thinks she is? The warden?" Laughter rippled around the table. "I don't sing about Jesus? Maybe she the new Judas!"

Willy contained her smile and held up her hands. "Let her explain, ladies. Why don't you sing about Jesus, Minnie Lou?"

Thompkins raised her chin. "'Cause I'm not a Christian anymore. I am now a Muslim." She confronted Willy. "And my name is not Minnie Lou. I changed it to Hosina. And I don't sing about no honky white preacher who was a Jew to start with."

Willy nodded. "I hear what you're saying, Minnie Lou. When you're in these meetings, you can be Hosina. Outside these walls, officially, you remain Minnie Lou Thompkins."

Lena angrily pushed back her chair and pointed to Thompkins. "What this bullshit that Jesus was a Jew?"

Willy said, "Hosina is right. Jesus was a Jew. There was no Christianity until after Christ died, but according to the Bible he was also the son of God."

Hosina spoke sharply, "No! Not according to the Koran, which is my bible!"

Georgia challenged Willy. "You a born-again and you lead this group. So what's an Arab doing in here with us, Miss Willy?"

"The reason I've brought my born-again ministry here is because born-again means a second chance to me." Willy scanned the angry faces of the women. "I hope that it means a second chance to you. And a Muslim like Hosina can use a second chance as much as a Christian."

Hosina glared. "Allah give me all the chances I want." Her eyes were pleading. "I don't even know why I'm here with you people, praise be to Allah. They won't even let me wear my head scarf which I wear to honor him."

Willy rose and brought a chair to the table. "Sit with us, Hosina. You're the first Muslim to join our group. And it shouldn't matter to us how you worship. Georgia's a Baptist. Lena's a Methodist. Cleo doesn't want to belong to any church. Mickey's a Lutheran. What brought all these women to Parchman is their own business, not mine. I'm not here to judge you, and I'm not here to sweet-talk you. You've been judged already. We don't get together every Tuesday to talk about the past. That's a time we want to forget."

Staring straight ahead, Hosina reluctantly took the offered seat.

Cleo spoke directly to her. "I been in this shit hole for two years of my twenty-year sentence. Twenty years, you hear what I'm sayin'? For killing my husband after I found he raped my daughter?" Hosina raised her head and stared at her. "Take it from me, girl, you're gonna need friends in here. My name is Cleo."

Chapter Forty-Six

In March, Lucas signed up for classes at Delta State in aquaculture. Eula commended him and arranged for him to have night duty so he could make daily classes. It was one more hurdle for Willy to manage, Luke sleeping in the afternoon when he wasn't doing his homework for Delta State. It was a harrowing schedule with the ministry, managing the two boys, settling the new house. Willy's sister came from across town when she could to help with the kids, but it was always tight.

But for the first time since leaving the plantation, her man was happy. The courses on aquaculture seemed to rekindle the excited young man Willy remembered from the early days when he first took the reins of the plantation from his father. There was excitement as he expounded about the bright new world of water agriculture that was beginning here in their Delta. Willy watched her husband embrace the new information, making plans and plotting strategies. "It's going to take hard work, boys, but we'll do it together. This is brand new!" He had looked fondly at his sons. "The days of plantation droughts and floods are the bad old days! That was my daddy's business, and it was my business. That's not going to be your business. It's going to be another world for you both to understand." He pulled them closer. "Your grandpa would never recognize it. There's going to be so much for us all to learn!" For the first time in a decade, Willy saw her husband totally and happily engaged in the future. Her Luke was no longer grappling with a past that had nearly destroyed him.

On the drives home from Parchman Prison, as the rising sun would anoint the endless cotton fields, Luke could almost see what was coming. The first catfish pond will be right there, he thought, about twice the size of a football field. The outbuildings just beyond. Going to take financing, maybe a proposal to Burroughs at the bank, because this could grow. And there will be a sign. He squinted as the sun rose to flood his windshield. Yeah, a large sign. Color for the name, black and white for the rest. He could see it clear:

CLAYBOURNE AND SONS
Catfish Farmers
Shiloh, Mississippi

Part Three 1974

Chapter Forty-Seven

It was an odd way to start the year in Mississippi, Z thought, but beautiful. A light dusting of snow had mysteriously moved across the Delta, leaving a pristine scrim of sparkling white over the withered ochre landscape. Z smiled, driving slowly up the approach to Fatback's Platter. Like Umbria in February, except there the snow would not disappear by noon as it would in this strange place. "The snow princess" they'd called her when they were in the forests, because she loved it. She remembered that the Partisans from the south only liked the hot weather. The Nazis, too. Even before the war, the Germans had come only for the sun. They never gave a smile or a lira to anyone or anything Italian. The Partisans taught her, "It's not hard shooting Nazis." She had been a good learner.

Nefertiti embraced her at the door, a shawl pulled tight against the damp. "Come out of the snow and warm up. You want some coffee?"

Z laughed. "Coffee sounds good. But this Mississippi white magic is hardly snow, Titi." They settled in the corner, the bar lit with the unfamiliar glow of the snow beneath the window. "When is your Perkins friend coming?"

"He called from the airport. He's driving up now and should be here by eleven."

"This is a good thing?"

Titi put down her coffee, her eyes bright. "Could be. It's something I've dreamed would happen." She looked lovingly around the room. "I've never been good at change, Z. This has been all I've known since I was sixteen. But it's why I asked you to be here. You've been good at change. I like the way you think, the way you've acted."

"This Dick Perkins wants you to leave this place, and go to the Gulf?"

"He's an old friend, Z, and he loves the Delta music I've grown up singing, loves the way I sing it. He thinks I can have a real career at Richard's Rook, and the money's more than good."

"So what is the complication?"

"Sheriff Dennis Haley."

Z leaned across the table and took Titi's hand. "Your silent partner, yes? Your Count Sforzi?"

Titi nodded. "It's a long-time arrangement, Z. We've had prohibition in Mississippi since 1907, and people like Haley like that setup. He just gets richer from all the places he lets stay open. A blood-sucker. When my daddy started Fatback's back in the thirties, there was no way to run a juke joint without paying off whoever was sheriff. If he didn't get his slice off the top every night, you were put out of business. It's still that way. During the war most of the men around here were gone, and to keep up Daddy sold off pieces of Fatback's to the new sheriff, Dennis Haley. By the time the war was over and the crowds were back, Haley owned eighty percent of the Platter. The twenty percent left for daddy just covered the cost of the booze and my wardrobe. After daddy died, my silent partner made it clear that the eighty percent included me. 'You want to work, bitch, this is the only place. You got the bed and I got the keys.' Finding the courage to say no has been hard. I've loved Fatback's and I've loved the work. And I never found your courage."

"And the policeman, Butler, who runs your door? The fascisto?"

"A racist pit bull. All he knows is to keep the niggers from tearing up the place and keep a sharp eye out for the bitch who sells all the tickets and make sure she don't stray." Her bitter laugh cut through the room. "There ain't going to be a new handyman like Bronko, that's for damn sure. If it happens on Butler's watch, the sheriff goes public on Butler and his Klan connections."

Z remained silent, watching the sunlight touch the tops of the pines that stood vigil beyond the parking area. When she turned to Titi, she seemed to have come to some private conclusion. She smiled. "Don't look so—how do you say—morose? Dear Titi. Look, the sun is already melting away your snow! And here comes your Dick Perkins!"

Perkins paused at the door, letting his eyes adjust to the dim room while he sought out every corner of Fatback's Platter. "It's what I remember, Nefertiti. I even dreamed twice about this room. I never saw it in daylight before." He crossed to the table and took Titi's hands. "You made me have nice dreams, lady."

She chuckled appreciatively, rising to kiss him on the cheek. "Didn't

I tell you he was a charming honky? Dick, this is Billy's wife, Z, and my dear friend."

He shook her hand. "I'm happy to meet any friend of Titi's. But who is the lucky Billy?"

Z smiled. "Billy of Billy's Chili. Some people think I'm the chili, Italian chili!"

Perkins nodded. "Best down-home food in Shiloh. That's not to say you're not his chili! Of course I know your husband. Everybody loves him but the police."

"Right on both counts, Dick. Let me pour us a drink to celebrate your arrival." Titi moved behind the bar, deftly seizing three tumblers and a bucket of ice. Returning to their corner table, she filled their glasses.

Perkins raised his glass. "To Nefertiti, Queen of the Nile, soon to grace Richard's Rook and bring the joys of the Delta blues to the virgin ears of the Redneck Riviera."

Laughing, Z applauded and raised her glass as well. "*Salud*, Titi!"

Perkins turned to the silent Titi, his eyebrows raised. "You're not joining us?"

With a forced smile, Titi raised her glass. "Thank you, Dick. From your lips to God's ear. Oh, how I want to go! But I can't say when."

"Take what time you need. The Rook won't be refurbished till Easter, and I want you to be the headliner. I'm going to invite the Claybournes to come for the opening." He grinned. "It'll be like old times. Have you seen Luke recently?"

"Luke? White Lightning?" Her voice was nearly inaudible. She shook her head. "No, I haven't. Not many folks have seen him or Willy since they lost the plantation. It's been a hard road. And working at Parchman for a proud man like Luke—" She paused, her eyes misting. "That's gonna be hard for a long time. I don't know if they'll be at your opening." She paused, searching for a firmer footing. Her smile was a question. "Our opening, Dick?"

Z said "*Coraggio*, Titi. You're not alone. Billy and his Italian chili will be at the center table. The Queen of the Nile will be a *diva magnifica*! And Sheriff Dennis Haley can console himself with Count Ricardo Sforzi as they recall the beautiful women that got away."

Titi's eyes glistened. "Since you came to Shiloh, Z, I've never felt alone."

Perkins smiled. "Can you come at Easter?"

She nodded, "Easter it is. Now tell me about the Redneck Riviera."

Chapter Forty-Eight

When all but the night shift had departed, Ted Mendelsohn approached Max's office, tapped, and entered. Max looked up from his typewriter. "You want to talk? Say yes, because I want to stop." He swiveled from the desk and turned to face Mendelsohn. "Grab a chair, Teddy."

Ted settled in the armchair next to the desk. "How many times have you said you want to talk and I've settled in this chair and talked. Maybe hundreds?"

Max chuckled. "Maybe thousands."

Ted nodded. "And how many deadlines?"

Max studied his friend. "Maybe thousands." He shifted in his chair. "Where's this going, Teddy?"

Ted met his eyes. "Maybe nowhere." He rose from his chair and walked to the window, scanning the always exciting dazzle of New York at night. "I've been more and more preoccupied with 'nowhere,' Max. At home. On the road. At my desk."

Max frowned. "Are you all right?"

Ted turned, held his arms wide, and returned to his seat. "No palpitations. No shortness of breath, Heart of a young man, Doc Adler says. But if I'm all right, why am I preoccupied with 'nowhere'?"

"I think you're worn out, maybe need some time away. This is not like you, Teddy."

"Max, I'm not worn out. I'm unhappy."

"Is it Julia? The kids?"

Ted pondered, shaking his head slowly in the negative. "No. They don't make me unhappy. I make me unhappy."

Max remained silent, sympathy softening his usually taciturn editor's face. "What can I do to help, Teddy?"

Ted leaned forward, his eyes bright. "Fire me, Max."

Max met his gaze. "You're not serious."

Ted said, "Fire me."

"You can't be serious." Max was angry now. "You know I could never fire you. I could never do that to you or to me. We're a team, for Christ's sake, maybe the best in the business. What kind of shit is this?"

"Max, I'm fifty-three. Free, white, and luckier than I deserve. I've got a family I love and hardly know. I've got a job that's paid my way and shown me the world. I've got a boss who's been my best friend. And all together they haven't made me happy. I'm haunted by my arm's-length relation with my life, Max." His voice broke. "Having a wife I love during the occasional intervals when I'm not in Karachi or Mexico City or Biloxi. Having kids who knew me better when they were two than when they're experimenting with pot at sixteen. Making my crisis visits to the trouble spots of the world and the people who are suffering, and I kiss them good-bye and say, 'Sorry, I've got a deadline.'"

"Teddy, you need a shrink . Or maybe a priest. Or a marriage counselor. Just don't ask me to fire you."

Ted rose and walked to the door. "You're making it harder for me, Max. You've got a reporter here who's trying to finish his story, and fucking up. And his editor won't help. So I'll do it myself. You've got my notice, Max. I'm gone in a month."

A letter from Ted reached Max at his home:

FYI Max,

I got a letter from the provost at Jackson State inviting me to come down for a symposium on nonviolence and the civil rights movement in Mississippi. He thinks the Fourth Estate can offer some perspective. You will not be surprised to learn that I think I'll go. It will be great seeing old friends like Jimmy Mack, who will be part of the symposium. He wrote me that he's considering a move into politics, sign of the times. I have been contemplating my future now that the smoke is clearing, and there is a nagging

itch to maybe pick up those threads in the Delta and see how they get woven. Free, white, and 53—right? What I'll miss most is reporting to you, pal. A whole lot.
   Ted

Ted picked up the rental car at the airport, eager to see it all fresh again, to recapture the rhythm of Mississippi in August. He left the air-conditioning off, letting the warm, damp air move through the Chevy's windows, watching the low hills around Jackson slowly flatten as he moved up the highway into the heart of Magnolia County. The familiar cotton began to unfold like an endless mural of velvety greens, stretching forever, the rows slowly spinning as he eased the car toward Shiloh. And then he saw the first series of what appeared to be small lakes, surprising flashes of cerulean in the green, mirrors for the pale blue sky that arched overhead. When he braked the Chevy at the first exit road, the sign announced the Ol' Reb Catfish Farm. Catfish were what the folks fished for in the muddy creeks when he had left Shiloh. A catfish farm in Magnolia County? It was a startling first, and he decided to ask Mayor Burroughs about it.

He drove slowly into Shiloh. Nothing seemed to have changed. He parked near the empty police truck in the shade of the bank and headed for the mayor's office, wondering what had ever happened to the aging police dog that used to prowl in its rear and exercise on the baking lawn of the square.

Burroughs rose and turned to face him after he knocked. In the years since their first bristly meeting, the mayor's salt-and-pepper hair had become grayer, the clean-shaven jowls more pronounced, but the watchful face was as he remembered it. His narrowed eyes regarded Mendelsohn over the wire-rimmed glasses.

"Mendelsohn," he said, nodding slightly. And motioned him to a chair.

"I'm pleased you remembered me," Mendelsohn said. "It's been quite a while."

With a fugitive half-smile, the mayor pulled open his desk drawer. He lifted a sheaf of newspaper clippings and spread them like cards on the desktop, his mouth tight. "Oh, I keep up with you, Mendelsohn.

And when I don't, folks send me clippings from around the country." His voice was flat. "You've been busy."

Mendelsohn's bylined *Newsweek* stories had datelines from Cape Town, Detroit, Newark, Los Angeles, and a stapled stack were all from Shiloh. He smiled at Burroughs. "I'm flattered, Mayor. I didn't know you were a fan."

Burroughs lolled back in his seat and lit a cigar. "Not exactly a fan. You could say, more a collector. I've got several from Mr. J. Edgar Hoover's office. I guess he's a collector, too."

Mendelsohn smiled. "We didn't pick our readers. We just appreciated having them. Looking at all this, you know a whole lot about what I've been doing since our last time together. But I don't know anything about what you all have been doing down here. It's the reason I wanted to revisit Shiloh, see some old friends if they're still around. I missed this place."

In an aggrieved voice Burroughs said, "You mean our little town is to get another humiliating exposure from this world-traveling journalist?" He swept the clippings back into the drawer and closed it sharply. "It's not like when you left here, Mendelsohn."

"No, sir. From what I've seen out there, the whole world's not like it was. But Shiloh's not my beat any more. I've left the magazine. I'm just down here for a symposium on nonviolence at Jackson State. The rest is pleasure and recreation."

Burroughs regarded him, his eyebrows arched. "For pleasure and recreation?"

Ted opened his hands. "No agenda other than sharing my wisdom on the tactic of turning the other cheek. No paycheck. No deadline. Just curiosity."

"The 'tactic of turning the other cheek.' Interesting choice of words, Mendelsohn." Burroughs frowned. "You regard nonviolence as a tactic?"

"I do. When the country becomes the loving community envisioned by those kids I covered in Mississippi, you won't need a tactical approach for surviving the violence of a closed society. Nonviolence will be just commonplace."

Burroughs soberly regarded Mendelsohn. "And from your perspective, the invasion of ideologues, revolutionaries, and a radical national media into a peaceful, law-abiding state was not an act of violence?"

Mendelsohn hesitated, then thrust ahead. "I don't regard Madison, Jefferson, and Adams as ideologues, but they were revolutionaries. As for the press that drew pictures of Mississippi for the nation, I don't regard them as radical. They were very reluctant witnesses, but the truth was unassailable. If Mississippi in 1964 was a 'law-abiding state,' all the protections of the Bill of Rights did not apply to your citizens of color."

Burroughs smiled for the first time. "I'm relieved to see that the implacable certainty and self-righteousness of the Fourth Estate continues to be your hallmark, Mendelsohn. But let's move on from Appomattox. You said curiosity without an agenda, a paycheck, and a deadline. That seems like a neighborly way to visit our little town. What do you want to know, Lieutenant?"

Ted answered his smile. "It's been thirty years since I was a lieutenant, Mayor. Seems to me by now I'd be a colonel."

The mayor chuckled. "Down here, colonels are very southern, Mendelsohn. I don't reckon you'd make colonel around here!"

"Mayor, I saw what I think were four different catfish farms driving up. They looked like nothing I ever saw before. Where did they come from?"

"Necessity. Our one-crop economy is too old and too fragile. Between weather and agitation among the laborers for unrealistic wages, there's a whole lot of hurt throughout the Delta. We've been losing a lot of good folks who never would have thought of leaving if things had stayed the way they were. But with the walkouts and the passage of the Civil Rights and Voting Rights bills, things don't stay the same."

"But where do catfish come in?"

"When some fast-food chains up North started to expand from hamburgers and hotdogs to fried fish, the demand for catfish just exploded, and they discovered what we had to offer. So we became the desirable virgin. You want land? We got lots of land. You want to invest in an economy that needs some help and can give you cheaper labor than in Illinois? We're your girl. You want to start an aqua-business and get some tax breaks? Hell, you've come to the right place. And colleges in the area are now starting courses to create the aqua-business managers they're going to need. Like I said, Mendelsohn, it's not like when you left. Let me show you something."

He walked across the room and pulled down a wall map of Shiloh. "You know something about the Sanctified Quarter, since you were living there. Look at this." A great swath on the side of the highway that was the beginning of the Sanctified Quarter was isolated with a green marker.

"That's all land that HUD is buying in order to build affordable housing for the black citizens of Shiloh. All those nontaxable shanties gonna come down and the new taxable housing is going to go up. Town's going to do good and do well. We're even paving the roads in the Quarter." He was watching Mendelsohn's astonished face with amusement. "You're not going to recognize the place."

"What am I missing?" asked Mendelsohn. "When did the frog get kissed and turn into the prince? And who did the kissing?" He rose and moved to the window, looking out on the Shiloh green. "The Sanctified Quarter was a dusty, muddy ghetto with sub-standard houses for more than a century, Mayor." Finally he turned to Burroughs, "And nobody this side of the highway seemed to know or give a damn."

Burroughs wrinkled his nose in distaste. "It wasn't a prince. It was that son of a bitch Lyndon Johnson's Great Society, his 'war on poverty,' 'we shall overcome.' Elections, Mendelsohn. Lot of people held their nose and pulled his lever. And it opened the spigots down here." He watched Mendelsohn, clearly enjoying his moment. "And this Republican mayor found the connection that could get us to HUD and closer to the trough."

Ted suppressed a smile. "Good for you, good for Shiloh. Who's the connection?"

"A black named Dale Billings who had a lot of family over near Neshoba. You must have known him when he was Communications Director over at the Commie's freedom house in '64."

"Dale! Sure I knew him. I saw him in Washington when he went back to law school."

"Well, he became a confidant of Bobby Kennedy and an enabler for the Democrats up in Washington when it comes to Mississippi."

"How'd you get to him?"

"Through your old friend Jimmy Mack. He came to me at the bank, looking for seed money for a construction company. He said he'd met some HUD folks through an old friend, and they'd likely be coming this way. There's no moss on that boy. Sharp as hell and hot to trot. We decided we could probably help each other, and we did."

Mendelsohn rose to his feet and extended his hand to Burroughs. "It beats all, doesn't it, Mayor? You wouldn't have believed any of that possible last time I was here. And I would have thought you were crazy if you did!"

Burroughs walked him to the door. "I don't rightly know," he said. "I read once in an article in *Newsweek* that politics was the art of the possible."

"You believe everything you read in *Newsweek*?"

"Depends on who wrote it." The mayor laughed and closed the door.

Chapter Forty-Nine

The voice on the phone made Willy smile. "I'm just like the others. But I'm ten years older."

"Not to me, Ted! You were very old even when you were very young! How wonderful to hear your voice. Where in heaven are you calling from? Soweto? London?"

"I'm calling you from the Fannie Lou Hamer Day Care Center in Ruleville, Willy." He chuckled. "What the winds of change bring! I can remember when you had never heard of Fannie Lou Hamer. Now she's part of history and has daycare centers named after her. News still travel that slow in Shiloh?"

Willy laughed. "Yes, it does. But I've heard of her. I've even heard of you, big shot! You've been all over the papers. But why are we talking on the telephone? Come on over. Luke will be back by two. He'd love to see his 'Hebrew journalist.' We have a lot of catching up to do."

"You found us, Ted." Willy's merry voice had not changed. "Not the big house you remember, but nobody shot at you as you approached. Our family motto is 'You're safe at the Claybournes.'"

"I always was," he said and embraced her. Over her shoulder he saw Luke Claybourne approaching. Gained some years, Ted thought. A little heavier, grayer. But there was a new relaxation, a quiet confidence in the way he walked, an absence of the suppressed emotion that had always seemed about to erupt when Ted was in his presence. When they shook hands, Ted's was lost in the grip of Luke's large and muscular hands. Tough and calloused, they were the hands of a farmer who had wrestled with the Delta for a lifetime.

Luke's voice was as deep and resonant as Ted remembered. "Welcome, Ted!" He stopped and surveyed Mendelsohn, cocking his head and squinting. "The horns are gone, Willy. I guess we can let him in."

Guided by old memories, the conversation that afternoon began as wary explorations of terrain incognita. Mendelsohn was back from lands and revolutions that had only been stories told in newspapers and magazines like *Newsweek*. Willy's eyes gleamed as Ted's personal encounters with Mandela, Fidel Castro, and Golda Meier came alive in her living room.

"It's not your daddy's world, Luke," Ted said thoughtfully. "It's churning. People don't want to be owned anymore. Not in Israel, not in Nigeria, not anywhere I've been for ten years. Who owns who? Who owns what? It's like a fever that spread after the war." His voice was melancholy. "Maybe from the millions of deaths, the ruined cities, the museums gone, the treasures ransacked, the histories lost, children without families, without a past. So many children." He held out his glass and Luke, his eyes troubled, refilled it. "But there are green shoots. I've seen them." He looked at Willy and Luke, his head nodding, his eyes alight. "There's something about the human spirit that won't quit. They're already rebuilding Hamburg, Leningrad, Berlin, even Hiroshima." He looked apologetically at Willy and Luke. "I've gone on too long. What I want to hear is how you are doing here?"

"We've had a sea of troubles, Ted," Luke murmured. "Being a farmer in Mississippi makes God laugh. Not only heat, but rain. Too much? Too little? Too late? Too early? And tenants who you needed, tenants who ran off, tenants who kept you awake because you knew they needed you, and you couldn't always be there for them?" He paused, trying to answer Ted's question. "How are we doing? Any black or white in Mississippi who can tell you that can be governor for life. We're trying to stand up on Jell-O. The footing we were raised on is gone." He looked at Willy and then at Ted. "Maybe you think it should be gone. We've got blacks in our legislature now, folks that weren't even allowed in the library ten years ago. Maybe our kids will find out if it should be gone. But for Willy and me, it's wrestling with the devil just trying to keep the family going."

When he left, Willy walked with Ted to his car. "And how is your family, Ted?" He leaned against the hood, frowning. "I wish I could tell you, Willy. The good part is that the kids are sprouting, like yours. Wonderful to see." He paused. "The bad part is that for ten years I haven't been around home long enough to see. And that's been tough on Julia and, in truth, it's been tough on our marriage." Ted shrugged, a sad smile on his face. "I'm a gentleman caller, Willy, who signed up to be a husband."

She took his hand in hers, squeezed and grinned wickedly. "You mean it ain't all sweetness and light out there in the real world beyond the Delta? You're an old friend, Ted, and I so value you as a wise mentor. But I'll share an insight I've found for myself. You can't choreograph life." Her gaze shifted to the house where Luke stood, waving a goodbye.

Chapter Fifty

Mendelsohn eased his car through the elmed shade of white Shiloh, crossed through the shimmering heat of Highway 49, and coasted into the Sanctified Quarter. Jimmy had said on the phone that he should pass Sojourner Chapel and continue to the beginning of the old McElroy plantation, due east of the Freedom School. "Hang a left and go past the old weighing station to a Quonset hut I bought from the Army. That's the modest headquarters of J. MACK. We welcome old friends, strays, and the unemployed. Man, it's good to hear your voice!"

Ted spotted the Quonset hut, comfortably located in the shaded lee of the old McElroy weighing barn. Through its open doors he could see dust rising as sweating men stacked lumber. From the dilapidated tool shed beyond, he could hear the screaming of a ripsaw as a crowd of kids waited at the door. Each, in turn, carried piles of new boards to two flatbed trucks that were parked in the rear. In what had been a cotton field were the slender frames of two new bungalows. In the noon glare, the carpenters moved over the scaffolding like animated silhouettes. There was a din of kids' voices, hammering, and straining motors as a bulldozer leveled adjacent areas for building and a backhoe prepared for the pouring of a foundation.

Ted pulled his Chevy alongside the spattered wreck of a jeep that had J. MACK stenciled on it. The door of the Quonset was open and the shouting voice of Mack added to the cacophony: "The Mendelsohn is back in town!" He trotted out, taking Ted in a warm embrace when he stepped from the car. "Hey, my favorite outside-agitating wandering Jew! Welcome to your old home away from home."

Mendelsohn laughed and pointed at the frenetic landscape. "There hasn't been this much activity since the Union troops took Vicksburg. It doesn't look like my home away from home. It's not at all like when I saw you last."

Jimmy grinned. "And the last time I saw you, you were high as a helicopter and singing 'Revel in the joys of copulation.' It was you, old buddy?"

"Revel in the joys? It sounds like me. Even though it was ten years ago and I haven't had a drop of bourbon since, it does sound like me. We Hebrews were never very good at drinking the hard stuff."

"I'm your witness, Mendelsohn! But come on in. You look hot. How about a drink of something softer, like Coke?"

"Doesn't have to be softer. Just wetter! Being hot is the price I had to pay to see you again, young James. I navigated the blazing desert, knowing there was an oasis waiting. And your letter is responsible, or irresponsible, depending on whether you were compos mentis when you wrote it. You weren't putting coke in the Coke, were you?"

Jimmy laughed and walked to the small fridge next to a cluttered worktable. "No. Knowing you were on the way, I ordered up your special beverage." He handed the chilled bottle to Ted and settled behind the table. "So put your feet up and stay a while. I've been following your byline halfway round the world. Now I want to hear everything from the horse's mouth. I've missed you. You've been missed in Mississippi."

"It's mutual. There are so many I want to hear about."

"A lot of friends we made back in the bad old days jumped ship when the Panthers came on the scene, Ted. They never got their hands around the Black Power movement. But you understood what it was and what it wasn't, and stayed aboard. I know because I've been your faithful reader all these years you've been traveling."

Ted looked at Jimmy, silently appraising him. "You haven't changed, Jimmy. You've never been out of mind, kid." He chuckled. "I always knew you'd abandon your careless ways and grow up. And I was right." He went to the wall and examined the blue prints of the bungalows that were rising in the abandoned cotton fields outside. "Jesus, look at all this! J. MACK!" He returned to his seat and studied the attentive man across the desk. "Why would you want to think about politics when you have this money tree growing in your backyard?"

"Because J. MACK is a hell of a lot more than a money tree. I think it's a ticket to ride." He grinned at Ted. "A ticket to ride to Washington. I really want to talk to you about my running for Congress."

"Are you really serious? Congress?"

"Dead serious. And I need you on the train."

Ted finished his drink. "Talk to me about why you want it, and why you think you can make it."

Jimmy got up and carefully closed the door. His voice was low and serious. "It started with Dale. Through him I got to meet the go-to people who are trying to bring the Great Society to Mississippi. They got their orders from Johnson even before they passed the Voting Rights Bill in '65. Word was out that he wanted things to happen real quickly down here, because he was planning on running in '68. That's how J. MACK got born, seed money from HUD and generous loans from our suddenly friendly banker, Burroughs. The president got a load of good public relations with the new black voters about 'our Negro entrepreneur in the Delta who was a Freedom Rider,' and J. MACK gets to transform the hovels of the Sanctified Quarter with good clean housing."

Ted smiled. "And Jimmy gets rich from doing good."

"Not rich, but getting there. And now I want to do some payback." He stood up and began to pace the room. "Housing is important. But so are the malnourished kids. So are all those brothers getting their only job-training from criminals in Mississippi jails. So are all the public schools, screwed out of funding because the white kids are going to private academies. And so are all the jobs that have disappeared because the men have had to go north to feed their families." He stopped, embarrassed by his passionate speech. "There's a ton of pain here." He took the seat close to Ted. "Only politics can help. And that's why I need you."

Mendelsohn's eyes were alight. "Last time I heard you that revved-up was at the mass meeting when you were nearly blitzed by Stanley Bronko. Truth is, if you're crazy enough to run for Congress in Sterling Tildon's state, then I'm probably crazy enough to help you. Being fiftieth of fifty in nearly everything important means Mississippi needs all the help it can get."

Jimmy clapped and grinned. "How come I'm not surprised?"

"So what's my mission?'

"You'll run my campaign so I can punch my ticket."

"That's all?"

"For now. But first you're coming home to see Eula and meet Junior." He grinned. "I told them this morning why I asked you to come down and Junior bet me twenty-five cents you'd say no. You can be there to see me collect the bet!"

Mendelsohn smiled. "Junior's probably smarter than both of us. What did Eula say?"

"Eula only said, 'I hope he still likes pot roast, that's what we're having.' She's not a politician like Junior and me. But she's dying to see you, now that you're back from the world. She wants to ask you about Washington and New York and Chicago, everything north of Memphis. She's tired of reading you, Mendelsohn. She wants to hear the real thing."

Eula welcomed him with open arms and an agenda of questions that rippled through supper. Junior was shy, watching Ted from the corner of his eye. When he brought his quarter to his father to pay off his debt, Jimmy gravely thanked him. "You're our witness, Ted. My son has acted honorably and hopefully has learned that you don't bet money on politics." He squatted and faced the wide-eyed boy. "This quarter is the beginning of my campaign for Congress, Junior. Let's hope it brings us luck."

By eight o'clock, the dishes had been cleared and Junior was up in his room playing. Eula led the men into the living room and settled on the floor, her back against the couch. "Have I talked your ear off, Ted? It's so good to hear about some place that's not Parchman or Shiloh or Mississippi! Thank you. But Jimmy wants to talk about Parchman and Shiloh and Mississippi with you, and I want to listen, too."

Jimmy frowned. "How come I've got no problem talking to you, Mendelsohn, but I'm tongue-tied when I'm asked to speak in front of an audience that looks like you?"

"Because you trust me and you don't trust them. But you can do it, Jimmy. It's no different than talking to your carpenters and plumbers."

"I've had a few white journeymen I've hired and fired. But they were listening to their boss. That's different."

Ted shook his head. "Wrong. People who show up to listen want to know what you have to tell. You're the boss of that moment, so you take charge and you decide what you're going to talk about."

"And you think honkies are going to listen?"

"They're not honkies, Jimmy—they're voters. You have to start thinking that way. You've got to be the candidate who happens to be black, not the black candidate, and they are voters who happen to be white. You have to set that table if you're going be their congressman."

Jimmy turned to Eula. "You hear this guy? Says I should set the agenda. I think he's been away from Magnolia County too long!"

Ted smiled. "I have been, but when I left here you would have thought it crazy to even think about running. So let's find out where we are." He stood and walked around the room, then turned. "Let's road-test this. Worst-case scenario: I'm a cracker in the back of the auditorium and suddenly I stand up. 'What makes you think you should run for Congress, nigger boy?'"

Jimmy's eyes narrowed. "Thank you, sir. I think I should run be-cause I have the education, the qualifications and the guts to confront somebody as ignorant and bigoted as you are, you son of—"

Laughing, Ted held up his hand. "No, pal, that won't do it. Let's try again. 'Coon, you think having you sit in Congress is going to change things in Mississippi? That's a legislature, not a zoo!'"

Jimmy's eyes flashed. "I sure do. Things've already begun to change. Schools, restaurants, back of the bus. Equal rights have to mean equal opportunity, and that's what my vote is going to mean."

Eula grinned and clapped, but Mendelsohn pressed on. "But what's your vote gonna do for me, Sambo? Let you marry my daughter?"

Jimmy's voice was tight. "It's going to put you in your place, you bastard!" He stopped abruptly. "I can't do this." He turned to face the two of them. "I can't say what I want to say."

For a long moment Mendelsohn remained silent and then seated himself opposite Jimmy. "Yes, you can. Listen to me, Jimmy. You're not preaching to the choir at Sojourner Chapel, and you're not selling bed sheets to the Ku Klux Klan. You've got to be who you are, but you've got to put a leash on that temper of yours. You have every right to be angry, but don't let it show. Not if you want to get white voters to cross the highway—a damn wide highway. And you do."

"Yessuh, Massa Mendelsohn."

"Knock it off, Mack." Ted's voice was sharp. "You said you're seri-ous? Then be smart."

Eula touched Jimmy's arm. "Hear what he's saying, baby." Her con-cerned gaze flicked from Jimmy to Ted. "Anybody ready for a cold one?" When they nodded, she left the two grim men but returned quickly from the kitchen with the glistening bottles.

Jimmy fixed his eyes on his intent mentor as Ted drank deep and then pushed ahead. "You got to tell it like you see it without hanging a guilt trip on every white voter sitting out there. You can't hold them re-sponsible for three hundred years of abuse."

Jimmy placed his beer on the coffee table. "You know, Eula doesn't even want me to do this. I think she believes I'm going to lose."

Eula shook her head vigorously in the negative. "No! Not so, Ted. That's not what I believe. I grew up outside Money where they killed

Emmet Till just for flirting with a white woman. What are those people going to try to do to my man when he beats one of theirs? No, it's not because he couldn't win that I don't want him to run." She looked at her husband. "It's because he could."

Mendelsohn said, "Is that what you think, Jimmy?"

"I wouldn't have written you a letter asking you to help me fight a losing battle. I think we can win, but I think it's going to be damn hard."

Ted nodded. "I think it's going to be damn hard, and I don't know if we can win."

"So where do we go next, Ted?"

"Let's try it another way. Tell me everything you really want to say, and then we'll try and twist it into what you can say that they can hear."

"Are you kidding?" Jimmy rose and walked to the front of the room, his chin up and eyes bright. "Listen up, you arrogant bastards. When are you going to learn to hear? To see? To feel? We know about you. We've washed your dirty laundry for three centuries. But you don't really know anything about us because you never wanted to know."

Mendelsohn said, "Jimmy, you can't."

But Mack charged ahead. "We've raised your kids, nursed them when they were sick, loved them when you were too busy to remember, gave them years we never had to give to our own kids. And then you taught them to have the same contempt for us that you have."

"Jimmy." Ted's voice was strained but it was lost in the rush of Jimmy's words.

"We were never contented animals, Mr. Charlie. Never! We were slaving in your fields, draining your swamps for less money than the dumbest white cracker could make." His angry glance swung to Eula. "Our women were never grateful property. They were abused property! Hell, we were all abused property. Did it ever occur to you that your black beasts of burden might have the same God-given brains that you have? That all we needed was a chance to show it? Three hundred years of waiting?" Jimmy's dark young face was shiny with sweat, but he seemed unable to stop the torrent of words. "You kept us poor, you kept us ignorant, you built us better prisons than schools, and you were surprised—surprised!—that there were more accomplished black criminals than qualified black students!"

Mendelsohn leaned forward and put his hand on Eula's, both of them swept up by the ferociousness of the speech. Jimmy's eyes glittered. "Can you really be that blind? That deaf? That unfeeling? If you have the guts, if you could see us, you could learn from us. Are you humble enough to learn from your darker brothers and sisters? Are you ready, neighbors? Because I'm one of them, and I'm ready to show you."

Only when Mendelsohn stood and placed his hands on Jimmy's shoulders did the tirade stop. The sudden stillness in the room was like the pause after a cloudburst.

"We've got work to do, Jimmy." Ted's voice was husky and low. "You're not preaching to the converted. You're talking to men and women in Magnolia County, Mississippi. Every white in that room is saying, 'I was never Simon Legree' and is heading for the hills, carrying the vote you need with him." He turned to Eula. "Mississippi needs Jimmy Mack, but we've got a lot of work to do."

Chapter Fifty-One

The fire in the bungalow behind Fatback's Platter was called in to the Shiloh Fire Department at 3:00 a.m. by a seed salesman passing on the road who noticed a glow behind the juke joint. When the call came to the sheriff at 3:30, he called Harold Butler at his home, demanding to know how this could happen. Butler protested that he had left the juke joint after meeting with Nefertiti when she closed at 2:00. "There was no goddam fire," he said, irritable and sleepy.

Haley snapped, "Meet me there." By the time the fire chief had reached the volunteers and gotten them to the scene, it was 4:30 and the bungalow had been eviscerated by flames. The challenge left for the firefighters was to find the nearest well and try to save Fatback's Platter and the surrounding pines from the surging fire.

When Haley arrived, the firemen were soaking the rear of Fatback's Platter with their hoses, and the small house in the woods was a sodden, smoking pile. "Wasn't anyone in the place," the Fire Chief told Haley. "Rotting wood, old electric circuits, no water available except the well out back. A lousy combination. But we saved the bar. Just lucky that no one was trapped. Don't know where that black singer who owned the place has gone to. Bet that nigger never even had insurance."

When Butler reached the scene, he slid into the seat next to Haley in the police cruiser and silently handed the Saturday night envelope to him. "What do you want me to do?"

Haley slipped the envelope into his glove compartment and confronted the apprehensive officer. "You just happened to not be here? Did the Klan preacher have anything to do with this?"

"Hell, no." Butler's voice was aggrieved. "Why would he? Just a no-account nigger house in the woods? He's got other fish to fry. Besides, he knows I work here for you."

"Stay here till the fire's out and make sure nobody gets into the Platter. Those rednecks will steal all the liquor if you give them half a chance." He stared at the desolate bar and his distracted nod was a dismissal. Butler swiftly closed the car door behind him and stationed himself at the front door of Fatback's Platter. The sky was just beginning to lighten behind the pines.

When he was alone, Haley opened the envelope. Printed neatly in Nefertiti's careful handwriting was the amount of receipts from the weekend, $2,420.00, the subtraction of 20 percent, $484.00 (as per agreement with the proprietor), and the amount of receipts enclosed: $1936.00. At the bottom was a brief note in her hand. It had been crafted over two long afternoons in the back booth of Billy's Chili.

TERMINATION OF CONTRACT

October 20, 1974

As of this date, I bequeath Fatback's Platter to Mr. Dennis Haley. The residence on the property built and owned by Mr. Calvin Bell, until recently occupied by Nefertiti Bell, the proprietor of Fatback's Platter, will have been destroyed by a fire of unknown causes. Among the possessions that will be lost in the fire, will be a rocking chair, a bed, and the services of Nefertiti Bell, all once owned by Dennis Haley. Nefertiti Bell is now under legal contract to Mr. Richard Perkins, owner of Richard's Rook at the Silver Spoon Casino in Gulfport, Mississippi. It is my wish that Fatback's Platter continue in its long tradition of providing the best of Delta blues to the citizens of Magnolia County.

A full, dated record of all transmissions of funds from Fatback's Platter to Dennis Haley during the years of prohibition of the sale of liquor in Mississippi will be found in Nefertiti Bell's deposit box whose number is held by my attorney, Mr. Leroy Ellis of Tupelo, Mississippi.

If there are any physical or monetary impediments to the execution of the terms of this termination of contract by Dennis Haley, his deputy, Harold Butler, or any other parties associated with Dennis Haley, my attorney is instructed to immediately send copies of this termination of contract to the Liquor Authority of Mississippi, the Federal Bureau of Investigation, Mrs. Dennis Haley, the mayor of Shiloh, Mississippi, and the editor of the Shiloh Clarion-Journal.

Nefertiti Bell
Natalia Johnson (witness)

When the last engine finally pulled out of the muddy parking lot, Harold Butler blinked as the sun topped the pines, flooding the forlorn scene with a cheery radiance he didn't feel. He was dying to sleep as he climbed into his truck. It was only then that he saw the sheriff's car, parked on the far side of the demolished bungalow in the shade of a huge pine. Butler eased alongside. A nearly empty bottle of bourbon was tilted on the dashboard, and in the driver's seat sat Dennis Haley, staring drunkenly at the sodden scene before him.

Butler rolled down his window. "Anything I can do for you, Sheriff?" Haley stirred, trying but failing to focus. Butler got out of his truck and approached the car. "Wanted to know if there's anything I can do."

Dennis Haley peered out at the voice then closed his eyes, and his head fell to his chest. Butler waited, but there was no response from Haley,who began to snore deeply. Butler shrugged, reached inside the car, and drank the rest of the whiskey. As he carefully replaced the bottle on the dash, he spotted the crumpled letter on the passenger seat. He checked the unconscious driver and then took the letter into the sunshine to read. It was nearly seven on the dashboard clock when he dropped the letter back on the empty passenger seat. *When I say jump, you say, how high?* He grimaced, spat, stretched, and drove home in the morning sun. He was grinning as he pulled up to his mobile home. Wait till I tell Luther Lonergan.

Four damn days. Even with the work of the prisoners, and the backhoe he got from Parchman to clear the burned wreckage and fill the foundation, it had taken four damn days. Dennis Haley watched as the prisoners finally entered their van and started down the highway, the backhoe lurching slowly in its wake. Now Fatback's looked like a bereft orphan. The sign he'd placed on the door, CLOSED TILL FURTHER NOTICE, spoke to no one. Who the hell was going to come with Nefertiti gone? He gazed morosely at the building. Some fucking gift from that smart-assed bitch. He caught a glimpse of his scowling face in the car mirror. Meet Br'er Rabbit in the briar patch. How the hell could he get out of this?

Late on Saturday afternoon he got the call from Billy Johnson. "Afternoon, Sheriff. This is Billy Johnson, of Billy's Chili? Thought maybe you might find a little time on Sunday morning to drop by here, have a cup of Joe together. I've got a few ideas that I'd like to talk to you about, and Sunday morning there's nobody at Chili's but me."

Puzzled and wary, Haley frowned at the receiver in his hand before replying. "Sunday sounds good, Billy. How about ten o'clock?"

"Coffee'll be ready."

Other than a few families walking to St. Ann's for the ten o'clock mass, downtown Shiloh was Sunday-still. When Haley opened the door at Billy's Chili, Billy called to him from the rear of the restaurant and brought two mugs of coffee to the table.

The sheriff settled back and raised his cup. "Thank you. My Sunday coffee is usually in bed, but you sounded like this was something important."

"Depends," said Billy. "Could be important."

"Could be? What's on your mind, Billy?"

"I want to buy Fatback's Platter. And you own it."

"Who said I own Fatback's Platter?" Haley shifted in his chair. "That's an unlicensed juke joint, Billy."

Billy put his elbows on the table and regarded Haley. "Let's just say you do own it, and I know it. Let's just say that, before she left Shiloh, Nefertiti had a close friend that she told, and the close friend told me. Let's just say that it's so, and that since it's so, I want to take this burden off your shoulders."

Haley's eyes narrowed. "And, if it's so, why would you do that, Billy?"

"Because unlicensed juke joints are disappearing, and the state is going to be legally selling the booze that used to be bootleg. That's going to make some folks who liked it the other way very unhappy, folks who had a good thing going for a long time. I thought that being so, Fatback's could be a burden."

"It could be." Haley's eyes never left Billy's as he finished his coffee. "But you want to buy it, if I own it and if I'm willing to sell it. Why is that?"

"I could make Fatback's into a real fine, legal chili and jazz joint, Sheriff. And you'd have some folding money so you could go to Belize and do the fishing you always said you wanted to do." He refilled their cups. "How long you been on the job, Sheriff?"

"It will be twenty-one years next January, Billy."

"Twenty-one is a nice long run. Maybe it's time to quit and go enjoy yourself."

"Maybe." Haley rose from the table. "A lot to think about on a Sunday morning, Billy."

"A good day for thinking." He followed Haley to the door. "I like Sundays," he said.

Chapter Fifty-Two

On Monday, Deputy Harold Butler picked up the police cruiser and was at the curb when Lonergan left the mayor's office. He climbed in, and Butler eagerly shared his news about Haley's dilemma. Lonergan listened and nodded, a secret smile in his eyes as he gazed back at the office. "Uh hunh."

Butler hit him with his elbow as he moved into traffic. "Uh hunh? That's it?" His voice was incredulous. "The nigger, Nefertiti, has Dennis Haley by the balls, and you don't care? The guy who has the job you want?"

Grinning, Lonergan turned to face him. "It don't change anything for me, partner. Burroughs just promised to appoint me sheriff soon as Haley's term is over, end of December."

Butler's eyes narrowed. "Burroughs said that? Knowing about you and the preacher . . . "

Lonergan cut him off. "He said any outside arrangements I might have are to be terminated as of now, and he doesn't want to know who or what they involve." He spread his hands and laughed. "Home free, baby! No skeletons in the closet, no preachers I got to explain, no nothing as of this date. It seems to be an understanding he has arrived at with the FBI to guarantee close cooperation. My mayor has bought himself a virginal sheriff-to-be—loyal, brave, clean, and reverent!" He shifted in his seat and looked at Butler appraisingly. "May be a good idea for my partner to shed some arrangements also, given that he is known to be my pal and partner."

Butler blinked furiously, then stumbled over the words that came tumbling out of his mouth. "You fink! You turncoat selfish bastard! You just walkin' out?" His voice rose. "Skipping away? Free at last? Well, let me tell you, you Judas prick, you got skeletons in the closet, and I'm one of 'em! And the preacher is sitting on his porch, right now, waiting to see us. And he ain't gonna be pleased that you've decided to take a walk. I think you've lost your mind."

Butler stared at the road, gunning the cruiser past the town green and heading south on highway 49, his foot flooring the gas pedal. "You forget what happened to Frank Tinsley when he decided to leave the preacher?" He shouted over the roar of the racing engine, refusing to look at Lonergan. "Feds found him tied to a tree four days later. Jesus, you saw his back!" His head swiveled. "You ain't with the preacher, ain't with me, then you're with the devil and all those Commie bastards who want to bury us!"

Lonergan reached over and turned off the ignition key. Startled, Butler fought to control the wheel as the car swerved to a lurching stop at the side of the highway. Lonergan calmly slid the key into his pocket and got out of the car. Once on the curb he leaned against the hood and tapped his knuckles on the roof. "Sorry you didn't get the message, Butler. You're cussing out your new boss who's going to be perusing the personnel records of those officers he wants to have rehired. And you, buddy, sound like an embarrassment to me and to my friend the mayor. As of now, the Klan is yesterday's newspaper, and you and the preacher are on the front page. The FBI is all over this, Butler. Maybe you and the preacher should go away for a while." He walked around the cruiser and opened the driver's door. He pointed to the dirt road that angled off the highway. "Preacher's house is right up the road. You won't have to call him."

Butler stumbled from the car and stood, staring, as Lonergan got in the cruiser, raced the motor, and swung into a screeching U-turn, heading back toward Shiloh.

In November there was an announcement from Mayor Roland Burroughs's office that Sheriff Dennis Haley would not seek reelection once his term was over at the end of the year.

Sheriff Haley posted a letter in the *Shiloh Clarion*:

> *I want to thank the good citizens of Magnolia County for the cooperation and support they have offered me for 21 years. It has been a privilege to be your guardian during turbulent times in our beloved county. I will miss you all. I am moving on to pursue a new business opportunity in the country of Belize. I wish you all the best.*

It was also announced that Deputy Harold Butler, after 17 years on the force, was retiring to Idaho due to pressing family business and a desire to spend more time with his wife and growing children. Mayor Burroughs declared: "The post of deputy sheriff, served so well by Deputy Harold Butler, will be filled by the best law enforcement applicant, regardless of race. It is time, once again, for Magnolia County to lead the way in Mississippi to achieve racial harmony among all our citizens."

Chapter Fifty-Three

The ceremony at Delta State had been brief, but for Luke Claybourne Willy knew it was a glory day. When he stepped from the stage bearing the diploma, his face was exultant, and he shepherded his family down the crowded aisle with an urgency of pure joy. "Race you to the car, guys!" He bounded across the lawn toward the car followed by Alex and Benny, hooting with laughter. She watched them. This was happy. God, how long since she had felt this? When she reached the car, the boys lay across the back seat, panting and giggling.

Luke leaned back from the steering wheel, grinning as he watched her approach. "Got a couple of sprinters here, Wil." He glanced up at the rearview mirror and smiled at the kids. "Your ma must be running cross-country, boys!"

Willy slid into the car and kissed Luke. "Just didn't expect all that speed from your daddy, him being the oldest kid in the class!"

He laughed. "Oldest, but the fastest!"

"You really the fastest, daddy? " Benny's eyes were wide. "Mama says you really are the oldest."

"Listen to your mama. She knows everything." He tapped her knee. "Knows she's married to the first Claybourne to get a B.A., and got it in two years. Now that's fast!"

There was whispering in the back seat and Benny erupted with laughter. "You the teacher's pet, daddy? Alex says the teacher looked real sweet at you."

"Did not!" shouted Alex.

"Did too!"

Willy turned in her seat. "Hush! This is a special occasion and daddy doesn't need fighting." She chuckled. "Come to think of it, though, the Dean did look sweet at your father!"

"She was just glad to get rid of me," Luke said as he backed the Chevy out of the parking lot. Once home, the boys went loping up the block to join a softball game and Luke followed Willy into the house. She settled into a seat and watched Luke pour two highballs to celebrate the occasion. Handing her the drink, he planted his feet in an oratorical manner and spoke enthusiastically to an imaginary microphone. "Ex-cotton planter and ex-Parchman guard Lucas Claybourne III announced today that he is entering the field of aquaculture that Mr. Claybourne triumphantly mastered in his studies at Delta State University after resigning his post at Parchman Penitentiary."

Willy grinned and applauded. Luke nodded majestically in acknowledgement and pushed ahead. "The ex-planter and ex-penologist now has plans to float a sufficiently munificent loan from the Tildon Commercial Bank to finance an ambitious new venture in Delta capitalism, Claybourne and Sons, Inc. This venture will be devoted to the production and distribution of the highest quality fish in the Mississippi Delta."

Laughing, Willy said, "Do you think you ought to send the announcement to the networks and *Time* and *Newsweek*?"

"Great idea! I'll send a telegram to the old outside agitator, Mendelsohn: 'A bit of breaking news from the blood-soaked soil of the Mississippi Delta! Times are changing and fish are now replacing cotton in order to answer the growing demand of the American public for fast food and fried fish! First among equals is entrepreneur Luke Claybourne, once an honorary member of the Shiloh White Citizens' Council, now head of Claybourne and Sons, whose motto will be: THE FISH WILL RISE AGAIN!"

"Glory be!" shouted Willy. "The Stars and Bars are shuddering to the ground, and Jefferson Davis is weeping. THE FISH WILL RISE

AGAIN!" She rose and embraced Luke. "I'm so proud of you, darling. We all are. Even Eula said you graduated Parchman honorably for a white cracker plantation owner. Not bad, Mr. Claybourne. And now you've got your Delta State degree, too. Congratulations." She placed her glass on the table and stepped back, her eyes seeking Luke's. The buoyant hilarity seemed suddenly to have leached from the room. In the silence they could hear the whooping of the children from the end of the street. Willy's voice sounded louder than she intended and the words she had not anticipated escaped unbidden into the early twilight of the cramped living room. "So if I understand the scenario of riches to rags to riches as performed by the Delta Claybournes, now you . . . and Alex . . . and Benny . . . will be starting all over again with Claybourne and Sons." The color had paled in her tight face. "Right?"

Luke frowned and set his glass carefully on the table. "Whoa, Willy! What are you getting at?"

She flushed, then lifted her chin to confront him. "Where exactly with Claybourne and Sons do you see me fitting into your exciting new life?"

He stared at her. "You know where. Where you've belonged for twenty years, as Willy Claybourne, my wife, mother of my sons, the heart of my family." His voice rose. "You fit in by taking pride in my accomplishments on behalf of our family and taking your rightful place as a quality woman who is important and gets respect in our Shiloh." His voice was now angry. "You fit in by giving up playing Lady Bountiful and leaving Parchman, as I have."

Willy erupted, "Lady Bountiful? How dare you! Your wife? Your woman who bears your sons? Your accomplishments? Your family? Your decisions?" Tears filled her eyes. "Luke, can you even remember our honeymoon?"

"Of course I remember! What in the world has that to do with this conversation?"

"Everything! Do you really remember New Orleans? The lovemaking? The long walks and the long talks when we'd go down to the river for hot croissants and watch the sun come up?" Her voice broke. "Do you really?"

"Willy—what?"

She sat down, her eyes squeezed tight, and he strained to hear. "That whole lovely week we talked. And we dreamed together about working together on your daddy's place. We'd build Claybourne's into the finest spread in the Delta. Together." Her eyes opened and she looked at Luke. "But from the day your daddy died and you had to take over, all those dreams stopped. And Willy McIntire Claybourne was taken back to Shiloh."

Luke stood above her, his mouth tight. "You objected to being Luke Claybourne's wife?"

"Never! How could you think that? I just wanted you to love me for being who I was, the woman you said in New Orleans you adored." Willy impatiently wiped the tears from her cheek. "You knew I could help you because I knew tractors. You said I knew cotton better in some ways than you did, and I wanted to be next to you, making Claybourne's successful. But you took me home like a little Shiloh schoolgirl. 'Claybourne women don't work in the fields. You're not Willy McIntire anymore.' So for all these years your pretty Cotton Queen wife has been playing Miss Scarlett, buying shoes, and tending the kitchen garden. Those days are gone, Luke."

"Willy, these last years have been like a nightmare to me. You know that. Now I want to get back to where we were before everything went to hell." His eyes were pleading. "Willy, I want what we had. I want to be what we were."

"Don't do this, Luke. Don't push me back. I'm forty-three and I've paid a lot being the Claybourne woman in Shiloh. But when I go to Parchman, I'm not being Lady Bountiful. I'm being me. I work with these women because they're people I care about, women who've never been treated with the respect they deserve. At least now they know that someone cares whether they live or die. They know that I care. They know they have a friend."

"You're not their friend! Are you so blind?" His voice snapped. "You're a white woman who is married to a white businessman in Shiloh, Mississippi. What is the matter with you?"

"No. I'm not blind. There's a world inside the Delta I'm just learning how to see." She paused when the back door slammed, and they heard the boys racing up the stairs to their room. When she heard their door close, she settled on the edge of the couch. "And there's a world outside the Delta, full of interesting people I've never met, and fascinating places I've never seen. Luke, I want to be part of it all. Wilson McIntire Claybourne is not about to be Miss Willy again. If you can't see me for what . . . "

He stared at her. "What?"

"I won't stay here." The words were naked.

"On this day of all days, you're giving me an ultimatum?" His voice was incredulous. "For twenty years I've been getting nothing but goddam ultimatums! First the blacks, then the bank, then the damn prison, and now my own wife, who apparently loves the orphans of the world more than she loves me!" He thrust his thumb toward the door. "You're going to bail out?" The words were nearly shouted and Willy's gaze flicked to the ceiling where the boys were romping overhead.

"No. I want to be in, really in, not out. I want all of us to be in. All around us the world is changing, Luke. You have to be deaf not to hear it, blind not to see it. Whether it's here in Mississippi or someplace out there for me is up to you."

Luke's rough hands covered his face .When he lifted his head, his reddened eyes looked steadily at Willy and his words were slow and deliberate. "There is a place for you, Willy. You've been in this family for more than twenty years. You should know it by now. Claybourne women have always known what was appropriate behavior. No Claybourne woman ever left her husband in my family. No Claybourne woman ever left her kids in my family. And no Claybourne woman ever will."

"Ever is a long time, Lucas." She moved to the bottom of the stairs and turned to look at him. "I just may have to go and find out what is appropriate for a Claybourne woman. Damned if I know. I may just have to go back to New Orleans and look for Willy McIntire."

Chapter Fifty-Four

The last driver had pulled into the parking area and logged out, and for the first time since early morning the yard was silent enough for Jimmy to hear the angelus carillon from St. James over in town. *Amazing grace, how sweet the sound.* He wondered if Eula was hearing it. Her favorite. He eased back in his chair, feet on the desk, eyes drifting to the construction schedules on the wall. He smiled, counting the completions, humming with the old spiritual. . . . *Was blind, but now I see.*

A tapping on his office door roused him and he glanced at his watch. Almost six. Who the hell could it be? The shadow on the frosted glass was large. The tapping grew louder. Annoyed, he swung his feet off the desk and crossed to the door, grabbing his jacket from the hook as he went.

Luke Claybourne's face was in shadow against the late afternoon glare. "You have a few minutes, Mack? I hoped I'd catch you before you locked up. Is this a bad time?"

"No. Come on in. I have a few minutes." He watched Lucas cross to the chair and then took his own seat behind the desk. "I'm meeting an old friend of yours for a drink at the Shiloh Club at seven," he said, suppressing a smile as Claybourne's questioning eyes widened. "Ted Mendelsohn's in town."

Luke shrugged. "Yeah, I heard that. I'm not sure I'd call Mendelsohn an old friend, but he did spend time at the plantation in the sixties. Not a bad fellow, if misguided." He shifted in his chair. "The word around town is that he's down here to talk to you about politics. Is that so?"

Jimmy was clearly annoyed. "That's of interest to you?"

"I found that troubling."

"You found that troubling." Jimmy stared at the man. "Jesus Christ! Should I be honored to hear what you have to say about my political discussions with my old friend?"

Angry now, Luke leaned toward the desk. "No need for that tone, Mack. I came here to share some information I thought might be important to one of Shiloh's new, successful contractors." He started to rise from his chair. "But maybe I'm wasting your time."

"Why don't you just say what you came here to say, Claybourne? I'm really flattered by the attention of the new president of the Shiloh Chamber of Commerce. After all, Claybournes have been pillars of this town for a hundred years." His dislike for Claybourne could not be throttled. "Hell, your daddy and Eula's mama were such good friends you and I could almost been kin!"

"You've got a dirty mouth, boy." Luke's fingers tightened on the arms of his chair. "Bein' the newest member of the Chamber doesn't give you the right to talk that way."

"Hardly know my place anymore, Claybourne? I sure wouldn't have been voted onto the old White Citizens' Council like you were." Jimmy leaned forward on his desk, noting an unwelcome tremor in his hand. He cleared his throat. "Before you leave, why don't you enlighten this poor old darkie about why you crossed the highway to see me?"

Luke remained silent. When he finally spoke, his words echoed in the quiet office. "I got a call from Senator Tildon's office about your contract with HUD." He nodded to the completion charts on the wall. "The senator's aide said there seems to be a problem about the allocation of the funds for the Shiloh housing. As president of the Shiloh Chamber, I found that troubling. Some influential members of the House seem to think a man who was once on the FBI list as a known radical ought not to be getting rewarded for his Red activities." He paused, watching Jimmy closely. "Tildon says he's trying to sort it out, Mack."

"Well, well, well." Jimmy's eyes met Luke's. "Tryin' to sort it out."

"My caller said the senator was going to call his old friend J. Edgar Hoover and clear the brush away, straighten out any misunderstanding."

"And what do you guess the senator'd like me to do to help him 'sort it out'?"

Lucas nodded. "I thought you might be interested." He stood up and moved toward the door, pausing at the threshold. "Young Timmy Kilbrew is announcing he's putting his hat in the ring for Congressional representative from Magnolia County."

Jimmy Mack nodded. "So that's it." He leaned back in his chair, half smiling at Claybourne. "I remember Timmy Kilbrew when he came to the Freedom House in '64, wanting to find out what we were doing. He was one of the few whites from Shiloh who had the guts to come and ask. And I remember his cousin, Bobby Joe Kilbrew. I'm sure you remember him, too, Claybourne. He served time for the conspiracy to kill Goodman, Schwerner, and Chaney. Yeah, I remember the Kilbrews."

Claybourne flushed. "There are black sheep in every flock. But the Kilbrews are an old family down here, Mack, and they've been good for the senator's long political career. I'm sure you can understand that Sterling'd like to help Oscar Kilbrew's young nephew."

Jimmy followed him out into the sunshine and locked his office door. "So having a strong, successful black businessman running for the same seat would be . . . "

"Foolish." Luke said.

"Inconvenient?"

"Counter-productive." Luke paused as he reached his car. "It would likely make it difficult for the senator to sort out the difficulties with your funding. And that would be bad for the Magnolia County housing and—"

"And for the J. Mack Construction Company." Jimmy shook his head and grinned at Claybourne. "Not like the old days is it, Lucas? Can I call you Lucas? Back when I was organizing on Tildon's plantation, the senator would have told Timmy Kilbrew's daddy at the Klan what was necessary and that would be that. Now we got all this foolishness like elections."

Luke said quietly, "Yes, we do. But it doesn't have to be foolish."

Jimmy chuckled. "Never did. I always wondered what all the fussin' was about."

Chapter Fifty-Five

For Willy, Dick Perkins had been the escape from the web of Mississippi constriction she had always longed for—a prince out of the west, knowing in the way that the men at the Shiloh Club were not, amused to share his outside world with an ardent and captivating listener. Perkins had been a sent-from-heaven Baedeker for Wilson Claybourne, who longed to know the things he knew. Tell me about New York. And tell me about the theater, and tell me about skiing at Aspen, about chamber music at Telluride, about riding in the Rockies, and did you really know Duke Ellington? Tell me about the Savoy Ballroom! For Willy, Perkins's presence at any time in any setting had always been felt, acknowledged only in her most private musings, when she was most alone and the dream of outside seemed almost in touch. Not once had she cheated on Luke. Not yet. But if she ever really ventured outside, she knew the hand that would reach for hers would be the hand of Dick Perkins.

Willy's telegram had made him laugh. He could almost see her as she'd gone to the high counter at Western Union. "Hi, Vera darling," she would've said. "Be an angel and send this right out. Got a Prince Charming waitin' to get it!" And Vera would have gone to the key to send it, grinning. "That Willy Claybourne is a caution!"

From the beginning, for Perkins it had been a dance without words, a meeting not quite a meeting, a flirtation without real consequence. By nature he was a reticent suitor, and any amorous longings since Helen's death had remained unspoken, unacknowledged, and unfulfilled. It wasn't guilt. Who was he cheating? He had married young, and was untutored in the cotillion of bachelorhood. Sex outside of the comfortable marital frame he'd known and enjoyed was simply behavior outside of his experience. Yet the attraction to Willy Claybourne was real, seeding thoughts about his friend's wife that he could control but not suppress. He'd known it to be so from that first brush with Willy at the Shiloh Club, from the first dance at Fatback's Platter, a full decade gone. He knew his role to be "the good friend of the Claybournes," the man made welcome to the gentried insularity of the affluent Delta world by their inclusive generosity. He was the available companion for the single women at the Claybourne dinner parties, the seasoned traveler who could show them Acapulco, the buddy who would hunt quail with Luke, the outsider who had come and profited with them from the largesse of the Delta. So how could he long so for Luke's wife? For ten years the dance had continued, the flirtation without real consequence. And now there was this telegram:

> *Dear Prince Charming:*
> *This hapless damsel is in great distress. If you still love me,*
> *please rescue. Can I come to your castle?*
> *The Cotton Queen of Magnolia County.*

The cotillion was over.

He watched her step from the cab, her blond hair floating in the breeze that moved across the lawn from the Gulf. When she stepped back to look at the casino, she spotted him on the balcony and grinned. "Hey, Prince, can a poor white girl come into the kingdom?"

"What's a poor white girl doing at a gambling casino? I think I've got to check your credit rating. I'll be right down." He smiled and waved her toward the front door.

Perkins took her bag and embraced her. "I'm so glad to see you, Willy." He stepped back and gazed at her. "You look terrific."

She smiled. "You always make me think I look terrific. Maybe that's what friends are for."

He answered her smile with his own. "From what I read in the telegram, it was more than friends. *If you still love me, can I come to your castle?* The answer is yes." He took her in his arms, and for the first time he kissed her.

When he'd led her to the terrace, she moved to the rail overlooking the Gulf, watching the slow caravan of shrimp boats returning to the wharves beyond the grove of palmettos. "Lordy, lordy. You live with this all the time? It's almost heathen it's so beautiful."

"It's never looked more beautiful to me than just this minute." When she turned to face him, he repeated quietly, "Never."

Willy moved from the rail and settled on the edge of the brightly striped chaise. "I've never had to play games with you, Dick. You've known all my secrets from the day you arrived from Colorado. You knew I loved you from way back. I guess I always will. But the friendship part is the most special of all. You know I've loved Luke, and you know he's loved me. But he's not been ready to be the good friend I need. You've been that from the get-go."

"I wanted to be, Willy, from the time I first met you. And we did become wonderful friends. I knew you loved Luke. In a lot of ways, I did, too. It's why I never thought of moving between you. But that was then, Willy. You're here now because you decided to come."

She looked at the glinting water that was making smudges of the shrimpers as they moved across the setting sun. "It's more lovely than I ever dreamed. Willy McIntire is a long way from home."

"And now?"

"Now it's hard to picture Shiloh, and, looking at you, it's hard to picture Luke. And now I don't know what to do."

"Times change, life changes." He gently raised her face. "We have to change with it."

She nodded. "It's all about change, isn't it? You manage it so wonderfully well." She rose and walked thoughtfully to the far edge of the patio, watching the last boat as it disappeared behind the trees. She turned and leaned back against the railing, "I struggle and struggle with it. And Luke, dear Luke, is just bewildered by it and hangs on to what used to be certain."

Perkins said, "He's like you, born and raised Mississippi White, Willy. Change is hard, real hard. It's tough biting the bullet if you're a Luke Claybourne. And he's had a lot of bullets to bite these last years."

"I know that. I came out of that soil, and growin' up was slow and hard. And there wasn't much change possible for me for a long time. Not till somebody noticed and said, 'You're pretty, Willy McIntire.'" Her laugh was tight and brittle. "Pretty! Let me tell you, Prince, pretty in Mississippi can take you a very long way. It can take you from choppin' cotton for shares at the Stennis plantation to sellin' cotton at the Claybourne plantation. And then you discover you are forty-three and that you can see in a way that you never could before, and pretty isn't enough."

He reached for her now and held her very close. "What is enough, Willy?"

Wrapped in his arms, her voice was muffled. "That's what I came to find out."

She followed him as he carried her bag to his apartment. When she hesitated at the door, he grinned. "This is my room, the one with the etchings. Yours is through that connecting door." She entered a room filled with sun and the sound of lapping water. A large bowl of hyacinths on the bed stand scented the salt breeze that ruffled the curtains. She sat on the edge of the bed and breathed deeply. "Not a lot of incentive to ever leave this room, Prince."

He chuckled. "I'll keep that in mind."

For three days, Willy navigated the world of Richard's Rook. Perkins kept her at his side at every meeting as the opening of the Rook got nearer. "Meet my dear friend, Wilson," he'd say to the decorators, the architect, the advertising committee, the sound engineer, the lighting expert. "Are you enjoying Gulfport?" they'd ask. "The Rook is going to be something special down here, don't you think? Gonna be like Café Society Downtown in New York! Richard's got great taste." And they'd look at her admiringly and smile. Perkins would beam. For Willy, it felt like being back at the Club in Shiloh, when Luke was introducing her as "my bride, the Cotton Queen."

The days were a welter of blueprints and schedules, paint samples and frantic phone calls. When is Nefertiti arriving? How do I reach her? And how do I handle the billing? And is the apartment across the hall ready for her? Perkins was racing, dashing from crisis to crisis, insisting on results. Willy was increasingly aware that he hardly looked back. He assumed she was following in the wake of these events in his exciting new life. The evenings were a lot better. Perkins was once again the sympathetic friend who had listened and counseled Willy for a decade. What was different now was that Perkins was an advocate, rather than an intermediary in the Claybourne household. He yearned for the intimacy with Willy that he had so long envisioned. "I love being with the most adorable woman I know. I even love having everyone envying me for having you with me. I love you, Willy."

She placed her hand on his, moved by the simple words. "And you know I love you." Her voice was hushed and her eyes sought his. "But I'm a clueless woman in my forties, Dick, with two children, a jealous husband, and a career working with desperate, nearly defeated women in a Mississippi prison." Her hand moved to touch his face. "So what am I doing here with you?"

"Being Willy. Being the most adorable woman I know."

That night she moved into his room. Over coffee the next morning she asked the question again. "So what am I doing here with you?"

He had laughed. "Being adorable."

She walked to the window, brushing back the curtain, gazing at the wheeling gulls that swept by the edge of the sand. "Adorable, like Mary Magdalene!" She turned, a half smile on her face. "Jesus would not be approving of what I've been doing with you."

"I'm not so sure." Perkins folded his arms, smiling and quizzical. "In my Colorado Sunday School they taught us that Jesus hates the sin but loves the sinner. It's hard to think of last night as a sin, though. They didn't change the text in your Delta liturgy, did they?"

She rejoined him at the table. "No. But that doesn't mean there isn't a wagon load of guilt under this gorgeous suntan." Her voice was tender.

"Last night didn't surprise either of us. And we weren't surprised that it was wonderful, like we'd imagined it would be." She frowned. "But there are other powerful things in my life, like Luke, like Alex, like Benny."

Perkins put down his cup and regarded her. "So that's the *but* I keep hearing through all this Biblical sweet talk?"

She nodded. "There is a *but*." Disconsolate, her voice was nearly inaudible. "It's because I don't know where I belong."

He rose, clearly annoyed. "Just hold it, Cotton Queen. You came here out of choice. You made a decision to come and be with me. I thought that was a grownup decision you made about where you wanted your life to go."

She stared at his angry face. "But . . . "

"No ifs, ands, or buts, Willy. Are you telling me that this was just a fling for you? That you came here to get laid, to find out if I was a better lover than your husband? Is that what's going on?"

"That's mean, Dick, and not fair. I came here thinking I would find

NOBODY SAID AMEN 263

some answers, but what I'm finding are more questions." Her voice broke. "Help me, Dick."

"I thought you knew you wanted to close one door and open another. That's what decisions are, Willy; they're choices we make. I made a decision when I left Colorado to go to Mississippi. I made another decision when I left Shiloh to come here. And I thought your 'Dear Prince Charming' telegram was the decision you had made. Or are you just testing the waters?"

She murmured, "The waters are wonderful, but that still doesn't tell me what I need to know."

"And what exactly is that, for God's sake?"

"I need to know where I fit. I need to know where Willy McIntire Claybourne belongs."

Perkins struggled to control his temper. "Your kids are growing up like kids grow up, Willy. You're not going to stop loving or supporting them, nor is Luke. But Luke has never given you the recognition and respect you deserve. His idea of you is the perpetual Cotton Queen, the trophy wife, perfectly dressed and the life of the party."

"And yours?"

"I've seen you as the woman you're becoming: intelligent, curious, adventurous, a woman who has been seeking to expand her horizons. And I've seen you as strong and decisive, someone who knew what she wanted. But now—" He hesitated.

Willy's voice rose. "The problem, Prince Charming, is that underneath what you describe is a Delta farm girl who still has Mississippi mud under her fingernails that won't let go. I didn't mean to, but even during these lovely days with you, my mind would fix on Shiloh."

Perkins reached for her hands and examined them. "If there's Delta mud, I don't see it. I think it's time for you to decide to change your life, Willy. It's time for you to make up your mind. It's past time." He raised her hands to his lips and kissed them, then raised her face to kiss her lips.

Willy said, "Don't." She rose from the table. "You always get what you want, don't you Dick?"

Perkins stood to face her. "No. But I always know what I want, and you can too. Do you know what you want, Willy?"

"No. I wish I did."

Perkins voice was pleading. "Stay with me, Willy. You don't have to go back. You're discovering a whole world outside of the Delta."

Willy turned from him. "For years I dreamed about seeing that world you described. I longed for change. I was sure that I could only find it if I left Mississippi." She raised her head. "But change is happening in the Delta. It's happening in Shiloh. Maybe it's happening in me. It's so slow and hard, Dick, that it hurts. But it's happening. And I've got to decide if I want to be part of that."

Perkins said gently, "There's your choice, Willy. You can flip a coin or you can simply say 'I know what I want.'"

She watched him leave the room and slowly close the door.

Chapter Fifty-Six

Taxco, Mexico
Dearest Luke,
How strange this is. My first letter ever to my husband of 21 years.

It's day 13, and I'm counting. You may no longer care to know that, but it's so. Eleven days on the Redneck Riviera, from Gulfport to New Orleans, then two days here in Taxco, looking for the shiny world Willy McIntire imagined. And I've found that Willy's world isn't here anymore, maybe never was, except in my dreams when everything outside Shiloh seemed magical and out of reach. And when I fell in love with you, I put my McIntire dreams away and proudly became Wilson Claybourne. I hope you believe that, because it's so. But dreams die hard, and 21 years later I had to see for myself. I've done that now.

I miss you, Luke. I miss Alex, and I miss Benny. I miss being important to people I really love. Wilson McIntire Claybourne wants to come home.

Love
W.

Luke returned from dropping off the boys at the construction site by the pond to find Willy's rental car in the driveway. He reached into his glove compartment and extracted his nearly exhausted pack of Luckies. When had he started this damn business again? When she left? Irritably, he lit the cigarette, staring morosely through the smoke at the luggage stacked by the door. When Willy came outside for the bags and saw his car, she stopped. Luke stepped from the Chevy, ground the butt of the Lucky on the macadam, and walked to the step.

"Why didn't you let me know when you were getting in?" He stepped past her and lifted the bags into the hall. "Did you think I wouldn't pick you up? In case you forgot, I'm still your husband."

She followed him into the living room, pausing at the door to assess her home. "It was an ungodly hour, Luke. The connection from New Orleans was in the middle of the night. Besides, I wanted to drive home as the sun was coming up." She settled with a sigh on the couch. "The Delta looked so scrubbed and beautiful." When Luke took the chair facing her, she said, "And I really didn't know if you'd want to pick me up after you got my letter."

"Tell you the truth, Wil, I was scared to open the letter."

"Scared?"

"Scared because I knew I'd missed you. And I wouldn't have bet a Confederate dollar that you'd be coming back. I was somewhere between rage that you actually left and relief that you said you'd be coming back."

"And now?"

"I don't know if I can trust it, your being back." The words seemed to weigh him down. "Are you really back?"

She hiked forward, watching intently. "I think so. I did a lot of thinking while I was away. And I think I discovered who I am, and rediscovered where I belong."

Luke sat rigid, fighting to control his anger. "You had to put me through hell to do that?" His voice rose. "You had to fly out of here like a runaway kid to do that? Why?"

Her voice was gentle. "Because here I was Willy Claybourne, and I thought it was all I could ever be." Her eyes were unblinking. "All you'd ever let me be, Luke."

"So what's changed? You left being Willy Claybourne and you're back being Willy Claybourne. That's what being married means."

"No. Now I know I'm Willy McIntire Claybourne. Remembering who I was, what I was that made you want to marry me in the first place." She searched his face. "I think you liked that grit and toughness once."

"And you needed Dick Perkins to help you find that?"

"Yes. I did. He was the friend I needed who saw me as I want to see myself, as I really am."

Anger tinged his voice and flushed his face. "So why come back at all? Dick Perkins doesn't live here! Your husband lives here! Your sons live here!"

When Willy spoke, her voice was hushed. "I came back because Luke Claybourne is such an important part of who I am. We grew up together, we've been tested by hell fires together, we've won and lost together. And in the end, I love you, Luke." Her voice broke. "I'm not complete without you."

Shaken, Luke moved uncertainly to the couch and sat beside her. "For thirteen days I've been replaying our twenty-one years. I remember winning Willy McIntire. That was the biggest hand I ever won, and I knew it. But I'm a sore loser, Wil, and I thought I'd lost you. And I've been angry with you that you made me lose." Frowning, he stopped abruptly, his face flushed. "But when your letter came, I had to be absolutely straight with myself and look at where I've been and who I've been. And I'm not happy with the me I found." She watched him rise and walk across to the window, becoming a silhouette against the bright morning. "I've been a lot more like my old man than I ever admitted to myself." He turned. "Or to you."

"I love the man you've become, Luke. Not the high school star I loved when I was sixteen. Not the hard-driving 'ol' redneck' you liked to call yourself." She came to him, placing her hands gently on his face. "The man who could humble himself to become a prison guard, the last thing in the world you wanted to do. The man who started over again, remaking his life from scratch to make it work."

"Then why, for Christ's sake, did you leave, just when things started to go well? For me? For us?"

"Because I needed to find *me* in all that." She moved back, her eyes intent on his. "I felt I was suffocating. I needed some place where I could breathe again."

"And running away did that?"

"Yes. I needed to find what the world outside felt like."

"And?"

"And I found that the world really is round. You keep moving and you reach the place you left from. " She smiled wryly. "Real nice scenery along the way. I saw the Gulf, I spent two days in Mexico, even saw our old haunts in New Orleans. But I found out Mississippi is part of me just like I'm part of Mississippi."

Luke walked to the luggage at the door. "I'll carry your bags up." He stopped suddenly, at a loss. "I don't know what room to put them in."

Willy reached for one of the suitcases, opened it, and took out a sombrero. "When I was in Taxco, I picked up a sombrero that's supposed to be like the one Pancho Villa wore. And the legend they tell in Taxco is that when Villa came to a new place, he'd sail his sombrero into the room and see if anybody shot it. If nobody did, he'd walk through the door." She turned with a grin, "I thought I might have to do that when I got home." She tossed the sombrero toward the stairs and they watched it settle gently on a step. She said, "I'd like them to go to our bedroom. You gonna shoot, Pancho?"

Luke picked up the sombrero and placed it on Willy's head. "No. We missed you. The boys did. I did."

"I missed all of you. How are they doing? They were already gone when I got back."

"I get them out early. They're fascinated watching the co-op's crew that's digging ponds at the catfish farm, but they're fine. They kept askin' 'When is Mom getting back?' They're not little kids any more, but they missed their mom. Two weeks away? They knew this was something different. I knew this was different."

"It was different." She cleared her throat. "What does a girl have to do to get a drink around here?"

Luke smiled and went to the small bar across the room. "You need Dutch courage?"

"Hell, no. I needed Dutch courage to leave. That was the hardest day of my life. No. I'd just like us to have a welcome-home drink together."

"We never had a farewell drink, Wil. You were like a bird, beating your wings against the cage. And I felt like I was still being a prison guard."

"It wasn't you that made me leave. I felt I couldn't be here in the Delta one more day—losing the plantation, losing the house, losing the years, watching everything changing except us."

"And what about your—" he hesitated. "What about Dick Perkins?"

Willy said evenly. "It wasn't Dick Perkins made me go. It was me, Luke."

"Did you sleep with Dick Perkins?" The words were unadorned. "Did you?"

Willy stood and faced him. "Don't go there, Lucas."

"Don't go there?" His voice was incredulous. "I'm your husband, and I have a right to know!"

"And I'm your wife. What rights do I have to know? Did I ask what you were doing in Jackson all those years when you were carousing with your buddies, selling cotton and getting quality time at Matty Semple's house? Do you really believe that the wives at the Shiloh Club didn't know about the delights of Matty Semple's house? There are things in everybody's life that we learn to live with that we consider exclusively our own." She paused. "I wasn't carousing, Luke. I was with a kind friend. Then I came home."

"So who came home? Don't I have a right to know?"

"The McIntire girl who you chose to be your wife, warts and all, who believes in herself, and wants to start fresh with the man she really loves."

He gazed at Willy with wonder. "Jesus. Am I ever going to get used to you?"

She smiled. "I certainly hope so."

He poured two drinks and handed her one. "Nothin' fancy. Not even a Taxco Marguerita, just my daddy's bourbon."

"Your daddy's bourbon is fine. I've had enough Margueritas to last a lifetime."

"A lifetime's a long time, "Luke said. "You sure?"

Willy laughed. "Sure? What's sure? I think so."

"Welcome home, Willy. I'll drink to that."

She touched her glass to his. "It's time I got back to work at Parchman. I'm surprised Eula didn't send a posse out looking for me."

"When she called I told her you needed a little R and R. She'll be glad to hear from you. She's a good friend, Willy."

She smiled. "And a good friend nowadays is hard to find?"

Luke said, "Maybe not."

Chapter Fifty-Seven

Jimmy's meetings with Ted were exhausting, testing the old friendship in ways that surprised him. Mendelsohn was unrelenting, probing the sensitive spots in the careful edifice Jimmy had erected and defended for his whole adult life.

What's the matter, black boy? You can't deal with this cracker? You 'llowed in this part of town, nigger?

It wasn't the taunts. Hell, he'd heard worse. It was Mendelsohn saying them. They seemed to come too easily to him. The more vulnerable Mendelsohn made him feel, the more suspicious Jimmy was about the role-playing. He was getting hit, and it made him irritable. "Why am I letting this white cat torment me?" he growled at Eula. "Maybe he likes it, enjoys baiting me, saying what he always felt but never said."

She laughed at his fears. "He loves you, baby. It's the way he's trying to protect you. You're talking about Ted, not just some cracker." And he knew she was right. But as the days got closer to the campaign, Mendelsohn probed deeper, watching the days slip by, anxious to arm him before he tangled with Timmy Kilbrew in November.

By the night of the kickoff of the Mack for Congress campaign, Jimmy was no longer uncertain if he loved or loathed Ted Mendelsohn. Ted's incessant racist barbs had induced a scar tissue that had grown into a sustaining patience deep within Jimmy, giving him the confidence to measure, think, and counter-punch. When they approached the auditorium, Jimmy felt the adrenaline rising, and he nudged Ted.

"You gonna be there to run interference for me, Honky?"

Ted grinned. "I've seen you in the open field, Nigger. You don't need me. You just need you."

Willy paused by the hall mirror, checking her hair, adding a little color to her lips. "I've got to be going, Luke," she called. "Are you going to come with me? We've talked this Jimmy Mack rally into the ground. If you're coming with me, we have to leave now." She turned and saw Luke standing, his arms folded, his back against the front door. "Are you coming?" she repeated.

"Willy, don't do this." His words were stark, echoing in the small foyer.

"We've gone through this, Luke. You know I'm going. You know why I'm going. The word is all over Parchman that I am going to the Mack rally and speak there."

"Oh, Christ. Just as I feared."

"Feared? Why feared? You're as fearful as the women in my group at the prison! 'Gonna call you nasty names, Miz Willy. Nigger lover! Whore! Judas!' They don't want me to go, scared to death that the crackers will kill me." Her voice softened and she stepped close to Luke. "I know you're worried like they're worried, and I hate making you worry. But I need to go."

He touched her shoulders. "For God's sake, listen to me. Those women could be right. This is not about redemption, Wil. It's about a man getting elected to represent us. Us!"

"Us? Which us? The ones you remember who had the Claybourne place? They don't live here anymore." She removed his hands from her shoulders. "Those folks who closed the Shiloh pool in July, to keep them out?" Her voice was flat. "The ones who started the white academies in Magnolia County so our kids could be taught in a pure place?"

"Willy, this is Shiloh, not Gethsemane. We didn't break all the eggs. You know that. What's done is done."

Her anger could not be leashed. "The black toilets are done, Luke! The

black water fountains are done! The all-white juries are done!" Her voice
rose, and tears were brimming in her eyes. "Segregation is not done!"

He waited for the storm to pass. "Wil, you were raised on a farm,
you're married to a farmer. We both know there are seasons." He spoke
gently. "The land's got to be prepared. Plants got to be healthy. And you
need patience and time, or you never make a crop."

She stowed the damp handkerchief in her purse. "Some of us think
time is all wore out, Luke." She moved to the door. "And how long do
you expect human beings to be patient?"

"As much time as it takes. It's sure as hell not time yet to elect a black
man to represent us, particularly, if the black man is Jimmy Mack. Remember, this is Magnolia County, Mississippi!"

"It's not about what we choose to remember. There's a whole lot I
choose to forget. But right now I'm going to the Mack rally." She stepped
past him and held open the door. "I wish you would come with me."

"Don't do this, Willy."

"It's late, Luke. It's very late."

As if rooted, he watched her turn at the step, hesitate, and look back
at him. He watched as she went down the flagstone walk and started the
Chevy. The sound of the motor roused him and he stepped to the stoop.

"Willy!"

She eased her foot from the gas and watched him close and lock
the door and start down the walk toward her.

Chapter Fifty-Eight

Mendelsohn and Jimmy Mack peered from the wings of the stage.
Ted touched him with his elbow. "They're coming in, Jimmy," he said,
his eyes bright with the moment, "and about a third of them are white.
Not shabby at all!"

Jimmy looked down at the 200 seats in the auditorium. "They're
filling the last rows first. How come?"

"There hasn't been a rally for a black candidate in this town since Reconstruction. They're not sure if they want to stay, want to be seen. It takes balls for a lot of them just to show up. "

Jimmy riffled nervously through his notes. Would Willy Claybourne really come? Eula, sitting there in the middle, calmly erect, had said she would: "I know Willy." Still uncertain, his eyes restlessly searched the filling seats as the evening slowly unreeled.

Fifteen minutes before the meeting would start, Ted saw that the rows were nearly filled. Only the first three had empty seats. There was a buoyant feeling in the room. Friends called to friends, and there was a pleasant murmur of comity as blacks often found themselves seated, remarkably, next to whites, and whites next to blacks, all waiting for the festivities to start.

Ted spotted her first. He expelled his breath, not realizing how concerned he'd felt. "Damn! She looks great!" He grinned as Jimmy stepped closer to see. "Willy is here!" Two steps behind, Luke followed, his face stolid. Ted moved quickly from the wings and extended his hand to Willy. "You really did come!" He grinned broadly. "I should have known. Jimmy said you would."

At the top of the steps she hesitated, then cocked her head, challenging him with a defiant half-smile. "You don't look like the others."

"Beg your pardon?"

"I said you don't look like the others."

"I'm just like the others," he said, his eyes twinkling. "I'm twenty years older, but I'm just like the others."

She stepped closer. "Take off your sunglasses. I've got questions to ask you, and . . . "

"And I want to see your eyes!" She stepped into his arms as they both exploded with laughter. Ted released her, nodded to Luke, and led her to the back of the lectern where they could talk.

Jimmy moved to the apron of the stage and looked down at Luke. "Mr. Claybourne."

"Mr. Mack."

"I'm surprised to see you in this audience, Mr. Claybourne. Timmy Kilbrew would be surprised, too."

Luke allowed himself a brief smile. "Timmy understands, Mr. Mack. He's married, too."

"Been a while, Mr. Claybourne, since the day you brought me the message from Senator Tildon that I was expected to step aside. It was a special day. It made me feel like I'd crossed the bridge from the bad old days."

For the first time, Luke seemed to respond. "Well, we all pay our dues one way or the other. It's been a long bridge in Mississippi." He turned his back, settled into an empty seat in the first row and looked up at the banner behind the podium: JIMMY MACK: A NEW MAN FOR A NEW MISSISSIPPI. He read the words aloud, his voice toneless. "But you've done all right, Jimmy Mack. No harm done in the long run."

Jimmy stared at the man. "That how you see it, Mr. Claybourne?" He descended the steps and sat down in the empty seat beside Luke. "No harm done?" He struggled to steady his voice, aware that people around them were party to the conversation. "Did Mrs. Claybourne ever talk to you about the night I got arrested coming off Senator Tildon's place?"

"Yes. Well, Sterling would get real agitated about anyone organizing on his property." He shrugged. "It was another time. Past's past, Mack."

"Not when you're cursed with a good memory for bad times."

Luke nodded. "I seem to remember that you had a little problem with the police."

"A little problem." Jimmy shifted in his seat to face Luke. "I went into our Shiloh jail as a nonviolent freedom fighter and I came out a nigger. Is nigger not a familiar word to you, Mr. Claybourne?"

Luke's eyes kindled. "Don't invent things, Jimmy Mack. I never called you nigger."

"You're right. It wasn't your words. It was their words."

"You're a man, Mack. And now you want to be a congressman. Sticks and stones can break my bones, but words'll never hurt me. Get over it!"

Jimmy struggled to moderate his voice. "Get over it? You've got the gall to lecture me about being a man?" With an angry glance at the intent faces in the row behind, he turned back to Luke. "When your Shiloh cops beat me with sticks for being a man? And no white man and no white woman I know ever had the courage to say we don't beat police prisoners in Shiloh? It's not the way we do it in the gallant South?"

Luke flushed, "We didn't beat prisoners when I was at Parchman. And you, of all people, know that."

"Shiloh. Not Parchman." Jimmy's words were measured, a teacher speaking to a struggling child. "Shiloh."

Luke said, "Don't patronize me."

"I'm telling you what you never seemed to know about your own home town."

"For Christ's sake, Mack."

"After they beat me, they dropped me out on the highway and I came to your kitchen." His eyes were unforgiving. "No harm done."

Luke slowly shook his head, fingers drumming on the arms of his chair. "Terrible." The word tumbled out, unbidden. "A long, sad time ago, Mack."

"Sad? Hell, yes. But not so long ago." He looked up at the stage where Willy and Ted continued their reminiscence. "Your wife got me to Mound Bayou so they could stop the bleeding. Healing the words has taken a lot longer. May even be the reason I'm running for office."

Luke stood up. "Can this redneck give you a little advice?" His voice was gentle. "Being bitter about the past won't move this state an inch forward, and it will never get your message across the highway. Blacks have memories and whites have memories, too. You remember my chasing your tail off my place because you were trying to organize my workers to vote. And I remember losing Claybournes because I was trying to stay afloat to keep my black tenants from starving."

"They weren't burning your place down. They were asking for the right to vote in an election. I remember," said Jimmy.

"And I remember when I had to throw in the towel when they walked out because I thought they weren't qualified to vote." Luke's voice was constricted. "It was the end of a hundred years of Claybournes."

Jimmy rose to face him. "So we just forgive and forget three hundred years of grief?"

Luke looked briefly at the podium and then at Jimmy. "No. We just forgive and remember." He turned and swiftly made his way up the aisle. When he reached the back door, he turned to watch the stage as the house lights dimmed.

Ted Mendelsohn walked to the lectern, adjusted the microphone, and moved off into the wings. The chatter of the audience began to subside as Willy rose from her chair at the back of the stage and made her approach to the lectern. Luke watched the slender figure step into the spotlight and stand quietly, looking across the darkened audience.

"I'm Wilson Claybourne, Willy to a whole lot of you. But you all know me. You've put up with me in some really good times and in some times we wish we never knew." She paused, peering into the audience. "Looking out at you from here, I don't know if you're white, or black, or striped. But I do know what Shiloh was, what Magnolia County was, when it was white Shiloh, white Magnolia. I remember and you can remember what we said to each other, and what we sealed in our hearts and never said."

Straining to hear, Luke whispered, "Be careful, Wil."

"I know what we did in Shiloh, and what we didn't do in Shiloh, and I know what we didn't want to know." There was a stirring in the audience as two white couples rose and noisily moved up the aisle toward the door. Willy watched them in silence, then continued. "But history has caught up with us, dear friends. So we need new mapmakers for our beloved Delta. New leaders who can help us find our way to each other and to a finer Mississippi for our kids and our grandkids. New leaders who are not defined by the color of their skin, but by the purity of their vision of what is possible."

She paused and her eyes sought out Jimmy in the darkness below. "And one of them who tilled this earth, who educated himself in this Delta, who never fled this place for an easier one, who never lost faith that the right kind of Mississippi could be born from our sorrows, our pain, and our common struggles, who believes in a New Mississippi, is a man who is one of our own. It's with pride and confidence that I introduce to you the next congressman from the Fourth Congressional District, Shiloh's own Jimmy Mack!"

The listeners rose from their seats and applauded as Jimmy stood, climbed the stairs to the stage, and shook hands with a beaming Willy.

He stepped to the microphone and began to speak, and Luke paused at the door and listened, reluctant to leave. As Mack spoke, applause continued to punctuate his speech. Luke finally stepped outside, frowning. The applause became fainter as he made his way down the deserted, moonlit streets, but images of the rally and fragments of Willy's introduction continued unreeling. The right kind of Mississippi could be born from our sorrows? Our sorrows, Willy? Our struggles?

When he reached his car, he scribbled a note and placed it under the windshield wiper. *See you later at home.*

Ted Mendelsohn stood at the front of the stage and watched the chattering and exuberant crowd move down the aisles and out the front doors of the auditorium, eddying about the television crew that was interviewing a flushed and excited Jimmy Mack. Their lights punctuated the autumnal darkness outside and touched the walls of the dimming auditorium. In the sudden quiet, he heard Willy clap and turned to see her. She still sat at the back of the deserted stage, seemingly reluctant to end the triumphant meeting. She was smiling as Ted pulled a folding chair alongside hers.

"You were clapping," he said. "Why were you clapping?"

She regarded him thoughtfully before answering. "Because I always clap at the end of the first act if I like the play."

"And you liked the play?"

She nodded. "I loved the play."

He said, "Not everybody loved the play. Luke was seen leaving his seat when you introduced Jimmy."

"But he listened at the door. The review is not in yet."

Ted turned in his seat to face her. "So you think Jimmy Mack is going to be your next congressman?"

"I don't know." The words were so forthright that he was startled. "I wish for all the world that I could say yes." Her eyes followed the still-noisy departing audience, then returned to Ted. "All the world," she repeated. "All my world. But I honestly don't know."

"You're a caution, Willy Claybourne," he said. "Were you watching what I was watching? The crowd loved him! The TV crew couldn't wait to get to him! I thought you loved the play."

She looked hard at Mendelsohn. "Of course I loved the play. But this is farm country, Ted. My Luke is a farmer. Before coming tonight he said to me: 'Farmers think seasonally. They learn patience or they don't make it as farmers.' Up East in Washington you're on deadlines and agendas that are immediate or sooner." She laughed. "Two hours ago Lucas was arguing that it was too soon to get a black man nominated. I thought he was wrong."

"And now?"

"I think the folks who turned out tonight want Jimmy Mack to be their congressman. I think they'll nominate him." Her eyes searched his. "But I don't know if there are enough of them yet. It's only the first act, Ted. It may be too soon to get a black man in Shiloh elected in Magnolia County like Luke believes, maybe always will believe. I know Jimmy Mack is ready. But are Mississippians ready yet?" She gathered her purse and stood up. "But the play's just beginning! I've got to get back to my farmer and my kids. Thank you. It's been a memorable evening."

He watched her walk to her car. When she swung by the entrance, she waved.

Chapter Fifty-Nine

When Luke reached home, he noticed the boys' shovels lying in a heap in his muddy Ford truck's bed. A wind sent leaves scampering over the drive, and he shivered in the sudden chill. Leaning on the truck, he looked up at the autumn moon, lonely in the vast sky of the Delta, and then at the house where he could see the boys moving in the warm light of the kitchen. He could use some coffee.

Alex and Benny turned from piling their dishes in the sink when the door opened. "Daddy! We ate without you," said Benny. "We didn't know where you were when we got home."

"And we were starved!" added Alex. "You go to that meeting at the school with mama?"

Luke moved to the stove to warm up the rest of the coffee. "Yeah. How'd you know about the meeting?"

"A kid at the academy asked me if my mama knew a nigger named Jimmy Mack. Said he heard my mama was going to be introducing Jimmy Mack at a politics meeting."

Luke carried his coffee to the table and nodded for the boys to sit down. He turned to Alex. "A black man named Jimmy Mack is running for Congress. You use that word? Nigger?"

The boy hesitated. "No, Billy Cosgrove did. He's the one asked me."

"How about you, Benny? You say nigger?"

Benny grinned. "Not since I came home and told mama a nigger joke I heard in school and she said that's not funny. She said that's a dirty word. Said her daddy taught her that. He said you have to use soap to get rid of dirt and if she kept using that dirty word he'd have to wash her mouth out with soap. Yuck!"

"Did mama ever get her mouth washed out with soap?" Alex asked.

Luke chuckled. "I don't think so. She's smart, like me. Ignorant people say nigger. Your ma's not ignorant." He pushed back his chair. "Get your jackets and meet me at the truck. I want to pick something up, and I need your strong backs. No questions."

The boys got their jackets and hurried to the truck. Luke drove, savoring the unusual silence of his sons, knowing their curiosity would leach out. It'll be Alex, he thought. Before they headed north on 49, Alex said, "Daddy, you just passed our old driveway! Where we going?"

Luke said, "I'm taking you to a part of the old place you boys have never been to."

Benny craned his neck to see out the truck window as the Ford swung to the right, bouncing its way further and further through the rows of cotton. The fields were a pale blue in the moonlight, the light so bright that Luke turned off the headlights as he carefully maneuvered the truck over a slight rise and then coasted down to a stop. Benny said, "Look at that old tree! Looks like a skeleton." The tree was like chalk against the sky. "Scary-looking."

Alex snorted. "What's scary? Just a dead tree. We getting out here, daddy?"

"Keep your voices down. We don't want to upset anybody. This place doesn't belong to us anymore." Luke opened the door. "Bring the shovels and the crow bar, and stay close. It gets wet down there in the hollow. There's a spring there. That's where our brook came from."

Luke led them to the clearing. "This was my secret place when I was a boy. Even your ma's never been here." He looked at his wide-eyed sons and smiled. "I think it's time the sons of Claybourne and Sons learn about our family history. It was your Grandpa Lucas who brought me here the first time. It was sort of his secret place, too. A place to talk together." A cloud passed briefly across the wafer of moon. "The last time was two days before he died." Luke picked up a shovel and stepped closer to the spring. "We had a special place to talk. Come over here."

The boys moved closer as Luke felt before him with the shovel. When there was a dull clang, he chuckled. "Right where I left them twenty years ago!" Partly hidden by the swamp grass were two flat stones. "My history, sons. Your history, too." He grinned at the questioning faces. "Let's dig them out and bring them to the truck."

Alex said, "These big rocks? Why?"

Luke handed him his shovel. "Just dig."

More and more clouds curtained the moon, and a chill rain began to fall as they struggled to free the stones. When Luke's crowbar finally wrestled them from their grave, the boys hauled the stones to the truck. Luke went into the cab and turned on the headlights as rain washed the mud from the stones. Then he knelt with the boys around the glistening rocks.

"Grandpa Lucas always said the bigger stone was his, and that the smaller one was mine." He grinned at the two intent faces before him. "Now both of them belong to both of you. Let me show you something on the smaller one. Grandpa showed me there was the print of a fossil on my rock. He said it was me, two million years ago when this Delta was the bottom of a huge ocean."

"You mean right here?" Benny stared at his father.

"Right here," said Luke, nodding. "So I asked him if I was a fish two million years ago. And he said no, I was a crustacean. And he showed me the little ridges on this fossil."

Benny tapped his father on the shoulder. "It does look a little like you, daddy," and Alex yelled, "It sure does!"

Once the rocks were secured in the bed of the Ford, Luke made his careful way back to the highway. It was raining hard now. "Tomorrow we'll drop these historical monuments at the catfish farm. They're part of our history."

"Those rocks really go back two million years, daddy?"

"Yeah. They do. So in a certain way, we go back two million years, too." He looked at Alex. "Something to be said about looking back. It's not all bad. I do quite a lot of that. Your ma is big on looking ahead."

He turned into the driveway and parked next to Willy's Chevy.

Acknowledgments

Learning to navigate the rocks, shoals and shallows that came with my desire to pursue the life of an artist has led me into a turbulent stream that has been both daunting and wondrous. The perspective has constantly shifted as I have moved from capturing the visual image to seeking words to define my vision. My perception of the people and landscapes along the way has been heightened by the demands of my many years as a working illustrator. Learning to really see has been a challenging and unending quest, and I think now of myself as a journalist whose task is to perceive what is true in my life and time. Now, at an advanced age, I find myself once again in flux, impatient with the "what is" and eager to explore the "what ifs" in my vision. I continue in the search for the reality beneath the journalism that has always intrigued me. If I am an elderly Don Quixote, then my journey has needed the strength and wisdom of many Sancho Panzas.

Without the compassionate guidance and encouragement of my journalist wife, Gloria Cole Sugarman, I would never have found the confidence to venture further in the unknown landscape of fiction. Her hand was always on my back as I was writing *Nobody Said Amen*.

The generosity and vast editorial experience of Sally Ateseros helped me in so many ways to navigate the entanglements of time and place that occur when one is creating a narrative. She was a teacher I cherish.

Sybil Steinberg, whose professional life has been devoted to educating the reading public about the innovative creators of today's often challenging fiction, has helped me to seek out and find the paths forward which have made me a surer traveler.

Martha Aasen, whose own life has been shaped by a youth spent in a politically vigorous and enlightened family in Mississippi, and by her professional years in the international community of the United Nations, has lent insight and authenticity in seeking the truth about Mississippi culture and traditions.

Mary Selden Evans has been stalwart in shepherding my journey from art to literature. Her understanding of the delicate balance necessary to wed the two into one compelling voice resulted in the publication of two books of important reportage, *We Had Sneakers, They Had*

Guns, and *Drawing Conclusions, One Man's Discovery of America*. I will miss her enthusiasm and support.

Why I wrote NOBODY SAID AMEN

As an artist and journalist, I have borne intimate witness to two seminal events that have changed the political and moral landscape of our world.

The struggle of World War II was to triumph over the military might of the fascism that had taken all of democratic Europe hostage, and to overcome the Japanese after their attack on America and dominance of Asia.

A generation later, the emergence of a non-violent civil rights revolution in the United States was a challenge to the very premise of *e pluribus unum*, rupturing the course of millions of lives in the South as it tore asunder expectations and habits of civil and communal behavior that had held sway since the Civil War.

As a reportorial artist, I was a participant and keen observer during both struggles, seeking to be honestly critical and truthful in the imagery I created to tell the story I saw. After a number of years of living in and visiting Mississippi, I came to recognize that this state was a Petri dish that revealed much more than the DNA of a poor, post–Civil War rebel state. It was a dramatic caldron of American passions, contradictions, and aspirations—and a uniquely American story.

Later, as an artist for the movement, I drew and painted more than a hundred pictures of Freedom Summer in the Mississippi Delta, wrote two books about the blacks and whites who were involved, and co-authored, with my wife, Gloria, *Look Away, Dixieland*, a play about the changing roles of men and women as a consequence of the movement.

The urgency of the continuing revolution I first saw in 1964 remains a living presence in my life. The images of bravery and idealism, the human fallibilities, the defeats, the frustrations, the changing moral landscapes were all colorblind. As a result, *Nobody Said Amen* was born to tell that uniquely American story.